Honolulu Heat
Between the Mountains and the Great Sea

A Novel by

Rosemary and Larry
MILD

Magic Island Literary Works • Honolulu, Hawaii • 2018

Library of Congress Cataloging-in-Publication Data
Mild, Rosemary P. ; Mild, Larry M.
Honolulu Heat, Between the Mountains and the Great Sea
Mild, Rosemary P. ; Mild, Larry M.
ISBN 978-0-9905472-3-5

First Edition 2018

10 9 8 7 6 5 4 3 2 1

Dedication

For our beloved grandchildren—
Alena, Craig, Ben, Leah, and Emily

For our wonderful children—
Jackie and Myrna

For our marriage—soul mates, partners, lovers

Acknowledgments

We could fill an entire volume with the names of all the family members, dear friends and acquaintances who are loyal fans of our books. You are all precious to us and give us the ultimate push to continue our writing. We owe special thanks to the following for their expertise, advice, feedback, and encouragement:

• Diane Farkas, our eagle-eyed proofreader and dear friend.

• Sisters in Crime/Hawaii and Chesapeake chapters.

• Hawaii Fiction Writers.

• Mystery Writers of America.

Disclaimer

Honolulu Heat, Between the Mountains and the Great Sea is entirely a work of fiction. The plot and the events therein are of the authors' imagination and invention. All characters are fictitious and any resemblance to persons living or dead is purely coincidental. No diacritical marks are used in any of the Hawaiian language words found in this text. That precedent was set in *Cry Ohana*. The authors made that choice in order to have their writings appeal to, and be understood by, a broader audience, beyond their beloved Hawaii.

Table of Contents

Table of Contents

Other Books by the Milds

- *Locks and Cream Cheese*
- *Hot Grudge Sunday*
- *Boston Scream Pie*
- *Death Goes Postal*
- *Death Takes A Mistress*
- *Death Steals A Holy Book*
- *Cry Ohana*
- *Murder, Fantasy, and Weird Tales*
- *The Misadventures of Slim O. Wittz*
- *Unto the Third Generation*

Other Books by Rosemary

- *Miriam's World—and Mine*
- *Love! Laugh! Panic! Life with My Mother*

Chapter 1

Wind and Water

MAN AND NATURE coexist in a not-so-delicate balance, each pushing, and more often punishing, the other. Beautiful, brilliant, respectful in one moment. Violent, vengeful, destructive in the next. The forces engage and recede. A victor emerges in the ongoing skirmish and then relinquishes the laurels—so true on the tiny Garden Isle of Kauai in the middle of the Pacific Ocean. The moment is 11:34 a.m. on the eleventh of September 1992, a Friday.

Alex Wong, an accountant in his early thirties, entered a few more numbers on the keyboard in his home office. But he couldn't focus on his client's quarterly fiscal report. His usual pragmatic head just wasn't in it today. The radio lulled him with Hawaiian slack-key guitar melodies. He leaned back in his swivel chair. *Ah, the joy of working in T-shirt and shorts.* Gazing out the picture window opposite his desk, he drank in nature at her most seductive. The ocean lay peaceful with nary a whitecap in sight. The sun glared brazenly. Malia, in her baby bikini, sat under a striped umbrella next to Noah, a neighbor's son. With shovels and pails, the two-year-olds wallowed joyously in the glistening sand. Leilani, in a broad sun hat, sat in a beach chair, dividing her watchful eye between the toddlers and the half-finished seascape on her canvas. The oils were drying quickly in the late-morning heat.

Alex breathed deeply. *It doesn't get any better than this.*

At 11:40 a.m., the guitar music stopped in mid-chord. A female voice announced: "This is a hurricane alert from the National Weather Service. Hurricane Iniki is currently 160 miles south and

80 miles east of Honolulu with winds up to 135 miles per hour. On its present northwesterly track, it is now likely that the main force of the storm will miss the island of Oahu and the islands of Kauai and Niihau. However, the storm's path is unpredictable. You are advised to secure whatever you can outdoors, then stay indoors, away from outside walls, and particularly, away from windows and glass doors. The storm center is moving at 100 miles per hour. Its track is constantly shifting and could swing north at any time— onto a collision course with Kauai. Be aware, this Category Four storm is still gathering strength. Stay tuned for further updates."

Alex stopped listening. He shut down the computer and placed the monitor face-down on the floor. Sliding bare feet into his size-thirteen sneakers, he hurried out of the house, striding fast to the beach.

Halting squarely in front of his wife, he announced: "Lani! We need to get the children inside. Now! I just heard on the radio that Hurricane Iniki may be headed our way. We need to get everything inside or else tied down."

Leilani, a tawny-skinned Hawaiian with lush dark hair, didn't even look up. "Not to worry, Alex." She applied a brush stroke of cobalt green. "Right after breakfast the TV said the storm was going to pass between Molokai and Oahu and we might just see a little rain."

"All that's changed now," Alex said. "The hurricane's eye is moving fast. It could be only a matter of hours before it hits here."

"Alex, the sky is clear blue. Look! Oh, maybe a few more clouds over that way. So what? I have to finish this. I'm entering it in a juried show next week."

"Lani, why are you being so stubborn? Can't we at least take Noah home?"

"There's nobody home. I told Ilima I'd watch him for the day. They went to a house-warming party up in Princeville." She dabbed a bit of silver-gray over a whitecap.

A rare wave of anger crossed Alex's unshaven face. "Damn it, Lani, your painting can wait." Scooping up the toddlers, one in each arm, he carried them squirming into the house. He set them down on Malia's throw rug on the *mauka*, mountain, side of the her bedroom and drew the Hello Kitty drapes shut. Dragging her twin-size mattress onto the floor, he hefted the two children onto it. They gave him a puzzled look, then decided they must be playing a game, and bounced up and down on the soft mattress.

Leilani was about to mix fresh colors, but paused to reflect. *It's not like Alex to be so short-tempered.* As if in response, the incoming clouds began to smother the beach with darkness, night descending in midday. She felt a sudden chill. Sharp gusts whipped up the sand, stinging her ample bare thighs. She gathered up her painting paraphernalia and hurried into the house.

When she appeared in the bedroom doorway, Alex looked up, his face grim. "It's about time. Give me a hand with the dresser." He stuck a large folded *soji* screen in front of the window, and the two of them pushed the dresser in front to hold the screen tight against the drapes. Lani gently laid Malia's matching Hello Kitty comforter over the children; they had already tired of the jumping game and fallen asleep.

During the next hour, Leilani and Alex silently set to work. They crisscrossed masking tape on all the windows; filled empty milk jugs with water; stacked towels and blankets; brought out flashlights plus candles; and laid everything on the floor along one wall of Malia's room. It was the safest room in the house, with only one window on an outside wall and that was now covered.

Out on the lanai, the steel sofa glider was too heavy to move. They flopped down on it to rest, both of them breathing hard, as much from tension as the physical effort of rushing around to secure things.

Leilani grabbed her husband's upper arm. "Look how fast the clouds are moving. They're coming straight at us."

They left the sliding door behind them open to hear the radio—just in time for a new report. "We interrupt this program... Attention! This is the latest update on Hurricane Iniki. The hurricane's eye is headed directly toward the south shore of the island of Kauai at 120 miles per hour. Winds have increased to 145 miles per hour with pulsing gusts to 175."

The time was 12:42 p.m. Leilani shuddered. "The humidity is so heavy you could choke on it."

Alex eyed the two coconut palms out back and the Cook Island pine at the side of the house. "There isn't a leaf or frond stirring out there, and it's so darn quiet. Not good, eerie even. The calm before the storm."

The words barely out of his mouth, a furious gust bowed the two palms inland in deep deference to Laamaomao, the Hawaiian god of the winds. At 12:55 the humidity yielded to a brief drizzle, then a drenching downpour, sending the couple indoors. First checking on the children, who were still asleep, they watched the storm from the center of the living room. Alex drew a protective arm around his wife's waist. The rain angled at their home from the south. Sand particles peppered the sliding glass doors with a plinking, piling up at floor level as though demanding to tunnel into the Wongs' domain.

Alex dared not utter his one optimistic thought, as though saying it aloud might jinx them. They had chosen this sturdy little house soon after their wedding four years ago. The outer walls were cement block covered in stucco; the roof was solidly covered in blue ceramic tiles. *Yeah, we just might weather this storm,* he thought. *Or not.*

The wind roared and screeched and bellowed. They heard unfamiliar objects strike the house in a clatter of thuds, clinks, and clanks. Although sunset wasn't due for almost six hours, darkness followed the storm's intensity, enveloping them. They retreated to Malia's bedroom. The toddlers slept on, indifferent. Holding hands, the parents leaned against each other as they sat on the box spring of Malia's bed. Leilani had spread two blankets across the box springs to make the bed more comfortable.

The picture window in the office gave up first. They heard it implode. Flying shards resounded against the common wall between Malia's room and the office. Plasterboard was no match for the angry wind. The wall bowed ever so slightly, then a small crack appeared. Like a malicious living thing, the crack spread vertically a few inches, threatening, but somehow containing itself.

The bay window in the living room surrendered next, unleashing the cyclonic forces, toppling lamps and ripping Leilani's framed paintings from their picture hooks. Shelves displaying her hand-built ceramics trembled. Glazed pots in glowing colors, comical dogs, cats, and geckos turned into missiles, hurtled against the remaining walls and windows—until there were no windows and no art works left to be destroyed.

Alex and Leilani knew from the clatter in the kitchen, beyond the opposite wall, that the winds had attacked from yet another direction—sounds of cabinet doors slamming open against their frames. Thumps and thuds as the wind became a giant sweeping hand across the countertops, littering the floor.

They heard an elongated groan ending in a loud thump outside. Leilani screamed as she sensed it was the massive ironwood tree next to their driveway crashing down—hoping it wasn't crunching her new Toyota Corolla. It was 2:05 p.m. The blunt force of the storm was upon them.

Another ten minutes passed and the electricity failed. Alex lit one of the candles and heated its opposite end with the match, so it would stick to the bottom of a water glass. This he set atop the dresser and sank back down on the bed next to his wife. He took her hand in his and squeezed it whenever he sensed her quivering responses to what they were hearing. An ear-splitting crash resounded at the opposite end of the house, followed by the clatter of loosened roof tiles falling onto the cement driveway for several seconds afterward. She began to shake. Even the candlelight shivered, creating eerie dancing shadows in the room.

"The avocado tree must have fallen on the master bedroom side of the house," he calmly offered, so as not to upset Leilani.

"Mommy, mommy!" The wailing, frantic cry jolted them. Noah thrashed about on the mattress in the middle of the floor. "I want my mommy!" he screamed.

"Maybe the crashing tree woke him," said Leilani.

Alex picked Noah up, cradling him. "You'll see Mommy soon," he said in a soothing voice. But the little boy refused to be comforted. His chubby body heaved and struggled as he sobbed. Alex steadfastly kept rocking, until Noah, exhausted from his own protests, nuzzled silently against Alex's chest.

Leilani's watch said 3:50 when Malia awoke with a whine and toddled over to her mother, arms raised, to be picked up. Leilani pulled her in and held her close, not able to speak for fear her own anxiety would be contagious and frighten her baby girl.

Minutes later the ruckus and howling winds outside the house ceased, and all they could hear was the persistent beat of the rain. Then, surprisingly, even that disappeared. It was as though nature had flipped a switch and turned the storm off.

Is the storm over or are we merely stalled in the hurricane's eye? Alex wondered. He had to venture a peek outside and see what was going on. He set Noah down on the mattress and handed him a stuffed teddy bear; the boy seemed content enough, at least for the moment. Selecting the one Maglite from the group of flashlights, he looked across at his wife.

"All quiet. It must be the eye of the storm." He cautiously opened the bedroom door and peeked out into the living room, strewn with sand and debris. He stepped out, closing the door behind him.

"Be careful and don't go too far from us," Leilani called out to him.

Switching on the Maglite, Alex stepped into what had been their lovingly arranged and organized living room. The irony of it. Weak sunshine illuminated what now looked like a city dump, covered with wet sand and puddles of water. Pieces of Leilani's artwork amassed and embedded against the inland wall; the two upholstered wing chairs on their sides; the TV set smashed on its belly; end tables overturned with legs broken. Huge shards of bay window glass stuck or lay everywhere.

Glancing through the void where the sliding doors should

have been, Alex saw sunlight overhead, but black clouds still blanketed the sky elsewhere. The lanai no longer had its wood-slatted roof. The air was soundless with the exception of water dripping everywhere. They had certainly entered the eye of the storm. Feeling his way to the kitchen, his sneakers immediately met up with the storm's clutter. He pushed all the cabinet doors shut, but not before noting that boxes and cans of food inside somehow had stayed in place; and luckily, their wooden table had remained upright. From the kitchen he crossed the living room to inspect the master bedroom. Their tall, full avocado tree had indeed fallen onto the roof of that room, denting and slightly caving the roof in, but not destroying it.

The hesitant patch of sunlight now surrendered to a shroud of blackness like a moonless nightfall. A distant whine pierced the heavy air once more and grew louder. Palm trees hunched in defeat, their fronds pointing stiffly in unison. Smaller objects were flying again.

Leilani, making sure the toddlers were still asleep, anxiously opened the bedroom door and stepped out. Her brain stubbornly refused to accept the destruction in the living room. A returning Alex wrapped his arm around her shoulders in empty reassurance. He shuffled Leilani back into Malia's room, shutting the door behind them. Just as they slumped down beside each other on the box spring, her dark eyes filled with tears. He gave her an extra squeeze.

Alex somehow knew this terrible storm wasn't finished.

Just then, Noah rolled onto his side and moaned. Husband and wife looked at each other, sharing the same feeling of alarm. *Where are Noah's parents? Are they safe? Did the hurricane hit Princeville?*

Alex knew it might be days before the electricity was restored. He stood and walked to check if the door was securely closed. When he turned around Leilani was standing and crying.

"Why now?" she sobbed, her hands in motion. "Why, when everything was going our way? Must we always live in fear?

What have we done to anger the gods so much?"

Alex acknowledged that there were no rational replies to such questions—and he certainly didn't have to answer to the Hawaiian gods. His wife's repeated reference to these gods was a cultural, traditional obsession stemming from her grandmother, *Tutu* Eme, and not religious in nature. But he felt obligated to give comfort anyway. He wrapped his arms around her and drew her close once more. Alex Wong, the son of a Japanese mother and Chinese father, was neither superstitious nor religious.

The storm howled and battered away, but there was yet another noise, a repeated and distinctive one.

"Listen, Alex! Someone's pounding on our front door," said Leilani, slipping out of his embrace and putting her ear to the wall.

"I'll take a look. Push the door shut after me." He pulled the door ajar and bent almost backward to stay upright against the whirling wind. He labored through the living room, kicking away obstacles that had once made their house a home. He was able to hear an urgent voice through the missing stained-glass window that Leilani had created near the top of their door.

"Please, Alex. Let us in, for God's sake. We've lost our whole roof and need shelter. We're soaking wet."

Alex recognized his neighbor from across the road. "Just a minute, Jesse, while I get this open." It took all his strength pulling and Jesse pushing to get the front door open. Ellie Duran slipped through first, carrying their swaddled four-month-old infant. As soon as Jesse followed her inside, they allowed the door to slam shut again.

"Wait! Be careful! The power's out," Alex warned. He switched on his Maglite, concentrating the beam on the debris-covered floor toward Malia's room. Hunching forward into the wind, he followed them and called to Leilani, "It's me and the Durans. They're going to stay with us."

Once everyone was inside, Leilani handed them towels and took the baby from Ellie so the family could dry off. Frightened by the darkness, too confused to babble, Malia and Noah sat wide-eyed on the mattress and watched the grownups.

"You folks have one of the only houses in sight with a roof overhead," Jesse said. His voice trembled. "What a disaster outside." He described the impassable roads strewn with downed trees, abandoned cars, and beach sand piled up in little dunes. "The Kaleos' house next door was hit bad, but looks like it survived—sort of."

"What about our cars?" asked Leilani. "Did you see what happened?"

"Sorry Lani, your Corolla is a total loss, but the Cherokee appears to be intact."

Alex braved a foray across the living room to the master bedroom to bring back dry clothes—pants, T-shirts, and underwear—for the Durans, with hand towels to turn into diapers.

The howling slowly dissipated. The drenching, driving rains eased, then ceased altogether. It was 7:30 p.m. The storm had finally passed over them. Ellie stayed with the children while the others ventured out to inspect the rest of the house. In the kitchen, Alex worked in the beam of his Maglite. He found a broom and dustpan and swept up the smashed glass coffeepot and other debris. Next, he lifted the dented toaster-oven and small microwave oven back up to the counter.

The master bedroom had a hole in that corner of the roof where the tree had fallen, but the tree still covered much of the opening. In fact, their king-sized mattress had stayed dry, and much of the bedroom furniture was still intact. But there was no guarantee that the roof wouldn't cave in entirely from the tree's sheer weight. Nothing in the living room or dining room appeared salvageable.

"I've got a small portable gasoline generator," said Jesse, "and some heavy-duty tarps in what's left of my tool shed. Maybe we can at least salvage the food in both our fridges and have a little electricity left over for some light. The tarps can cover some of the holes here. Problem is, they're probably under a mess of debris right now. Are you willing to tackle this with me?"

"Let's go!" said Alex." He actually felt buoyed up with the relief of having something useful to do.

The two men had to slog through muddy ponds and climb over tree limbs and house parts just to get to Jesse's property. There was no sign of the Durans' roof. The men skirted the three remaining house walls still standing. They found the roof of the tool shed wedged between two trees, with the shed's corrugated steel walls collapsed inward. Using a pole as a lever, they managed to slide the steel walls out of the way. They found the tarps first and searched for the portable generator next. At last they exposed its red metal exterior.

The generator was too heavy to lift. Even in its carriage it couldn't be moved; the carriage wheels were too small to be of any use without bogging down in the mud. Jesse made a sled out of a flat piece of steel and some heavy cord. With huge effort and a lot of muscle, they slid the generator onto the makeshift sled and got the rig moving. Jesse was able to retrieve an axe and a saw from the tool shed he'd uncovered earlier. They made quick work of a tree branch that barred their way. The two men dragged the sled across the road to the window outside the Wong kitchen.

Jesse removed the gas cap and discovered the tank empty. No surprise. Alex came to the rescue. He kept a siphon in the trunk of his Jeep Cherokee, along with a gas can. When they were ready to start the generator, Leilani tossed the end of an extension cord out the kitchen window. Alex turned the key. The engine choked. He tried the starter cord. After a dozen hopeless pulls, he surrendered the job to stronger Jesse. Five pulls later, the generator engine took hold. Jesse adjusted the choke and throttle until it ran smoothly. Alex plugged in the extension chord and immediately Leilani yelled out, "The fridge is running. We've got lights! Let's see if we can rustle up some food."

The men did a high five, and Jesse said, "Let's cover the hole in your master bedroom roof next, pal, then I'll be ready to call it quits for the night." Hacking away at two large roots, the avocado tree soon slipped away from the roof and fell to the ground.

Using a tree branch, they poled up and draped one of the tarps over a corner of the bedroom roof. Standing on the front window sill, Alex stapled the tarp to a sloping beam and repeated the stapling from the window on the side of the house.

The families huddled up to the kitchen table, children on laps, Ellie nursing the baby. At 9 p.m. they devoured left-over chicken with rice and wilted, warmish salad.

But Leilani was merely keeping up a brave front. She'd already made up her mind. No matter how much repairing and rebuilding they could do to their dear little house, it would never be enough. She wasn't going to live each day in anguished suspense, fearing another hurricane. She knew that every time high winds or heavy rain assaulted their vulnerable island, she would feel a sense of doom—that maybe next time they wouldn't be so lucky. She hadn't graduated with honors from the University of California at Berkeley to spend her life under a cloud of anxiety—from weather they couldn't control or vengeful gods they couldn't appease.

She'd wait a few days to break that news to Alex. For sure, they would go back to Oahu. Of course, they'd wait for little Noah's parents. Leilani's eyes welled up with fresh tears. He was still whimpering for his mommy.

Chapter 2

Aftermath

MORNING dawned with the rhythmic putt-putt of Jesse's faithful generator—and the county bulldozers outside grunting, grinding away. The giant construction machines pushed aside debris, opening a single-lane path in the main road for emergency vehicles. This same debris wound up piled high on driveways, lawns, and crossroads. The Wong driveway proved no exception.

Nestled with the two Wongs in their king-size bed, the toddlers awoke just after six-thirty. Malia stirred first and regarded her surroundings. Where was her Hello Kitty comforter? And what was she doing in her parents' bed? Hungry and confused, she started sucking her thumb, a habit she'd abandoned months before.

Noah awoke a few minutes later, most likely from Malia's knee in his back. Looking at the unfamiliar grownups in bed with him, he soon realized they were neither his mother nor his father. Frightened, he sobbed, "I want my mommy."

Leilani's eyes flew open. As soon as she rolled over to regard the little boy, her eyes filled with tears, but she blinked them back and crawled out of bed. There was breakfast to be made. She slipped into her clothes and left for the kitchen. There was plenty of time to think about Noah later.

Alex felt sorry for the boy, so he sat up and scooted across the bed to a place between the toddlers. He put a comforting arm about each of them and, in a soothing voice, calmed Noah down. A tug on Malia's arm and the wet thumb fell out of her mouth. He eventually saw to their early morning needs. Some clothes, brushed teeth, washed faces, and combed hair—his charges were ready for breakfast.

The grateful Durans had squeezed into Malia's youth bed with the sides down. Jesse, up first and full of angst, dressed and stepped out onto the front lawn. At the break of day he gazed across the road and saw the shattered remains of what had been their home for the last three years. The unstoppable winds had totaled their single-walled, wood-frame dwelling. The missing wall was nowhere in sight. About fifty yards from the wreckage he saw his pickup. It lay on its right side in a ditch, but it did appear to be in one piece. Jesse wondered, with a tinge of envy, why Alex's Jeep remained upright and in place while his own heavy truck had surrendered.

"Hey, guys," Leilani called out. "I've scrambled some eggs and made toast and coffee on the grill. Come eat."

They crowded around the table as one family, but the adults were introspective, upset, and afraid to bring up the future—the "future" at this point meant the next few days. "Pass the…whatever." What could they say in front of the children, when they had no idea themselves? The two-year-olds intuitively sensed disruption.

After breakfast Alex replenished the gasoline in the generator tank. To his amazement, the office closet, where he kept his tools, remained undisturbed. He chose his bow saw for cutting branches and clearing brush, and handed Jesse the axe. Together they took on the eight-foot-high pile left by the bulldozers: tree limbs, wrecked home sections, crushed furnishings, and smashed appliances, along with sand and mud and a mélange of indescribables. Already 83 degrees, the air hung humid and heavy. Before long, their shirts had been shed and their skin gleamed with sweat. Along the road as far as the eye could see, telephone poles leaned at varying angles, resembling some macabre ballet.

No traffic appeared on the road while they were working, so it surprised them when a Kauai County Police cruiser crawled to a stop as close as it could to the Wong driveway. Two officers climbed out and plodded their way around the debris. Their faces were grim. Deep wrinkles appeared on the driver's brow as he spoke. "Good morning. I'm Officer Otani and this is Officer Mehara. Could you tell us, please, where the Kaleo family lives?"

"That's it over there." Alex pointed to the tiny house next door. The roof had sagged to the street side, as if on one knee—battered and missing many of its tiles. The near side wall had caved in some—unstable looking, but the structure somehow remained standing.

"Ilima and Tom were up in Princeville overnight," Alex added. "I'm assuming they're all right."

Officer Otani shook his head. "I'm very sorry to report that they're both dead. A bulldozer operator found them trapped in their car about ten miles north of here. An uprooted tree trunk fell on their car roof, demolishing it and crushing them in the front seat. I guess they were trying to make it home. The address on Mr. Kaleo's driver's license is what brought us here."

"Oh, no! That's terrible news," said Alex. "They were good neighbors, good friends too. "I can't believe it! We're babysitting Noah, their two-year-old son."

"Do you know of any next of kin we can notify?" Officer Otani asked.

Alex's voice choked. "Tom's parents were killed in a plane crash three years ago. But Ilima and my wife were close. Maybe Ilima mentioned more family."

"That would be helpful," said Officer Otani. "If you hear of anyone, call us. He handed Alex a business card. The officers climbed back in their cruiser and slowly drove off.

Grabbing the neck of his T-shirt, Alex ducked his head under it to mop his sweaty brow. *How am I gonna tell Lani?* he pondered. Just then, he looked up and saw her cautiously pushing open the ripped screen door that now hung from one hinge.

Carrying two bottles of water, she handed them over. "I thought you might need these. What did the police want?" She saw the anguish on both men's faces. "Alex, what's wrong?"

"They were looking for the Kaleo place."

"Did you tell them they were in Princeville?"

"I tried to, but…Terrible news, Lani."

"What?"

"Ilima and Tom were killed in their car some time last night. I guess they were on their way home. A bulldozer driver found them this morning—crushed by a tree trunk that fell across their car."

Leilani gasped. "Oh, dear God, no." She covered her eyes with her hands as tears drenched her cheeks. "Oh my God," she moaned. "Alex, how are we going to tell Noah?"

"The police were looking for next of kin," he said. "Do you know of any relatives?"

"They didn't have any siblings. Ilima's mother died several years ago. I'm pretty sure there's no one else. Ilima even told me once that she envied us for having so much family."

Alex cast a sidelong glance at Jesse, who quickly picked up the message. "This is a real tragedy, man, but we've got our hands full with our baby."

"Yeah, I understand," said Alex. "I guess that means there's no one to take care of Noah."

Leilani stopped crying. "*We* can, Alex. For now, anyway. At least he knows us, and that's a start."

"Lani, that's one hell of a lot of responsibility. We can talk about it later."

"Shame on you, Alex Wong! I seemed to remember when I had no place to go, how your parents took me into your home. It was *not* easy for them." She stomped her foot on the soggy ground and wound up splashing her slippered feet and shins. "And they were good to me. They still are."

"Of course they are, Lani. You're their daughter-in-law. They love you. They always did. But you were sixteen, not two." He chose not to remind her that his parents had been paid for taking in a foster child. "Honey, we just lost two-thirds of everything we own. Let's be reasonable. We should think about this before we make such a big decision."

The accountant and artist glared at one another. Leilani

spun about and started toward the house—but only a few steps. With second thoughts, she returned to Alex, her cheeks flushed and eyes bright. "Dear, I hate it when you're so level-headed and practical, but I have an idea. The Kaleos left their house key with us in case of an emergency. One thing we can do right now is get some of Noah's things. His toys, his clothes, anything that will make him feel less foreign in our house."

Alex's stubbled face took on a look of alarm. "Lani, we don't know the true condition of their house. It looks bad from here— it could collapse at any time. We could get stuck inside, crushed under the roof or something. Why would we take that chance?"

She squared her shoulders and took on the no-holds-barred look he recognized. "It would only be for a few quick minutes."

He saw there was no point in arguing. "I'll only agree if you let me go in first and...hey, wait a minute, babe. It would be crazy for both of us to risk getting hurt. You're not going in. I am. I'll collect everything I can of his as fast as I can."

Her wide, sensual mouth broke into a pout, then a surrendering grin. "Okay, that makes sense. I'll get you the key."

"And a big bag."

Prancing back to the house, she gingerly pulled the screen door open to raucous shouts and giggles coming from Malia's room. Startled, Leilani realized that she'd foolishly left the children alone. The wrecked living room was a treacherous obstacle course, and she'd better keep a closer eye on the children. But she needn't have worried. Ellie Duran was breast-feeding baby Becca next door in the kitchen. Leilani found the toddlers crowing with delight as they chased each other around the bed, lurching this way and that, abruptly stopping to throw stuffed animals at each other. For the moment, Noah seemed happily occupied, and she had a little breathing space before the moment she dreaded.

Reappearing at the screen door a few moments later, she held out the Kaleos' house key, along with a garbage bag for Alex. "Don't forget Noah's sippy cup. And darling? Be careful."

Back inside, Leilani decided not to stand on ceremony and

poked her head into the kitchen, where Ellie was still nursing the baby. "Ellie? Could you please come into Malia's room and watch the kids for me? I tried to call my dad in Honolulu. They must be worried sick, but of course there's no dial tone. I'll be in Alex's office seeing what else I can do."

Ellie nodded. She welcomed any distraction that would smother the reality of their own misfortunes.

Nearly all the rain water driven through the shattered office window had collected on the opposite wall and run off into the living room. Alex's desktop computer and monitor lay face-down and dry on the floor under the heavy desk where he had left them, but there was no electricity. In the top drawer she found his laptop. *He'll be pleased*, she thought. She opened it and tried to boot it up. It responded with a desktop display, but when she tried the Internet it was dead. *Hey, we have a satellite dish! Maybe it got turned around in the wind.*

Outside, she picked her way around the rubble that had been the lanai and looked up at the roof. The dish was gone—ripped from its metal mounting brackets. But then she saw cable coming out of the office and followed the length of it around to the side of the house until she saw the dish hanging over the edge of the eave by its own cable. *It looks like it's intact. Maybe I can set it upright.* The idea of attacking this project herself fired her up.

Forty minutes later Alex returned from the rickety Kaleo home without incident; he ignored the house shifting on its block pilings twice while he was inside. The stuffed black Hefty bag was so full, it had to be dragged behind him. There was more, but he'd have to go back for it later. He left the bag in the corner of the living room to be dealt with later—there were more important things to be done now. He headed out front to help Jesse.

Meanwhile, Jesse had finished shoveling and clearing away the rubble blocking the Duran driveway. Earlier, the two men had cleared a path to the road for the Wongs' Jeep and successfully started its engine. They began to clear a path from Jesse's truck to the street. By 2:30 p.m. they reached the ditch where the pickup lay almost on its side.

"Hi, guys." Leilani had crossed the street to bring them more water. "Alex, your laptop computer appears to be okay. I was able to turn it on, but you know what? No Internet. Our dish on the roof might make it work. It's torn loose from its mount, but it's still attached to the cable and looks to be in one piece. Maybe you could take a look before you go back to work. It's our only way to communicate with the outside world as long as the power is out islandwide. Or at least I assume it is."

"Good grief! We've been so busy, I forgot all about Mom and Dad worrying about us," said Alex. "Your dad and Kekoa too, of course. Yeah, I had better see if I can fix it."

"How would you get up there?" asked Leilani. "Our ladder is gone. But I do have the duct tape from the kitchen drawer. Maybe you could tape it back to the mounting. Hey, dear, I've got an idea. Could the two of you boost me up to the roof? I could do the taping if you directed from below."

"Too risky," said Alex. "Let's see if we can find our extension ladder first."

He discovered it wedged between two trees about sixty feet from their house. He abandoned the cracked upper section, dragged the ten-foot lower section back, and leaned it against the house.

"Yea!" Leilani cheered. She climbed it quickly and in ten minutes had the satellite dish taped in place on its mounts. It just needed a little adjustment.

"Up and a little to the left." Alex called to her. "That's it."

"Well, that was easy enough," Leilani said on the way down the ladder. She had a prideful grin across her face.

Alex lifted her off the ladder and hugged her. Inside, they tried the laptop again, this time with success, including the Internet and e-mail accounts. "I'll let you attend to all the messaging while Jesse and I go rescue his wayward truck."

Alex found about fifteen feet of one-inch nylon rope tied to the splintered remains of Tom Kaleo's rowboat. Jesse returned with more rope from his demolished shed and some chain that had been tied to a pair of swings hung from a swing set.

The truck lay parallel to the Duran driveway, facing the road, with the bottom showing. Because of a stump holding up the right side, they were able to pass the chain around the cab roof twice before knotting it. Alex backed the Jeep up. They tied the remainder of the ropes together, fastening the hemp ends around the Jeep's rear axle and knotting the nylon end around the chain. A half hour later, they were ready to give it a try. Alex slowly took up the slack, then put on the brake. They slipped two old blankets under the Jeep's wheels to get traction. Alex slowly fed the gas. The ropes tightened and stretched amid a clatter of metallic groan as the truck began to stress and roll.

"Stay clear, Jesse, the rope might snap!" shouted Alex, leaning out the window. No sooner said than one of the dissimilar rope knots slipped apart, snapping the two ends in opposite directions like a bullwhip crack. Ten minutes later, the pickup still lay in the ditch like a wounded beast.

They had nowhere near the right equipment and knew it might be weeks before a tow truck got to it, so Alex backed the Jeep up again, and, this time, they retied each knot back on itself, only looped through the connecting rope. The second try was more successful in easing the truck down on four wheels. The right side had been crunched in a number of places and the passenger door was jammed. But Jesse had no illusions—he got in right away and tried to start the pickup. It was a contest—would the battery surrender, or would the truck start first? On the fourth try the engine coughed a few times, and on the fifth finally caught hold. It ran rough at first and then settled in well enough. He shifted into gear and drove toward the road, as the ditch alongside the driveway was far too steep to climb. When he reached the debris at the road, he stopped and got out. Using the Jeep and the attached ropes, Alex dragged away several large tree branches, making an opening for Jesse's truck to enter the road from the lower grade.

Having driven onto the road, Jesse then backed the pickup

truck into the end of his driveway and parked it there. He untied the chain around the cab roof and managed to get the windows up. By the time he'd done that, Alex had undone the tow rope and backed the Jeep into his own driveway.

"Well, *brah*, I guess we both have transportation now," Jesse said as they dragged themselves back to the house.

"Guys, come in the office! The satellite dish works!" Leilani called. "Alex, you have to hear this!" She sat at the desk in the only chair, reading an email from Hank Pualoa, her father. The men slumped down to the floor, leaning against the only dry wall, too exhausted to stand any longer.

"Jesse," Leilani explained, "this is an email from my dad. He and his wife live in Ewa Beach." She read aloud:

Dearest Lani and Alex,

Thank God all of you are safe. Possessions can always be replaced. You are precious to us. I highly recommend that you secure the house and come to Honolulu—as soon as it is practical and transportation is available. The Wongs say they have plenty of room for all three of you. Masako and Paul send their love. Oahu escaped for the most part, but the west coast from Barber's Point to Kaena Point got hit hard.

From the aerial television accounts we've seen, Kauai is a major disaster area with widespread damage. Food, water, and medical supplies may be hard to come by, and I don't think too many businesses will be operating for a while. I believe building materials will also be scarce for some time. Insurance payments will be far slower, if at all. Many firms are calling the storm an act of God and might not honor household insurance claims.

Don't worry. When the time comes and materials and services are available, I will bring a construction crew of mine over to fix up your home. By then, there may even be some Federal disaster assistance. Meanwhile, take heart, everyone here is willing to help.

Love, Dad and Lori

"It does make a lot of sense, dear," said Leilani.

Alex scowled. "In your email to your dad did you explain about Noah? Do my parents know they'll have a second baby in the house?"

Leilani reddened. "Uh, no, not yet."

"What about all my clients?" he asked. "They've got businesses to run."

"You don't even know if there are any client businesses still running. Some will even be shutting down for good. And how would you reach some of the others with the roads the way they are?"

"There's the Internet, dear," he said.

"We have it," said Leilani. "But do they? And if they do get Internet, you can reach them from Oahu just as well."

"Maybe," said Alex. "But people will soon be desperate. There may even be some looting. How can we secure the house so there won't be any looting here?"

"Ellie and I could be the solution," interrupted Jesse, feeling a surge of optimism for the first time since Iniki hit. "I'll help you two with your cleanup here. If you do decide to go to Honolulu for a while, Ellie and I and the baby could stay here, so it'll be lived in—that is, if you'd allow us to. It would only be temporary, of course, until I have time to rebuild my place. I've been in residential construction all my working life, so there's going to be plenty of work for me on the island. In the meantime, I could get your place back in shape. Then, when the bulk building materials arrive, I'll get started on our own house."

Leilani's heart quickened. "Sounds like the perfect answer to me," she said, cutting in before Alex had a chance to have his say.

"Sounds more like I'm being railroaded," Alex complained. "On the other hand—Jesse, I sure would be happy to take you up on your offer to do some repairs here. You and Ellie are good friends. We do want you all to be safe. I suppose we could try it for a month or two and see how everything plays out."

At that moment, a piercing shriek came from the living room—Noah's frantic wailing, "Mommy, Mommy!" Ellie's soothing voice, "There, there, darling," met with "No! No!"

Leilani and Alex rushed in. Noah had discovered the Hefty bag filled with all his possessions and, suddenly, in his intuitive two-year-old head, he knew something very bad had happened.

* * * *

A week later, Alex, Leilani, and the children left their home on the Garden Isle of Kauai. They moved back to Honolulu, where they were welcomed by Alex's parents into the spacious Manoa Valley home where Alex grew up and Leilani had been a foster teen.

What Masako and Paul Wong had not expected was a second toddler, whose moods wildly swung past any typical two-year-old's tirades. Noah would angelically play with Malia for a few hours, then lapse into fierce tantrums of foot-stamping; shouting "No" this and "No" that; or, in his high chair, throw food he didn't like. All understandable, barely out of babyhood and in light of his orphaned state, but setting the family's teeth on edge.

Alex and Leilani debated late into the night in the privacy of their bedroom. Should they or should they not continue to live with his parents? Tempting, this living comfortably under one roof, plus the outrageous housing costs on Oahu. The clincher came when, a few weeks later, Alex's mother fell ill with cancer. Masako had to quit her teaching job at Oahu Preparatory Academy, where both Alex and Leilani had gone to school. Leilani converted the garage into an art studio, so she could paint and still be there to help care for Masako. Paul Wong continued teaching at Oahu Prep as the science department head.

The Duran family ultimately purchased the Wong home on Kauai. Alex still returned to the island a day or two a month to service his loyal clientele there, but now he had a substantial list of clients on Oahu as well.

After a trial year as Noah's foster parents, Alex and Leilani officially adopted him. They felt that somewhere, deep down, the boy appreciated what they had done for him, but there was something amiss—something they couldn't comprehend in his demeanor. He never quite grew out of the terrible twos, just segued into a more grownup version of it when he started school.

At that point the annoyances turned into flagrant problems. The boy was bright enough, but rarely paid attention and soon lagged behind in his studies. His lack of motivation and concentration led to disruptiveness in the classroom, then on to spontaneous fighting with other students over little or nothing. A faint scar over his left eye and a broken finger that never healed quite right were permanent reminders of his hot-headedness and skill with his fists.

Oh, he was clever and imaginative, all right. He poured fatal vinegar into his third-grade teacher's treasured violet plant. His fourth-grade teacher found a live frog in her bottom desk drawer. Then there was the rock thrown through Mr. Mack's sixth-grade classroom window and the spontaneous fire in his wastebasket. Subsequent parent-teacher meetings began with thoughtful advice, but quickly morphed into explosive tones until, finally, Noah was expelled from Oahu Prep at the age of eleven. Paul Wong breathed a deep sigh of relief. As a prominent faculty member, he had suffered his grandson's exploits in silent humiliation.

* * * *

Masako, although weak and frail, went into remission. Leilani harbored a seed of guilt. Had the constant aggravation over Noah's behavior contributed to her mother-in-law's cancer?

Chapter 3

Troublesome

(November 2004, Twelve Years After Hurricane Iniki)

MALIA Wong thrived at Oahu Prep, a model student with top grades, but because of her adopted brother, she was not as popular as she might have been. In the classes they shared, Noah had been overly protective of her, bloodying a few noses in the process. Many fearful students kept her at arm's length. After his expulsion she regained her popularity. She bore the same comely island features as her mother—long, dark-brown hair, dark eyes, a warm broad smile, and a mild tendency toward plumpness. Her sweet gullibility proved to be her only downside—yes, a real Goody Two-shoes.

Leilani and Alex enrolled Noah in public school, where he too thrived, but in all the wrong ways. He was now fourteen, wildly good looking, deeply affectionate, strongly loyal, and just as obstinate as before. Understandably, he looked quite different from his adoptive family—shorter, with a bull-strength build, darker complexion, and even the too-early hint of a mustache. Still, oddly enough, his thick brown hair and wide-set dark eyes resembled his stepsister's.

Alex knew Noah's father had been an athlete, a star wrestler in high school, and he saw the same traits of agility and physical skills in Noah. All good. But it was their son's personality that constantly ate away at their insides. Although Noah proved to be smart and articulate, his closest friends teetered on the delinquent, even the criminal, but his parents' efforts to alter his choices were futile. Alex and Leilani received regular calls from the principal's office informing them of his truancy, but they were ineffective in stopping it. Noah frequently cut school on Fridays and this was one of those days.

Today, the wayward high school freshman was joined by junior Dante (Duke) Santos and another freshman, gangly Gino Akino. The trio, led by Duke, was up to no good—as usual.

"Wong," ordered Duke, "you distract the shopkeeper while me and Gino pick the shelves for the good stuff. You go in first so he don't think we're together."

Noah entered the drugstore and walked up to the counter in the back. "Are you the pharmacist?" he asked.

"Why, yes, young man, what can I do for you?" asked the white-haired proprietor.

"I've got this real bad rash on my butt and I'm always scratching it. It's so bad I can hardly sit. Don't worry, I can pay." He waved a ten-dollar bill in the man's face. It was folded over to look like two tens.

"Have you seen a doctor about this?" asked the pharmacist.

Meanwhile, the front door opened with a lone jingle. Duke, casually slouching, headed for the magazine shelves, where he pretended to be making a selection. The pharmacist looked up, but what he didn't see was Gino slipping in after Duke and hiding behind a display at the end of the third aisle.

With an innocent expression, Noah respectfully said, "I've got a doctor's appointment a week from next Thursday, but it's killing me. I can't wait that long. Can you give me something for it?" The boy had grown up a quick study and had learned from his adoptive parents the value of speaking with educated grammar—so disarming, so much more useful than the Hawaiian pidgin he spoke with his friends.

As the conversation at the pharmacy counter continued, Gino made his way up the aisle to the mirror surveying the third aisle. He leaped up and tilted it so it covered only one side of the aisle. With two visible distracters afoot, the now-invisible shoplifter cleared the small display stand of cheap watches and slid them into the deep pockets of his cargo pants. He moved to the candy section, undid a few shirt buttons, then shoveled a dozen or so candy bars into his open shirt, and re-buttoned it. He couldn't carry anything more, so he returned to his original hiding spot next to the door and signaled Duke he was ready to leave.

The pharmacist kept a sharp eye on Duke to make sure the young hoodlum put down the motorcycle magazine he'd been reading. What the man missed was that Duke had picked up two magazines at once, slipping the second one into his pants under a warm-up jacket. He flamboyantly rearranged the first magazine back on the rack before turning to leave the store. The lone jingle signaled the departure of one customer, whereas two had actually left the store.

"Here you are," said the pharmacist. "This ought to curb all that itching. Apply it every four hours—a *skosh* bit on the end of your fingers." He slipped a white tube into a small bag and laid it on the counter. "That comes to $13.56, young man."

"But I've only got this," Noah said. Unfolding the ten, he pushed it forward on the counter, hoping the pharmacist would cancel the transaction.

The elderly man thought for a moment and smiled as he picked up the ten, and slid the bag toward Noah. "We'll call it square. My good deed for the day."

"Thanks, mister," said Noah, but he begrudgingly took the bag and walked out, now ten bucks in the hole.

He caught up with his conspirators at a predetermined alley several blocks away. Duke and Gino were already kneeling on the concrete, divvying up the booty: two watches and five candy bars each, except that Duke kept four extra watches for himself.

"Hey, that's not fair," whined Gino. "I took all the friggin' risks—I should get the bigger share if anyone does."

"It was my idea," returned Duke. "I planned the whole damn caper, and you're complaining about a couple a watches?" He stood, puffed himself up, and curled his fists in a defiant manner.

"Uh, no," grumbled Gino.

"What about me?" asked an anxious Noah, standing a little too close to Duke. "I lost a sawbuck in this job and all I get is two cheesy watches I don't need and some lousy candy bars I don't even like."

"That was your fault, not mine," sneered Duke.

Noah took a swing at Duke which he easily deflected. The more muscular and experienced Duke quickly swung back, hitting Noah square in the mouth and, knocking him to the concrete. Noah spit blood. A tooth came out in his fingers. He looked up and saw Duke standing over him, ready to dish out more. Noah held up his right hand, signifying that he had had enough. Duke scooped up Noah's share, turned his back to him, and left the alley with his arm around Gino.

* * * *

The Wongs were eating a quiet supper in the dining room when Noah entered the house through the back door. Instead of joining them, he darted through the kitchen to the stairs with the intent of slipping up to his room before anyone saw his state of disarray.

"Whoa, young man," said Alex. "Stop right now! Aren't you going to join us?"

Noah stood still for a minute without turning around. "In a couple minutes, Dad."

"Can't you at least face us when you're talking?" asked Alex.

"I was just going upstairs to wash up for dinner." He turned around to reveal his bloody T-shirt, and when he saw the gasping effect it had on his family, his amusement produced a grin that exposed his missing tooth.

"My God, what happened to you?" exclaimed Masako.

"How badly are you hurt?" asked Leilani. She stood and hurried to the boy to see for herself.

"Oooo, gross!" said Malia.

"You really need to do something about Noah's temper," advised Paul.

"You've been fighting again," declared Alex. "How many times have I told you not to antagonize people? Stand down and walk away from arguments you can't win. Will you never learn that you always get the worst of these skirmishes?"

Noah's dander flared. He intended to answer some of the remarks, but his mother spun him away and hurried him up the stairs to the master bathroom. She pulled the T-shirt over his head to see where he was injured and found no wounds. When she stepped back, she saw his outstretched arm with a tooth lying in the middle of his palm.

"Where did all this blood come from?" she asked.

"From here, Mom," he said, pointing to the gap with his other hand. "I got sucker-punched in the mouth. I didn't even land a punch on him."

"Noah, what started this?" She stared intently at him. "Were you gambling?"

"Uh, yeah. He cheated and stole some money from me. The ten spot Dad gave me yesterday." He couldn't tell her about his friends robbing the drugstore.

"What's the boy's name?"

"I can't tell you that, Mom. You'd act on it, and I couldn't face anybody at school any more."

"Nonsense! He stole from you and attacked you. And look at your mouth. It's going to cost us a lot to fix your teeth. What kind of loyalty does that merit from you?"

"I just can't, Mom. I'd rather go around looking goofy for the rest of my life than squeal."

"If that's the way you want it, you may have to go around with a hole in your smile for a while. Let's see if the dentist can even replant your tooth. I'll call her in the morning."

That night, long after Alex had fallen asleep, Leilani lay awake brooding. *How has all this happened? What have we done wrong as Noah's parents? What are we still doing wrong? Or is it some-*

thing else—maybe a black sheep gene in his birth family? She and Alex had never been overly indulgent, but certainly not overly strict either. A tiny piece of her resented their adopted son. She knew tragedy better than most anyone—when she was only four, she lost her own mother driving home from a family picnic, an auto accident.

* * * *

Six friggin' weeks and three painful dental appointments with this oral surgeon butcher, and all I'm gonna have for it is this lousy implant and not even a fake tooth, ran through Noah's thoughts.

"Okay, young man, we're done," said the surgeon—glad to be finished with her squirming, complaining patient. "Your implant is in place."

The only good part about hearing the oral surgeon's pronouncement was knowing the worst part was over. But Noah Wong couldn't even count on no more pain. Two hours flat on his back. The rogue tooth Noah had managed to bring home in his handkerchief that day simply couldn't be sewn back into his gums. It would take several months for the implant buried in his jawbone to heal, then a temporary tooth, and finally, after full healing, a permanent crown would be attached.

Dr. Li removed her protective mask and Latex gloves. "We'll give you a list of instructions. No solid foods for at least a week, nothing you have to chew on, anyway. We'll see how well the implant is healing then and make sure there's no infection."

"Nothing solid for a week?" repeated Noah, now sitting up in the surgery chair's normal position.

"That's right, and it could even be longer. It depends on how well you do."

"Longer? I'll starve, Miss, I mean Doctor," Noah said, feeling like he had a mouth full of marbles.

"Not very likely," said Dr. Li. "I think I can count on you sticking with milkshakes, nutritional drinks, puddings and the like."

"Yeah, sure. What about the numbing?"

"That will pass in two or three hours, and then you might have some discomfort. I've written a prescription for any pain. Start with two pills and then one every four hours for the next day or so. That's it."

Noah, still under the effects, slid off the surgical chair and slowly slogged to the waiting room, where his mother was co-paying the bill and placing the prescription in her purse. Leilani saw the pained expression on his face.

"Oh no, my dear Noah," she declared, as they left the office in Kukui Plaza. "You'll get no sympathy from me. How many times have we warned you not to get into fights?"

Leilani monologed her nonstop lecture until she deposited him in front of his high school entrance.

Chapter 4

Brothers and Sisters

(Saturday, December 16th, 2004, Six Weeks Later)

MANUEL "Manny" Portfia couldn't afford to lose another sale. The forty-year-old car salesman was already relegated to cold calls, unlikely drop-ins, and Sunday leisure lookers. Dreskoll Motors was the leading supplier of commercial fleets and upscale automobiles in Honolulu. The smoother, more experienced salespersons had developed and refined long lists of repeat clientele and only laughed at Manuel's lame efforts. Handsome but clueless in the sales world, he'd been cautioned about his flashy dressing habits and unpolished humor. This was his third sales position in twelve years, and the only reason he was given a trial run here—his brother had exerted influence over the younger Hans Dreskoll, Manuel's immediate boss. Hans Dreskoll Senior knew nothing of the reason for the hire. Nor did he know the extent of his son's gambling debt to Manuel's brother, Raimonde.

For better or worse, Raimonde Portfia was nothing like his brother. Raimonde had expertly shoved, elbowed, and muscled his way to success in his own shady arena. His slicked-back, black hair, beautifully tailored Armani suits, and elegant demeanor gave him a striking presence. His quick mind and sharp, commanding tongue didn't hurt either.

A sprawling home in a gated compound, a large swimming pool, and a fleet of fast and flashy cars attested to Raimonde's success. The fact that the bulk of his business empire comprised illegal activities had proven unimportant to his own conscience, if he ever had one. Gambling, prostitution, and drugs provided the

31

wellspring of his wealth. Now at the pinnacle of his career, he kept his manicured hands clean by relying heavily on a man named Domingo "Domo" Martinez for all of his enforcement chores.

A profound soft spot for family, including Manuel's family, could be called his only virtue. Raimonde often took Manny aside and whispered, "Come work for me. I pay good wages and skip the crap. All I expect is loyalty."

Manuel always responded, "Thanks, *brah*, but I can't. Esmeralda would make a big stink, take the kids, and leave me nowhere. I don't judge what you do, but she does. I just can't lose my family."

Raimonde always countered, "She doesn't have to know about it."

Manuel ruffled his already uncombed hair. "Hey, man, you don't know her. She has a nose. She always knows."

Esmeralda, "Esme," was the eldest and feistiest of the Ballesteros children. When she met Manuel, she thought he was gorgeous, a diamond in the rough. They were married in a dazzling Filipino wedding in May of 1985 in the Ballesteros backyard. Frank and Delores were born a year apart, five and six years later. But now, with Manuel so passive, Esme took the reins and ruled their roost.

"Uh…What was that you said?" Manuel asked the man seated in the Mercedes on the showroom floor. "I'm sorry. I didn't hear your question." He'd allowed his mind to wander with thoughts of his family. *What would we do if I got fired again? How could we manage?*

"I said, How do I adjust the damned seat? Aren't you paying attention? What kind of a dumb, screwed-up salesman are you, anyway?"

"I said I'm sorry," pleaded Manuel. "There's no need to get insulting."

"Insulting, is it? Hah!" the customer shouted. "I want to talk to the manager." He pounded a fist down on the steering wheel.

"Please give me another chance. I'll lose my job," Manuel

whispered.

The customer shoved open the Mercedes door, banging it into Manuel's side in the process, and strode out the front door. The incident didn't go unnoticed by Hans Junior, who just happened to be peering out of his second-floor office window. Several minutes later Hans swooped down and found his prey.

"Mr. Portfia, what was that disturbance all about?"

Oh-oh. Now I'm gonna get it, Manuel thought. *It's Mister when he's angry and first names otherwise.* "Sorry, Hans. All I did was ask him to repeat his question, and he got all bent out of shape."

"Had to be more than that," said his boss. "Besides you're way behind on your monthly sales goal for the third month in a row. My dad and I agree that you're in the wrong line of work. You're done here. You'll get a week's salary and any commissions due. You can pick up your check in the office. Get your things and clear out. Oh, and good luck." Hans walked away, leaving Manuel stunned and disheartened.

* * * *

The Osaka Family Bakery had been a popular fixture for half a century in the Kaimuki section of Oahu. Leilani's brother, Kekoa, now operated the bakery for the childless owners. Sam and Mauro Osaka had been like family to him ever since the homeless fifteen-year-old Kekoa arrived, pounding on their back door, asking for work and shelter. Sam took him on as a helper, and the eager youth not only learned quickly and proved his worth, but found a way into their hearts as well—the son they never had. A dozen years later Mauro died, and Sam had a disabling stroke that put him in a nursing home. His dedicated and trusted assistant, Kekoa, took over the bakery operation with skill and efficiency.

At 9:30 a.m. Kekoa had just completed the day's baking, with the goods and their heavenly aromas ready for the display cases. He had begun at four that morning. Tall and lean at thirty-four, he removed his flour-covered apron and paper mesh hat and washed up in the little sink under the staircase. Those stairs led to his family's apartment on the second floor. But now he headed for the store facing the street.

Maria, his wife for the past twelve years, ran the store side of things, selling the delectable breads, rolls, cakes, and pastries. Maria Ballesteros Pualoa, younger and prettier than her sister, Esmeralda Portfia, wanted a child. Maria was thirty-three and envied Esme, who already had two, but wished her sister had a different husband. There was something about the Portfia family she didn't like. Perhaps it was that Esme's husband, Manny, couldn't hold down a job for very long. More likely, she hated that Manny's brother, Raimonde, headed up the powerful Portfia crime family.

Maria was speaking with a customer when Kekoa walked in. He watched Maria's adept fingers wrap cotton twine several turns around a square cardboard box and end with a simple bow. *That's a gene reserved for the ladies,* he thought. *She looks especially pretty today, almost glowing.* He wished he could reach out and hold her—but not during a sale.

"Hi, Mrs. Yashimoto," said Kekoa with a respectful nod. "Fine day we're having."

"Oh, hi, Mr. Pualoa. Yes it is." Then turning to Maria, she asked: "When are you due?"

"It's very early, Mrs. Yashimoto," said Maria with a slight Tagalog twang as she handed over the box. "*Arigato,*" she added and then paused. *I hope Kekoa wasn't paying attention,* she thought.

Husband and wife anxiously waited for the door to close on the elderly, ever-smiling Japanese lady.

"Is it true?" Kekoa asked.

"Yes!"

"When were you going to tell me?"

"Do you know what Sunday is?"

He looked up at the wall calendar. "Oh yeah, my birthday."

"And?"

"Our anniversary. Number twelve, right?" he blurted out. "Sorry!"

"It was going to be my present to you," she confessed.

"And now I've spoiled the surprise. How long have you known?" Kekoa wrapped his long arms around Maria's tiny waist. His chin rested on her head of jet-black hair. She hugged him back.

"I saw the doctor on Tuesday, and he said the baby is due the end of June."

"This pregnancy isn't going to end like the last ones, is it?"

She disengaged and backed away from him. "What kind of question is that? There's no way to know at this point. It's only been two months. The doctor said the baby's development looks normal so far, and I can keep doing almost anything that I do now." With a tremor in her voice she reminded Kekoa that the previous three miscarriages happened within the first few weeks, touch and go, right from the beginning. "Don't you remember?"

"I'm sorry, I didn't mean what I said to come out like that." He drew her in once more and she relented.

"It's no one's fault," she murmured. "We need to think positive."

Kekoa launched into the practical side. "Looks like we'll need some extra space upstairs and soon. Our one-bedroom apartment just isn't big enough. Children need their own space."

"Yes, but there's no rush, darling," she assured him. "The baby can sleep with us for some time to come."

Kekoa scowled. "A family bed? No way! I know it appeals to lots of people here in the islands, but I don't go for it. At all!"

Maria giggled. "Me neither, actually. We could chop up the living room to make a second bedroom. "Wait! Where are you going?"

"Out to the street. I want to see something." Kekoa darted out the door and faced the building, then walked next door and out of her sight. When he returned a few minutes later to continue the conversation, Maria was bagging a loaf of Hawaiian cheese bread.

"Thank you, come again, Mr. Ng," she chirped to the young man.

Kekoa darted behind the display cases, his wiry body tensed with excitement. "I've got this terrific idea," he said, taking her two hands in his. "The shop on our left is still up for sale. Been that way for months. What if we bought it and broke through the walls upstairs and made a second and third bedroom and another bath, a modern one with all the gadgets? Downstairs, we could break through the same way and expand the storefront. I've always wanted more room to display our fancy baked goods. And I would have a larger storeroom and office in the back part." His excitement was contagious.

"Whoa, there, husband of mine. What about modernizing the kitchen and bath we have now?"

"I promise we'll do it all," he said. "But everything will have to be done in stages. I'll have to consult with Dad. Maybe he'll have some good ideas too."

Maria brought her long, single braid forward over one shoulder and played with it when she was unsure of herself. "How are we going to pay for all this expansion or are we just dreaming this thing?"

"We could dip into our savings," suggested Kekoa. "The bakery has been doing great, and we've been putting away a tidy sum every month for years now."

"But what if one of your machines has to be replaced—like that old oven?"

"Sam put a new electronic pilot in it. The way it's built, it should last longer than the newer oven—maybe even longer than me. Besides, if we do everything in stages, we won't have to dig so deep into our savings. I'll have to talk with Dad to see if all this is feasible. Maybe I can even do some of the labor myself."

"Hmm." A gleam of a smile flashed across her oval face.

"What?" he said. "Out with it. I can almost hear those wheels turning."

"Well, I was thinking about the larger shop on the other side of us. Mrs. Sachi told me her husband wants to close their dry goods shop and retire next summer. I thought—"

"I don't think that would work as well," he interrupted.

"Wait, hear me out! There's more, and this does nothing to change what you're suggesting."

Maria reminded Kekoa that her brother, Andy, would be graduating from Kapiolani Community College in May with a degree from their culinary school. Papa Ballesteros had promised to help him set up his own coffee shop business.

"Darling!" Maria almost shouted. "Think about it. Next door would be a great location for him, and the timing is just right too."

"Ah, I think I know where you're going with this," said Kekoa. "We could supply them with all their baked goods. Right!"

"Yes! Fresh out of the oven!" she agreed. "And speaking of ovens, you're usually through baking by ten every morning. He wouldn't need any oven for his coffee shop—he could use ours. Maybe even connect the kitchen with the bakery."

"He'd still need a professional grill for eggs and meats and pancakes and things."

"Sure. And if we connected the bakery front with his dining area, his customers would have to parade past our pastry displays before going inside." Her face clouded. "What?"

"I think we're getting in a little deep here," cautioned Kekoa. "We'd better slow down and find out what all this is going to cost first. Otherwise, it's all a pipe dream. Don't get me wrong. I like the concept. Dad can visualize *our* costs pretty well, but Andy will have to get some kind of loan to cover his part."

"Darling, I just know it's not a pipe dream. We can make it happen." She threw her arms about his neck. "Look how you got your business degree going to school nights. I'm proud of you."

* * * *

Hank Pualoa drove his Dodge pickup onto the work site and parked at the edge of the lot alongside the construction trailer. The senior partner in Finast Construction Company turned off the engine and eyed the small package on the seat beside him. Hank picked it up, removed the bag, and lifted the sleek black box out of its velvet pouch. He opened it to reveal a gold locket with a ruby in the center of its cover and, on the back, the inscription: "Love you always 18." The romantic husband smiled boyishly and fingered the elaborate gold chain. The locket was an anniversary present for Lori, his wife for the past eighteen years. December 20th was their magical date. Inside the locket, their tiny photos sat nicely side by side.

Hank snapped the box shut, slid it back into the bag, and stuck it under the seat. As he stepped down from the truck, one of his three partners appeared at the door to the trailer to inform him of an inconsistency in a blueprint. Solly Hokumalu, the managing partner, was a much younger man, who kept a sharp eye on details as well as on the work crew and their productivity.

Shortly before quitting time, a young day laborer headed for his own pickup and noticed that the driver's door to Hank's truck was slightly ajar. The worker looked around and saw no one coming. He opened the door farther and poked around until he saw the package under the seat. He slid it out and read Royal Crown Jewelry on the bag. The thief was about to slip it into his pocket when he heard gravel crunching behind him.

Hank's meeting with Solly had taken only twenty minutes to clear up the blueprint mistake. When he came upon the worker rifling through his truck, he shouted, "Stop! Get away from my truck!"

The thief lunged toward him and landed a powerful left hook to Hank's face, knocking him off his feet. He then sprinted to his own truck and drove off. A frustrated Hank managed to note the last few digits of the thief's license plate, P349, maybe YGP349.

Seeing Hank sprawled on the ground, Solly came running. "What was all that about?" He held out a hand to help him up.

"Did ya see who that was, Solly?" Hank cried out. "The dirty son of a bitch stole my wife's locket."

"Yeah, Ernie Peshelli."

"Does he work here?"

"He did, but he's not likely to come back after getting caught like that. He's a day laborer and a real tough bird. Everyone thinks he's a pain in the *okole*. How much was the locket worth?"

"Two-hundred-thirty bucks, but that's not the worst of it. Now I gotta go out and get another one for Lori. If they have another one."

"You better have Lori take a look at that right eye of yours. You're about to raise one helluva shiner. Hey, pal, you okay to drive?"

"Yeah, thanks." Hank slowly climbed into his truck and drove home.

* * * *

Lori Yamashita Pualoa stirred the rich, thick poi stew cooking on the stove, so she had her back to Hank when he came through the door. With a nonchalant "Hi" he kissed her on the neck and went straight for the refrigerator. She heard the door open and close again. Puzzled, she spun about to find her husband sitting at the table holding a bag of frozen peas over his right eye.

"My God, Hank, what happened to you. You're much too old to be barroom scrapping."

"Since when is a guy too old for a black eye?" he said, grimly. "I didn't ask for it. And I wasn't in a bar. I caught a thief stealing something from my truck and I confronted him. Before I knew what happened, he threw a punch at me."

"And you forgot to duck."

"Something like that. I guess at seventy-one my reflexes aren't what they used to be."

"Here, let me have a look at it." She turned off the stove and took the frozen peas from him. "Oooh, that's nasty, hon. You poor dear. Did you catch the thief at least?"

"No, damn it! The SOB got away and drove off before I could get up off the ground."

"What did he take?" she asked.

"Uh, just some stuff." He hoped that answer would suffice.

"What stuff?" she insisted.

"Aw, can't a guy have any secrets?"

"Not if he's married to me, he can't."

"Damn! It was your anniversary present—a gold picture locket and chain. I even had it engraved. I didn't want to wait for the last minute again and have you accuse me of forgetting our anniversary."

Perching herself on his lap, she kissed him gently on the lips. "Well, you get a free pass this year. Here, put this back on that sad-looking eye." She handed him the package of frozen peas.

"Oh, I almost forgot," said Hank. "I got a call from Kekoa this noon. He and Maria have been discussing some plans to expand both the bakery and their living spaces. You know, with the *keiki* coming and such a crowded apartment and all."

"Did they want your help?"

"Not really, just a bit of advice."

"So what did you tell them?" asked Lori. "You already helped Leilani and Alex after their Iniki disaster. You most certainly could do the same for Kekoa and Maria, *nei?*"

"Nothing so far. There's some things I want to check on first. I've been thinking of a way to finally redeem myself for all the misery I've caused them. But would Kekoa and Maria even accept my help?"

* * * *

Hank had destroyed his family—and Lori knew it. Thirty-three years ago, his drunk driving had killed Malia, his first wife. Malia had been Lori's lifelong best friend. His guilt over causing his wife's death drove him to the Mainland. Although he ran construction crews in Baltimore and deposited money weekly for his children in a Hawaii bank account, he had done it incognito. When Kekoa and Leilani were teenagers, their grandmother died. In one sense, the two became orphaned. Leilani went into foster care with the Wongs and Kekoa roamed the streets of Chinatown and Kaimuki until he happened upon the Osakas.

After a ten-year self-imposed exile, Hank returned to reclaim his family and his active partnership in Finast Construction. It was a difficult transition, but Lori and his children finally accepted him back into their lives. Hank had made amends to his kids in umpteen ways, but he could still never quite forgive himself for abandoning them to their grandmother.

Chapter 5

A Curried Favor

(May 2005, Five Months Later)

THE PUNGENT odor of *huli huli* chicken sizzling over the open fire enveloped the Portfia family as they drove up the curved driveway to the home of Manny's older brother, Raimonde. Manny and Esme had argued over the invitation. Esme hated Rai and wanted to decline. She loudly disapproved of his criminal ties, and the way he dominated Manny whenever they came together.

But Manny protested, "We shouldn't deprive our kids of their cousins. If they grow up together, they'll be friends for life. Besides, Frank and Delores always have fun here. And Rai would consider it an insult. After all, he is my big brother."

That's the whole problem, Esme thought. She had no choice but to relent. For now, anyway.

Actually, Manny had an ulterior motive. He'd come to curry a favor from Rai, but he couldn't admit that to Esme. No, he hadn't even told her about losing his job five months ago, and hoped he wouldn't have to.

The Portfia compound resembled a fortress: four separate residences surrounded by a pink and yellow brick wall eight feet high and two feet thick. Raimonde really wanted a charcoal-gray wall, but Carlotta, his wife, refused to allow their compound to look like a prison to the outside world. Fuchsia bougainvillea bloomed against the wall, but even "Lottie" didn't much care for gardening. Mango, jacaranda, and plumeria trees edged the court-yard that separated their home from the other three. Rai and Lottie lived in an eight-bedroom rambling colonial of glass, stucco, and pink brick with their boys, Raul and Salvadore, and their daughter, Nina. The other residences were of stucco painted gray. One two-bedroom structure housed Rai's second in command, Domingo (Domo) Martinez. Another served as a guest house. A two-story, five-bedroom structure served as a dormitory for the kitchen staff, housekeepers, security squad, and goons, whom he called his "soldiers."

Sounds of splashes and laughter came from the rainbow-tiled pool, where the older children played Keep Away. Their parents sipped gin and tonics in one screened-in lanai. Domo and one of his soldiers tended to the poolside barbeque, comprising three fifty-gallon drums cut in half and welded end-to-end. The large men slowly turned a dozen whole chickens on spits and flipped chunks of pork tenderloin on a grill top. Clouds of smoke-laden flavors filled the courtyard. Even Esme's mouth watered over the Portfia family's Filipino barbecue recipe: a creative mix of soy sauce, brown sugar, pineapple and lime juice, banana ketchup, garlic, onion, red pepper flakes, and 7-Up.

Rai eagerly embraced his brother and patted him on the shoulder.

The jolly, rotund Lottie approached her nephew and niece with enthusiastic hugs and squeezes. Lottie believed that Esme's disdain for Rai included her as well, so she limited her greeting to a nod and a noncommittal peck on the cheek for Manny. Lottie's instinct was right-on.

Esme felt that Lottie must be giving at least tacit approval to her husband's underworld business life, perhaps because of the luxury lifestyle it brought them, so she slipped off to one side, preferring to be ignored than to being pinched on her bottom—Rai's sly habit when she was still on speaking terms with him right after her wedding—another justification for disliking him so much.

Moving onto the more secluded screened lanai attached to the guest house, Manny pulled out a bottle of San Miguel beer from a Styrofoam cooler and sank down into a rattan love seat. He ignored the pupus on the coffee table: lumpia—spring rolls with a coconut-vinegar dip, steamed shrimp, and a huge bowl of purple taro chips. Esme poured from a pitcher—sangria over ice in a tumbler and circulated among the womenfolk. Next to the pool, the two teenagers quickly shed their T-shirts and shorts for underneath swimsuits and dove in. In a matter of minutes they had organized a game of water polo with their cousins, Raul, Nina, and Sal.

Manny sat alone wallowing in his private misery for the better part of two hours, speaking to no one. Esme was nowhere in sight. He was on his fourth beer when Rai strolled by with a dark-haired young *chiquita*. Seeing Manny's state, Rai excused himself, patting her rump to move her on, and sat down next to him.

"Hey *bunso!*" Rai called, using the Tagalog word for little brother. "What's wrong? You don't look so good. Maybe you should go easy on the beer. That doesn't solve nothing, little brother."

"Beer ain't the problem. I lost my job again," Manny whimpered.

"That's a lot a bull," said Rai. "You want me to have a talk with the Dreskolls? Hans Junior is into me for thirty large. I've got plenty of clout there. Just say the word, *bunso*, and I'm all over him."

"No, Rai. It won't do any good. I'm a lousy car salesman. I can't keep up with the other guys with their fancy suits and polished talk and their know-how about cars. The only thing I'm good at is numbers."

"Like I've always said, you could come to work for me."

"My answer is still no—Esme would throw me out of the house."

"Don't be such a damn wimp, Manny. Besides, the bitch doesn't have to know what you're doing. It's none of her business."

"Don't call my wife a bitch. But it's not only that, Rai. I'm not too fond of all the rough stuff involved. I don't want to know anything about that part of the business."

"Dont worry, Manny. I have something else in mind for you. You were always good with numbers. I need someone I can really trust to do my bookkeeping. My guy Sonny is too old, screwing up, and making too many mistakes. I gotta put the old buzzard out to pasture and plenty soon. So you see, you can be my bookkeeper. You could come here to work every day and take over Sonny's office in Domo's cottage."

"I'd like that kind of work, Rai, but coming here to the compound every day would be too risky for me. My kids—all our relatives—come here all the time. Someone's bound to tell Esme sooner or later."

"The question is, where the hell would I put you out of the stupid limelight?"

"Couldn't we rent an office for me someplace? That would be the easiest thing."

"Just 'cause you're a wimp in your own home? Manny, ya gotta stand up for who you are."

"Quit it, Rai. It is what it is, and I like it that way, and name calling isn't going to get you what you want. What's wrong with renting a place somewhere?"

Rai popped a shrimp into his mouth and chewed for a moment. "I do have a building in Chinatown with a few empty offices. I s'pose I could fix you a workplace over there. The down side is that it isn't as secure as the compound. Also, we'd have to figure something out for getting the numbers to you and the payroll to the guys. I gotta think about that one, *bunso*."

"What about renting a drop box at the Chinatown post office?" asked Manny. "Oh, wait. They only have the boxes during the holidays. But the Richards Street post office has 'em all year. We can use a random drop schedule too. I think I can come up with a way to code and hide both the categories and the actual numbers, so even if the Feds ever attempt to get a warrant to open the box, they'll never know what they have; the numbers won't mean anything to them."

"You think that's safe, Manny?"

"Safer than in your compound, Rai. The Feds can come in *here* anytime they want. I can create a dummy trading or cleaning service company in Chinatown so we can handle payroll, taxes, money laundering, and any other creative accounting you want done."

"What if they raid your offices?" Rai asked.

Manny's eyes, set too close together like Rai's, gleamed as he relaxed—in his element now. "Let's say we keep two sets of books like you always do. We keep the legit files out front, and we get a carpenter to create a hidden room for the real books."

"How do you know so much about this sort of thing?" Rai pressed.

Manny took a final swig of his beer and wiped his mouth with the back of his hand. "Hey, my business degree at UH included six semesters of accounting, plus tax law and licensing. I guess all that won't be wasted after all. I just wasn't cut out to be a salesman. I'm not what they call a 'people person.'"

"I like the way it sounds, Manny, but let me sleep on it for a few days. I'll let you know." Rai wandered off into the guest house to find his curvy, glamorous *chiquita*.

Manny brooded. *If this thing doesn't work out, I'm dead meat trying to get a job.*

Chapter 6

Expansions and Contractions

THE LAST nail had been driven and the final wall had been spackled and painted. Kekoa and Maria's expectations and planning had come to fruition, made possible by Hank and his carpenters, plumbers, masons, and painters. In fact, Hank had it planned so well that the bakery operation continued unimpeded throughout the renovations with the exception of the very last week when the grand entrance and four first-floor access ways were integrated into the newly acquired adjacent stores. The whole expansion had taken six months to accomplish. Today, the family had just finished walking through the renovations. Maria's petite birdlike body, swollen with pregnancy, had waddled from room to room to take it all in.

Kekoa said, "We have you to thank for this, Dad. You did everything, even shelling out the money."

"It was the least I could do after what I subjected you kids to," said Hank.

Kekoa's eyes narrowed behind his horn-rimmed glasses. He wanted to say, Give it up, Dad. Don't remind me of my miserable life hiding out in Chinatown alleys. Instead, he said, "We'd like to repay you a little something every month."

"Not to worry. Consider it a gift from Lori and me," said Hank. "Besides, Finast Construction is doing very well—more profit than we know what to do with."

"That's true," said Lori. "I'm even talking about retiring from the law office so your father and I can travel some."

"You gotta know we're grateful," said Kekoa. "It would

have taken us years to accomplish all this on our own."

Surrounded by his family, in his newly renovated place, Kekoa smiled. Even with his mouth closed, his wide smile triggered deep dimples that traveled down to his square chin. The wild, thick hair of his youth was now clipped short and had given way to a slightly receding hairline. A neatly trimmed mustache lay above his upper lip, extending to the corners of his mouth. Even his warm brown eyes joined in his smile and gave off a sense of a man you could trust.

Upstairs Hank had transformed the tiny Osaka apartment above the bakery, adding two spacious bedrooms and an enlarged living room with tall jalousied windows, front and back. The renovated kitchen gleamed with new appliances. They now had a real master bedroom with plenty of closet space and an elegant master bath—all of it beyond Maria's wildest expectations.

"I couldn't have asked for more," she chirped.

"My dear sweetheart," began Hank. "I understand you are solely responsible for coming up with the idea to acquire and fix up the store on the other side as well."

"Yes!" said Maria. "I had this vision that it was the perfect place for Andy to open his coffee shop—the ideal business to complement our bakery. Kekoa doesn't even know it yet, but I have ideas for special coffee shop pastries. And you know what's best of all? My papa has agreed to pay for all the fixtures and get him started with supplies."

"If you don't mind my asking, Maria, how does your father have that kind of money?" asked Hank. "I know he's retired now."

"Well, with Momma gone and Esme and me married, there's just Papa and Andy left in that big old house in Mokuleia. The North Shore is too long a commute for Andy. We thought that Papa could sell the house, and the two of them could live in the apartment above the coffee shop."

"Sounds like a plan to me," said Hank. "Has Andy seen the latest improvements?"

"No, Dad, he's been too busy," Marie said. It was the week

before Andy's graduation as a full-fledged chef from the prestigious Culinary Arts Program at Kapiolani Community College. "Besides, the fixtures haven't arrived yet. Andy couldn't believe it—that you were able to make such a large room out of the first-floor store space and still have room for a working kitchen in the rear."

"I did have to put in six load-bearing stanchions to redistribute the load for the second floor," Hank explained. "Otherwise, I couldn't have moved or removed any of the downstairs walls."

"Oh, here comes Andy now with Papa," remarked Maria.

Andy Ballesteros let Papa in first. The five-foot-nine young man, with a cowlick sticking straight up, strode into the large open room with no furniture and swirled around and around as he took in his new surroundings. The expression on his face left no doubt that he was pleased.

When all of the hugs and greetings were finished, Lori asked, "When do you plan your grand opening, Andy dear?"

"Well, it's hard to say," he replied. "There are still so many details to be worked out. I bought fifteen tables and sixty-five chairs and three vinyl booths at a hotel auction yesterday. They'll be delivered late this afternoon. I still need the electrician to hook up the walk-in freezer. The four-door fridge comes tomorrow morning. I can't get the gas grill and exhaust hood fan installed until Monday. And I've been working on recipes and menus, and ordering supplies all week. So it'll be a while."

"Have you thought anything about décor?" asked Maria. Then "Ooh, ooh!"

"What's wrong, Maria?" asked Lori. "You suddenly don't look so well."

"Maria?" echoed Kekoa.

"Yes! Yes! It's just that the baby is super active," admitted Maria in a small, shaky voice. "She just gave me two swift kicks in the belly. I had a couple of contractions late yesterday and more today, but they're still too far apart to be concerned. I'm fine. Really I am. I asked you about décor."

"I haven't given it much thought yet," confessed Andy.

"What do you suggest?"

"Leilani said she had a whole mess of oil and pastel paintings she could let you have on consignment," said Kekoa. "They would have 'For Sale' and price tags on them, and you would get a commission on those you sold. She also talked about an island mural she had in mind for one wall if you were agreeable."

"That sounds fabulous. Everyone's been so helpful and giving," blubbered Andy. "I've got one terrific family." He hugged Maria.

"Oooooh! *O Diyos ko!* (Oh my God!) Oooooh! "

Maria's pixie face took on a frightened look as she stood with her legs apart. She held her stomach, looked down at her feet, and saw a good-sized puddle.

"Oh-oh! My water broke," she said. "The baby's coming."

* * * *

Over the past six months Manny Portfia had enjoyed success in two new areas. One, he'd created a phantom business that fulfilled all of the secret financial and money laundering needs that his brother had asked for and had established a legitimate shell service company to cover for it. Rai was content with the result and happy to have Manny in the family business at last. Two, Manny had managed to keep his current employer and actual job description from his wife. As far as Esme knew, he managed a cleaning and maintenance service for high-rise buildings in the downtown business district.

With almost hit-over-the-head advice from Rai, Manny abandoned his flamboyant clothes and dressed in the subdued, successful fashion of a proficient accountant: designer aloha shirts in subtle patterns and neat black pants.

There were two visible public rooms in the shell business office and one hidden office. The front room had two upholstered chairs, a koa conference table with seating for six, and no windows. The visible inner office belonged to Manny, furnished with a glass-topped executive desk, a swivel chair in the finest leather, two large windows, and three teak filing cabinets. But these cabinets contained none of Rai's business records. His records were securely relegated to the hidden room to the left of Manny's desk. That room had no visible door and was accessible only through a thirty-inch-square air-conditioning grate. Even with the hinged grate opened, the access hole merely exposed snug-fitting metal ductwork leading to the roof unit. But if the grate's catch was unhooked and released in a particular way, a large section of ductwork would swing out and away, clearing a path to an eight-foot by twenty-four-foot hidden space that could only be detected by actual floor-plan measurements.

Manny had been working on the cleaning crews' payroll when he heard someone enter the outer office. He quickly cleared the top of his desk and shoved the ledger and checkbook into his top drawer. He looked around the room to see if everything else was in place. It was.

"Have a seat. Be with you in a minute," he yelled.

Manny got up and went to open the door to the outer office. He was startled to see a colossus of a man, at least six-foot-eleven, filling the entire door frame. The scarred, knobby-boned, and pockmarked face sent an immediate fright through Manny. He stepped back and out of the way. "Aloha," he said weakly.

The silent, ogre-like giant, in a plain white T-shirt and tan shorts, stepped over the threshold into the inner office, ignoring the meager greeting. Manny's first reaction was to push the giant back out of the room and lock him out, but he had no chance. A second Asian stood in the doorway, a slight, well-dressed man with sharp but attractive features. With a polite nod and a small smile of acknowledgment, he followed the giant into Manny's office.

"My name is Hugo Trang," he said, "and my companion is Edward Li Mong," indicating the goliath with a broad sweep of his hand.

"How may I help you?" asked Manny, his breath shallow.

"Quite the contrary," replied Hugo with a sly smile. "It is rather how we intend to help and protect you." His English was elegant and perfect except for slight Asian intonations.

"I don't understand," said Manny, who couldn't take his eyes off the giant, now standing at a window, staring at the busy commerce outside.

"Then allow me to explain," responded Hugo, his tone respectful. "First of all—on behalf of the Chinatown Benevolent Brotherhood and Protective Society, I would like to welcome you to your new neighborhood offices. We sincerely wish you and your business every success here."

With beads of cold sweat forming in his armpits, Manny said, "Thank you, but—"

"To guarantee that success, we would like to offer you some *special* insurance."

"What kind of *special* insurance did you have in mind?" asked Manny, his head slightly tilted to one side.

"Why, protection insurance, of course," replied Hugo. "Fire, water, theft, and vandalism. The usual, I suspect. Very inexpensive. Only $500 a month."

"But I already have all that kind of business insurance," protested Manny. His belly began to churn.

"But not enough to cover this sort of thing," retorted Hugo. He flashed a quick nod to Mong.

Mong's massive forearm swept across the desk, carrying with it to the tiled floor a stapler, three-hole punch, IN/OUT trays, a glass and pitcher half-full of water, and several framed pictures. The sounds of glass shattering, the sounds of violence shook Manny to the core, in a way he wasn't used to. As he stared in horror at the mess on the floor, he didn't notice Hugo dropping a lit match into a nearly full wastebasket. The flame struggled, but by the time it caught Manny's attention, it had roared toward the ceiling.

"Okay! Okay! Okay, I'll pay," cried Manny. "You said $500. I'll pay the first month's insurance, anyway, but I'll have to talk with my associates about any future payments."

Mong quickly flipped the wastebasket upside down, capturing the entire contents within and smothering the fire. Stepping closer, his malevolent green eyes scrutinized Manny's every move as he opened the bottom drawer of his desk and pulled out the metal cash box. He counted out four one-hundreds and two fifties and laid them on the table. Hugo picked up the six bills, nodded, and bowed with the irony of gratitude. The two intruders left the inner office, closing the door behind them.

A miserable Manny sank into his swivel chair, suppressing a retching feeling in his gut. What was he going to tell Rai? The last thing he wanted to do was start a turf war between Rai's organization and a rival Chinatown gang. But Rai needed to know.

* * * *

It had taken Noah Wong six dental appointments to reach this final stage

"Okay, Noah, we're finished. Your new crown is in place."

"Neat!" Noah slid out of the surgical chair and rushed to the waiting room, where his mother co-paid the bill.

Leilani deposited Noah in front of his high school and drove away without another word. Alex had talked about the possibility of a military school if the scrapping incidences didn't cease. But she wasn't so sure about that. She would miss her wayward son terribly and believed there was still hope for him snapping out of this foolishness. Strangely, Noah had been behaving himself for the last month and a half. Was it a sign, somehow a turn of events in his life?

Noah dropped off the excuse note at the office, waited for the start of the next period, and went to English class. He couldn't concentrate, barely hearing the teacher adding Steinbeck's *Of Mice and Men* to the summer reading assignment. After English, slowly walking to World History, Gino Akino appeared at his side and bumped him on the shoulder.

"*Bruddah*, Duke Santos is still pissed off at you," taunted Gino. "I wouldn't want to be in your shoes, yah."

"Why would he be so pissed at me?" said Noah. "I'm the sucker he beat up and cheated. And now even my folks are down on me for all the dental work they had to pay for. Besides, that was over seven months ago. What's he got to be so damn mad about now?"

"Didn't ya hear? Da cops picked him up fer trying to sell one of dem watches we took, yah. And dat pharmacist identified him as being there when da store was robbed, but they couldn't prove nuttin'. Duke say he bought da watch off some guy, so dey had to let him go. Youse was there too, but da cops didn't pick you up, so he thinks you ratted him out, yah."

Noah seethed inside. The anesthetic was beginning to wear off, he felt slightly woozy and miserable. But he heard Gino loud and clear. "I hate Duke's guts," he said, "but I'm no rat. I didn't go to the police."

"Hey, I believe ya," said Gino. "I'm not da one ya gotta convince. It's Duke."

"Thanks, *brah*, I'll keep an eye out for him."

Noah reached for the doorknob to room 121 for World History. He held the door for Gino, and just as he was about to follow his friend in, he held it a little longer for a bright-eyed girl in a too-tight blue sweater and short skirt. Noah took his seat across the aisle from Gino, but his eyes followed the girl as she slid into her seat four rows over.

"Who's the looker in the blue sweater?" whispered Noah, leaning over toward Gino.

"She's new," said Gino. "Dey introduced her in Spanish during first period. Nina Portfia. You don' wanna mess wit' her, *bruddah*. Her ol' man is Raimonde Portfia, da big-time gang boss."

Noah continued to stare across the room at Nina all through Mrs. Wallace's lecture. His daydreaming came to an abrupt end when the teacher took notice of him.

"Noah Wong! How many major Crusades were there?" she asked, starting up the aisle toward him.

"What? What was that question again, Mrs. Wallace?" he stumbled. He could feel the chicken skin crawling up his arms.

"Just as I thought," she said. "Do my lessons bore you, young man?"

"Yeah. I mean No, ma'am, I was just distracted for a minute. That's all." *I hope the new girl doesn't think I'm a goofball.* The thought raced through his mind.

His classmates tittered to the teacher's displeasure. She retreated to the front of the class and continued her lecture. Noah tuned her out. He was busy concocting his own plans. At the end of class he whispered his scheme to Gino.

Out in the hall a few minutes later, Gino followed instructions. He rushed past Nina, bumping her arm. She dropped her two books. Gino wandered off. Noah stepped up and knelt down beside her to recover the wayward books. Straightening up, he handed them to her with a closed-mouthed, half-grin.

"My name is Noah Wong."

"I know," she said, laughing.

"Yeah, old lady Wallace made sure of that, didn't she?" he said, joining her mirth. "You're new here, aren't you?"

"Yeah, I had enough of all-girl parochial schools to last a lifetime, so I convinced my parents to transfer me to a public school."

"Wow! That's a big move. Say, I hope we can be friends." He extended his right hand to seal the offer and she accepted.

"Sure! Hey! Thanks for the help, Noah. I'll see you around." She started to turn away.

"Wait, you didn't tell me your name."

"It's Nina."

"Nina what?"

"Just Nina for now." *I want to get to know him better first,* she thought. She feared her last name would scare him off, the way it did all the other guys she'd liked.

Chapter 7

Surprises

THE PUALOA baby wasn't due for another three weeks, so the family was taken by surprise when Maria's water broke ahead of time. Though multiple and random contractions continued afterward, her concentrated labor didn't progress until well after midnight. When the serious screaming began around 2 a.m., the expectant father turned squeamish and had to be ejected from the delivery room. A late sonogram informed them that the baby had turned to a precarious position, indicating a breech birth. It also revealed that the umbilical cord might interfere with the delivery. There was nothing the family could do but wait and see. Andy had taken an exhausted Papa Ballesteros home. Lori, Hank, and Kekoa stayed to wait.

Lori entered the maternity waiting room carrying three coffees. As she handed a vending machine cup to Hank, she asked, "Anything yet?"

"Nothing!" he grumped. "I haven't seen anyone but the nurse behind the desk, and even she hasn't moved in the last half hour."

"What's the matter now, dear?"

"Why is it that most waiting rooms have ladies' magazines," whined Hank. "You'd think in a damn maternity waiting room there'd be at least one men's magazine. Do you see any men in the delivery room having babies? Who does the waiting around here, anyway?"

Lori smiled and set the remaining two coffees down on the end table. "Calm down. Do you want me to try and find a newspaper for you? Or do you want to take a nice nap like Kekoa here?"

"The boy really is snoring away," said Hank. "I don't know how he does it at a time like this."

"He isn't a boy anymore, Hank, he's about to be a father himself. Besides, he got up at 4 a.m. yesterday to do the day's baking. The poor guy's been up almost twenty-four hours straight."

"I don't think I can sleep right now," said Hank. "I'm far too excited. Maybe a couple of laps around the halls would help burn off my excess energy."

"Go ahead, dear," she said. "I'll stay with Kekoa."

Hank started up the hall peeking in the rooms and reading the patients' and babies' names on the doors. He wondered what the kids would name his brand-new granddaughter. As he lapped passed the elevator for the second time, he noticed a younger man stepping inside it. The face looked vaguely familiar. *Where do I know that face from? I must be getting old. I should know that face.* It wasn't until he got back to the maternity waiting room that he had an inkling of who it was.

"What's wrong, dear," asked Lori. "You look as if you've seen a ghost."

"It might as well have been," he answered. "Do you remember just before our last anniversary when I came home with a shiner?"

"Sure, it was a doozy. You said the guy punched you in the eye and ran off with my anniversary gift."

"Yeah, that's right. I'm pretty sure I just saw the slime-bag getting on the elevator, but it didn't register with me until it was too late."

"Too late for what?" she challenged. "And what would you have done, anyway—call him out, right here in the hospital? I doubt that."

"I suppose you're right," he said. "It's been six months, and he probably wouldn't recognize me, anyway, so if I blackened one of his eyes, he wouldn't remember why."

There was a noise at the end of the hall. The double swinging doors pushed open with a squeak. A tall man in blue scrubs and cloth booties over his shoes burst through and approached the family. Hank shook the sleeping Kekoa awake.

"What?" shouted a stunned Kekoa.

"Wake up! The doctor's coming down the hall to tell us something," Hank said.

"Mr. Pualoa?" asked the doctor.

"Yes," said an overanxious Hank.

"Yes," said Kekoa. "I'm the expectant father."

"Mr. Pualoa, I'm Dr. Sumito. You have a six-pound, four-ounce baby girl. The delivery was quite tricky, but both mother and daughter are doing fine."

"When can I see them?" asked Kekoa.

Dr. Sumito looked at his watch and said, "In ten or fifteen minutes a nurse will come out and get you. Your wife is exhausted and needs lots of bed rest, so stay no more than five minutes. There'll be plenty of time for visiting this afternoon."

"Thank you, Doctor," said Lori. "Would I be permitted a peek too?"

"Are you Mrs. Pualoa's mother?"

"No, I'm her stepmom, but we're close."

"Just a peek, then," he said. "No more than a minute or two." Dr. Sumito turned away and retraced his steps through the swinging doors.

It was close to thirty minutes before the nurse ushered Kekoa and Lori in to see Maria and the baby. Kekoa rushed to Maria and their new daughter. He was suddenly fascinated by this tiny red, nearly hairless, wrinkled creature lying next to his wife. Her eyes were closed and the round face seemed at peace.

"She's beautiful, isn't she, honey?" declared Maria.

"She sure is and she's all ours," said Kekoa, as he bent down to kiss his wife and then his daughter on the forehead. "I love you, sweetheart."

Ten minutes later Kekoa felt strange going home alone for the first time since their marriage. Another hour and he'd have to start baking again.

* * * *

Noah finished the last of his Thursday classes and started down the front steps of the high school. There she was, the new girl he'd met the day before, standing on the lawn in a tight circle of classmates. Nina was wearing another terrific sweater today, just as clingy, but a different shade of blue. He wanted to talk to her again, but quickly sized up his chances. *From the way those other girls flock around her, she's made friends quickly. No way to get near her today.* He continued to the street and started homeward.

Halfway home, the fourteen-year-old Noah's thoughts were so full of Nina that he'd completely forgotten about Gino's warning. Noah figured Duke Santos already had his revenge. Passing an alley between two storefronts, he didn't realize that someone had stepped in behind him until he heard footsteps matching his own. At first he didn't think anything of it. Then he turned the corner and continued. The footsteps didn't miss a beat. Now he worried. Another turned corner put him at the entrance to a nearly empty parking lot adjacent to a low-rise apartment building. He quickened his pace, and the echoing footsteps did the same, beat for beat, taunting him. He stopped and turned to face his pursuer.

Noah wasn't surprised to find the imposing figure of Duke Santos standing over him. His so-called friend was half a foot taller, with a vee-shaped head, tapering in to a small, mean mouth and an even narrower chin. A tangle of straw-yellow hair was bleached with black streaks. Noah wished he hadn't naively led his pursuer to such a desolate spot—making himself so dangerously vulnerable.

"Hey, Duke, what's going on? I didn't do anything to you. Nice shirt," he said, hoping to defuse what was sure to be an ugly encounter. In a flash he took in Duke's outfit: black jeans and a new-looking long-sleeved Ralph Lauren polo shirt embroidered on the right with a fancy crest: a gold crown and crossed mallets. *Stolen, no doubt.* But Duke wasn't buying the chitchat.

"You didn't do anything to me? You're a real shitface." With

59

his open hand, he shoved Noah backward in short pushes in the chest until the boy felt himself slam against the concrete block wall of the apartment house. Duke's long, sinewy fingers wrapped around Noah's throat. Noah felt the fingers alternately squeezing his airway shut, then releasing, never knowing whether he had another breath coming. He grabbed hold of Duke's wrist and tried to pull it away from his throat, but Duke kept batting it out of the way with his free hand, rage granting him the extra strength.

"You bastard, I should never have trusted you," Duke screamed. "I'll teach you to go to the cops, you rat fink you."

Noah wanted to deny the accusation, but with a hand over his throat, all he could manage was an unintelligible squawk. He made another attempt to extricate the chokehold. Duke grabbed his middle finger and bent it back until they both heard a knuckle snap.

Duke's free hand started slapping Noah's face mercilessly, until the younger boy collapsed to the ground unconscious. Duke heard a car pull into the lot behind them. Turning around, he saw a woman lean on her car's horn. The blaring horn proved both deafening and threatening to Duke. He ran from the lot, leaving Noah lying on the ground. As he reached the curb, he looked over his shoulder once, then disappeared down the street and out of sight.

The driver parked her car, climbed out, and walked over to see if Noah was still alive. Seeing him stir, she did an about-face and walked briskly to the building entrance. Not wanting to be involved, she made an anonymous 9-1-1 call from the safety of her own apartment. A half-hour later she looked out the hall window. The boy was gone from the spot. She shrugged. It could have been the emergency medical technicians taking him away, or simply the boy got himself up and left. In her mind she had done her part, and that was all anyone could ask of her.

Noah had actually pulled himself up. Dragging one foot after the other in a zombie-like manner, he resembled someone walking off a drunken stupor. His face looked like red, raw liver and his neck—finger-marked blue with the worst sore throat of his short life. He inhaled painfully through a narrow, swollen passage of measured air. His index finger began to swell and hurt, and he just couldn't find a position to convey it, no matter how he held his hand. A portion of the dizziness wore away, and somehow he navigated the few remaining streets that led to the Wong residence. Noah managed to slam the front door behind him before collapsing again—this time on the front hall rug.

"Noah? Malia?" called Masako from the kitchen. She had heard the door slam. "Noah? Malia? Is that you?" she called a second time, wondering which of her grandchildren had come home from school.

Masako rushed into the hall and saw her grandson lying there. "Paul, come quickly," she yelled to her husband, who'd been reading in the den. "Noah's hurt. He's unconscious on the hall floor. Give me a hand."

Paul hurried in and clumsily lifted the boy up, half-carrying, half-dragging him to the parlor sofa. "He looks terrible. I suppose he's been in another one of his scrapes."

"Now is not the time, Paul," Masako scolded, as she went for wet compresses and her full medical kit.

"Where are Leilani and Alex?" asked Paul.

"Leilani went for groceries and Alex went to see a client," she yelled from the first-floor bathroom.

Masako returned to the patient with her supplies. Searching through the kit, she retrieved and broke apart an ampoule of smelling salts, which she then waved under Noah's nose. The boy rolled his eyes open, shook his head vigorously, and groaned with the pain. He didn't speak, but continued staring at the ceiling, apparently seeing nothing.

"Sweetheart, sweetheart," Masako cooed, "what's happened to you?"

It wasn't that Noah couldn't talk. He fully recognized his adoptive grandparents standing over him, but hadn't quite figured out what he should tell them. The was no way he would admit to taking part in the robbery, and he couldn't very well squeal on who had jumped him. They'd go directly to the police, and that would be like fulfilling Duke's accusation of ratting him out. He didn't know what to do, and his frustration brought him to tears.

"Speak up, son," his grandfather pleaded. "You won't get in trouble. I promise you."

Masako applied the cold wet towels to his burning cheeks. "Please tell us, dear."

"Oooh! Aaah! That hurts, Grandma," Noah tried to bring his right hand to his face. The swollen middle finger drooped.

"It might be broken," Masako said. She took his hand in her own and leaned in to examine the finger more closely. *Grandmothers know about these things,* she thought. She wriggled it slightly in several directions while he bit his lip to keep from yelling outright.

"Look over there," she ordered, pointing to a French door that led to the garden.

"Why?" he whined.

"Never mind why," Masako ordered. "Just look over there." She had decided his finger was only dislocated, and with a short, powerful tug coaxed it into place once more.

Noah had bitten down so hard that he drew a few drops of blood from his lower lip. He released a single uncontrolled yelp and then realized it didn't hurt as much. Sure, it was sore, but not as sore as before.

Masako dipped the towels in the bowl of ice water and applied them to his cheeks again.

"Who did this, son?" asked Paul.

"He snuck up behind me and beat me up," replied Noah.

"Who beat you up and why?"

"I don't know, Grandpa, his face was covered," the boy said. "I guess all he wanted was my money. He got angry because I didn't have much. All I had was a few dollars." Noah knew it was a pitiful lie, but it was the best he could come up with on such short notice.

"Don't you think this is a matter for the police, Paul?" asked

Masako.

"What good would that do?" asked Noah. "I never saw his face. He had a stocking mask on, so I couldn't even tell his hair color."

"Maybe the boy is right," said Paul. "I'll talk it over with his father when he gets home." Paul lowered his head of thick white hair and slumped down in a wing chair, struggling to hide his disappointment. *It never ends, does it, with this grandson of ours?*

Chapter 8

Cindy Chou

HOMICIDE Detective Lieutenant Gertrude Mahaila, a native Hawaiian, with island coloring, broad shoulders, and short brown hair, bounded up the stairs of the small office building in Chinatown. Gert stopped at room 201 on the second floor. The gold-painted sign on the glass door read Chou & Rice, Commercial and Residential Real Estate. Turning the brass knob, she stepped into a waiting room with well-appointed teak Danish Modern furniture.

The tiny bell announced her arrival, and a statuesque Chinese woman appeared out of the inner sanctum. She had sleek black hair that fell to her shoulders. An expensive pants suit revealed a lush figure.

"Hey, Gertie," called Cindy Chou to her old high school chum as she moved into the waiting room. "It's been months since we've gotten together for a drink. I'm afraid that's been my fault. I've been so busy you wouldn't believe."

"I suppose I could take some of the blame," said Gert. "I could have picked up the phone too. But today I'm here on police business."

"Come on in, Gertie. How can I help the Honolulu Police Department?" Cindy led her friend into her private office and motioned to the studded leather chair in front of her desk.

Gert sat down in a chair facing her. She wore her daily, no-nonsense uniform: black blouse, khakis, and sturdy black oxfords. "You're looking lovely as usual, Cindy," she said. Inwardly, she thought, *Damn, how does that girl deserve to get such a fair, al-*

most translucent, complexion? And those long natural lashes and high cheekbones and she dresses so elegantly. I'd almost kill to look like that.

"Thank you, Gert. You're looking fit too. Do you still run those awful marathons?"

"Of course, I came in thirty-third in the last Honolulu Marathon. And I keep up with my body-building classes as well."

"Congratulations, dear. Now what was it you wanted to see me about?"

"I understand you own the building next door," Gert said, crossing her legs.

"Why, yes, and this one too," Cindy said.

"Then you certainly know the Chang family, Lee and Min."

"Of course," said Cindy. "They rent from me. They have a souvenir shop. What's wrong? I can't imagine they'd have broken any laws."

"No, no. Min Chang left the store for an hour this morning. When she returned, she found Lee severely beaten. He died in the ambulance on the way to Kuakini Hospital. We won't know the specific cause until after the autopsy. The woman is miserable with grief and chattering half in English and half in Mandarin. About all I could make out was 'He pay! He pay!'"

"Oh my God. This is terrible," said Cindy. "What happened?"

"I was hoping you could tell me." Gert's slate-gray eyes bore into Cindy's. "Is there some kind of protection racketeering going on in the shops on this block?"

A sour taste filled Cindy's mouth. She didn't like where this so-called conversation was going. "Not that I know of. It's possible, but I don't speak Mandarin. Why would I be privy to those sorts of dealings?"

"There was a time when you had an ear for such things," replied Gert. "You had connections. You know what I'm talking about. Let me know if you find out anything." She stood and strode out of the office, through the small waiting room.

"That's a low blow, even for you, Gert," shouted Cindy after her, hoping the detective would stop and make peace, or at least soften her harsh words. Gert didn't. "There are some things I prefer to put behind me. I'm not proud of what I was. I want to forget those days." She heard the downstairs door shut.

There are some things that everyone would like to forget. Cindy Chou had more than a lion's share to put aside. As a bold teenager unable to get a job after high school graduation, she was barred from her own home and disowned by her straitlaced father for sleeping with her boyfriend. When even the boyfriend abandoned her, she turned to the streets and prostitution. Fortunately, her exquisite features and artful performance earned her enough to quickly transition from the cruel streets to a comfortable apartment in the heart of Chinatown—as a high-priced call girl. Eventually, in May of 1985, Li Tien Chou, her rueful father, died, leaving her a heartfelt apology and a considerable sum.

She traded a good portion of that sum for a four-year college degree, followed by a law degree. The remainder she invested in several small Chinatown shops with residences above them. As the years passed and the rents accumulated, she acquired more of the same. Still stunning and smart at age forty-eight, Cindy formed a real estate partnership with an ex-john by the name of Coland Benfield-Rice, who brought needed capital to her business. Coland, a debonair, expatriot Englishman, was the last remnant of her darker days.

After they became business partners, she denied him her bed. Of course, Coland never stopped trying. He still believed he could woo her into a romantic relationship, but for Cindy it was strictly a business arrangement.

Coland, a widower, had retired from managing the First Sugarman's Bank and had time and money on his hands. It no longer seemed relevant that Cindy had once betrayed him—blackmailed him, in fact. She had done her penance, and he had forgiven her. Perhaps his ardent physical desire for her had something to do with that.

Cindy heard the doorbell jingle once more and recognized the familiar footsteps climbing the stairs. Coland came through the office door and sat down opposite her desk.

"Wasn't that your friend the police lieutenant I saw coming out of here just now?" he asked.

"Some friend!" Cindy snapped.

"Hey, I thought you two were close."

"*Were* is the operative word."

"Why? What's the matter?"

"Gert accused me of cavorting with the criminal element here in Chinatown. The bitch even brought up my past. She wanted to know if I knew about protection racketeering going on in the shops downstairs. She told me Lee Chang was beaten to death this morning."

"That's terrible," said Coland. "I wonder—are Wen Tse Fong and his gang of hoodlums at it again?"

"I don't know," said Cindy. "I did see his chief henchman, Hugo Set Trang, milling around last Thursday. You can always bet that he's up to no good."

"Just stay out of their way, Cindy," Coland advised. "We can ill afford to offend that bunch."

* * * *

The firm of Chou & Rice owned and managed properties on both sides of the street. The two- and three-story buildings featured street-level shops. The upper floors were either residences or offices. In general, the shops had wall-to-wall open fronts with tables of wares extending onto the sidewalks. For the most part, the proprietors were savvy, honest, and humble merchants just trying to eke out a living. They worked long hours and paid their rents on time. Their profit margins couldn't sustain paying an exorbitant amount every month to an illegal protection scam. At least two beatings had occurred in recent days when helpless shop owners refused to pay. And now Lee Chang was dead. Fear reigned among the proprietors and their families.

Cindy Chou walked into the quaint little souvenir shop

next door. She wanted to show Min Chang her concern for what had happened to Lee. It was his second beating in six months for refusing to pay a local gang for protection. Cindy fully understood that the Changs' refusal—they could ill afford to pay—would put them out of business. What else could they do but endure the punishment? Today, Min was alone in the store, and her predominant half-frown melted into a smile as soon as she laid eyes on her friend and landlady. Cindy embraced the short Chinese lady withered with age.

"How are you?" Cindy inquired. "I'm sorry. I only heard of your brutal encounter this morning."

"I'm strong, I survive," Min replied. I have only bruising this time, veddy sore. Las' time—broken arm. Coulda be worse. But my sweet Lee, he's gone. I alone now. Wha' I do?"

"Dear God," said Cindy with a shudder running through her. "I don't know how you endure it. These beatings have to stop."

"I know, Missy Cindy, but what can I do?"

"You could go to the police and complain," Cindy answered.

"Den dey kill me too or hurt me worse."

"Who are *they*? Do you know who is doing this?"

"Veddy beeg man call Mong and leetle man call Hugo Set Trang. Leetle man tell beeg man what to do."

"Could you identify them if you saw them again?"

"Sure, but no good idea, Missy Cindy!"

"That's good advice, Missy Cindy," boomed a gravelly voice behind them. "What business is this of yours, anyway?"

They both turned toward the street and saw Hugo and Mong standing there, eavesdropping on their conversation. The little man had done the speaking.

"My company owns the building," retorted Cindy, "and the Changs rent from me. So it is my business."

"Then maybe you need the protection from fire, water, theft, and vandalism yourself," said Hugo, his weasel eyes glinting.

"Don't you?"

"Over my dead body," she answered with all the insubordination she could muster.

"That, my dear, can be arranged." Hugo wore a sly grin as he motioned to Mong.

"You bastards," she cried as she saw the expressionless Mong close the space between them.

Every step backward she took was matched by a longer one of his. Both of Mong's arms hung in an arc by his sides, ape-like, until he was in range. He swung his fist in an uppercut to the left side of Cindy's jaw. It landed with such force that it lifted her off her feet and drove her atop one of the tables on wheels piled high with T-shirts. The table rolled until it collided with another table and another in domino fashion. All in all, the T-shirts and the successive tables absorbed the staggering blow, or the damage would have been much more than a cracked mandible and a slight concussion.

By the time Cindy recovered enough to stand on her feet, the two horrible men had gone from the shop. Frail Min Chang had retreated to the storeroom, peeking and cowering from behind the storeroom door. Ignoring Min and attending to her own painful needs, Cindy staggered out of the shop and next door to the doorway that led upstairs to her office.

Coland heard the loud moaning and groaning with each individual step Cindy took and met her at the landing, where she collapsed into his arms. He picked her up and carried her to the sofa in his personal office. Her moaning continued. She was trying to tell him something, but he couldn't make out what it was.

"What's happened?" Coland cried in confusion. He scanned the entire length of Cindy's body looking for something broken or dislocated, but nothing was that apparent. Then he realized she was unable to move her jaw without major pain. Blood trickled from her lower lip. The left side of her face had begun to swell. When she tried to speak, the series of sounds she uttered were unintelligible. On his desk phone he punched in 9-1-1. He returned to the sofa and knelt down. Coland kissed her twice lightly on the forehead and clasped her hand while they waited for the ambulance.

Chapter 9

Hot Seat

RAI PORTFIA sat in his lavish office inside the family compound in Honolulu's Salt Lake neighborhood. Having just put down the phone from speaking with Manuel, he wondered, *What's so all-fired important and secretive that my brother needs a mano-a-mano talk with me?* Rai leaned back in his executive leather chair and stared at the opposite wall. A pair of bamboo-framed pictures, yellowed with age, stared back at him and engaged his thoughts.

One was a group photo of his paternal great-great-grandfather, Don Diego Portfia, encircled by a group of rough-and-tumble henchmen, taken nearly 150 years before. Don Diego had created the original criminal empire that Rai Portfia ran today. The storied Don knew all about evading the law and sustaining loyalty among his cohorts. He'd surrounded himself with able soldiers ready to do anything for him—even die for him. Originally, Don Diego came from a wealthy Hispanic Filipino family that owned a fleet of commercial shipping vessels, so he already knew about the open seas and navigation. He also knew about wealth: how to amass it; how best to use and abuse it; and how to keep it intact. But his weak father, Don Luis Portfia, had gambled away all their original wealth and wound up in shame, taking his own life rather than face his creditors.

The second picture was a drawing of the *Asian Star*, a sailing ship, a fast and streamlined beauty that became a key factor in the opium smuggling trade. The *Asian Star* carted opium and slave laborers from the southern Chinese port of Canton to British Columbia during the Second Opium War beginning in the late 1850s. After three lucrative years as second mate on the *Star*, with a one-third stake in that endeavor, Don Diego Portfia accumulated the seed money, connections, and acumen needed to start again—this time with his own illicit enterprises. Moving to Oahu, he began with the opium distribution racket, mainly importing Chinese laborers, and eventually branching into prostitution and gambling. Don Diego engaged out-of-work Hawaiians and willing immigrants from the Philippines to do his muscle work. He was also a generous man, contributing to local politicians, public works, schools, and charities. His handsome bribes were well-placed among the elite Honolulu citizenry where they would benefit him most. Substituting processed drug distribution for the raw opium trade and targeting the masses, the resulting rackets were largely the business that Rai inherited five generations later and commanded today.

Two sharp knocks on the office door snapped him out of his daydreaming. "Yes?" he inquired, straightening from his slouched position.

"Your brother is here," replied his wife, Lottie.

"Ah, Manny. Come on in," said Rai.

Lottie closed the door behind Manny and returned to managing the household details.

Manny took a seat across the desk from Rai, who checked the time on his Rolex, then chose to skip the pleasantries. "So, Manny, what's so damned important that we need a face-to-face meeting at the beginning of the week? And why such a serious face? It can't be all that bad."

"I've been trying to reach you since last Wednesday. Where the hell have you been? Even Lottie didn't know where you were. I need to talk with you. It's imperative."

"I was on the Mainland for business, Frisco to be exact. I don't tell my wife everything like *you* do. Couldn't you have talked with Domo?" asked Rai. "I have no secrets from him."

"No, I figured he might overreact," replied Manny, trying to ignore Rai's stinging insult.

"Overreact? What the hell do you mean? What is this that's so all-fired important?"

"What would you say if I told you I had a visit from two of Wen Tse Fong's men demanding a protection payment for our new business offices."

Rai frowned. "Shit! I see what you mean. This could become a serious problem. I didn't account for the Chinatown muscle boys when I okayed your setting up shop away from the compound. Are you sure it was Fong's crew? Did you get any names?"

"Yeah, the silent hulk of a guy was called Mong, and the other one said his name was Hugo Set Trang."

"I recognize those names," said Rai. "We're dealing with Wen Tse Fong's Chinatown bunch all right. What the hell did you tell them?"

"When I told them I had all the insurance I needed, things got rough. Mong started to mess up the office. Threw stuff off my desk. Broke my glass pitcher. When I still didn't cave, he lit a fire in my wastebasket. I thought the whole goddamned place was gonna go up in flames, so I paid them a month's premium out of petty cash and told them I'd have to talk with my partners before I could make any long-term commitment."

"How much did you give them?"

"Five hundred. That's what they asked for." A flush crept over Manny's moon face. "Rai, I'm not sure I want to be there when they come back next month."

"Let's consider our options then," said Rai. "One, you continue to pay the five hundred every month out of your petty cash. But that rubs me the wrong way. Two, we meet with Fong and try to work something out. Amiable, friendly, but I'd have to explain too much, and that might put a bull's-eye on what we're trying to hide here. Three, we could simply pull out and set up back at the compound or even elsewhere."

"No, Rai," said Manny. "Not back at the compound. We already talked that one out. It would be too easy for Esme to find out. I can't risk it."

"Okay, yeah, I agree, that option would be very expensive— I've got too much invested in this office already to ditch it now. And four, we could out-and-out refuse to pay anything and—"

"Whoa there, Rai!" interrupted Manuel, his body half-rising from the chair. "There's no 'we' here. That would put the bull's-eye square on me. I'm not gonna just sit in that office and never know when the sky's gonna fall in on me. Remember me, Rai? It's Manny, your only blood brother."

"Calm down, Manny, I've got you covered. Have I ever let you down before? Besides, there's always option five."

"What's option five, Rai? How can you protect me?"

"Let me work out the details first. I'll let you know."

"Don't wait too long, brother, I wanna live. Know what I mean?"

* * * *

Cindy Chou received emergency room care as soon as the ambulance dropped her off at Kuakini Hospital that Thursday. Her mandible was set and temporarily held in place by a mechanically adjustable brace. The next day she underwent surgery to wire her jaw so she could be ambulatory without danger of jostling the long-term mend. At first she needed nourishment and liquids intravenously, then she was fitted with a straw and given supplementary health drinks to keep up her strength and hydration.

Nurses repeatedly applied ice packs to bring down the swelling of her face. The harrowing ordeal required several more days in the hospital. In any case, Cindy was unable to speak, only animal-like groans and sighs through clenched teeth, so she was given a dry-erase writing tablet and a point-and-tap chart to communicate with the medical staff. Coland even brought her the laptop he'd bought for her birthday, but the prescribed pain medications kept her in a half-trance, inhibiting her use of a keyboard and increasing her frustrations.

As the days passed, the facial swelling decreased, enabling Cindy to form more and more intelligible words and phrases, even with her immobilized jaw. When the meds eventually were decreased, she was forced to accept the futility of raging and began fighting through the pain. She was nothing, if not determined, to get past this horrible incident.

Coland had accompanied Cindy to the hospital on that first night. Now her partner and friend spent every visiting hour thereafter with her, sometimes ignoring their real estate business altogether. The effort to talk easily tired her, so he simply sat quietly and read the *Wall Street Journal*, mentioning an article of interest here and there. He didn't notice her scrutinizing him so intently. With a combination of talking and scribbling she conveyed the title of a book she wanted him to bring to read to her: *The Girl with the Dragon Tattoo* by Stieg Larsson. Startled, he realized he was seeing a dramatically different side to the woman he thought he knew. And then he realized maybe there was a comparison of sorts between Cindy and the Swedish heroine: gritty, tough, inventive.

Every day, upon coming and going, he kissed her on the forehead. She acknowledged his kisses with a slight curl of her swollen lips. On Friday she was feeling much better, so the doctors eased her off the painkillers altogether. When Coland came in to visit that afternoon, he found her asleep. The first thing she sensed was the whiff of after-shave as someone kissed her lightly on the lips. Her eyelids batted open to find Coland up close, studying her. The face she saw was clean-shaven, intent, and seriously concerned. His alert gray eyes had allowed a lone tear to escape down his right cheek.

At first Cindy wanted to return the gesture, but held back. As much as she wanted this kind, handsome, and distinguished gentleman from her past, they had a pact, an agreement she had insisted on for clearly business reasons. Cindy's one-time life as a prostitute and Coland's role as one of her leading johns, even though he was married, had, at first, stood in the way of an effective business partnership in commercial real estate. They had agreed: No sex. Partners and friends. Nothing more.

When he arrived the next morning he found her fully awake and unmedicated. As he leaned over her to plant his usual kiss, she searched deep into his eyes, wondering, *Is there something more in his kisses? Am I putting too much meaning into them? Is it pity I see? I can't abide pity and I don't want to slip back into the old ways. What does he want from me—just a temporary girlfriend with benefits, or a real commitment to something decent and lasting? I must admit I have feelings, strong feelings for him. Oh, hell!* She reached up, put a hand behind his neck, and pulled him closer yet to her full lips for a longer kiss. Her tightly banded jaw bone objected; the pain produced a long, unnerving moan that upset them both. He backed away, apologizing.

Coland didn't know whether she was talking more clearly or if he was just getting use to her awkward hampered speech, but he did understand when she said: "Colan'? Wha' abow our 'act?"

"The hell with our pact," he said, seating himself cautiously on the edge of her bed. "I love you. I always have. I want to be near you all the time."

At the risk of treading on dangerous ground, she murmured, "Wha' abou' your wife? Did-din 'ou love her?"

"Of course I loved Constance. We had our rough years, even some good ones. But it was a different kind of love—friendly, highly formal, and quite socially demanding. She never stopped being a proper Englishwoman."

The retired bank president, a dignified Englishman to the rest of the world, reflexively touched the inch-long scar on one gray temple. The scar had faded, but not the memory of his weekly visits to a divine call girl and the ultimate confession to Constance. His wife had responded by heaving a Waterford ashtray at his head, sending him unconscious to the hospital. Oddly enough, it was terminal cancer in her later years, not his former visits to Cindy that ended their happily reclaimed marriage.

Closing off that latter memory like a kitchen cabinet shutting, he opened another at Cindy's bedside. "With you, there was always excitement and yearning. Afterward, I could easily relax and say, the hell with the social hogwash. You and I were free to be and do what we wanted."

"ou neher reg-etted Tuedays with Cindy, den?"

"No, never, and I never will."

"Colan' is this a pa-osal? Ah 'ou asking 'e to 'arry you?"

He took both her slender hands in his and said, "It *is* a proposal, my dear. I am asking for your hand in marriage. What do you say to that?"

"Yes!" she whispered, painfully trying to produce a smile. *Cynthia Benfield-Rice*, she tried out within the confines of her own mind.

"You've made me a very happy man, Cindy dear. The next question should be a lot easier to answer. What kind of wedding would you like to have? We could simply make a trip to the courthouse and get a judge or county clerk to do the ceremony, or you could find a preacher of your choosing. In either case we could have a reception to include any number of friends and relatives who are still speaking to us after we announce our intentions."

She drew him closer, weakly. Then she wrote on her dry-erase tablet: "Courthouse clerk. Small reception. Maybe twelve guests."

"I'll be a good husband to you, I promise. Can I offer you a world cruise for a honeymoon?"

She shook her head, her glossy black hair falling over half her face. "I don think so, swee-heart." Cindy wiped away the previous message with a tissue and wrote: "We've got a business to run. Just being with you will be honeymoon enough for me."

"When are the doctors going to let you come home? I can't wait." He kissed her again.

She erased and wrote: "Tomorrow if no infection. Home? Where home—your place or mine?"

"Excellent question!" he said with a broad smile. "What do you say we try both places and decide later where we fit best?" Then he noticed a troubled look in her eyes. "What, dear? What's wrong? Does it hurt more? Do you need more pain medication?"

"No." She reverted to the tablet once more: "Worry about two men. Filed complaint with police. No descriptions."

"We'll call Gert. Explain it all. She'll help."

Cindy sighed. She wondered if meeting with Gert would result in a better conclusion than last time.

* * * *

"Noah Wong," scolded Alex. "Are you going to sit indoors watching TV for the next two weeks, brooding while you wait for your face to heal or are you going to get out and get some exercise?" Alex took the remote from him and turned off the TV.

"Aw, Dad. I *have* been exercising," his son returned. "I've been pumping weights all weekend—at least three times, anyway."

"Why the weights, son? You promised your mother and me that you wouldn't go looking for trouble again."

"Sure, Dad, but what if he comes looking for *me* again? What am I supposed to do?"

"Try to avoid him, or if you can't—of course, defend your-self, but you told me his motive was robbery. Why would a random thief accost you a second time?"

"Maybe I got in a couple of good punches too. Just maybe I hurt the bastard some, and he wants to get even." Noah couldn't believe he had come up with these fabricated answers so easily. He searched his father's face for signs of disbelief—he saw none.

After a few moments of silence, Alex asked, "Did you hurt him, son?"

"I don't know for sure."

"I see. By the way, isn't there a baseball game tonight at your high school?"

"Sure, Dad. We're playing the Falcons at home. I guess I could go and watch it by my lonesome." Noah wrestled himself out of the recliner and brushed his father's arm on the way to the front door. As an afterthought, he turned back, waved, and disappeared through it.

* * * *

The bottom of the third inning had left Rosevelt High's Rough Riders a run behind the Kalani High's Falcons when Noah reached the third-base bleachers. The boy climbed eight tiers until he found the first available aisle seat. Most of the spectators were below and in front of him, but of course, there were the usual emboldened few making out in the top row. He scanned the crowd but saw only a handful of faces that he recognized.

A low outside pitch to Billy Lau was met with the crack of his bat and a line drive that dropped short of the center fielder, who tripped getting to it. The bleachers roared and rumbled as Billy ran past first base and returned to it, beating out the toss there. The Riders now had a man on first.

It was during the cheering that Noah noticed a girl two rows below him, standing on her bleacher seat, attempting to see beyond the person in front of her. Just then she turned, and he saw her profile—it was Nina! He ached to move down one row and maybe sit just behind her. *But what if she sees how bad my face looks? She'll be turned off forever, and I'll never get to be her boyfriend.*

Big Jeff Naiah was up next, and he drew a full count, including three hefty fouls just off the third-base line before blasting one over the left-field fence for a two-run homer. The Rough Riders now led four to three, and havoc prevailed in the stands. Nina once again stood on her seat to cheer, but this time she turned fully around to scan the bleachers behind her before resuming her seat. She quickly recognized Noah and waved to him. He waved back, and then she did the unexpected thing by motioning him to take one of the several seats directly behind her and her friends. The boy couldn't believe his good fortune. Noah quickly climbed down to the row she had indicated. He was soon dumbfounded once more—just as he sat down, she stepped over her bench and sat down next to him.

"Ooh! What happened to your face, Noah? It's all black and blue."

His face now turned a purplish-red. "An older guy, bigger than me, picked a fight with me, and I got the worst of it."

"That's terrible," she exclaimed. "You're sure you didn't start the fight?"

"No, no," he replied. "The scumbag was robbing me, and I

had to defend myself."

"Does it hurt much?" she asked.

He shrugged his shoulders. "Sometimes, but not too much. I was real miserable when it happened, but it's been a couple days now."

Her hand started for his cheek and then she hesitated. "You poor dear, may I touch your face? Will it hurt you?"

"Eh, yeah. Uh, no. I mean go ahead. It won't hurt," he mumbled.

Nina's fingers were dainty and smooth. Her touch skimmed lightly across his face from his right sideburn down to his trembling lips, where she lingered for just a moment before withdrawing her hand. His whole body shuddered with an unfamiliar sensation, and the teen hormones raging within couldn't help producing a long sigh of enjoyment. Her hand crept into his, and he squeezed it gently. Noah stared at her, unbelieving. She returned the look as the innings slipped by without their paying attention to the rest of the game. The Rough Riders scored twice more, and the Falcons managed only one run in the top of the ninth to seal their fate.

As the stands cleared, Noah and Nina walked hand in hand to the ballpark entrance where Noah asked, "Can I walk you home?"

She looked at her watch. "No, my brother Raul is picking me up any minute now. Besides, it's way too far for us to walk."

"Why, where do you live?" he asked. "Can't be *that* far."

"But it is," she answered. "I live in Salt Lake with my parents and two brothers. It's at least a half-hour drive from here."

"Then how come you're going to school here?"

"My father thought I'd get a better education here, so he arranged for a geographic school district exception."

Half fudging the truth, Noah said, "I used to go to Oahu Prep where my grandparents were teachers. But I really wanted to go to public school. So I go here now."

"Where do you live, Noah?"

"Manoa Valley," he replied. "We live with my grandparents

in their big house—they're always giving me advice on how to behave."

"We?"

"Yeah, my sister. Malia's a pain. My Dad's a CPA, and my Mom's an artist."

"Malia, Malia Wong—I know her from typing class. She's really nice. We sit together at lunch afterward."

"Wow, who would have believed that? Uh, what are your folks like?"

"Mainly, too damned strict," she complained. "Daddy's a businessman and Momma's a homemaker. And my brothers, Raul and Sal, are much too nosy, but I guess they're only being protective."

A late-model black Mercedes sedan pulled to the curb before them, and the front passenger door swung open, followed by the horn yielding two short toots.

"I think that's your ride," said Noah, dreading her departure.

Nina quickly made her way to the waiting sedan.

Noah watched the car grow smaller as distance consumed it. He felt alone and empty again as he began the long walk home.

Chapter 10

Trepidations
(Almost a Month Later)

TODAY, weeks of tears and stomach-wrenching anxiety were about to end for Maria and Kekoa. The most special someone in their lives was coming home for the first time. Maria had been home from the hospital for three weeks—but without their newborn baby. Respiratory complications had kept her in intensive care until this very morning. The parents had named her Rosa for her maternal grandmother; and Nani, the Hawaiian word for pretty. For now, Rosa Nani was deemed strong enough to leave the hospital, but surgery on an underdeveloped respiratory passage would have to be scheduled for the not-too-distant future.

The entire Pualoa clan had gathered to celebrate, crowding into the newly renovated Osaka Family Bakery. Auntie Leilani had taken time from her painting and parenting to mind the bakery store and fully intended to give Maria a breather now and then with baby Rosa. Lori had driven Maria to the hospital to pick up the baby. The excited father was torn between this morning's baking chores and the urge to be the first to greet his new daughter at the front door.

"Here they are now," cried Malia, when she saw the familiar Toyota Corolla pull up to the curb on Waialae Avenue.

Leilani stepped out from behind the bakery counter and met Malia outside. Noah, playing the eager gentleman to greet his baby cousin, opened the rear door of the car. He'd been waiting outside by himself. Maria passed the baby to Leilani while she exited the back seat. As soon as they were inside the bakery, she proudly took fragile Rosa back in her arms. As tears of joy and gratitude welled up in her eyes, she felt Kekoa's arms embracing them both. Then he chose to run a forefinger across Rosa's tiny cheek.

Maria's mood instantly shifted to new-mom mode. "Did you wash your hands?"

Everyone laughed, and Kekoa laughed with them, even though she reminded him of his grandmother's frequent rebukes before he and Leilani sat down to meals. *Maria sounded just like my Tutu Eme—and maybe with good reason*, he thought. *She's with us in spirit.*

"Of course I did," he answered. "I only want to hold my darling Rosa Nani too."

"Then why is there flour on the end of your nose?" Maria asked.

Malia took a napkin from the top of the display case and brushed off Uncle Kekoa's nose. "There, that ought to do it," she said.

The glowing father took his daughter, swaddled in layers of pink blankets, and paraded back and forth in front of the glass case. "Now, Rosa, it's time you learned all about baking," he said, stopping in front of a sumptuous display. "Here's *anpan*. It's a sweet roll filled with red bean paste. And these purple things are taro rolls."

Listening to her brother, Leilani giggled with affection as she stepped behind the counter to serve a customer. The elderly lady with a paisley-patterned cane said, "My oh my. You have my blessing, little one. Just for this special occasion, I'll buy more than I planned to. Give me four poi mochi donuts and a Hawaiian sweet bread."

"Thank you so much, Mrs. Yoshimoto," beamed Leilani, handing her the white box with the string tied in an extra-large bow.

"Everyone!" Uncle Andy called from the connecting door to his coffee shop. "Come on in. There's plenty of seating in here. Take a load off. Besides, my papa wants to see his granddaughter too. He's coming downstairs to meet her now." Maria's brother was all set to have his coffee shop's grand opening the following week.

Lori chose one of the red vinyl booths, and Hank placed the baby seat atop the Formica table for Rosa Nani. Kekoa eased her into it before sliding himself into the bench seat beside her. Maria, sliding in on the opposite side, rolled and puffed up the blanket edges to consume the extra space around the tiny package. Hank, the other grandfather, pulled a lone chair up to the booth to be close. Papa Ballesteros descended the last stair, shuffled over to their booth, and slowly seated himself next to Maria. He put his thin arm around her shoulders. Tears flowed freely down his gaunt cheeks.

"Si, if only mi Rosalita was alive to see a this day, I'd be the most a happiest man," he said. Papa placed an arthritic finger near the palm of Rosa's hand, and the little fingers curled around it. He began to hum a melody his wife used to sing to their own babies. In a short time he had everyone in tears.

A strange beeping sound in the distance soon turned into a siren's scream.

"Oh-oh! Kekoa, have you finished all the baking yet?" asked Maria.

"Oh my God! The last batch of croissants…"

Kekoa scooted out of the booth and ran toward the workroom. As soon as he entered, he snapped the overhead fan switch to ON. Then he raced to shut down the huge new oven. Thick gray smoke streamed from the cracks around the stainless steel doors. He swung open both doors to the rear alley before opening the oven to prevent it from filling the room with still more smoke. His theory proved right; the pair of massive overhead fan blades pulled air in from the alley, sucking the cloud of smoke up through the ceiling vent. Slipping on a pair of insulated mitts, he flung open the oven door, slid out the smoking tray, and carried it into the alley. There he set it on top of the rain barrel and leaned against the wall to catch his breath. It took a few minutes for the workroom to clear, and when it did, the first face he saw belonged to Noah.

"Need any help, Uncle K?"

The boy's deep voice surprised Kekoa. It seemed to have changed overnight. "No, but thanks a lot anyway. I'm just paying for my stupidity and neglect. Thank God it was just a tray of small rolls. It could have been a lot worse."

"Hey!" said Noah. "It wasn't your fault. You're having a lot of excitement today with the baby coming home and all. And I got a new cousin!"

"Thank you, Noah. Thanks for your confidence, son," said Kekoa, putting an arm around his nephew.

"Uncle K, kin I ask you somethin'?"

"Sure, what do you want to know?"

"Do you ever need any help in the bakery? I mean working—doing the mixing, baking, and stuff."

"Are you asking me for a job?"

"Well, yeah, but you wouldn't have to pay me much."

"What about school?"

"School's out now until August, and even then, I could come after school and on weekends. Yah?"

"After school is far too late, except maybe for a few chores and some occasional afternoon deliveries," said Kekoa. "My workday starts at four every morning. Besides, how would you get here?"

"On my bike, I guess," replied the boy. Four...in...the... morning? Wow!"

"Yah, four every morning," his uncle repeated. "Your parents would never agree, because you couldn't keep up with your schoolwork, and I agree with that. If you're sure you're willing to get up that early every day, you could help me out through the summer. That is, if you get their permission."

"I'd like to try it anyway."

"I'll talk to your parents and we'll see."

"Thanks, Uncle K." Under the unruly mop of dark hair, Noah's handsome face—with its square, strong jaw and large but straight nose—lit up with hope.

* * * *

Early in the morning, a white panel truck parked on River Street, around the corner from Manuel's Chinatown office. The magnetic signs on both sides identified it as JULIO's AMBULANCE SERVICE. Two men dressed in white sat in the front seat playing Internet games on their cell phones. There was no emergency—not yet anyway. They weren't in any hurry to go anywhere and seemed oblivious to their surroundings. On the half hour the taller of the two left the truck to feed the parking meter.

Upstairs in his office, Manuel Portfia uneasily drummed the desktop with his fingers. Tiny beads of sweat formed above his upper lip. Today was Friday the 24th of June, the precise day Hugo Set Trang had threatened to return to collect the next premium on the office protection policy. The day before, Manny had pleaded with Rai to either authorize him to pay up or provide him with some sort of physical protection.

Rai had listened and reluctantly agreed to send over Bruno, one of his henchmen, to babysit in the outer office. To the frazzled Manny, the offer sounded like an afterthought. But Rai didn't have afterthoughts. He calculated his every move like a well-oiled machine. "Hey, *brah*," he said before hanging up, "stay at your desk. Don't pay any attention to what might be going on in the outer office. Ya hear?"

"Sure, Rai, thanks." Of course, that morning Manny couldn't resist peeking now and then to be sure Bruno was still there. And he was: a hulk with shaggy hair, deep-set eyes, protruding brow, and long, ape-like face.

A little after ten Mong walked through the outer door and boldly headed for the inner office. He never made it. Bruno had heard him coming up the stairs alone and had stepped behind the door. A hypodermic needle plunged into Mong's thick neck, discharging its syringe contents to instantly disable him. He thudded to the floor. Bruno sprang to the outer door and flung it open. An alerted Hugo Set Trang had reversed his direction, spun around and was headed down the steps to escape.

"Stop!" thundered Bruno. "Stop or you're dead!"

Hugo jerked to a halt and turned to face the business end of a military-issue Colt .45. Bruno motioned him upstairs with his free hand, and as Hugo complied and passed in front of him, that same hand reached into a pocket to retrieve a second syringe. Hugo stopped in view of the fallen Mong, and the needle found its mark in Hugo's neck. A few seconds later the two immobile forms lay on Manuel's outer office carpet. Bruno peeled off his lifelike rubber face mask and went through all their pockets, meticulously removing IDs, credit cards, cash, and keys. He pocketed the lot.

When Manny heard the ruckus he shuddered, but knew better than to take even one more peek. He didn't want to know. Rai was the brother with ice water running through his veins, not him. Then he heard a number of cell phone tones and a rough voice say, "They're ready for delivery, guys."

Outside, the private ambulance pulled around the corner—stopping adjacent to the fire plug opposite the office staircase. The two men exited the truck and removed a gurney. Leaving the rear doors ajar, they carried the collapsed gurney up the stairs. The three men, all members of Rai's expert "cleaning crew," conveyed the two protection racketeers to the fake ambulance in two trips. To passersby they were merely responding to a routine hospital transfer call. Bruno remained behind to inspect the site for any overt signs of the kidnapped men.

The driver and helper drove west down Ala Moana Boulevard and Nimitz Highway, bordering the ocean, to the Port of Honolulu—a massive beehive of berths for every size and range of vessel, from fishing boats and tugs to container barges and cruise ships. The fake ambulance turned left at a particular green pier sign, and parked at a warehouse next to the cargo terminals. Inside the warehouse, the two unconscious henchmen were stripped naked, given additional hypos, and boarded up in a sturdy wooden crate already affixed with proper lading labels. The crate, dotted with air slots, sat on a wooden shipping pallet. Later that afternoon the pallet would be loaded onto a rusty tramp freighter, destined for a port on the Malay Peninsula.

Rai received a call from Bruno: "Hey, boss. Mission accomplished. It'll be months before they're heard from again. And best of all, the trail ain't never gonna lead to you or your organization."

"Good work, Bruno. I knew I could count on you," Rai said, then dialed Manny. "Hey, it's me, *brah*. I've taken care of our mutual problem. All you have to do if anybody comes calling is play dumb. You haven't seen anyone or talked to anyone. You don't know nothing about paying nobody. You don't admit to ever seeing Hugo Set Trang or Edward Mong."

"Sure, Rai, thanks, but what if someone else comes and wants me to pay protection all over again?"

"You be polite, Manny. You cooperate, pay for one month, and say you have to talk with your partners about future payments. Just like you did the last time. Little brother, you leave the rest to me. Don't I always take care of you?"

* * * *

"Your place or mine?" turned out to be a no-brainer. Coland's British friends had assumed Coland Benfield-Rice was living large, still in the lavish twelve-room Kahala home with its own pool and stunning view of the Pacific. But since his wife's death sixteen years ago, he'd let the housekeeper go and entertained no one. He occupied one bedroom, one bath, the kitchen, and den. He figured that if you shut the other doors and pulled the drapes, the rest of the house wouldn't exist—bachelor digs at best. Cindy called it "the dark palace." They agreed that her apartment would suit them better.

Cindy owned a spacious fifteenth-floor condo overlooking an even more expansive view of the Pacific; on a clear day she could see the shadows of Molokai and Lanai. Twenty years ago when she abandoned her life as a hooker and gave up her Chinatown walk-up with its seductive mirrored walls, black-lacquered furnishings, satin sheets, and crystal lamps, Cindy sought respectability. Her mother had never lost faith in her. Cindy's alcoholic father had forgiven her and left her his worldly goods. During her fifteen years in the profession, her supple young body and exquisite breasts had earned her a substantial stake, and her quick mind had led to rewarding investments, including her real estate alliance with Coland.

* * * *

Coland brought Cindy home from the hospital with her jaw still on the mend and her speech somewhat improved through practice. In one more week the external staples and stitches would be removed and the mechanical brace would be limited to just nighttimes a week after that. The wedding was set for three weeks away.

Their first night in bed together proved strange and awkward. They were not exactly youngsters. Coland was fifty-six and Cindy fifty-one, and they saw no reason why they should sleep apart now that all the wedding arrangements had been settled. But Cindy had lost interest in sex since giving up the profession, and Coland had remained chaste after losing Constance. Although they had mated frequently in their weekly relationship many years before, they thoughtfully explored each other's bodies as though it was the first time. And when that intimacy concluded, they spoke of things deeply personal, things long forgotten, and plans for the future. They exchanged thoughts until sunrise.

The day following Cindy's release from the hospital, Coland called Lieutenant Gert Mahaila and asked her to come to the office. It didn't take long for her and Cindy to smooth over their heated last encounter. Cindy described the two men who attacked her and the shopkeeper Lee Chang. She also laid out the elaborate protection racket Wen Tse Fong was running. She agreed to go to court and testify against these two men. She knew that, generally, Chinatown criminal witnesses were hard to come by.

On Wednesday, June 29th, Gert was at their office door once more. Stalling for time, she slid her black blazer off and laid it across a chair. "Cindy, I identified the two men you described. I even have addresses for them both."

An agitated Coland broke in. "Then why haven't you arrested them? They still present a grave danger to Cindy, and if they find out who your leading witness is, it will be like putting a target on her back."

"I know. I obtained the necessary warrants," said Gert, "but when I tried to arrest them, there was no one at either address and no one has seen either Hugo Trang or Edward Li Mong for several days now. Word on the street has it that they've gone into hiding."

"Why would they?" asked Cindy.

"How would they know you're looking for them?" asked Coland. "Is there a leak in your department?"

Gert pulled out a hard red rubber ball from her pocket and started squeezing it, her signature habit when faced with a dilemma. "I don't know. And I can't imagine a leak."

"What about their boss, Wen Tse Fong?" said Coland. "It's rumored he runs everything crooked here in Chinatown."

"Fong conveniently doesn't speak English when asked for information," replied Gert. "He shrugs his shoulders a lot and uses a mis-interpreter as a go-between. You'll get nothing from him. We've been after that bastard for years. He's a sly one."

"Where do you hide someone as huge as Mong?" asked Cindy. He must be at least six-ten and weigh well over 275. Even if he's hiding in a flophouse or opium den or his mother's basement, he's got to eat or come out sometime. Someone must have seen him."

"I'm not exactly pleased with this situation," warned Gert. "My whole reason for coming over here is to inform you what it is, so you can be on the alert for them. I don't know how much they know or whether they even have your names. They're a dangerous bunch. Be careful, both of you. And don't go out alone, either one of you." She picked up her jacket and moved toward the door.

"Wait!" called Cindy. "I have something important to ask you. Save July 10th. We're getting married."

"Where and what time?" asked Gert.

"Here, in my apartment, Sunday, 10 a.m.

"Congratulations you two," said Gert, smiling. "I know

you'll be happy."

"We've got Judge Fujita to perform the ceremony. There'll be about a dozen close friends here," said Coland.

"I'm honored to still be considered a close friend, Cindy. I'd love to come."

Chapter 11

Celebrations—or Not

(Ten Days Later)

THE FOURTH of July fell on a Monday, the perfect day for Andy's grand opening of Sweet Choice and Coffee. Kekoa furnished all the cakes, tarts, pies, breads, and rolls, in a variety of ethnic treats. The Kona coffee came in exotic flavors: chocolate and vanilla macadamia nut, hazelnut, and coconut. Andy worked the kitchen himself and he hired an experienced waitress, Bunny Kobyashi. Noah reluctantly agreed to bus the tables until a permanent busboy could be found. Malia was thrilled to act as hostess for the day. It gave her a new sense of importance.

To celebrate the holiday, the coffee shop was decked out in red, white, and blue buntings, flags, and streamers. Kekoa had even decorated a number of cakes and cupcakes in these same colors. It took an hour and a half after the doors opened for the first customer to wander in. The bakery did business as usual, but the near-empty dining room panicked Andy. Then slowly, neighbors and friends began to arrive, but not the flood of patrons he had expected. Dejected, he said, "Looks like I fired up the stove for nothing and mixed up too much pancake batter to boot."

"Hey, boss," Bunny said, "today's a holiday. People sleep in and read the paper. They'll come. Give 'em a chance."

Sure enough, around 11:30, Sweet Choice and Coffee began to fill with lunch and brunch customers, and Andy became so occupied making sandwiches and running the grill that there was little time for him to talk story. Kekoa took over the sandwich making and grill so that Andy could make the rounds every so often and greet his patrons. The supply of dishes began running low. Noah came to the rescue and took over the entire machine dishwashing operation. Papa Ballesteros manned the register.

By 1:15 there wasn't a seat left in the cafe. That was precisely when the mayor of Honolulu and his entourage of three showed up. A collapsible bridge table and folding chairs were rushed in from upstairs to accommodate His Honor's party. Maria covered it with her screen-printed tablecloth of *honu,* sea turtles. Somewhere in the crowd, the dining-out maven for the daily paper sat unnoticed. Her next-day's column would award the coffee house four-and-a-half whisks out of five and quote an overheard comment by the mayor: "I could get addicted to this place."

But the star attraction wasn't even the delicious food or rich coffee. It was a breathtaking mural—floor-to-ceiling and twenty-eight feet long—painted by Leilani Pualoa Wong; her debut as a local artist to be reckoned with. Customers' eyes were transfixed by the majestic figures of the chief Hawaiian gods: Kanaloa, god of the ocean, emerging from the aqua-colored sea; Kane-hekili, god of thunder, tossing a lightning bolt from the azure-blue sky; Lie, goddess of the mountains, sitting atop a gray *pali,* cliff, with her arms crossed in defiance; Keuakepo, god of rain and fire, looming opposite her, with rain pouring down from one hand and holding a fiery torch in the other; Pele, goddess of the volcano, emerging from Haleakala on Maui; and Laamaomao, god of the wind, blowing huge, white clouds from full cheeks. More figures and scenes were mere charcoal sketches that Leilani would fill in during the days to come.

The crowd thinned mid-afternoon and swelled again during the supper hour. It had been a supercharged day—highly successful, yet Andy knew it wasn't typical. In a week or so he would know better what typical meant and adjust his permanent staff accordingly. For now it would remain Bunny, Noah, and himself. Before Kekoa turned in for the night, he poked his head surreptitiously into Andy's kitchen next door. Noah was hunched over the sink scrubbing out a coffee urn. Kekoa smiled. Oh, yeah, he made a good dishwasher, and he'd bussed the tables just fine too. A better fit than 4 a.m. in the bakery. There was hope for his nephew yet.

* * * *

Sunshine filtered through the silk drapes in Cindy's master bedroom. Not yet ready for morning's light, Coland rolled over in the plush king-sized bed. Opening one eye, he soaked in Cindy's delightful form as she lay asleep beneath a single clinging sheet. The sight was so pleasing that he opened the second eye to take it all in. He lay still, allowing his thoughts to fully waken. He knew their impending union would bring a lot more than desire's pleasure to their lives. They had a tested friendship and mutual understanding, and they had attained that age of maturity when life had begun to simplify and financial worries could take a back seat.

The brace was gone for good, and the pain in her jaw was slowly sinking into memory. Kissing and speaking had peaked at a pleasant norm. Without warning, two alluring Asian eyes fluttered open. Eying him, Cindy's smiling lips pursed into a soft kiss that traveled clear across the bed. Coland responded by sliding under the sheet and taking her into his arms. Their electric bare bodies initiated a fondling that culminated in a mutual coupling.

"How's that for a wedding present?" she asked, lying back on the pillow.

"Delightful, I must say, old girl. In fact, quite good."

"Old girl? Quite good?" she smirked, elbowing him in the ribs. "What's this 'old girl' business? Is that what you think of me?"

"Hey, that hurts," he cried, grabbing her arm. "I'm only teasing, sweetheart. Remember, I'm the man you promised to marry today."

"Marry! Wedding!" she shrieked. "What time is it? Everyone will be here at ten."

Coland picked up his Rolex off the night table and said, "It's seven-oh-six."

"Oh, no!"

"I am going to have a normal breakfast first," he declared.

94

"There's no time for anything normal," she replied. "I've got to get ready. My hair! My nails! Just pour me a cup of coffee." Cindy jumped out of bed and flew across the room to her bathroom, slamming the door behind her.

By 9:30 bride and groom were dressed and ready. In the living room, gilt-painted side chairs were arranged theater style. White bows with tiny bells decorated each chair. At the corner of the living room where the ceremony was to take place, four white pedestals held sumptuous bouquets: birds of paradise, protea, orchids, and helikonia. Judge Terumi Fujita arrived at 10:40, followed by Gert Mahaila, Kekoa and Maria Pualoa, Paul and Masako Wong, three of Cindy's closest "colleagues" from her former life, a college chum, two of Coland's associates from his banking career, and a British couple from his former society days. Only an occasional whisper was heard in the rows of seated guests. Judge Fujita, in a black judicial robe, and Coland in tropical white evening wear with a lavender cummerbund, chatted while they waited for the bride to enter.

On cue, the recorded traditional *Wedding March* by Felix Mendelssohn filled the room from the CD player just as Cindy appeared in the frame of the foyer arch. She wore a demure lavender lace knee-length dress. She had never been married. Decades before, in her darkest moments, she assumed she never would be. Now she glided into the room, smiles gracing her guests, to arrive at the corner altar. Coland took her hand in his as Judge Fujita began to recite the wedding ceremony, culminating in the ring exchange and their marital vows.

"I do," said Cindy.

"I do," promised Coland.

"By the authority vested in me and in accordance with the laws of the City and County of Honolulu, I now declare you husband and wife, and may you live peaceful and productive lives henceforth," recited Terumi. "Go ahead and kiss the bride. It's legal now," he added with a wink.

Coland scooped up his bride and they engaged in a long

passionate kiss. The room came alive with cheers, well wishes, and opportunities to kiss the bride.

A young Filipino waiter rolled in a cart with a half-dozen bottles of bubbly and a tray full of fluted glasses. He kept pouring to meet the challenge of repeated toasts by the guests.

"Ladies and gentlemen," announced Coland after an hour. "Downstairs in front of the building are two white limousines just waiting to whisk you off to our favorite restaurant."

The celebration luncheon took place at a famed third-floor upscale restaurant on King Street. Cocktails accompanied the sophisticated fusion buffet: lobster bisque; quail egg with a sweet sauce; a ramen hot pot with cake noodle; *ahi* and *umami* steaks; and grilled *kalbi* short ribs. Desserts consisted of Kona coffee and *haupia* (coconut) sorbet in chocolate cups, and *lilikoi,* passionfruit, wedding cake.

The couple hugged their goodbyes to the last of their guests shortly after four in the afternoon, so that the restaurant could turn its attention to the regular evening supper crowd.

* * * *

In Chinatown the next morning Manny Portfia sat in his secret inner office working on the weekly payroll for his brother's organization. He manipulated the necessary spreadsheets on his computer screen and enabled the commercial check-writing machine to create the individual checks and envelopes. He would deliver the envelopes to Raimonde at the compound tomorrow. The physically isolated computer, together with its attached hardware, was neither connected to the Internet nor to any external machine—making it essentially protected from outside intrusion.

A buzzer on the wall behind him sounded, alerting him that someone had stepped into the downstairs hall. He stopped typing, flipped the switch beneath his desk to ON, and peered at the security monitor. Two people stood there. He quickly swung the vent section out of the way, stepped through the opening, and restored the vent and grating behind him—thereby hiding the inner office.

Two men awaited Manny in the reception room. A slender man, sporting a goatee, smiled back at him, bowing politely. He wore a muted-print aloha shirt and pressed slacks. Behind him stood a Hawaiian, who could qualify as an offensive lineman on any professional football team. The big man was clean-shaven and wore black shorts and tank top.

"May I assist you gentlemen?" asked Manny, his chest muscles already tightening.

"Ah, yes," answered the thin man. "I am Wen Tse Fong, and this is my loyal friend Mathew Saint." He turned to face Mathew, who was grinding one fist into the palm of the other paw.

Wen continued. "You no doubt are acquainted with two of my other colleagues, Hugo Set Trang and Edward Li Mong."

"Yes! I've already complied with their demands," replied Manny, his breath growing shallow.

"*Demands* is such a harsh word," said Wen. "Let's just say you happily purchased insurance from those gentlemen one month ago."

"Anything you say," agreed Manny. He stole another look at the hulking Mathew, who was now shifting from one foot to the other, as though itching for violence.

Wen stroked his tiny goatee. "Have you seen those gentlemen recently?"

"Why, yes," replied Manny. "I made a premium payment to Hugo on Friday morning."

"What time was that?" asked Wen, no longer smiling.

"A little after ten, I believe," replied Manny.

"And you paid Hugo?" said Wen.

"I just told you I did. He didn't exactly leave me a receipt, but I did give him five hundred in bills. Honest! Just ask him."

"I believe you, Mr. Portfia, but unfortunately I can't."

"Why is that?" asked Manny, thinking *I'm probably better off not asking.*

"They have not been seen since then," replied Wen. "It is most disconcerting, to say the least."

"Do you think they ran off with your money?" suggested Manny, trying to throw suspicion elsewhere.

"*That* is extremely unlikely," claimed Wen. "Hugo is loyal to a fault, and Mong does not have the brains to defy me. I can only believe my agents were disposed of and the monthly premiums stolen."

"How unfortunate," said Manny, trying to steady his breathing.

Wen's stilted smile suddenly returned. "I assume you will have your premium ready when we call next month, Mr. Portfia."

Manny had his well-rehearsed answer ready. "It is always contingent upon what my business associates have to say about it. But, yes, I have every confidence that our premium will be ready for you."

"Might I ask who these associates are?"

"They wish to remain anonymous, Mr. Wen, just as you would wish your name to be in these transactions. I'm sure you understand that."

Wen eyed Manny suspiciously and then nodded to Mathew for a reminder. The hulking bruiser smashed one meaty fist into the other, making a large slapping sound. Manny reacted with a nervous shudder that ran the extremities of his spine. Swallowing hard, he dared not respond as the two left the reception room and headed down the stairs.

Manny flopped down in the outer-office desk chair to regain his bearings. *How much does Wen really know? Is this circus to go on every month? Am I still in danger? Why doesn't Rai confront these bastards once and for all? I'm the one that's exposed, not him.*

Manny's heart rate had just begun returning to normal when the front door buzzer alerted him to check the outer-office monitor. This time Esme's face filled the screen, and welcome relief spread through him—but relief filled with apprehension. He stood and stepped into the reception room to greet her.

"W-w-what are you doing here, Esme?" he stammered.

"Is that any way to greet the love of your life?" she asked, swishing her hips just a little in her flowered skirt, peasant blouse, and sandals.

"Of course not, sweetheart. It's just that you took me by surprise. You don't often visit me at work in the middle of the week."

"What's wrong, honey," she asked. "You're ghostly pale, and you look like you're ready to jump out of your skin."

"Nothing! It's nothing, sweetheart," he lied. "Just a little work stress. Really, nothing to worry about."

Esme knew he wasn't telling the truth, but then she felt sorry for him and embraced him in a huge hug. She felt his body trembling in her arms. *He'll tell me in time. He always does. I'll change the subject and put him at ease.* "Who were those men I saw coming out of your front door just now?"

"What men?" The words exploded out of Manny's mouth.

"The thin guy and the big oaf, silly."

"Oh, uh, just some salesmen." His body betrayed him as he began to shake uncontrollably, while he tried to end the subject.

Hands on hips, she defied him. "Manuel Portfia, you're lying to me."

"Honest, Esme, they were trying to sell me something."

"It must have been one helluva hard sell to upset you this much."

"Yeah!"

"What were they trying to sell you?"

After some moments of silence Manny said, "Protection insurance!"

"Do you know them?"

"Yeah."

"We should go to the police and turn them in."

Manny's chunky cheeks flushed. "We can't bring the police into this."

"Why not?"

"Because there's repercussions, that's why. This office would be destroyed, and I would be beaten up. That would be the end of my business and maybe me."

"All the more reason to go to the police first and get their protection," she pleaded.

"We can't go to the police. We can't afford to have them looking into every detail of our business." His voice cracked as he tried to explain.

"We? Our?" asked Esme. "Who are we and our? Is this something to do with your brother's crooked businesses? I warned you, mister, that if you went to work for him, I would kick you out of the house. And I will too."

"Whoa, sweetheart, 'we' and 'our' are personal slips of the tongue. I meant you and me. Rai isn't the least interested in my cleaning services."

Esme's rigid, interrogating stance eased. "I'm going to finish my downtown shopping. I just stopped in to see if you wanted to go to lunch with me."

"I wish I could, babe, but I can't leave just now," he replied. "I'm expecting a few phone calls. Some new business maybe."

Esme wanted desperately for everything to be all right. She rose on tiptoe and planted a passionate kiss on his lips. *Maybe he'll feel better now.* She spun about and swished out the door.

Chapter 12

Awake

(Two Days Later)

ARHYTHMIC metallic throbbing and thumping pulsed throughout the tramp freighter as it churned through the southern Pacific, carrying its cargo. A periodic creaking accompanied the ship's slower fore-and-aft, up-down motion. A constant shrill whirr of machines turning over filled a background void. All this and the pungent smell of diesel fuel. These sensations were even more intense below deck in the sweltering Number 2 cargo hold among the hundreds of barrels, boxes, and crates. Temperatures baked in the high nineties. For the first two days, neither Hugo Trang nor Edward Li Mong sensed any of it. They began to awaken after metabolizing the drugs they had been given—only to find themselves boarded up in a wooden slatted crate, with barely room to breathe, a space without light; a five-by-five by six-foot world in which they couldn't even stand up. The sounds, motions, and sensations further irritated their internal systems, already disrupted by lingering drug effects.

Hugo awoke first and discovered his scrawny nakedness. In total darkness, he tried to force the limits of his confines without success. Wood slivers poked his flesh with his slightest move. He smelled rank, but not as bad as his crate mate. Rumblings from deep inside his gut warned him that he soon would be deathly sick—with the dry heaves—if he couldn't get out of this stinking prison soon. His brain quickly grabbed hold, and he realized what had happened. They'd been drugged and shanghaied, taken from behind. A sharp needle prick—that's all he remembered. *Why?*

When? How long ago? The rocking and tossing confirmed to his empty stomach that he was at sea. *Going where?*

Mong stirred, one huge leg, then the other. He tried to stretch to his full six-foot-ten. Impossible. He attempted to sit up and succeeded only in bumping his head. Resting on his elbows, Mong's sickly green eyes finally focused and he realized vaguely, even in the blackness, that he wasn't alone.

"Hugo?"

"Yeah, it's me."

"You got any clothes on?"

"No. You?"

"Nah. Where the hell are we, Hugo? What's happenin'? Where we goin'?" Mong whined, distressed, out of his element, where sheer strength usually made all the difference.

"We're stuck in this friggin' crate. We must be at sea in the hold of some damn tramp tub," Hugo said. "And I don't know where the hell we're going."

"A crate?"

"Yeah, Mong. Don't play dumb with me," although Hugo knew there was rarely any other way Mong could behave. "Can you break out some of the boards and get us out of this cage thing?"

Barefoot, Mong tried with his heel to kick out the bottom, but it was too reinforced. Next, at Hugo's direction, feeling their way, they pulled up their knees and rotated their personal positions at right angles. At that orientation Mong tried again to kick out one of the longer sides. This time they heard a nail complain with a short squeak. After several more powerful kicks, he pressed with his heels while his back was leveraged against the opposite side of the crate. One after another, the loudly protesting nails gave way. First one board, then another, and another bent away from the crate until the hole was large enough for even Mong to fit through. Hugo crawled out behind him.

In unison they breathed deeply, freed from their stifling prison with only its meager air holes. The crate sat on a wooden pallet which, without their weight, swished and swayed in two inches of thick, slimy water. The two men stretched their limbs and strained their eyes to see a way out of the darkness. The ship's tossing and pitching seemed to be greater than the rocking motion. Hugo decided the sides of the ship were to his right and left. The engine noise seemed louder out of the crate and Hugo placed it well behind where he stood. He guessed that each hold would be at least thirty feet deep. A ladder, or at least ladder rungs welded into a bulkhead, would be their only way out of such a depth.

Mong ripped a narrow wood slat from the crate and handed it to Hugo. It became a makeshift, blind-man's cane, despite the protruding nails. Hugo led the way in the darkness, tapping carefully in front of him, sensing his way to the nearest side bulkhead with Mong's hand gripping his bare shoulder. The two naked men had to step around loaded and empty cargo pallets along the way. Once they had found the port bulkhead, or wall, they plodded forward, Mong first, feeling the bulkhead surface, searching for any sign of a way up. Their snail's pace consumed much of the night—with the moon and stars shut off from them, light they couldn't make use of.

Dawn decided to break at last. A pitiful streak of daylight squeezed through a torn piece of canvas covering one of the overhead hatches. Hugo and Mong could now faintly discern the structure of their prison. Ship's ribs, curved vertical supports running from the keel up to the main deck, formed a skeleton for the bulkhead's steel skin. They also found a set of iron rungs welded to the bulkhead, but these curved bars of iron ended six feet above them. The muscle-bound Mong boosted Hugo as if he were a feather to where he could reach the rungs; then pulled himself up. In the meager daylight the two could not see where the iron rung ladder ended above them.

They climbed hand-over-hand, one foot, one rung at a time, taking care to avoid any embarrassing body contact. Their shoeless feet—enslimed in a mix of dirt, oil, and water—pressed down hard on the narrow arch-penetrating rungs with each painful, slippery step. Still, they continued to climb. Finally at the top rung, Hugo could go up no farther. The weak light of dawn was so thick with dust that each structure he encountered was barely silhouetted. Desperately holding on with one hand, he reached with his free hand for any object that could contribute to their escape. When that failed, he extended one foot out at a time—right, then left, and found a shelf at least two feet wide protruding out from the bulkhead. He thumped one sore foot down hard on it. Finding it sturdy, he stepped onto it and inched along. Not far in, he found another ship's rib that he could grip with confidence. He called to his partner.

"Mong, I'm on some kind of catwalk. When you reach the top rung, there's a shelf you can step on."

"Got it, man. Hey, what now? Ow! Hell! That hurt!"

"What hurt, Mong?"

"Something banged my head real hard."

* * * *

Manuel drove into the Portfia compound and found a parking space in front of Domo Martinez's cottage. He needed to deliver the routine payroll package to Rai's second in command. Manny could have had Domo pick it up for him, but he also needed to talk *mano-a-mano* again with his brother about the recent visit of Wen Tse Fong. He wasn't satisfied with Rai's complacent reassurances. Fong was certainly more persistent than either of the brothers had given him credit for. Manny felt insecure and personally threatened, but didn't quite know how to approach Rai without sounding like a wimp. Even growing up, Manny's older brother had kept a tight reign over him, claiming it was for his own protection. Passive Manny had never thought to defy him.

Still sitting in his car, mulling things over, he was startled when his nephew, Salvadore, rapped on the passenger-side window. He rolled the window down and forced a weak smile.

"Hey, Sal, howzit?"

"Great, Uncle Manny. Dad just bought me a new car." He pointed to a yellow Porsche convertible parked in front Rai's mansion. "You wanna closer look?"

"She's a beauty," Manny said, climbing out of his ten-year-old Chevy Impala. "Wait for me while I drop this package off to Domo." He reappeared a few minutes later without the package.

As they walked over to his dad's gift, Salvadore talked nonstop. "She's a brand-new 2005 Porsche Boxster Spyder with a 375-horsepower, flat-six-cylinder engine. It has a six-speed manual transmission. This baby'll do zero to sixty in 4.3 seconds. Feel that suede interior, Uncle Manny. Real smooth, huh? Dad even paid for a custom color change for me."

Manny ran one hand over the back of the driver's seat. "All I can say is, wow! I'm glad you have such a good relationship with your dad. Business must be great for him to spend so much on a gift for you."

"Yeah, business is good, as you well know." Rai's voice came from the lanai. "To what do I owe this visit, Manny?"

"I was just dropping off the payroll and I thought I'd drop in and pay my respects."

"Well, then, come on into the den and share some suds with me."

In the teak-paneled, richly carpeted den, Rai brought out two bottles of San Miguel from the half-size refrigerator built under a small recessed bar. He prided himself on serving only the premier beer from the Philippines. He flipped the caps off, handed a bottle to Manny, and they settled into the twin easy chairs facing one another. Manny didn't speak right away. Rai couldn't help but notice the anguished look on his brother's face.

"What's wrong, *brah*?"

"Well, actually, I have to confess, I did have a reason for coming over here today. We need to talk about Wen Tse Fong."

Rai's response was sharp with a tinge of annoyance. "I told you I took care of that situation. Those two losers are on a slow boat to somewhere far away from here."

"I know what you told me, but Fong showed up on Tuesday with another one of his bruisers looking for Hugo and Mong. He said they hadn't been seen since early Friday."

"What did you tell him?" asked Rai.

"I told him I paid the five hundred on Friday morning and that I haven't seen them since."

"That was the right answer," Rai said. "So what's the matter then?"

"Wong didn't believe me. In fact, he threatened me and said I'd better have the premium payment ready for next month. The bruiser he had with him looked pretty damn mean."

"So they're still pushing the protection thing. They're ignoring my warning. Not wise at all."

A pulsing headache began forming within Manny's thick brow. "Yeah, Rai, he's ignoring you, and if you go to war with him, it'll be *my* skin, *my* neck, in the line of fire! If you can't protect me any better than this, I'm gonna have to find another line of work."

"Keep your shirt on, *brah*," Rai ordered. "I've got a big investment in you and that office of yours. You're not going to be in any real danger. I think it's about time I showed Mr. Wen Tse Fong who the boss is at this particular address. I'll be there waiting for him and his goon with a reception committee when they show up next month. As far as they know, you're paid up for this month so I don't believe they'll show up any sooner. So you'll be safe until then."

"That's easy for you to say. It's my life and body you're gambling with." Manny slammed the half-consumed beer bottle down on the end table and sprang to his feet. "Damn it, Rai, put yourself in my position for once." He left the den, fled out the front door, and squeezed into his old car.

* * * *

On Thursday morning Cindy Benfield-Rice sat alone in her Chinatown real estate office while Coland showed a commercial property to a client in Kailua, on the windward side of Oahu. This was only her second week back at work since the wedding. In conservative beige slacks and a white short-sleeved blouse, she bent over the piled-up paperwork.

The broken mandible had healed nicely, occasionally leaving Cindy with only a slight twinge, a reminder of her ordeal. But she didn't need that to remind her. Though the beating had taken place almost eight weeks earlier, her latent fury was unwilling to forget. She wouldn't settle for anything less than putting the responsible pair behind bars for good. To that end, she had been in frequent contact with her friend Gert, but as the lieutenant had reported to her and Coland, the two thugs had disappeared without a trace. There was no record of either man leaving the island. The frustrating police search continued.

Cindy caught herself daydreaming. A sudden aggressive knock on her office door jarred her out of her reverie. "Just a moment, please! I'll be right out."

The door opened anyway. Two strangers barged in: a slight, well-dressed Asian man with a small goatee and a hulking, no-neck islander in a gray tank top and baggy pants. Cindy rose and came around her desk to greet them, but something seemed wrong. These men did not resemble her usual real estate clientele. She stopped and asked, "How may I help you?"

"I am Wen Tse Fong and this is Mathew Saint. We—"

"Wait!" she interrupted. "I know that name and I damn well know who you are. After what your man Mong did to me, you have one hell of a nerve coming here. Get out!"

"That terrible incident was most unfortunate. Edward surely overstepped his bounds in his dealing with you, and for that I must profusely apologize," Wen said, holding his palms up in a conciliatory gesture.

"Why the hell are you here?" she asked, her voice cracking in near-hysterics. "What do you want from me now? Maybe to break something else? What on earth does it take to get rid of you lice?"

"Calm down, dear lady," said Wen. "Such insults are most unnecessary. We are not here to harm you. We need only a tiny bit of information."

"What kind of information?" she asked.

"I am seeking the whereabouts of Messieurs Hugo Trang

and Edward Mong. They seem to have disappeared. Like poof! No one has seen them for almost a month. I thought you might enlighten me in this matter."

"Why me? I know absolutely nothing about their whereabouts other than the police are looking for them as well," replied Cindy.

"Police?" asked Wen. "Why police? What have they to do with this thing?"

"In the hospital the doctors are required to report all beatings to the police, and now I must testify against these men for what Mong did to my jaw."

"But you don't have to testify, Miss Cindy. Do you?" Wen motioned to Mathew, who took a step closer.

"Oh, but I do," she said. "I can't let him get away with it, or you either in this intimidation." Then she wished she'd kept her mouth shut. Gripping terror set in, replacing her blatant boldness. *Oh, where is Coland when I need him most? Why isn't he here?*

Cindy saw Mathew Saint lumbering toward her from across the room. She backed away. *His eyes, they're strangely empty. Dilated pupils, probably drugs,* she thought. Suddenly forced up against the desk, she was trapped. Cindy held up one hand in a meek show of submission. Slowly placing the other hand behind her, she let her fingers roam the desktop, searching for anything useful, a weapon maybe. Her letter opener slipped within reach: a long shaft of sharply pointed steel. Her fingers closed tightly around the ivory handle.

As Mathew clenched his red-knuckled fist to strike her with an uppercut, she threw her body sideways. He missed her entirely and stumbled forward. As his right hand grabbed for the desk to restore his balance, Cindy sprang back, raised her arm holding the letter opener, and, with all her strength, plunged the blade into the back of his hand, piercing the flesh all the way down, deep into the wood desk. He bellowed with pain and grabbed the hilt, trying to remove the bloody blade. She screamed, realizing it wouldn't be long before he'd be free and furious. She looked for another weapon—anything within reach.

To the two intruders, Cindy had looked soft, frail, and malleable. She was anything but. Years of gym workouts and martial-arts classes had given her body sinewy strength and lightning reflexes.

She spotted the heavy-duty three-hole paper punch on the near corner of her desk. She picked it up in both hands, darted behind Mathew, and swung it with all her strength at the back of his skull. She struck a half-dozen times before he sank into a heap on the floor, his right arm still pinned to the desk. Blood oozed from the letter opener wound, seeping into the plush blue carpet. He looked helpless now. She whacked him twice more on the head to be sure, then laid the punch down on the desk, where trickles of blood were already spreading onto several real estate documents.

Cindy heard a metallic click-clack. Spinning around, she saw Wen across the room, wielding a gun barrel in her direction. He fired one shot with deliberate carelessness into the ceiling to frighten her. She grabbed the next thing off her desk, a snug-top medicine jar filled with cough drops, and flung it at him. It struck Wen in the left shoulder and fell to the floor. This time he meant business. While still moving, she caught a stinging second shot in the flesh under her upper left arm. She fell on her knees. He nervously fired a third shot that splintered the front of the mahogany desk to the right of Mathew. Still on her knees she heard repeated clicks—either the gun had jammed or it was out of bullets. He slowly backed out of her office, still holding the gun upright, faking its lost potency.

Despite the stabbing pain in her upper arm, Cindy rose up in an adrenaline rage against the slight figure of the man now holding an ineffectual weapon. Grabbing the three-holed punch once more, she took off after him, swinging away, driving Wen to cowardice. He turned and tried to run through the outer door. Her first swing glanced off his sore shoulder. She chased him until he reached the top of the stairs. The next swing pounded into the middle of his spine, shoving him forward, causing him to trip and tumble down the flight of stairs. Before she could pursue, he managed to get to his feet and disappear outside.

Cindy's heart thumped fast and heaved hard as though it would burst through her chest wall. She couldn't believe her own courage. She felt like vomiting. She dragged herself to the desk and flopped down in her chair. Looking across the desk she saw the pinned and bleeding hand. Regarding her own wound, she saw a small piece of flesh torn from her underarm. It too bled, but slowly and steadily, so she pulled a narrow runner from the top of a nearby bookcase, toppling a photograph in the process. She wrapped the fabric four times about the wound and let the rest hang. A small red spot appeared on the surface, but grew no larger. A few minutes later, she calmly dialed Gert's cell and leaned back to wait.

Chapter 13

Frustration

LT. MAHAILA arrived just as Mathew Saint took his final breath. The homicide detective knelt to place her fingers in the region of Mathew's carotid artery. Looking up into Cindy's face, Gert shook her head. Assuming him dead, she followed protocol by calling in the medical examiner's crew, then turned her attention to her friend.

"Cindy, your arm is bleeding. Sit down. Let me have a look at it."

"I caught a bullet during the fight," said Cindy. Wincing, she unwound the cotton runner and pulled up the bloody short sleeve of her white silk blouse as high as her armpit.

"It's a flesh wound," said Gert. "The bullet took a bit of skin and a chunk of flesh with it. Still, you may need an ambulance. It appears there's no bone or major muscle involved, although it may take a stitch or two to close up and some rehab. Meanwhile, we have to stop the bleeding. Do you have a bathroom here?" Cindy pointed to the door on the far wall. Gert rushed in and returned quickly with a fresh towel. She folded it twice before wrapping it snugly around Cindy's upper arm. "Who shot you, girl?"

"Wen Tse Fong!" Cindy said. "He shot at me three times and missed twice. I'm guessing his first shot was just a warning. I think there's a bullet hole in the ceiling near the light fixture. *Au-wie*, that's way too tight."

"It needs to be tight to do any good, girl," said Gert as she slapped some clear tape from the desktop around the makeshift bandage. "You mean Wen Tse Fong, the Chinatown crime boss himself? He usually gets someone else to do his dirty work. I'd love to haul him in on an attempted murder charge. For your sake I'm glad he was such a poor shot."

"Me too!"

"Who's the dead bozo?" asked Gert.

"An enforcer Wen brought along," replied Cindy. "Wen said his name was Mathew Saint. Some saint. Are you going to arrest me for murdering him? It was self-defense."

"I don't know yet. Maybe you need to tell me everything that happened here." Gert frowned, causing deep worry lines on her brow and around her eyes. This was not looking good for her friend. She pulled the red rubber ball out of her windbreaker pocket and began squeezing it, as she often did when faced with a nasty situation.

Slumping in the leather armchair, Cindy felt woozy and frightened. Still, she was determined to tell her side of the gruesome story. "The two of them barged in here, uninvited, looking for Wen's missing henchmen, Hugo and Mong. But as soon as Wen told me his name, I ordered them both the hell out of here. They refused, and when I told them I'd already gone to the police, Wen went ballistic and sicced big Mathew on me. I had to defend myself, He backed me up to my desk, so I got creative with that letter opener."

"The letter opener?" Gert eyed her suspiciously. Saint's bloodied, massive head trauma had kept her from noticing the knife before this.

"There." Cindy pointed to the blood-soaked limp hand still stuck to the desk. "He was about to wallop me one when I stabbed his hand—kind of pinning it to the desk. He was trying to free his hand, so I hit him a couple of times with the paper punch." Breathing heavily, Cindy looked up at Gert, trying to gauge the detective's reaction. "Well, not just a couple times. Then he dropped down onto the floor. That's when Wen began shooting at me. Apparently he ran out of bullets, so I threw a jar at him."

"The one on the floor?" asked Gert.

"Yeah. It hit him on his shoulder. I chased the bastard out of the office with my paper punch. Got in a few good hits, too, and he fell down the stairs. But he got up and ran away. Are you still going to arrest me, Gert?"

"I don't think so, because it was self-defense. You were shot at and wounded, so you feared for your life. But, of course, it really will be up to the legal beagles. I'll need a formal written statement from you when you're able."

"Sure. Anything to put that bastard behind bars," whispered Cindy.

"Right now I have to call this one in," said Gert, taking out her cell.

Some thirty minutes later, the medical examiner's crew and the Crime Scene Investigators arrived. Cindy remained slumped in her chair, near tears now, while cameras flashed all around her, covering the entire room, the hall, and staircase.

Upon examining the dead Mathew Saint, one of the technicians said, "The head trauma was so severe that death might have been the kindest thing for him. Pure spaghetti mush! His mind and body functions would have been a scrambled mess had he ever recovered. The man had no future after *that* kind of trauma."

Gert turned to the same technician and asked, "Do you think you could take a look at this lady's arm wound here? I think it might take a stitch or three."

"Sure thing, Lieutenant," he replied.

"Are you a doctor?" Cindy asked as the young man unraveled her towel bandage.

"I'm an intern doing a pathology rotation," he replied. "Don't worry, the bleeding has pretty much slowed down. All I'm going to do is clean the wound with disinfectant, cover it with a real bandage, and close with a tight surgical tape wrap. I do recommend that you go to the emergency room and let them do some stitching to promote a better healing and minimal scarring. While I'm at it, let me check your vital signs." He started with her pulse, then blood pressure, and finished with listening to her heart before pronouncing, "Your blood pressure is a tad high. Remain sitting there for a few more minutes. I'll check you again before we leave."

"Thanks," whispered Cindy when the intern had finished.

"Do you need transportation to the ER?" asked the intern. "A taxi, maybe? I don't think you need an ambulance, do you?"

"I'll run her over to Queens ER in a few minutes," interrupted Gert. "She's a key witness in my case and she needs police protection as well."

"Cindy, what's going on here?" demanded the tall, stately figure standing in the doorway. "Are you okay? Who are all these people and what are they doing here?"

Cindy was so relieved at the sight of Coland that she rose up out of her chair, but her legs crumbled beneath her and she slid to the floor in a graceful heap. Startled, Coland dropped down beside her and tenderly took her head into his lap. The intern knelt on the other side and waved a white capsule under her nose. She shook her head vigorously, then her eyes popped wide open, her thick black lashes flickering with confusion.

"What happened?" she mumbled.

"You fainted, ma'am," replied the intern. "You were supposed to sit quietly for a while. Maybe you should lie here while you tell him the whole story," he said, checking her pulse and blood pressure once more.

The large strapped-on body of Mathew Saint, overlapping both sides of the gurney, was awkwardly carried out and down the stairs by two technicians.

* * * *

In the hold of the tramp steamer headed for they-knew-not-where, Hugo cried out to Mong in the dank semi-darkness.

"Hey, *brah*, what's wrong?"

"I hit m' head on somethin' hard above me," Mong said, exploring overhead with one hand. "Feels like a small wheel thing, but it don't spin none."

"Is it attached to a pipe?"

"*Bù shì!* No it ain't. Some kind of large circle with arms

across it, boss."

"Sounds like a waterproof hatch," said Hugo. "Maybe it's a way we can get out of this putrid hole up to the main deck. "Does the wheel turn at all?"

"*Bù huì*, no can, boss, it's stuck tight."

"Try turning it in the other direction." As Hugo waited for an answer, he listened to Mong grunt and groan. Finally he heard a scraping, screeching sound. "That the wheel releasing?"

"*Néng*, yeah! Now what, boss?"

"Turn it all the way in the same direction until it doesn't turn anymore."

"*Duì*, right, it's there. It don' turn no more."

"Now push the wheel straight up over your head. It should open to the outside."

The hatch resisted at first, and then began to release with a snap as the gasket seal broke suction and the rusted hinge mewled its low-pitched squeal. A circular beam of sunlight exploded in their faces. Mong continued to push up and to his right until the hatch cover passed the midpoint in its arc and fell noisily to rest on some metal stop. The abrupt clanging sounded much louder than it actually was, so they waited several minutes before showing themselves above deck. The desperate men suppressed their feelings, the reality, of being stupidly naked and vulnerable.

Mong, taking advantage of his extraordinary height and build, chinned his head through the hole first. He saw no one, only rusted iron and painted steel. That is, except for a wooden lifeboat swinging lazily from its davits, a foot or two above its cradle. The late morning sun beat down on the chopless sea, tiny sparkles like freshly charged seltzer. The horizon remained a thin, shifting black line, signifying the lack of any land within sight.

"See anybody, Mong?"

"*Bù huì*! No can boss!"

"Boost me up there so I can have a look."

Mong formed a foothold with his finger-linked hands and Hugo stepped into it. Mong thrust him upward through the hole onto the ship's main deck. Hugo dragged himself out of the way, and sat up. His bare bottom scraped on the bare wood. Soon after, Mong's head reappeared through the hole, but his shoulders wouldn't fit through. He pushed against the large rivet heads on the ship's rib below to gain upward leverage, but that didn't work.

Hugo knew Mong wasn't exactly a man of ideas. "Cross your arms and hands and make your shoulders smaller," he said.

Mong did as he was told and, sure enough, he wriggled his shoulders through to the point where his arms could help his legs once more, and hoisted himself onto the main deck. He eased the hatch shut to cover their exodus. They huddled to rest in the shadows of the lifeboat. It was almost midday now, and they could sense cooking nearby, a strong stench of stale fish, hot peppers, and other spices too difficult to identify. After three days without food, the odor was still tempting—so tempting that Hugo could not restrain Mong from prowling, still naked, near the source of the smells. Ten minutes later he returned with a large porcelain bowl of white sticky rice covered with a heavily gravied fish stew strewn with tiny red and green Thai peppers.

"You fool, they'll know we're here," Hugo complained. "They'll see the food's missing and come looking for us!"

"*Bù huì!* No, boss. Plenty bowls, lots food for crew. They never miss one lousy bowl."

Seated squeezed between the lifeboat and the ship's rail, they shared their meal. They passed the bowl back and forth, digging into the drenched rice with three fingers and scooping it to their mouths. This stolen meal became the pattern for many more in the landless days ahead of them. By night, Hugo and Mong slept in the lifeboat, hidden under its tarp. By day they kept hidden, depressed, with limbs aching from lack of exercise, and wondering how long this hell on board would last. As near as they could figure, there was a captain and at least two mates on board. They had counted eight or nine additional crew members from the number of bowls set out for each meal, but there could be one or two more.

Eleven precarious days and nights at sea they hid on deck

and stole what they dared. One morning they awoke to the sounds of a teeming city nearby. Peeking out from under the lifeboat tarp, they saw the tarpaulin hatch covers were gone, exposing the cargo holds. A ship's crane off-loaded cargo pallets onto the adjacent quay. There were crewmen rolling barrels down improvised gangways. The ship's officers stood amid them barking orders at the teams of laborers.

Assuming the entire above-decks crew to be engaged in the unlading process, Hugo and Mong decided to risk a trip to the forecastle, a forward space where the crew lived. The two could hardly sneak ashore in their sunburned, bruised birthday suits. Using the seaward side of the ship, they snuck forward out of sight from the work gangs. If discovered, they had planned to dive overboard. They weren't—they arrived undetected, and the venture proved worth the risk. Not only did they find the forecastle unpopulated, they found the crew's belongings, including their stowed-away clothes. Size and cleanliness were not priorities. Mong's outfit consisted of a too-tight T-shirt and full-length cargo pants that came only to his knees. Hugo pulled on a black polo shirt and shorts two sizes too big. They even stole work boots, ill-fitting but way better than barefoot. No socks anywhere. They climbed out of the forecastle and retraced their steps back to the lifeboat.

Later that same night, under cover of a sky thick with clouds and no moonlight, the two men lowered themselves to the pier, hand-over-hand down the aft mooring line with their legs looped over it. Their only difficulty was maneuvering around the rat-catching disks. At last Hugo and Mong had their feet on dry land. They knew they were somewhere in Southeast Asia—but where?

* * * *

The month of July passed far too quickly for Manuel Portfia. He would have been only too happy to stay away on the day the next protection premium came due, but Raimonde had insisted he be there. Domo and two of his top enforcers showed up at the door behind Manny when he unlocked the office for the day.

Domo was a quiet, forceful man possessed of a cruel streak. The hardbodied underboss, standing at the six-foot mark, exuded exactly two expressions: a strangely ghoulish smile and a wild stare that penetrated like projectiles from a crossbow. He had a habit of running three fingers across his greased-down black hair as though he sensed some offensive strand out of place.

Domo's loyalty to Rai couldn't be challenged—they were more than family. Rai had saved his skin several times and given him wealth and position in his organization, and he was grateful to a fault. He took and gave orders without questioning their intent, but was bright enough to interpret, suggest, and advise on their execution. Today's instructions were clear, and Rai knew Domo would carry them out better than he could himself.

Inside the office, Domo sat slouched in the client chair across the desk from Manny. Another thug sat on the sofa to the left of the door. The third man waited down the hall, smoking one cigarette after another, grinding butts into the tiled floor with his shoe.

With nothing to do but wait for Wen Tse Fong, Manny sensed at least one of the men staring at him at all times. He found it difficult to concentrate on his work. At one point he tried to converse with Domo, but he got only one-word answers. He wanted to be somewhere else—anywhere else. In fact, he wanted to scream.

At ten minutes to ten, Domo stiffened and sat up straight. He heard the downstairs door to the street open with its own unique noise, and there were footsteps, two persons climbing the staircase. The door to the outer office opened and closed and then all eyes were on the knob to the inner office as it turned slowly counterclockwise. Wen's head appeared around the door first.

"Oh, I'm so sorry. I didn't realize you had customers with you," said Wen politely. "I can come back later if you wish."

"Please come in," offered Domo as he stood up. "We're already finished in here and I'd very much like to speak with you myself."

A second man, a squat hard-bodied Asian, appeared behind Wen. Sensing something awry, Wen turned back toward the door with an eye toward leaving, but Domo's enforcer from down the hall stepped inside and cut off all retreat. Brandishing a pair of brass knuckles, the second enforcer rose from the sofa and slid between the new visitors, cutting off any reasonable escape.

"Mr. Wen Tse Fong, I presume?" asked Domo offering his ghoulish grin.

"Why yes, how can I help you?" said Wen with a nervous smile."

"Do you realize just how *special* this man is?" asked Domo, pointing to Manny.

"If you say so," said Wen.

"I do say so," Domo said. "And what's more, this man, this office, and this business are *very* special. Do you know what that means?"

"Whatever you say it means, young man," answered Wen, in a tone of exaggerated respect.

"Young man?" intoned Domo. "I don't think you *are* taking me seriously. Are you listening? Do you need convincing?"

Wen, the brains in his own domain, felt himself overpowered mentally and physically, even skinnier and smaller than his five-foot-six height. He glanced around the room for his own man and saw him in the grip of one of Domo's enforcers. "Of course I'm listening," he said, a wary edge to his soft voice.

"I asked you what special means to you," said Domo. "Now you can tell me."

"I don't know exactly what you mean," Wen said, stalling.

"Then I'll explain, you wormy little shit. Special means that this office, this man, and this business are off limits to you and your protection racket. They are under *my* protection, and if I ever hear of you or your bunch bothering them again, we'll send the whole lot of you on a slow boat to Thailand, just like we sent Mr. Hugo and Mr. Mong."

"You mean you're taking over the protection business in Chinatown? Muscling me out?" Wen countered.

"No! I don't give a damn what you do with the rest of Chinatown. Just stay away from this building or we'll change our minds and take over everything. Understand?"

"Yeah, I understand," said Wen. "Wait! You shanghaied Hugo and Mong off to Thailand?"

"Of course," replied Domo, allowing his sinister smile to reappear. "We mean you guys no harm. It's just a warning to get your asses in gear and stay out of our way. You'll probably hear from them some time real soon. Now make like the wind and blow out of here."

Wen and his muscleman made for the exit as fast as they could.

Domo sent his enforcers to the outer office while he spoke with Manny.

"Rai made you a promise and he kept it," he said. "You've got one helluva brother. I hope you appreciate him going out on a limb for you."

"I do," said Manny. His gut calmed with relief.

Chapter 14

Tribulations

COLAND drove Cindy to the emergency room, where she was immediately ushered into a white-curtained treatment cubicle. Gert's tightly wrapped towel and the intern's compression bandage had prevented a larger blood loss. By the time the wound was uncovered, the broad, shallow gap of arm flesh had nearly stopped bleeding. A young Vietnamese intern and a *haole* nurse worked their magic on her. The topical pain retardant spread over her upper arm made the half-dozen stitches far less painful.

The intern affixed two narrow strips of surgical tape to hold a thick gauze patch in place and prescribed a strong antibiotic. "Mrs. Benfield-Rice?" He spoke almost apologetically. "I'm required by law to report any gunshot wound to the police."

Cindy nodded weakly. "I understand. Thank you."

The nurse drew back the curtain to reveal Gert and Coland sitting in adjacent chairs across the room. Gert clenched her small rubber ball unobtrusively with her arm lowered at her side. She and Coland jumped up to hover at Cindy's side.

"Consider the wound your badge of courage," Gert said.

Cindy emitted a long sigh. "I felt more blatant rage than anything else, Gert. My heart is still racing. How do we let monsters like Wen continue to roam our streets?"

"We don't if we can stop them. It's going to take courage for you to come forward and testify. I trust that you'll want to."

Cindy's eyes turned cloudy. "I do, but I hope it won't be too soon. It's going to take me a little time to get over this." A look of alarm crossed her wan face. "Do you think a prosecutor would bring up my past?"

"No," Gert said bluntly. "That was two decades ago. It had nothing to do with what happened today. Today your life was threatened by a gang boss's strong-arm tactics. By the way, you were absolutely marvelous, my dear."

"Can I take Captain Marvelous home now?" asked Coland with a wink.

"Not yet," said the intern. Finding her blood pressure still too high, he ordered her to lie quiet for another hour. Exhausted and depressed, Cindy slept.

"Now can I take Captain Marvelous home?" Coland repeated, pleased with his clever label for her. The intern said, "Yes."

But Coland didn't count on Gert, who still had her job to do; timing was everything. "Not until I get a written statement from her."

"Can't it wait a day?" pleaded Coland. "This whole calamity has been quite trying."

"The sooner we get it, the sooner the bastard will be behind bars," said Gert. She paused for a moment. "What the hell, so what if my captain has a hissy fit. He'll just have to wait a day."

"I'll drive her down to the station myself tomorrow morning. Promise!" said Coland.

During the ride home, Cindy, enveloped by a blanket of doubt, slouched down in the passenger seat and closed her eyes. As Coland's business partner, she'd felt anchored and financially secure. Marriage and mutual tenderness had made her feel emotionally safe as well. Now the Chinatown underworld was ruining everything. Would she ever feel safe again?

* * * *

Wen Tse Fong knew he had become a fugitive in his own backyard—a degrading situation he wasn't used to. The moment he shot that dame in the arm he knew he'd gone too far with his protection racket. He was losing his grip in Chinatown. First Hugo and Mong dissapeared. Now the pea-brained Mathew was dead.

Moments after fleeing from Chou & Rice Realty, Wen

crouched on a dim staircase in a two-story apartment building a few doors away, on the opposite side of the street. Through a small window in the front door he watched a detective arrive in an unmarked car. He also saw a pair of uniformed patrolmen weave in and out of the dozen or so open-front shops, stopping often to question the shop owners and clerks. Wen knew what that was all about. One of the shopkeepers even pointed down the street in his direction. Perspiration drizzled down from his thinning hairline across his forehead, stinging his eyes, but the July afternoon heat could not take all the blame. The soaked white shirt stuck to his hairless chest, and he needed to pee in the worst way.

Wen climbed the thinly carpeted staircase and scanned the second-floor layout: four units. Quietly. he resorted to the door-knob-rattling ploy from his early gang days, seeking a careless resident's unlocked door. At the end of the hall, he found one, inched it open, and slowly stepped inside. It appeared that no one was home. The unit had a transient rental look to it—no pictures on the walls or photos on tables, no evident books or personal papers. The living room contained a cheap couch on metal legs, a Formica coffee table, and an old TV—but a fairly new upholstered recliner.

Wen made a beeline for the bathroom. After peeing, as if he owned the place he removed his dress white shirt and doused his head and chest with tap water, freely using the tenant's towel to dry off. An armoire in the tiny bedroom held several medium-size polo shirts. He chose a blue one with a black serpent on its back and pulled it over his head. The bedside table held a pair of sunglasses, and he tucked one temple into the front of the polo shirt. A search through the tiny apartment failed to yield any practical weapon to replace the empty gun bulging in his pants pocket. He did remove a baseball bat from the hall closet and carried it around with him. Everything he observed led him to believe a bachelor lived here.

Next, the fugitive sought out the refrigerator and drained a half-filled bottle of water, then thoughtlessly placed the empty bottle back on the shelf. Wen also taste-tested a leftover pot sticker and a few pan-fried noodles, but found them less than fresh. In the front room the recliner caught his eye. Perfect—for now, anyway. He would wait here until after nightfall.

Wen hunkered down in the recliner, setting the baseball bat next to him, and waited. After an hour he started to doze off when he heard the downstairs door slam and someone climbing the steps. He bounded to his feet, grabbed the baseball bat, and positioned himself behind the door. The footsteps came close. A key was slid into the unlocked knob, causing a puzzled, hesitating gesture before the occupant entered. A young Asian boy in a grocery apron stepped inside, jerked to a stop when he saw the intruder, and shouted, "Hey! Get out of here!"

Wen swung the bat at the base of the boy's skull. He fell to the floor, never knowing what hit him. Wen shut the door, locked it, and dragged the lightweight victim by his feet to the center of the room. Realizing the boy was still alive, Wen lifted him onto a kitchen chair, removed his apron, and used it to tie the boy's hands behind him through the chair slats. With a pair of dish towels, he secured each short leg to the legs of the chair. Some butcher's tape in a kitchen drawer made for a perfect gag.

Satisfied his hideaway was secure, for another few hours anyway, Wen returned to the comfortable recliner and continued his vigil. He fell asleep until a loud thud in the kitchen jarred him awake, followed by a string of muffled cries. The chair lay on its side as the boy struggled unsuccessfully to free himself. Wen smiled cruelly and left the victim to pursue his unproductive misery.

* * * *

Two days later, Esme Portfia left the house around noon for a personal shopping trip at Kahala Mall—to Macy's to replace her purse with its broken clasp, and maybe to Calista, her favorite boutique for a fun dress. Ordinarily, Esme enjoyed shopping for herself. The new school year had just started. *The kids won't be home 'til about three. Ah, a few hours without all their petty disasters.*

But today was different. Needling thoughts preyed on her mind, teetering on the verge of wrecking her trust in Manny and their marriage. *I want to believe him, I do, but is he deliberately lying*

124

to me? Who were those men, really, and why can't he go to the police with their threats? And if he's not out-and-out lying, what is he not telling me? Oooh! My head hurts already.

Esme drove east on the freeway to Kahala Mall—smaller and friendlier, she thought, less overwhelming than Ala Moana. On Waialae Avenue she turned right for the upper level, the less-congested parking lot. Maneuvering her Honda CR-V up the ramp, she pulled into a space near the glass elevator.

Something bright yellow flashed by, catching her peripheral vision. Putting it out of her mind, she locked the car. As she made her way toward the elevator, she saw the yellow vehicle again, dazzling in the sunlight: a Porsche convertible parked on the end of the row. As Esme hesitated a moment to admire it, the driver climbed out.

"Auntie Esme!" called the driver.

"Salvadore! Hi! Wow! That's some fancy set of wheels you have there, Sal. Is it yours?"

"Yeah, she's all mine—a gift from my dad. Ain't she great? She's a brand-new Boxster Spyder. He even custom-ordered the color for me."

"She a beauty!" said Esme.

"That's funny," said Sal, smiling.

"What's funny?" Esme asked.

"'She's a beauty'—that's exactly what Uncle Manny said when he looked her over."

"Uncle Manny? When? When did you see your Uncle Manny?"

"Oh, a couple weeks ago, a Thursday morning, I think," replied Sal.

"Oh? And just where did you run into him?" Esme felt herself beginning to seethe, but did her best to conceal it from her nephew.

"Out in front of my house. Actually, he parked in front of Domo's house a few spaces away."

"You mean at the compound?" she probed to be sure she

heard correctly.

"Yeah. He had a package to deliver to Domo. Then Dad came out and he and Uncle Manny went into our den. I drove off after that."

"Well, Sal, enjoy your new car. I guess I'd better see to my shopping," she said in a controlled perky voice.

"See ya, Auntie! I'm off to get some foreign car magazines," he said, heading toward Barnes & Noble.

"Say hi to Nina and Raul," she called back, mechanically.

Suddenly, Esme stopped in her tracks. *Manny did lie to me, and after I warned him too. Manny, you're gonna get a terrible piece of my mind.* She spun around and stomped back to her car. *Shopping be damned. I've got more important things to do.* Esme unlocked the car and slid in without starting the engine. She sat there for several minutes, pounding on the steering wheel with all her strength. *Should I—and can I—go through with all my threats? Would it do any good? He told me he runs a cleaning service. What if he gives up the job with Rai and gets another one? But who will hire him? How will it affect the children?*

Dabbing her eyes with a tissue couldn't begin to stem the flood of spilling tears. Suddenly, she felt an acid fire ignite in her stomach and chest. She shifted her body from left to right and even bent forward and back, hoping the burn would subside. After several moments of agony, she upended her broken purse on the passenger seat and swept her hand through the articles until she found the little bottle of pink, chewable antacid disks. Popping two of them in her mouth, she chomped until the grainy glob disintegrated. She swallowed and prayed for miracle relief to come soon.

While Esme waited, she shut her eyes and laid her head down on the steering wheel. Some minutes later, an elderly lady passerby rapped on her window.

"Are you all right, dear?"

Esme lifted her head long enough to wave and yell, "Fine!" Humiliated, she forced her mind to a more peaceful place. Only then did the fire within begin to ebb. A half hour later Esme turned the ignition key and started for home. Misery made her so distracted that the drive was rife with self-inflicted hazards: frantic sudden braking and a near-collision.

* * * *

The tramp freighter *Black Rose* had tied up to a quay in the port of Prachuap Khiri Khan, a sleepy beach town on the Gulf of Siam in the thinnest part of the Thai peninsula. During the all-hands unloading of its cargo three days earlier, Hugo Trang and Edward Mong had managed to disembark undiscovered. Since then, they had wandered the waterfront, begging for food and coins among the poorer dock workers. Aside from being chased off as a public nuisance, their unfamiliarity with the baht currency and the Thai language made even begging a difficult chore. They slept fitfully in a long, deserted alley on stacks of empty gunny sacks swiped from one of the waterfront wharfs. As it became fully apparent that begging wouldn't sustain even their modest needs for more than a day or so, the two turned to stealing what they could from the peon dock workers—anything left unguarded at first, but then they resorted to blatant mugging and rolling waterfront drunks. The more affluent dock workers who served the container piers couldn't be their prey, as they were insulated from them by high, barbed-top, chain-link fences.

With no money and no other choice, they walked for two days south to the resort area, an exquisite well-kept secret from all but the most knowledgeable tourists.

The stunning natural beauty, the shrines, the gentle charm held nothing but misery for Mong. "How we gonna git home, boss?" he complained. "Maybe this way no good. Takes too long, and it ain't enough."

Also disgusted, Hugo replied, "Mong, there are three ways to get back to Hawaii. One, we get enough money to phone Wen and have him wire plane fare or ship's passage back from here. Two, we steal seamen's papers and sign on as crew to one of these tramp freighters and earn our way back. That is, if no one aboard discovers how little we know about ships. Or three, we move to a resort area and knock over some rich tourist for plane fare."

"How much you got for a phone?" asked Mong.

Hugo reached into his pocket and pulled out a handful of coins. He spread them out in his palm. "Fourteen one-*bahts*, two fives, three tens, and fifty-one *santang*. That's about fifty-four and a half *baht*."

"Is that enough, boss?"

"Don't know," he replied. "We gotta find a public pay phone somewhere. I don't remember seeing any around here, though. Either that, or we gotta find somebody that speaks English."

Hugo and Mong searched the warehouse business district two blocks behind the waterfront from one end to the other and came across only two public pay phones, but neither had coin slots, only credit card swipes. Hugo encountered a well-dressed Caucasian man in a white suit waiting to use the phone.

"Sir, do you speak English?"

The man stared blankly at them and quickly turned sideways to fit into the tiny phone booth. A half-block later a well-dressed Eurasian woman in a floppy sun hat responded, "Yes. Yes, I do."

Hugo bowed slightly to show his deference and asked, "Ma'am, is there such a thing as a coin-operated public phone booth in this city?"

"I wouldn't have any way of knowing that. I use a cell phone," she answered. "I'm just a tourist. Now I really must be going. I have an appointment."

From the way the woman wrinkled her nose and sniffed, Hugo realized their body odors had become quite repulsive. Quickly, she stepped away from them.

"Wait! Just a moment, please," begged Hugo.

She turned her head, but kept walking. "Can't, I'm in a hurry."

Mong caught up with the woman and stood in her way, silently side-stepping her efforts to get around him, that is, until

Hugo closed in.

"My sincerest apologies for detaining you, ma'am. Does your cell phone plan include Hawaii? Please don't lie. All I want to do is make one collect call to Honolulu."

The panicky woman took another look at the apish Mong. Her eyes scanned the street for possible help. No one was about. She surrendered the cell to Hugo.

Hugo punched in Wen's number and waited for a dozen rings before giving up, repeating the number with the same result. How was he to know that Wen wasn't responding to his usual cell phone—he didn't want to be traced.

"Thank you, ma'am, you were very kind," Hugo said as he handed the phone back. He added a slight bow.

The frightened woman turned and quick-stepped as fast as her sandals could carry her to put the greatest distance between them.

"We stink like rotten fish, Mong. No wonder nobody wants to get close to us," said Hugo. "It's been more than two weeks since we had baths. Let's head for the beach. No one will bother us."

Among occasional snorkelers and swimmers, they swished about in the calm Gulf of Siam for an hour, then flopped on the sand away from the few tourists to let the baking sun dry their filched clothes.

"Where is the next beach resort town?" Hugo asked a passing neatly dressed gentleman, hoping he spoke English.

"About two hours south of here by car," replied the man, pointing to a sign showing the southern route out of town.

"Thanks," said Hugo, as the gentleman walked away, shaking his head at the oddly dressed Mutt-and-Jeff pair.

They had hardly walked a block in the direction of the sign when they heard a noisy vehicle behind them. They turned to see a *tuk-tuk*, a rickshaw-style taxi, pull up in front of a bustling restaurant. A tourist with a camera slung around his neck got out and paid his fare. The driver, a wiry, knobby-kneed man in a coolie hat, left his vehicle and entered a small shop next door.

Hugo and Mong eyed the *tuk-tuk* with curiosity. It looked like a three-wheeled motorbike with a hooded top and padded bench attached to the back. While the driver was gone, they seized upon the opportunity, climbed onto the passenger seat, and waited.

When the driver came out of the shop, he took one look at the two foreigners in their wrinkled, ill-fitting clothes and his eyes widened with anger. He was about to protest, but thought better of it after seeing the size and demeanor of Mong.

"Where you go?" he asked.

Unable to pronounce the name of the town, Ao Manao, Hugo merely pointed to the sign leading to their next destination. The driver mounted his single seat up front and started the engine. Two backfires later, the *tuk-tuk* chugged on its way south out of town with no talk of payment—yet.

Chapter 15

Confrontations

ESME ARRIVED home from the mall in an almost uncontrollable funk. She pulled into the carport and turned off the engine, but decided to stay put for a few moments. *I need to get a grip.* She was determined not to take out her frustration on the kids, especially because this was their first week of parochial school. She closed her perfectly lipsticked mouth and slowly breathed in for eight seconds, then out for eight, then took the plunge.

"Hi, everybody," she called with stiff cheerfulness.

Frank, a freshman, thundered down the stairs. "Hey, Mom! I made the basketball team! Isn't that cool?"

Eighth-grader Delores bounced into the foyer from the kitchen. "Hi, Mom, guess what? I'm gonna take sax lessons at school. I'll be in the band."

Esme briefly hugged them both. "That's great, you two," she said without enthusiasm, wondering how much those activities would interfere with their homework. She threw her old purse on a chair and marched into the kitchen to heat and pour herself a cup of chocolate macadamia nut coffee. And there her composure and resolve ended.

"Frank," she snapped, "why is all your junk strewn around the family room? And Delores, how many times have I told you not to leave your snack dishes from nachos and gooey cheese in the kitchen sink?"

Esme stomped into the master bedroom to change out of her mini-dress and stiletto heels. As she pulled on jeans and a T-shirt, she knew she was being bitchy, and felt vaguely ashamed of herself. After all, they were good kids. They had started to clean up their messes when Esme interrupted them with a new order. To make sure they would be out of hearing range when she confronted their father, she scribbled a long grocery list and sent them to the Village Market on Wilder Avenue just minutes before she expected Manny home.

Sister and brother weren't surprised. Both keenly intelligent, they'd been sensing, even witnessing, the recent tension between their parents. Frank grabbed the list and they willingly fled on the errand.

Manny, working all alone in his satellite office, could come and go at will as long as Rai's books—and double set of books— were up to date. As for the dummy cleaning business, he chose to work from 9:00 to 4:30. He drove the twenty-minute ride to their Makiki home. Esme could predict his arrival within a few minutes.

"Hi, sweetie, hi, kids," Manny shouted as the front door slammed shut behind him.

"Don't you 'Hi, sweetie' me, you lying sack of crap," Esme said, standing in the kitchen-to-dining room doorway with her hands fixed on her hips. Her words were like missiles hurled at her unsuspecting husband.

"What lie? What did I do now?" exclaimed Manny. He tried to close the distance between them and hug her, thinking he could disarm her unexplained fury. But when he came near, she beat off his extended arms, clenched her fists, and hammered away at his chest until it really hurt. When he grabbed her wrists, she kicked him hard in the shins.

"Hey!" he yelled, shoving her against the nearest wall. "Stop it! That hurts."

"Good!" she cried. "Now maybe you'll take your stuff and leave."

"What the hell are you talking about? Why are you in such a dither, Esme? And where are the children?"

"They're at the Village Market. Don't you 'Esme' me, and

don't change the subject, you bastard."

"I don't understand what's going on. Why don't you just tell me what I've done."

"You made me a promise that you wouldn't go to work for that gangster brother of yours. You lied to me. I told you I'd kick you out if you ever did go to work for him."

"What makes you think I'm working for Rai?" Manny's voice took on an air of false innocence.

"You were seen at the compound delivering a package to Domo and then you spent time with Rai inside."

"Who told you that?" asked Manny.

"Your nephew, Salvadore, that's who, and he'd have no reason to lie to me. Besides, those two unsavory goons I saw leaving your office the other day? I'm sure they had something to do with Rai's crooked businesses."

"I already explained about those two Chinatown leeches. And where did you see Sal?"

"At Kahala Mall with his yellow Porsche. And you're changing the subject again."

"All I did was show Rai's new bookkeeper a few tips in the accounts," he said. "I just did my brother a small favor. That's not actually *working* for him, is it? You can't condemn me for *that*, can you?"

"You bet I can! I know when you're lying to me, Manny. I can see it in your face. You can take your bags and get the hell out of here. Now!" She pointed to the two pieces of luggage deposited on the floor beside the dining room table, and began shoving him toward them.

"I thought you actually loved me."

"I did. I still do, but I can't live with a lying gangster of a husband."

"I'm not a gangster. I'm not doing anything illegal. Don't I have any rights to live in this house?"

"Not any more you don't."

"Remember, Esme, I pay the mortgage on this place and

for the food you put on the table—clothes too."

"Are you saying you'll stop paying for those things—denying your own children?"

"Of course not, but where do you expect me to go?" he asked. "Don't I get a chance to make things right with you? Where will I live? When do I get to see the kids?"

"The kids? That's between you and them. I don't give a hoot where you live. For all I care, you can go live at the compound with all the other gangsters in your family."

His mouth went dry. "If I go there, we'll never reconcile," he reasoned.

"That's true." She held the front door open.

Trembling, Manny picked up the two bags his wife had hastily stuffed and slowly left the premises. In a mood of total hopelessness, he drove back to his office. The couch would have to do until he could figure everything out—and win his wife back.

The moment Manny's car drove away Esme's tough performance collapsed. She slid into a chair at the kitchen table, cradled her head in her arms, and sobbed. It wasn't supposed to be like this, married with two children without any peace of mind. Just wall-to-wall anxiety. She thought back to their beautiful wedding—and the catastrophic end to the backyard reception. Thirteen-year-old Kekoa, Maria's guest, had seen someone there who frightened him. He bolted. But his loafer caught the edge of the bridge table. It held the traditional glass punchbowl, heaped with fruit donated by wedding guests to bring the couple good luck. The punchbowl crashed to the stone walkway, fruit and juice flying. Auntie Philiamina had screamed, "Now the bride and groom will have bad luck! It will follow them always!" Horrified, Mama Ballesteros charged at Auntie, shouting "Don't you dare put a curse on my children!"

In the kitchen Esme wept for twenty minutes. She couldn't help wondering, *Is the curse coming true? Mama wasn't the only superstitious one.*

* * * *

At the Osaka Family Bakery, morning dawned with white flour dust filling the air. Overhead exhaust fans pushed the dust out the roof vent and the delicious aromas out to the street to entice the pedestrians. Master baker Kekoa, removing the last trays from the ovens, transferred them to the cooling racks while Noah damp-mopped the floor. A bonding beyond uncle and nephew had taken place in the short time the boy had been working there. Andy had kindly released Noah from dishwashing duty in the cafe.

Noah was eager to learn and quick to understand. Kekoa welcomed the early morning company and enjoyed the role of mentor—it reminded him of how Sam Osaka had once taken *him* in, first as an apprentice, and then as family.

At one point Noah stopped mopping and leaned on the wooden handle. "Uncle K, I've got a problem and I don't know what to do about it."

Kekoa slid the last tray of Hawaiian sweet breads into the rolling rack. "How can I help you, son?"

"Well, there's this older and bigger guy at school who thinks I ratted him out to the police. His name is Duke and he's out to get me. He already knocked out my front tooth and is not satisfied with that. He wants to beat me up even more."

"What do your parents have to say about this or haven't you even told them?"

"I've told them, but Dad thinks I'm always the one starting the fights and this is all my fault. Mom agrees with him, but she wants me to go to the police. I can't do that."

"Why not, my boy?"

"This is just between you and me, right, Uncle K? I can't tell you otherwise."

"In that case, sure, I'll keep your secret." Kekoa silently added to himself, *as best I can. This doesn't sound good.*

"It's...I got sort of involved with something illegal." The boy couldn't make eye contact.

"What do you mean sort of?" Kekoa asked.

"Well, I created a distraction while Duke and another guy

stole stuff from a drugstore."

"I'd say that makes you just as guilty as they were. Don't you think so?"

"But I didn't actually take anything and I didn't get to share any of the loot."

"Did you know what you were doing at the time? Did you know you were making the robbery possible?"

"Yeah, I suppose so, but I was sort of roped into the thing. I didn't want to do it in the first place."

"But you aided them anyway." *Peer pressure*, Kekoa assumed.

"Yeah, but what do I do now?"

"The way I see it, you've got three choices. One: you can man-up and go to the police and accept the blot on your record. Of course, the police will demand the names of the other boys. And that could make you a target with them.

"Two: if questioned, you can lie and insist you had nothing to do with the robbery. But lying to the police is really not an option and might get you in even deeper trouble.

"Or three: you can do nothing and hope Duke decides not to beat you up anymore. I don't know what more I can tell you."

"Uncle K, didn't you ever get into messes like this when you were my age?"

"I was just about the same age. Yeah. I got into a serious mess that drove me into hiding for almost three years. I had to run away from home."

"Wow! I'd sure like to hear about that," said Noah, eager to move the painful attention away from himself.

Kekoa looked up at the round clock on the wall—10:15. "I guess we have a little time to talk story now. Why don't you put away the mop and I'll tell you."

When the boy returned, Kekoa put his arm around his shoulders and walked him over to a cushioned bench beside the doorway.

"One day when I was fourteen I was playing on the big

machine in the family tool shed and—"

"What kind of machine?" broke in Noah.

"Just let me tell the story, son." Kekoa told the boy how he witnessed the murder of his Uncle Big John and had to flee from the killer. He explained that he had to leave Leilani and *Tutu* Eme and the comforts of his grandmother's home to hide in the sugarcane fields in Ewa and then live on his own in Pearl City, Chinatown, and Kaimuki, not knowing where he'd put his head each night or where his next meal would come from. He related running away after being falsely accused of stealing and needing to dodge the social services workers. Noah smiled when Kekoa told him of Ol' Chou's antics and of Ilio, his dog.

"Did the murderer ever catch up with you?" inquired the boy.

"Yeah, a couple of times," said Kekoa. "Once he dropped a wrecking ball on a car I was in, and another time, he tried to run me over with a truck and, yet another time, he tried to shoot Grandpa Hank and me."

"What happened?" asked Noah.

"I got away. I'm here, aren't I?"

Kekoa finished his story, telling of the Osakas' kindnesses, and how he became a baker. "And you know what that's all about now."

"But what happened to the killer?" the anxious Noah asked.

"He's dead," said his uncle. "I'll tell you all about that some other time." That part of the story was too painful for him to tell even now.

Noah got the message and took another tack. "Should I run away and go into hiding too?"

"Absolutely not!" Kekoa said. "The killer wanted me out of the way because I witnessed him murdering Uncle Big John. I didn't have a support group like you do, so I ran. You said Duke knocked out your tooth. Maybe he'll think that's enough and leave you alone."

"Hell, no!" Noah burst out. "That shithead pretended he was my friend, and I actually fell for it, when all along he just wanted me for an accomplice. My parents have been complaining for years about my friends and I just didn't want to hear it. I wanted to be part of something, a group, and look where it got me."

* * * *

The *tuk-tuk* sputtered its way south on a paved, two-lane roadway for the better part of three hours before petering out of fuel. The driver slipped off his motorcycle seat and faced Hugo and Mong. He shrugged his shoulders and tilted his head with an embarrassed grin. Walking around to the rear of the *tuk-tuk*, he returned with a can printed with the word Petrol. Hoisting it in sinewy arms, he marched off in the direction they were headed. The two passengers continued to watch until the little man was no larger than a mite in the distance.

Hugo and Mong got off the *tuk-tuk* and found shelter from the late afternoon sun in a nearby jackfruit orchard. Their legs were still stiff from confinement and hiding on the ship, and the walking felt good. They could still smell the low tide from the ocean at least a half-mile away on their left. There were low white buildings, maybe small apartments, over that way as well, and a much taller building, maybe a hotel or office building. On the other side of the road perhaps two hundred feet behind them, a dozen or so men and women were thrashing rice from a drained paddy. They pounded bundles of long reed-like stalks against the ground to shake the kernels from the reeds. Some of them had huge wooden rakes and pitchforks.

"Hey, boss, you think driver bring back police or maybe not come back at all?" asked Mong.

Hugo drew his right hand down his sallow cheeks, while he thought about the two possibilities. "Perhaps it would be wise to remain hidden in the shelter of this grove and see what develops. It would be a dumb move to abandon a perfectly good ride to the resort town, but walking into a trap with the local law would be even dumber."

They lowered themselves to the ground. Leaning against tree trunks, they fell asleep. It was a little after sunset with pink and gray strands still swirling in the sky when Mong heard the clanking sound of the gas can spout against the *tuk-tuk's* fuel tank. He shook Hugo awake and they awkwardly stood, peering out of the trees to see if the driver had returned alone or with company.

He *was* alone and quite surprised to see that they hadn't gone off when they emerged out of the brush. Apparently, the driver was torn between missing a sizeable fare and being possibly cheated out of it by two questionable characters. He drained the can and banged it against the lip for the last drop before screwing the lid back in place. He hooked the empty gas can on the rear of the carriage and motioned for his passengers to re-board. Hugo climbed in, but Mong waited. He scanned the countryside for witnesses, but the farm workers had left for the day.

As the driver removed the vehicle's key from his pocket, Mong stepped close behind him and wrapped his massive right arm around the unsuspecting man's head. The few muffled sounds ended as his head was slowly turned left—then suddenly and powerfully jerked around to the right in a well-practiced move that apparently snapped his neck. Mong took a backward step as the limp figure slipped off the seat and into his arms. The huge man carried the small, spindly Asian some fifty feet into the grove and left him there, but not before going through the man's pockets. He retrieved 4,200 baht in small bills and a few santang coins, the equivalent of almost $102.

Returning to the *tuk-tuk*, Mong gave the newfound fortune to Hugo. Then he picked the key up off the ground and inserted it into the ignition. Climbing aboard the motorcycle seat, he turned the key, and kick-started the engine into several explosive backfires, which eventually settled into the more familiar *tuk-tuk* sound. He turned on the single headlamp, shifted into gear, and they were on their way once more. Mong's huge knobby knees protruded comically outward as he straddled the vehicle.

The buildings along the shore were getting both taller and

closer together. The sunset's pink glow, smearing the horizon, heralded the much larger resort town they were approaching. There would also be a fine meal ahead and not the scraps they had been begging for.

Chapter 16

Consequences

NINA PORTFIA headed for the front door with a white cashmere cardigan folded across one arm.

"And where do you think you're going, young lady?" asked Rai, appearing out of nowhere.

"Oh, Daddy, you scared me. Must you keep track of my every move? I'm not a child anymore. I'm fourteen."

"Whether you want to acknowledge it or not, my dear, you're not of age yet, and you are my daughter. I'm responsible for you. I do care what happens to you, so I want to know where you're popping off to at nine o'clock at night."

"Sal's dropping me off at the Ward movies. Mom said I could go. I'm meeting Malia and some other kids. We're going to see *The Hitchhiker's Guide to the Galaxy*. It's PG, Dad, perfectly harmless."

"What kids?" Rai asked. "Any boys involved?"

"I don't know, but everyone's going as a group, so it doesn't matter. I do know I'm not supposed to date, Daddy."

"Good. Now, honey, how are you getting home afterward?"

"Mr. Wong, Malia's dad, said he'd pick us up and drive us home. He said he'll be working late in town anyway, and I have his cell number with me. Okay?"

"Us?"

"Yeah, Malia and me. I'm spending the night at her house." Nina held up a small tote. "See? My sleepover stuff."

"On a school night?" Rai demanded, hoping to derail her

whole plan.

"Gee, Dad, I'm in public school now. The new school year doesn't start 'til Monday, next week."

As a last-ditch attempt, Rai scanned his daughter's outfit. Faded jeans, short-sleeved, modest scoop-neck blue shirt, and bare feet in strapped sandals. All quite proper. He had run out of objections. "Okay, then. Have fun and give Malia a hug from me."

Nina reached up, threw her arms around her father's neck, and kissed him on the cheek. She giggled. His mustache and clipped beard always tickled her chin.

Half an hour later, Sal dropped her off. Nina rode the escalator from the street to the second-floor theater complex. Malia and Noah were standing there, impatiently waiting for more of the group to come. Nina waved and started for the box office, but Noah held out a ticket for her.

"Already got you covered, Nina," he said.

"Who do I owe?"

"I bought the tickets for us," he said, looking pleased with himself.

"But isn't that a lot like dating?" asked Nina. "You know I'm not allowed to date."

"Not to worry," Malia replied. "Noah didn't buy the tickets. My dad paid for the three of us. His treat. Besides, we're almost cousins."

"What's this *almost cousins* bit?" asked Nina. "I thought you and I figured out how we were distantly related. Up to now I've even *called* you cousin."

"That's just it," replied Malia. "We're not *strictly* related, but we *are* connected by marriage. We share a common auntie and uncle, Auntie Maria and Uncle Kekoa. I'd say that makes us *ohana*."

"Except for me," said Noah, grinning. "I'm adopted."

"Noah, that's crazy. Mom and Dad officially adopted you, so you're my official brother, you silly," reassured Malia, squeezing her brother's hard bicep and laying her head on his shoulder. "We wouldn't be a family without you."

When the escalator delivered Malia's two other school friends a few minutes later, they all strode through the grand lobby. Malia wanted to stop at the concession stand for a tub of popcorn loaded with butter and salt, but her friends were already on their way to Theater 13. Inside the stadium-style theater about the sixth row up, everyone shuffled seating positions. It wasn't any accident or surprise to the other kids that Nina chose to sit next to Noah at one end. They remembered the way it had turned out on the pair's three previous non-dates. Malia was unhappily getting used to being left out. She moved away to sit with the others. She now realized, when there's a boy involved, your best friend is never quite the same.

The lights went dim and then off as the preview trailers blasted onto the screen. Then, as *A Hitchhiker's Guide* began, Noah stowed the armrest that separated the two teens. Nina reached over, found his large, warm hand, entwined her fingers in his, and settled them on her knee. Not long after, Noah conjured up the courage to slide his hand away and place his arm around her shoulders. Nina liked the feeling. She turned her face toward his. He wasn't watching the movie at all. He leaned toward her, their eyes met, their lips almost touched. They kissed, a first time for both, and if you had asked them later what the film was about, they couldn't have told you.

The movie's alien world with its many-headed president ended without Nina and Noah giving a hoot. The five teenagers filed out and through the hall to the main lobby.

"Hey, everybody, how about Dave and Buster's for some dessert before we go home?" asked Malia.

Nina slipped into her sweater. "I don't know," she said. "I better not. My stomach's a little queasy from dinner. I need some fresh air. Maybe a little walk is what I need."

"Okay if I walk with you?" asked Noah.

"I'd like that," said Nina, smiling shyly before turning to Malia. "You can call your dad to pick us up when I join you guys later at D & B's. Can you keep my tote for me?"

"Okay," Malia said, wishing she hadn't suggested D & B's.

Noah and Nina took the escalator down to street level, turned left at the corner, and left again without a thought as to where they were heading. They soon strolled out of the bright lights of the Ward entertainment complex and into dimmed streets of closed shops and deserted businesses. Holding hands, they stopped every now and then for a quick kiss and continued on with hardly a spoken word between them.

The warmth, the sweetness, was all so new that they were unaware of their surroundings. A shadowy figure had chosen to join them from some thirty feet behind. At first the shadow darted between empty doorways, maintaining the same approximate separation. As the two oblivious youngsters strolled, the stalking figure quick-stepped to close the distance. A heavy hand suddenly landed on Noah's shoulder, spinning him around.

"Duke! Duke Santos!" cried Noah. "You scared the shit out of me!"

In the poisonous glare of a distant streetlight, Duke's mouth forced a humorless grin. "I ain't exactly here to play patsy wit you, yah."

"What the hell do you want from me?" Noah asked. "I told you the last time, I didn't rat you out."

Duke shoved Nina back in the direction of the theaters. "Git out of here, pretty girl, before you git hurt. My gripes are wit dis here punk."

They were standing outside an auto body shop, closed at this late hour, when Duke threw the first punch. Noah saw it coming and ducked, but agile as he was, Duke was half a foot taller, heavier, and two years older. Noah knew he couldn't win in a fair fight with this evil guy he'd once called a friend, but he had to try or Duke would kill him. But after ducking and dodging a few more swings, Noah caught a sinking fist to the stomach that folded him to the sidewalk. He could hear Nina screaming and crying, but couldn't tell exactly where she was standing. Duke followed up by repeatedly kicking him in the ribs. Hunching into a fetal position, Noah rolled right, then left, to ward off the kicks. His hand struck something hard—a chunk of iron, a length of tailpipe from the auto repair shop. He wrapped both hands around it. Rolling back toward Duke, with all his strength he swung the metal pipe at the closer knee.

Duke crumbled to the ground, howling, "You broke my leg, you rotten bastard."

As Duke thrashed about, Noah saw him struggling to pull some object out of his back pocket. Noah couldn't see what it was, but managed to get to his feet, ready to pulverize his attacker with the tailpipe. Limping closer, he saw the unknown object. A revolver. Before Duke could level it at him, Noah swung the pipe at the hand holding the gun and knocked it out of reach a half-dozen feet away. Angered even more, Duke reached up, grabbed him by the belt, and pulled him down, then nimbly flipped on top of him. The tailpipe flew out of Noah's grip and clattered to the sidewalk out of reach. He tried to roll free of the smelly, suffocating body, but Duke straddled his target, punching both cheeks at will. Noah's head jerked right and left with alternate blows.

"Stop! Stop now!"

Noah heard Nina's screams, then a deafening explosion near his left ear.

* * * *

Mong drove the *tuk-tuk* through the night toward the pink and yellow horizon as the sun set. He churned wearily up the last hill, and motored toward the first sign of civilization they'd seen for hours. Around midnight they approached a modest-sized resort town. It suited Mong and Hugo just fine. Lively twanging music, lantern lights, and drunken shouts filled the road beside noodle shops, cafes, and jumping bars. The Happy Feast boasted a sign in the window, in both Thai and English, announcing Thai beer, burgers, pancakes, eggs, sausage, and a list of local dishes. A growling stomach and a pocketful of *bahts* propelled Monk to turn off the road. He drove the *tuk-tuk* straight into the alley next door and parked. They spotted an empty table at the rear of the brightly lit, smoke-filled eatery.

On the way to the table, Hugo eyed a large leather purse with its strap draped over the back of a chair occupied, most likely, by an American tourist. She was engrossed in conversation in English with two men. What attracted Hugo's keen attention was a recent cell-phone model protruding from an unzipped purse compartment. The ex-pickpocket casually extended his hand barely an inch or two from his side, while his fingers deftly lifted the cell without leaning or hesitation in motion. When he and Mong settled at their table, he slipped the phone into a pants pocket and turned his attention to ordering.

Twenty minutes later, the two castaways were enjoying local *Singha* beer straight from the bottle. Hugo munched on a local beef burger, spiced with garlic, cilantro, ginger, and chili peppers. Mong attacked a disappointing platter of Thai *roti*. Not exactly the stack of pancakes he always ordered at Zippy's in Honolulu, but delicate grilled crepes stuffed with banana slices and scrambled eggs.

As they guzzled a second round of *Singha*, the cell phone in Hugo's pocket began a muffled ring. Fearing the discovery of his theft, he quickly pulled the phone from the pocket in his shorts, silenced it, and sandwiched it between the sandal and his bare foot. A few minutes later a large Western male shadowed their table.

"Okay, give up the phone, and I'll say no more about it."

"I don't know what you're talking about, mistah," replied Hugo, in a quiet, deferential manner. Mong shook his shaggy head and shrugged his shoulders.

"My wife's cell phone was stolen sometime in the last hour," claimed the stranger as a second Western man came to stand with him. "I punched in her number on my phone and heard hers ring in this direction. One of you must have taken it. Give it up and you can walk away free as a bird."

"You can frisk us both," offered Hugo, as he rose in a disarmingly courtly manner, placing most of his weight on the opposite foot.

The first stranger slid both his hands over Hugo's shirt and down over the pockets of his cargo shorts. Surprised to come up empty-handed, he checked the chair and the surrounding floor space. Nothing. "Okay, your turn," he addressed Mong.

Hugo sat down while Mong took to his feet with his towering height and massive strongman build. Hugo smiled, as he saw the newfound-fear struck in the stranger's face. With Mong so willing, the stranger proceeded with a full search that led to the same negative result.

Just then, a ring tone emanated from an adjacent table. All four men turned their attention to the well-dressed Thai male, holding an extended conversation over his cell phone. He was accompanied by an attractive Asian female, who wore a spaghetti-strapped black cocktail dress.

The first stranger stared. "The ring tone is the same, but the phone is a different brand," he said.

"Apparently, that is the phone you heard," said Hugo.

The first man turned back to address Hugo and Mong. "My apologies, gentlemen. I acted impulsively. Forgive me."

"Accepted," said Hugo. "It is an easy mistake to make, but false accusations can sometimes lead to unnecessary conflict. You are fortunate to be dealing with ourselves, two peaceful men. Good morning, sirs." He nodded, dismissing the strangers, who shuffled back to their own table.

"You sure poured it on thick, boss," muttered Mong.

"Let's not push our luck," said Hugo, slipping the phone back in his pocket. "It's time to blow this joint."

Hugo held out the cash they'd taken from the *tuk-tuk* driver and counted out the cost of their food and drink. Leaving the Happy Feast meant the two castaways had to pass the strangers' table again. As they did, each made a polite bow and continued out the door into the early morning humidity.

* * * *

Holed up in the Chinatown apartment, Wen Tse Fong had

long since tired of his captive's complaints and wailing. Using the apartment's landline, he called on two of his remaining henchmen to dispose of the hapless grocery clerk, whose ranting had made it impossible for Wen to catch any sleep. Over several days, Wen had become more and more enamored of the strategically located little apartment he'd commandeered. From the front window he not only had a view of Chou & Rice Realty, but he also had a narrow view of the office down the block, where Domo had issued his ultimatum.

"The nerve of that son of a bitch threatening me on my own turf," said Wen to his two thugs when they had returned from their mission to dispose of the defenseless little clerk. Wen had no interest in how or where they'd done it. "Domo works for Portfia, and I can't have him muscling me out of Chinatown. It's my territory, always has been. If he wants a fight, I'll give him a good one. Let's start with a contract on his brother, Manuel, and see how that sits with him."

"I could pick 'im off wit a scope from dis here window when he comes out of his office—pop pop," said Zeke Young, one of Wen's *hapa* thugs, adding the comic sound effects.

"No, no, you idiot," scolded Wen. "The cops would trace the bullet path right back to this apartment. I'm not done staying here yet. You keep an eye on him and nail him at home or some other place. Now get the hell out of here and do what I told you. I got some serious planning to do."

"Sure, boss, we're on our way."

An hour later, his cell phone rang. *I wonder what those two dumb goons want now*, Wen thought. He flipped open the phone. "Yeah?…Hugo? Where the hell you been?…Kidnapped? In a crate on board a ship?…What the hell you doing in Thailand?…I see. You want my help to get back to Honolulu. That's real tough, Hugo, but this ain't a good time. I'm holed up right now. The cops are looking for me, and I'm battling with the Portfia mob, so I gotta stay off the streets for a while. And I'm cash-strapped. I can't get to a bank. Sorry, man." He abruptly cut Hugo off.

Honolulu Heat

* * * *

Two hours later, down the street in his office, Manny Portfia dozed on crossed arms while sitting at his desk. The rattle and clatter of a garbage truck woke him up. He lifted his disheveled head and looked outside. Dusk was settling over the city. No need to remind his miserable self that this was home for now. *How much longer will it be?* he wondered. Hours earlier, he had stocked the half-size office refrigerator with perishable groceries and stowed the dry and canned food in empty slots on his bookshelves.

On impulse, he scanned the office. A jolt of fear shot through his body. *Something's out of the ordinary.* Something moving caught his eye: a tiny red dot on the far wall. *What the hell is it?* The red dot danced back and forth across the file cabinets along the right wall and just as suddenly jerked to the left along the bookcases, like it was scanning, searching for something. Or someone! *It's moving—looking for me!* All at once it registered with him: this was the mark of an infrared, sniper-scoped rifle. *And I'm the intended target!* His heart thumped so rapidly he thought he would have a heart attack. His breathing raced to gather in as much air as it could.

When sheer icy panic melted into more liquid logic, Manny slipped out of his chair onto the floor. Crouching well below window level, he crawled several feet to the outside wall between the two windows. Slowly, he reached up for the venetian blind cord on the first window. The red dot continued to dance across the opposite wall. Manny lifted himself up a few inches, just long enough to grab the cord. He lowered the blinds and closed the slats, then ducked under the second window to do the same thing. Once the room was very nearly dark, he peeked through one of the slats and saw the silhouettes of two men on the ledge of a roof across the street. One was kneeling, holding a rifle; the other stood next to him.

My desk light! I've got to turn it off or the shooter will track my shadows. He crept back to his desk, and slid one arm up to snap the switch off and, while he was at it, grabbed his cell phone, which

149

was sitting next to his ledgers.

With the room dark, still terrified, but feeling braver now that he had a course of action, Manny opened the air conditioning grate to his hidden office and pushed the hinged vent aside. Stepping through the opening, he shoved the vent home once more and turned on the lights and air conditioning to the windowless secret room. Inside his private hideaway, he felt safe, comfortable enough, but food, water, and the bathroom remained out of reach in the main office. He turned on his computer, and soon the outer room's image formed on the monitor screen—via the camera Rai's technicians had implanted in the drapes. Slowly, his breathing returned to near normal and his heartbeat calmed. He began to think about the longer term.

My supplies won't last more than a week, and I'll go nuts in this damn hole before then. I assured Esme I wasn't working for Rai so I can't very well move out to the compound. Or can I? It's the only place I can be protected. But would Esme find out? Would she ever forgive me? She already knows I lied.

Manny clutched his cell phone and poked in Rai's business number.

"Portfia," the abrupt voice answered.

"Rai, it's me. I'm trapped in the hidden office and I'm in real big trouble. I think Domo's scare tactics didn't work with Wen. Two of his boys are on the roof across the street with a sniper rifle. They're trying to kill me, Rai. I don't know what to do. I can't go home because Esme kicked me out."

"Easy, take it easy, little *brah*," said Rai. "There's plenty of room for you upstairs in Domo's house. You got a car?"

"Yeah, but the minute I step out the front door, I'll become a bull's-eye for those two goons across the street. Until it gets real dark, anyway."

"I get it," Rai said. "Wait an hour. I'll send someone to take them out. I'll call you and let you know when it's done. You can ride back here with my man. Okay, little *brah*?"

"Thanks, big brother." As he flipped his phone shut, Manny

felt a rush of relief—and a rush of despair all at once. He had become too hardened to cry, but at this horrible moment he choked back tears. *My life wasn't supposed to be like this. How did it all fall apart?*

Chapter 17

Impulsive Moves

THE SILENCE that followed the explosion in Noah's ear seemed to last far longer than the seconds it actually did. But during that virtual eternity, the beating to his face ceased. Duke's heavy body collapsed on top of him. Noah shoved and heaved and rolled to get free. And when he finally succeeded in liberating himself, he felt a thick liquid trickling across his neck. He struggled to his feet and regarded the motionless body of his attacker at his feet.

A pair of passing headlights briefly illuminated the scene. Noah saw a long shadow shift across the body. Someone was standing there, and when he turned and looked up, he saw that it was Nina, glassy-eyed and frozen to the spot where she stood. She was shivering, even in her cashmere sweater. He approached and placed his arms around his girl and pulled her to him, but she remained stubbornly stiff, both arms hanging straight at her hips. Sensing her terrified state, Noah backed off a little. It was then that he noticed the gun in her left hand. The explosion. *Oh my God!* He realized with horror that Nina had picked up Duke's revolver and fired the shot that saved his life.

Noah's brain surged with a flood of conflicting thoughts and feelings, but through it all, he came to one conclusion: *Nina cannot get blamed for this screwed-up mess I got her into.* He carefully lifted up her left arm and pried her fingers from the gun's grip and trigger. With his own hand shaking, he tucked the gun into his back pocket. *There must be gunpowder all over her sweater,* he thought. So he coaxed her out of it and tied the arms around his waist. Seeing the catatonic look on her face, he kissed her on parted lips and then hugged her tightly for several minutes. Slowly, her stiffness began to soften, and her eyes took on a slight focus. Her lips began to move.

"What have I done?" she asked in a trembling, squeaky voice that surprised even her.

"You didn't do anything," he said. "I pulled the trigger. That's all you need to remember."

"But I—"

"Never mind. Let's go," he pleaded. "Before someone sees us here."

"Are you just going to leave him lying there?"

Oh hell! Noah hadn't thought about it. He grabbed Duke by his ankles and pulled. The body refused to move. Noah squatted for better leverage. Inch by inch, he dragged the body behind a wall of worn-out truck tires ready to be hauled away. Breathing heavily, his chest aching, he straightened up and used the toes of his sneakers to sweep away the dusty drag marks.

"Come on, let's go! We gotta get outta here!" He grabbed Nina's arm and tried to coax her back in the direction of the theaters. As they came in range of the towering, glaring street lights, she pulled her arm back and gasped. "Noah, there's blood all over the front of your shirt."

He jerked to a stop and looked down. "Shit!" he muttered. His UH football shirt was forest green, but dark red blotches, still damp, were smeared over the tall, white "Warrior" letters. In one swift motion, he pulled the jersey over his head, flipped it inside out, then reversed it, and roughly pulled it back on. It felt uncomfortable backwards, too tight, and the label was now in front just under his chin. Nina peeked around his back. "Better," she whispered. "You can hardly see anything."

With one hand in the small of her back, Noah hurried her along to the entrance of the entertainment complex. When they finally stepped off the UP escalator, Malia was standing a few feet away, alone, hands on her hips, her thick brown hair falling over half her face. "Where have you guys been? Everyone else has gone home."

"Calm down, sis," said Noah, as he coaxed her into the shadows. "We've got a little emergency here, and I need you to listen to me very carefully."

"What emergency? Is anybody hurt?"

"Stop, sis! Can I trust you? You won't tell anyone?"

"Wow! Okay, our secret. Now tell me what's going on?"

"I had to shoot Duke Santos with his own gun. It was self-defense."

Malia's mouth dropped open. Her dark eyes widened in a look of sheer panic and disbelief. "Oh my God, Noah! Is he dead, actually dead?"

"Yeah. I couldn't help it. The bastard beat me up. Look at what he did to my face."

"Oh God, it's all red and puffy. You poor thing."

"It'll be black and blue by morning."

She grasped both his hands and squeezed them. "What are you going to do?"

"I don't know," he said, disengaging his hands. "But right now I need you to do me a big favor, sis."

"What?"

"Call Dad now to come and get you and Nina. When you get to our house, make sure she showers thoroughly. Run all her clothes through the washing machine, at least twice."

"Can I ask why?"

"Nina has this crazy idea that she pulled the trigger herself. She witnessed everything up close and nasty. She was like a zombie afterwards, so now she's real confused about what actually happened. Help her and see that she gets back to her parents tomorrow. Okay?"

Malia's body went rigid with shock over the preposterous, unfathomable responsibility her brother had just thrust upon her. "Aren't you coming with us?" she asked, wondering how, at the very least, she was supposed to manage Nina's laundry without her mother getting suspicious.

"No, there's a few things I have to do yet." He hugged her and bussed Nina's cheek as he backed away from them toward the DOWN escalator and escape.

Once at street level Noah headed for Ala Moana Beach Park merely a block away. A vague plan germinated in his mind. He thought the park closed about eleven, and it must be past midnight by now. It would be deserted. He waited for the green light, crossed the boulevard at Kamakee Street, and dashed into the park onto the narrow road bordering the sandy beach.

To avoid being seen, he kept to the grassy area. He wanted nothing to do with the beach itself. If security vehicles happened to be cruising about, the huge flat expanse would announce him blatantly trespassing. Taking advantage of any available shrubs and shadows, the teenager walked in a steadied, quick gait the length of the extended block to the parking lot entrance of Magic Island. Slipping into the empty lot, he broke into a trot across it and onto the pedestrian pathway.

Magic Island, actually a small peninsula jutting out into the Pacific Ocean, comprised a sweeping lawn, studded with palms and umbrella-shaped monkeypod trees.

The sounds of traffic behind him mixed with the sounds of the sea ahead. Feeling totally alone and scared, Noah tried to focus on his mission. The boy increased his pace up one of the walking paths encircling the peninsula. Darting between the trees toward the Ewa or westerly side of the island, he arrived at the seawall, the highest point in the park.

With nothing but wave-breaking rocks below him and the vast ocean beyond, this was the perfect spot for what he had planned. Admittedly, his plan was a little weak, but it was all he could think of in the short time that he had. Tonight, the ocean only washed waves gently over the outermost rocks as if resting from a hard day.

Noah had to hurry. Bike-riding police security could come along at any moment. Although the moon was nearly full, charcoal-gray clouds enabled him to carry out his plan under dark shadows. He sat down on the edge of the seawall and dangled his feet, trying to figure out where to climb down. Noah pulled off his sneakers, leaving them on the wall. He slid down over the edge for at least six feet to the lava rocks below, landing hard and flat without mishap—stretching from one rock to another and then to the last large boulder.

Once there, he lowered himself again until he sat with his feet dangling in the water. Little gray rock crabs skittered about him. Pulling Duke's gun out of his back pocket, he emptied it of the remaining bullets and flung them as far he could out into the gray night above the sea—their tiny splashes unheard. Noah began scrubbing the gun with wet sand—the barrel, trigger housing, chambers, and grip. Satisfied that all the prints must be gone by now, he scraped the gun's barrel on the rock next to him to raise barnacle grit, which he stuffed into the barrel itself. The boy then used his house key to scratch the grit around inside the barrel to hopefully disturb any future ballistic testing. Somewhat satisfied, he cast the gun out to sea.

Untying the sleeves of Nina's sweater from around his waist and spreading it out on the rocks, he piled wet sand, shells, and any small rocks he could find on it. Folding it neatly into a tight ball, he wrapped the long sleeves around it in a secure square knot. Satisfied that it was heavy enough and the little rocks wouldn't fall out, he stood, picked it up, spun about, and shot-put it out to sea as well. This time he heard the splash and saw it sink below the gentle rolling surf.

He pulled off his bloody jersey and then rethought abandoning it. Walking half-naked along Ala Moana Boulevard after midnight would be stupid. So he soaked it in the cold sea water, scrubbing it between his fists until the mostly dried blood began to fade. He rinsed and wrung it out several times. Turning it right-side-out once more, Noah pulled it on over his head. It was cold, clammy, and full of fresh holes—but at least he was dressed.

He calculated his next move, a place to climb out, but not where the seawall was at its steepest. The exhausted boy turned inland toward the beach and worked his way along the rocks to where the wall ended, where he knew surfers and paddleboarders found it easier to climb out onto the grass. He walked back to where he had left his sneakers and sat on a nearby bench to put them on.

Suddenly, he saw a light approaching from the distance, weaving as it followed the walking path. He dashed to the nearby restroom and kept moving to the lee side of the building as the security patrol's bicycle circled around him. Watching the patrol leave the park, he waited a good ten minutes before attempting to leave. Then darting among the trees once more, he headed to the boulevard, somehow escaping the park without getting caught.

As Noah trudged along, he questioned his own reasoning. Drained and dazed, he asked himself, *How did I get into this mess?* This was the favorite park of all Oahu locals. On weekends his parents would bring him and Malia here for whole days. They barbequed, rode bikes, swam in the ocean, fished for fun but never got a bite. The family had watched small-sized weddings from a respectful distance, and once even joined a church service at sunrise. Noah and his sister loved to sit on a bench on the seawall watching tugs haul container barges to and from the Port of Honolulu. Now the beach park would never look or even feel the same again.

Tonight had started so happily with Nina and sweet kisses. It had turned out to be the worst night of his life. And hers too.

* * * *

Zeke Young lay on his stomach in darkness, at the roof's edge atop a vacant building, eying the offices across the street through the scope of a high-powered rifle. Himé, a solidly built Hawaiian, boldly sat on the same ledge with his feet hanging over the front. Passing cars and street lights exposed his thick, hard face as he munched on an egg roll. At one point in their vigil, a short, noisy gasp emanated from Himé's mouth. Zeke glanced up. The Hawaiian's hands had dropped to his side, his jaw agape. His eyes were fixed on a shadowy object atop a roof on the far side of the street.

Zeke squinted. "What the hell you looking at, *brah*? That bird?"

"T'ain't no ordinary bird, Zeke. Dat's a *pueo*, a black owl. Dey bring *pilikia*, big trouble w'en you see dem."

"That's a lotta bull, man," returned Zeke. "Besides, what the hell you doing sitting up there in the light where anyone can see you?"

Two other dark figures had silently ascended the rusted fire escape at the rear of the same Chinatown roof. The first to arrive on the rooftop moved wide left, undetected, but the second figure stepped on a piece of tubing from an old television antenna, making a crunching sound.

Himé dropped his egg roll to reach for his handgun. It was only halfway out of the shoulder holster when a fatal bullet found its mark in his chest. He fell sideways, then backward with one leg still on the ledge, his gun only inches away.

Zeke smartly rolled onto his back, swung his rifle around, and easily picked off the shooter using the infrared scope. Not realizing there was a second assassin, he stood up. A lone shot whizzed passed him. He shifted direction, lurched toward the fire escape, and leapt to the first landing. Just as he started through the fire door, a second shot caught him in the shoulder. He felt blazing pain and dropped the rifle. It clattered to the ground. The remaining assassin pursued him, but Zeke disappeared into the entrails of the building.

* * * *

Across the street, concealed within his private inner sanctum, Manny waited anxiously for his phone call. Around eleven, the welcome ring tone sounded. It was Domo. "I'm parked out front, the black Ford Taurus."

"What about those goons across the street?" asked Manny.

"You don't have to worry about them. One's dead, and the other's wounded and on the run. Besides, they abandoned the rifle. I picked it up in the back of the building."

Manny had collected the documents he needed to continue

conducting Rai's business and quickly tidied up the office before he left. With the office now locked up, he rushed down the steps and outside. He located the car and pulled open the back door with the intention of getting in, but the rear seat was already occupied. Two bodies sat propped up in opposite corners, looking as though they might still be alive.

"Sorry, guys," said Manny, as he backed away and shut the door.

"Yeah, you'll have to sit up front," Domo said. "I'll get rid of 'em after I drop you off at the compound." Then he turned somber. "I don't like losing one of our guys. Jorge was a solid friend and a crack shot, but he made one misstep on that roof that got hisself killed. The other guy was one of Wen's gorillas."

Domo started the engine and pulled the stolen Ford out into light Chinatown traffic. A dozen blocks and a couple of turns put them on the freeway going west.

"Where do you dispose of them?" asked an overcurious Manny. "Never mind. Don't answer. I don't want to know."

"I wouldn't tell you anyway," replied Domo. "Your brother doesn't even know. Rai's smart. He doesn't ask questions."

Domo drove into the compound and stopped in front of the main house. A short, thick-bodied man approached the car and opened the passenger door, motioning for Manny to get out.

"I thought I was staying at your place," said Manny. "Why are you stopping here?"

"The boss wants to see you first," Domo replied.

Manny left the car. He mounted the three steps to the screened lanai and one more step into the marbled front hall, where he met Rai. The two men embraced, concluding with affectionate slaps on the back.

"So you had a rough day of it, *brah*," consoled Rai. "Well, you'll be safe here. We can pick up Esme and the kids and move them in here for the time being as well."

"Don't I wish, Rai. Esme already threw me out of the house because she found out that I'm working for you. Why the hell would she want to live here, even temporarily?"

"You gotta be firm with these wives," advised Rai in an arrogant tone. "You can't be a wimp in your own home. They'll walk all over you."

"I'm who I am, Rai. I can't change that after this many years of marriage. My whole friggin' life is a joke."

"What I really meant was, do you think they're safe where they are?" asked Rai. "Don't you think Wen Tse Fong would take his revenge out on *them*?"

"Oh God, I hadn't thought of that."

* * * *

Hugo and Mong had spent the breezy night on the open beach and awoke to glaring sun, scorching heat, and sticky sweat—not to mention the sand in their clothes and bites all over their bodies. Nocturnal insects had had a field day. The temptation to scratch was hard to resist. Hugo rolled over on his stomach to see the clock on a nearby building. It read 6:30. The beach appeared deserted. He sat up in time to see Mong strip down completely, dash into the surf, and dive in. *Maybe the cold water will help the itching,* Hugo thought as he also stripped down and headed for the water.

Mong proved to be a swift swimmer, demonstrating a long, reaching stroke with a power kick. The motion relaxed him and as the muscle kinks and knots of the past two weeks worked out of his system, he began to think. *Hugo ain't been ordering me around lately, and I been doing my own thing. We're kinda like equals out here. And he's always got a plan. He knows what to do.*

Hugo's ability to swim had never exceeded the dog paddle. He floated on his back in shallow water, rolling over the gentle wave crests, shutting his eyes from the sun and salt. He accepted the fact that they'd been screwed. There'd be no help from Wen Tse Fong or anyone else back home. In some odd familial way he felt a responsibility for getting the two of them out of this jam. He figured they would need passports, Western clothes, and the equivalent of 3,000 U.S dollars. The cash and clothes they could steal, but finding U.S. passports with Asian photos presented yet another tough problem.

Hugo opened his eyes to find Mong standing only a few feet away. Deciding to stand up himself, he could see that the beach had became more populated. As they exited the water and traversed the sand to their clothes, no one seemed concerned about their nudity, although one strolling woman seemed quite taken with Mong's masculinity.

They donned their ragged clothing and took shelter from the sun on dunes covered with healthy sea grape bushes bordering the beach. Mong relaxed. Hugo observed the people-behavior patterns, particularly those leaving their possessions on the beach while they swam. He noted that the better swimmers preferred the deeper waters. Others left their things high and dry on the sand, well away from the shoreline. These were the best marks, the ones most vulnerable to theft. He stood and scanned beyond the sea grape bushes to see a jumble of parked cars next to a row of stores. A pickup truck with a tarp covering its bed stood out. It sat sunk in sand up to its wheel hubs—not likely to be going anywhere soon, Hugo reasoned. It was time to put his plan into action. He explained the details to Mong, and they waited for an opportunity.

A Caucasian man, whom Hugo judged to be in his late forties, spread a beach towel high on the sand, disrobed to a swimsuit, and headed into the foaming surf with a practiced dive. His belongings were in a folded, neat pile covered with a towel. Easy pickings. The mark's physique resembled Hugo's, so he nodded to his partner in crime. Mong moved down the beach and assumed a position blocking a clear view of the pile. While the man stroked for the open sea, Hugo performed a cursory scan to see if anyone was watching. Apparently not. He swooped down, scooped up the entire pile, and quickly disappeared into the cover of the sea grape bushes. His skinny body moved fast to the pickup, deposited the pile he'd stolen under the pickup's tarp, and strolled back to his beach perch as though nothing had happened.

The victim now swam parallel to the beach. Mong strolled

in the same direction, keeping pace with the swimmer. When he noticed that Hugo had returned to the shady spot under the bushes, he reversed direction and strolled back to join his boss.

Some twenty minutes later, the swimmer emerged from the water and walked up the beach to where he presumed his belongings lay. Not finding them there, he scouted up and down the breadth of the beach, at first questioning his own memory and judgment. Then a blood-red anger flooded his face as he realized he'd been robbed. He swore under his breath as he looked in every direction. Approaching several groups of bathers, he questioned those who spoke English, but to no avail. Finally, the dejected, frustrated victim shuffled to the parking lot.

When Hugo and Mong realized that many of the nearby bathers had been alerted to the theft, they moved down the beach a hundred yards or so before attempting another. Shortly after noon, they observed a second mark, a lone young woman surreptitiously hiding her purse under her spread blanket while overtly scanning the sandy real estate for any onlookers. Her clothes became a second lump under the same blanket. Even as she strolled toward the surf, she kept looking over her shoulder to be certain.

The two thieves were ready to execute their second plan. Hugo followed her into the water and immersed himself, even his head under water, then ran up the beach to her blanket. Lowering himself onto it like he belonged, he fished out her towel from underneath it, and dried himself off—all the while keeping an eye on the woman paddling about in the surf. Meanwhile, Mong did pushups in the wet sand at the water's edge as a distraction. If nothing else, his physique drew the attention of most sunbathers.

Hugo handily removed a plump wallet from the woman's purse that she'd hidden under the blanket. He slipped the wallet into his pocket, stood up, and meandered farther up the beach behind the sea-grape vegetation to the pickup. Neither man stayed to watch the woman's frantic discovery. At nightfall the two thieves collected their booty from the truck bed. They had netted some 20,000 *bahts,* or about 480 in U.S. dollars; a Polo shirt; a pair of tan Levi slacks; sandals; and a male U.S. passport—a decent day's trickery. But it would take a little more time to accumulate all that they needed to make their way home.

Chapter 18

Confession

SHIVERING in his wrung-out but still-soaked jersey, Noah walked through most of the night—first, from Ala Moana Boulevard over to King Street, then at its end, Waialae Avenue—all the way to the alley behind the bakery. He shuffled to the back door at 3:15 a.m.. With nowhere to sit, not even a wayward cardboard box, he flopped down on the ground, flicking away pebbles and dirt, and leaned against a wall across from the bakery workroom. Around him, tufts of grass poked up between cracks in the concrete. He was waiting for a bedroom light to come on in the Pualoa apartment upstairs. The youngster knew that his Uncle Kekoa started baking at four. *Just a short wait now*, he thought. The bedroom light did come on at 3:45 a.m., and he heard his uncle moving about in the workroom a quarter-hour later. Noah quickly stood up, tried to dust off the back of his pants with the palm of his hand, and pounded on the door. Kekoa opened it with a smile, expecting him at this hour.

"Morning, Uncle K." Noah put on an apron and a paper hat, then began work by carrying a multi-layered carton of eggs from the fridge to the worktable.

"Good morning yourself," said Kekoa, not able to even look up as he poured half a bag of sifted flour into a mixer. A moment later, he threw a sidelong glance at his nephew.

"What's with the wet jersey?"

"I got caught in the rain."

"That's a hot one. You stink like the shore at low tide. If you're going to lie to me and betray my trust, I can't do anything about it, but I won't let you near any of my ingredients. Take off the apron and hat. Go upstairs and tell Auntie Maria that I told you to take a shower. Put on a pair of my briefs, shorts, and a T-shirt." Kekoa suddenly stopped before flipping on the giant mixer, and stared at Noah's face. "My God, somebody must've beaten the crap out of you. Ask Auntie Maria if she can patch you up a little. I want to know what happened. We'll talk more when you come down."

Noah silently did as he was told, and thirty minutes later he returned to the workroom in an apologetic mood. "I'm sorry, Uncle K. I didn't intend to show up here looking like a slob. I didn't mean to lie to you either. I had a real rough time last night, and it just seemed a lot easier not having to explain everything. I suppose if anyone could understand, it would be you." He picked a large brown egg from the box and held it over the rim of the mixing bowl.

"So now are you willing to tell me what transpired last night?"

"Sure. You remember that problem we talked about a few days ago?" asked Noah, carefully cracking one egg after another into the stainless steel mixing bowl.

"You mean the trouble you were having with that bully?"

"Yeah, only this time it really blew up in my face."

"Speaking of face, let me have a closer look at yours." Kekoa gently nudged his nephew's chin one way and the other, examining the damage there. "I don't know why I didn't notice it when you came in. My God, he did a real number on you. What happened?"

"I can't tell you unless you promise not to tell *anyone*."

"I won't promise that. What if it's not in your best interests?"

"Then I can't tell you."

"All right, then, I promise," surrendered Kekoa, realizing he'd better find out the truth.

"Duke Santos is dead. I shot him in self-defense. He was beating me up, and if I'd let him go on, he would've killed *me*."

"Where did you get the gun?" asked Kekoa.

"It was Duke's gun, but I got it away from him and shot him." Noah dropped the contents of another egg into the bowl.

"Let me get this straight. *You* shot *him?*" Kekoa started a second mixer.

"Yeah." Noah picked up yet another egg and cracked it against the bowl's lip.

"We should go to the police. Like you said, it was self-defense."

"We can't go to the police," said an agitated Noah as he dropped the cracked egg he was holding, shell and all, into the bowl.

"Why not?" demanded his uncle. "Is there something you're not telling me? Was there a witness?" Baker and helper stopped what they were doing, while Noah retrieved the wayward eggshell.

"No, no, and no!" cried Noah. When he turned back to face Kekoa, the tears were streaming down his face.

Kekoa placed both hands on the boy's shoulders and gazed at him intently. He studied the boy's puffy, swollen face, already turning black and blue—but also took in the faded scar over his left eye, the strong square jaw, the early hint of a mustache, and the tears flowing helplessly. "You know something, nephew? I don't think you pulled that trigger at all. I think you're protecting someone else. Is it that new girlfriend of yours?"

"Yeah. but she only did it to protect *me,*" cried Noah. "Duke was sitting on top of me, punching both sides of my face nonstop. He went sort of crazy, like he was enjoying it and he hit harder and harder. I had knocked the gun out of his hand a minute before and it slid across the ground. Nina watched the whole thing and then she picked it up and shot him in the neck. It must have caught one of the main arteries because he died right away—a lot of blood too."

"Nina, Nina who?"

"Nina Portfia," the boy replied.

"Nina Portfia? Rai Portfia's daughter?"

"Yeah. She's not allowed to date, so we went to the movies with a bunch of kids, Malia too. After the movie we just walked around holding hands and stuff."

It was the "and stuff" that made Kekoa's stomach muscles clench. And it had to be Portfia's daughter, of all the girls in Hawaii. He finally spoke. "And you chose to do the heroic thing and take the whole responsibility, right?"

"Yeah, I couldn't let her be blamed," Noah said. "It was all my fault she was there with me. And besides, Duke was after *me*, not *her*."

"I see," said Kekoa. "And where is this gun now?"

"I threw it in the ocean, along with her sweater. I cleaned the gun real good before I did."

"Where did you do all this?"

"Magic Island. On the seawall."

"So now you're telling me you tampered with evidence as well?"

"Yeah, I had to."

"Why did you get rid of her sweater?"

"On TV they always talk about gunpowder residue getting on your clothes when you shoot somebody."

"Uh-huh. Think carefully. Is there any way either you or Nina can be tied to Duke's death?"

"Not so long ago Duke and me hung around together. Is that what you mean, Uncle K?"

"Yes. Have there been any eyewitnesses to your feud with this Duke character? That is, in addition to your girlfriend."

"Well, there's this friend of ours, Gino Akino. He used to hang with us too. He warned me that Duke wanted to beat me up."

A sick feeling now joined the tension in Kekoa's gut. The situation was getting worse and worse. A few days ago, Noah had confided in him about the drugstore shoplifting and how Duke wrongly believed that Noah had ratted him out to the police. "This Gino—does he know Duke was still stalking you to get revenge for being arrested?"

"Yeah, but I'm not sure he'll still be on my side when he finds out Duke is dead. I'm scared, Uncle K. What do you think I should do?"

"I'm not sure," replied Kekoa. "We need to consult a lawyer. A criminal lawyer. We'll talk more tomorrow."

Silence hovered over the workroom for the rest of the morning. The room's usual baking warmth was overcome by the emotionally frigid atmosphere. For Noah, a trapped sensation. For his uncle, a complete lack of helpful answers.

* * * *

The owner of the Queen Street auto body shop, a Mr. Dan Kono, discovered Duke's body at 7 a.m. when he opened up for the day. The medical examiner arrived an hour later, followed by a forensics team.

Leaning over the body, the ME said, "A single .38 slug severed the carotid artery and a few critical nerves in the neck. He died instantly. Also, there are a number of defensive bruises on the knuckles of both hands."

Gert Mahaila reached the Queen Street site just as the crime scene tapes were going up. "What do we know so far? Any ID?"

"His wallet says he's Dante Santos, a sixteen-year-old high school junior," replied the ME. "I found both a driver's license and a school ID, but I ran his prints through the local system just to confirm who he is. The youngster had a juvie record. AKA Duke Santos, a few petty theft convictions, but never served any time. I estimate he's been dead about six hours, but I can't be sure until we do the autopsy. However, judging from the gravel and dirt on the back of his head and jacket, I would say he was moved, probably dragged, after being killed."

Mr. Kono stood anxiously a few feet away.

"Sir," said Gert respectfully, "do you recognize this man? A customer maybe?" When he shook his head, she asked him to check his records.

He quickly returned from his one-room office and said, "We have no record of anybody by that name being a customer of ours."

Gert strode to the sidewalk, bent down, and touched several dark spots on the pavement. "Doctor?" she called to the ME. "Got something. Looks like blood." A forensics technician confirmed it.

"He was probably shot here on the sidewalk," said Gert. "Maybe a random robbery. Either he was the victim or he died trying to rob someone else."

"My guess, it was the latter," said the technician. "There was at least eighty bucks still in his wallet. That rules out *him* being robbed."

"I suppose it could have been a grudge fight," said Gert. "Those badly bruised knuckles could be either defensive or aggressive. From the looks of it, Santos must have gotten in a bunch of good licks anyway. By the way, is there a home address in that wallet?"

"There's one on his driver's license," he answered.

* * * *

Twenty minutes later Gert knocked on a recently painted, green door on the second floor of a subsidized apartment house. No one answered, even though she could hear someone moving about.

"Juan Fernandez? Honolulu Police!" shouted Gert, while pounding harder on the door. She could hear the chain and bolt being undone. The door slowly opened, revealing a man in his mid-forties with a sinewy build and blood-red eyes. She flashed her credentials. "I'm Detective Mahaila. Don't you answer when someone knocks?"

"Yeah, well, lady, I was takin' a dump. What da kine HPD want with me, anyway? I ain't done nothing, yah?"

"I'm just here to ask you a few questions, Mr. Fernandez. May I come in?"

He grudgingly held the door for her, but when she entered, he stopped her in the dim front hall.

Gert accepted that. Better than standing outside with bad news. "Does Dante Santos live here?"

"Sometimes, but he not come home last night. What about it?"

"You his father?" asked the lieutenant.

"Nope. Duke's m' sistah's boy. Why?"

"Is she home?"

"Nope. She ain't nowhere anymore. She die' of ovahdose five year ago."

"Is his father home?"

"Nope. He locked up in Halawa fo' sellin' coke."

"So you're his guardian then?"

"I suppose so," he answered, shifting from one bare foot to the other in his gray tank top and denim shorts. "Wha' you wan' with all dese questions, lady?"

"I'm very sorry, sir, but your nephew, Dante, was found shot to death early this morning on Queen Street, a few blocks from the Ward theaters. He'd been fighting with somebody and ended up taking a bullet in the neck."

Juan shook his uncombed head. "I kinda thought he migh' end up tha' way. He nevah listen to me. Always gettin' inta trouble, yah."

Gert examined the man's slack face. She found it hard and unemotional, and yet he appeared somewhat familiar. "Do I know you from somewhere?"

"Don' know where, lady, maybe."

"Wait. Don't you run with Raimonde Portfia's gang?"

"I do couple a tings fo him now and den, but I no belong to any gang."

"Forget I mentioned it. Mr. Fernandez. Who were Dante's closest friends? Do you have any names for me?"

"Duke ain't got any friends, 'ceptin maybe th' Akino kid upstairs."

"Does he have a first name?"

"Duke call' him Gino sometimes, yah."

"Which apartment?"

"Don' know. Try the mailboxes downstairs maybe."

"Thank you, sir, you've been very helpful," said Gert as she took her leave and returned to the first-floor entranceway.

She found the name Akino painted in red nail polish across the fifth box in the fourth tier. So, by her logic, the Akinos lived in apartment 405. A slight, grandmotherly woman in a loose jacket and simple pants tight at the ankles responded to the knock on 405. Gert introduced herself, flashed her credentials, and asked if Gino was at home. The woman bowed and gestured Gert into their living space. "Please, a moment," she said, bowing again, before disappearing into another room.

The elderly woman reappeared with the tall, gangly Gino just behind her. At first Gert thought the boy appeared embarrassed to face a police officer, but then she realized that the lad had brought disgrace to the household by attracting police attention and was embarrassed about this in front of his grandmother.

"I am *not* here to arrest you, Gino," Gert assured him. "I just have a few questions for you and your grandmother. Do you understand me?"

"Yah!" replied Gino.

"*Hai!*" replied the grandmother.

"First question—how well do you know Dante Santos?"

"He's a friend. We hang around together sometimes."

"Just the two of you?" Gert pressed.

"Some days more of us."

"What are their names?"

"Why do you want to know names? Are we in trouble?"

"Why? Have you done anything wrong?" countered Gert. "I asked you for their names, and you promised to cooperate with me."

"Just the one—Noah. I don't know his last name. He's Hawaiian, but I think his last name is Chinese."

Gert thought for a minute. *Noah is not that common a name, and the Wong boy has been in trouble before.* "Could his last name be

Wong?"

"That's it, Wong," Gino said hesitantly, and then regretted saying anything at all.

"Think carefully. Do you know any reason why anyone would want to hurt Dante or even fight with him?" When the lad didn't reply, Gert studied his body language and perceived him to be wrestling with a touch of street code syndrome. She understood—he didn't want to rat out a friend. "Dante was your friend. Don't you want to do right by him?"

"Was?" repeated Gino.

"Yes, Gino," said Gert. "I have very bad news. Dante was found dead this morning somewhere on Queen Street. Someone shot him in the midst of a fist fight." Again she studied the boy's stricken face. His shocked reaction seemed genuine. "One more time—could it have been the Wong boy?"

Gino shrugged. *Duke is dead, so he can't hurt me.* "Duke was mad at Noah and threatened to kill him," he said aloud. "A couple days ago at school I warned Noah to steer clear of Duke. I guess he didn't listen."

"How bad was this argument? Did he really mean to kill Noah?"

"I thought Duke just meant he wanted to beat him up, but he sometimes got carried away." Gino looked away, blinking to suppress tears.

"Gino," Gert said gently, "I'm very sorry. What was this fight about anyway?"

The boy's jaw dropped. *This* was something he didn't want to go into. But one peek at the stern detective's face and he knew he couldn't hold back. "D-D-D-Duke and Noah did some shoplifting together, and when the shopkeeper ID'ed Duke for the police, Duke thought Noah had ratted him out. Boy, was he pissed at him—fightin' mad."

"Did Noah rat him out?

"No way."

Gert felt the boy was generally telling the truth, but leaving something out. "By any chance, were you a part of that shoplifting venture?"

Gino looked first at his grandmother and then back at Gert. "Oh, no! It was just them." His voice had slowed and shifted an octave higher. Maybe he'd given away more than he'd intended.

The grandmother's eyes turned from soft gray to sheer steel. She knew her grandson.

Now, from their combined body language, Gert was sure the boy had lied, and there was nothing she could do about it, unless the shopkeeper ID'ed Gino as well. But that was Robbery's job, not Homicide's. She had now pegged her main suspect and would take the necessary steps to pursue him.

* * * *

Gert knew the whole family well. Hank, Kekoa, and Leilani Pualoa had figured prominently in one of her earlier successful cases and that led to a friendship. Of course, Leilani was now married to Alex Wong, and Noah was their adopted child. That complicated matters. Gert glanced at her watch. Popping in on the Wongs at the noon hour would be considered inappropriate, so she stopped off at the Young Street Zippy's for *Zip Min,* a strong chicken broth stuffed with boiled noodles, wontons, fried egg, sliced fishcake, breaded fried shrimp, beef strips, chives, and bok choy greens. The generous portion was served in a covered stainless tureen, along with an Asian-style porcelain spoon and chopsticks. Forty-five minutes later, Gert decided she had eaten her fill and had the rest doggie-bagged to take home. She felt satisfied that she'd done a good day's investigating. She just wished the circumstances weren't so distasteful.

Chapter 19

Missing

NORMALLY, Lieutenant Mahaila took pleasure in driving her unmarked Toyota Camry through the quaint, venerable neighborhoods of Manoa. Set deep in a heavily wooded valley, flowers bloomed at most every home: hibiscus, orchids, ginger, birds of paradise, heliconia, bougainvillea. But she took no pleasure in the journey today. Winding slowly through the narrow, often potholed, streets on official business, she was about to give her friends appalling news: that their son was the lead suspect in a murder investigation.

She climbed the half-dozen steps onto the lanai that wrapped around the handsome white house and tapped the lion's-head brass knocker on the koa door; no one answered. The door chimes met with no response. Still, she had an idea where she might find Leilani.

Walking around to the backyard, Gert found her sitting at her easel, painting, inside a ten- by ten-foot screened gazebo. Alex had bought it just for her, where she could do her artwork in all weather. Dense trees surrounded the gazebo: an umbrella-shaped monkeypod, mango, and avocado, and a showy white plumeria, the centers of its blossoms splashed with yellow.

With brush and a pallet of oils, Leilani daubed at a canvas depicting the valley's watershed forest reserve sprawled behind the community. As soon as the police lieutenant entered the open gate, she laid aside her brush, popped out of the gazebo, and rushed to greet her. The two women embraced, gently patting one another's backs a few times, an appropriate Hawaiian greeting.

"How wonderful you're here. I just made lemonade. Would you like a glass?"

"No thank you, Leilani, this is not a social call. When you hear the real reason for my coming, you might not be so hospitable."

"That sounds ominous. What could possibly be so terrible?"

"Unfortunately, I've come to question Noah. It's about his possible role in one of my murder cases. Is he home?"

"Dear God! What now?" moaned Leilani. "As a matter of fact, he isn't. He's usually still at work at this time of day, but he should be home shortly. A murder case? Surely, you're joking. I know he's been in trouble in the past, but I think he's learned his lesson. What's this all about, Gert?"

"A schoolmate of his was found murdered this morning down on Queen Street, a few blocks behind the Ward theaters. I questioned some of his friends." Gert deliberately exaggerated; it had only been Gino. "I learned that the deceased had threatened Noah and had beaten him up once before. In fact, I heard Noah lost a tooth in that fight."

Leilani's beautiful island face screwed up in displeasure. "Oh yes, a twenty-eight-hundred-dollar dental bill for an implant and crown. But Gert, Noah is certainly not capable of murder. Are you sure he was even there? He went to the movies with Malia and some friends last night. Perhaps what happened to the boy was an accident."

"An accident?" said Gert. "Maybe, but that's why I have to talk to him."

"Of course, as soon as he comes in," said his mother. "Actually, he should be home by now."

"How late did he come in last night and did he do or say anything unusual when he arrived?"

An involuntary shudder crawled up Leilani's spine. "He didn't come home last night."

"Isn't that a little unusual?" asked Gert.

"Not really," Leilani replied. "Sometimes when he's out late, he goes over to my brother's place to sleep. My brother and Noah start work at four in the morning at the bakery. Noah's helping Kekoa during the summer months and sometimes does a little busing of tables for Andy over the lunch hour."

"Leilani, could you call your brother and discreetly see if Noah is still there?"

"Discreetly? I think you're asking quite a lot of me, Gert Mahaila. Do you plan on arresting him?"

"Not if he can explain his whereabouts last night. Truth is, I don't have any solid evidence against him—only a strong motive and possibly an opportunity window. Not enough for an arrest. But if he runs or tries to hide from me before I can question him, he will become a fugitive from justice."

"Gert, you know he isn't capable of out-and-out murder."

"You said Malia and her friends were at the movies with him last night. Is Malia available? I'd like to speak with her also."

"She went hiking up on the North Shore with her Girl Scout troop this morning. She won't be home 'til tonight."

"Now I'd say that's awfully damned convenient," said Gert, thinking aloud. She shut her eyes tight, immediately realizing the impact of what she had implied.

Storm clouds crossed Leilani's face. "Whoa! With that crack I think you'd better leave before I say something we'll both regret."

"Sorry, Leilani!" Gert nodded sadly and returned to her cruiser. Once inside, she used her cell phone to reach Kekoa at the bakery. After a polite exchange of greetings she asked, "Is Noah still with you?....Good. I need to speak with him in person. It's very important. I'll be there in fifteen minutes. Why? I'd rather not say until I get there."

The moment Leilani heard the cruiser pull away, her broad, chunky shoulders slouched. She dragged herself back inside the gazebo and sat down at the easel. But she wouldn't be doing any more painting today; she was too upset. Now that she thought about it, she did suspect something last night when Alex brought the girls home from the movies. She'd waited up for them and found them strangely quiet, not their usual giggly selves, happy to be together for a sleepover. And Malia doing laundry at one-thirty in the morning? Nina had apologetically said she'd gotten her period and needed to wash her jeans.

Gert's visit had frightened Leilani enough to call Alex, which she never did when he was at work, unless there was an emergency. And this was one.

* * * *

Alex had just wrapped up an appointment with a corporate client and answered his cell's ring tone. Leilani's voice trembled.

"Darling!" Alex said. "What's the matter? You sound terrible." As Alex listened, his anxiety barometer rose. "You're right, he needs a lawyer. If he's still at the bakery, he may have told Kekoa what's going on. Noah trusts him. I'd better call and find out what Kekoa knows, if anything, especially if he has a lawyer in mind. If he doesn't, I'll call Terumi Fujita when I get home….Yes, dear, I know he's a judge now, but he'll recommend the best criminal attorney for us. I'll be home in a couple hours. Now dear, don't cry. I'm sure this will all work itself out."

Sounding upbeat for his wife was exactly the opposite of how Alex felt. He reflected on this morning's drive with the girls in the back seat. They were hugging, and tears were skiing down Nina's cheeks. *They know something more about what went on last night,* he thought.

He'd said, "Nina, I'll have you home in a few minutes. Is there anything you want to talk about before I deliver you to your parents?"

"I don't think so, Uncle Alex. It's terribly personal."

When he pulled up at the Portfias' she jumped out and flew past her waiting father into the house.

Driving Malia to her hiking trip proved even worse. For the entire hour she sat silent—completely uncharacteristic. She loved talking with her father, and usually jabbered nonstop. Not this morning.

* * * *

In the bakery, Maria Pualoa sat behind the display cases rocking baby Rosa in her stroller. Finished with work for the day, heading for the door, Noah stopped and bent down for a moment marveling over his new cousin. He reached in and tickled Rosa under the chin, eliciting the sought-after smile.

Meanwhile, Kekoa leaned on the wall next to the phone, talking: "Fine, and you? What's this all about?…Got it." He hung up and motioned for Noah's attention.

"Noah, wait. Things are moving much faster now, and they've gotten far too complicated for someone like me to help you. As I told you, we need the advice of a good criminal lawyer. Now! However, he'll probably advise you to turn yourself in. That was Lieutenant Gert Mahaila. I don't know how much she knows, but she wants to talk to you. Don't shake your head. If you run now you're sure to be in big trouble. If everything you've told me is true, then you're innocent, and Nina acted in your defense. We can trust Gert to be fair. She's a long-time friend."

The phone rang a second time. Kekoa picked up and listened to his sister's frantic voice. "I know, Leilani. Gert's on her way over here….Don't worry, I'll be here with him," he assured her.

Kekoa hung up and turned to the boy. "That was your mother warning us about Gert. She's not arresting you—just wants to talk with you. Your father is calling an attorney."

The boy shifted uneasily from foot to foot, his face a mask of fear. He heard the squealing of tires as an unmarked police cruiser parked hurriedly on Waialae outside the bakery. The car door slammed shut.

Through the tall windows displaying fresh cakes, rolls, and cookies, Noah saw Gert approaching. He pivoted and bolted toward the workroom.

Kekoa rushed after him. "Noah, for God's sake, come back!"

His nephew slowed down just long enough to call out over his shoulder: "I have to leave. If I say I did it, I'm guilty of murder.

If I tell the truth, then Nina will be found guilty. I just can't stay and talk to the police. See you guys." He reached the rear door and disappeared into the alley.

Gert entered the bakery. Looking from Kekoa to Maria, she asked, "Is Noah still here?"

Kekoa shook his head with an air of innocence. "Apparently, he's gone out."

"You didn't say anything to him, did you?"

Avoiding her direct question, Kekoa responded, "What would I say to him and why? You never told me what this was all about."

"Do you have any idea where he'd be going?"

"Probably home or off to hang with one of his buddies," offered Maria.

"Gert, you've kept us in suspense long enough. Now maybe you can tell us what's going on here," said Kekoa. *I need to know how much the police have found out,* he thought.

"A former schoolmate of your nephew was found murdered this morning—on Queen Street a few blocks behind Ward theaters. I understand Noah and the victim weren't on very good terms. They had already been reported fighting recently. I also have information that Noah was in the vicinity around the time of the murder."

"Are you going to arrest him?" asked Maria.

"Not yet. But he does need to talk with me. And soon."

* * * *

Noah's impulsive decision to run left him with less than fifty dollars in his pocket, with no place to stay, and completely without a strategy. In the alley he saw Auntie Maria's Honda Accord. At first, he thought of sleeping in the back seat after dark. *But I'd have to break in, and what if I oversleep and daylight gives me away? I have to stay out of sight. Too many people know me. Especially busing tables for Uncle Andy. One thing's for sure, I can't stay in Kaimuki. I need a place to hide. Nina lives in a guarded compound; maybe her family would be willing to hide me. No, no, I can't involve her any more than*

I have already—she's much too fragile. I have to protect her. It wasn't her fault.

The boy cautiously walked the lonely back streets and remote neighborhoods of Kaimuki for hours, trying to think things out. In mid-afternoon he remembered a quiet place: the Manoa Chinese Cemetery, nestled against the Koolau mountain range at the back of Manoa Valley. Dusk, early evening, and his three hours of walking had put him exactly nowhere. Twenty minutes later put him at the cemetery. Now that he'd arrived, he worried that he'd made a bad choice. *Boy, am I stupid. I live only a mile or so away from here. I could be recognized by a neighbor or maybe a classmate.*

In the early evening, the towering gateway looked like a semblance of pagoda and shrine. Moonlight danced on the rich green tiles of the up-curved, overhanging roof. A stone guardian lion sat on each side of the entrance. Kekoa walked quickly toward the farthest reaches of the cemetery. He selected a tall tombstone and stepped behind it. Exhausted as he was, he took a moment to kick away a Reese's Pieces wrapper and, *ugh*, a used condom. *Gross*, he thought, *especially here*. He lowered himself to the ground and rested his back against the tombstone, its cold granite soothing him. He knew the cemetery well, and had never considered it a fearful place. As little kids, he and Malia had played among the graves while their grandparents paid their respects to esteemed and beloved ancestors. He'd found the perfect hiding place. No one in their right mind would be strolling down the paths of a graveyard at night, even a moonlit one. He'd be safe from the police here.

Yet shortly before midnight, a car came crawling along the turn-around where the cemetery road stopped. The engine turned off. He could see two people in the front seats, teenagers, he assumed, No one got out of the car. The two figures melted into one large black shadow, and he figured out why. Of course. This was a lover's lane. That explained the condom. He started to smile, but these thoughts only reminded him of Nina and how far out of reach she was now.

Noah relaxed and pulled his knees up close to his chin, but

only minutes later he heard a second car. It stopped. A spotlight flashed among the gravestones. When it came to a halt in the direction of the turn-around, he peeked out to see a police cruiser with its spotlight beam on the parked car—the lovers were being chased out.

In the desolate, wee hours of morning, Noah crept to a more isolated spot, a grave thick with grass, and flopped on his back. He yearned for sleep. Yet every rustling noise denied him rest. It could have been a scorpion or biting centipede. He blamed the police cruiser—that was too close. In a way he yearned for morning, the end of his struggle for sleep, but morning would bring its own brand of peril. This neighborhood would come alive and the cemetery would get its fair share of visitors.

Just when the boy thought sleep was impossible, his eyes fluttered shut. His dreams were cruel; he wasn't transported away to safety. It was as though he wasn't asleep at all. The gravesite grass remained a mattress below him, and the stars blanketed him. The three-quarter moon slipped from behind a dark cloud, creating patterned gravestone shadows. Noah sat up and turned toward a strange white-pebble path leading to the top of the hillside and a majestic tamarind tree. In sitting up, he rolled onto a sharp, flat stone jabbing him in his butt. He quickly pulled it out from under him and flung it Frisbee-style in the direction of the path. He saw it land. It appeared to slow to a stop just short of the path, then picked up momentum again, and continued across the path to the far side, as though driven by some ethereal force.

The unnatural movement of the stone bewildered Noah, but when he saw two silhouetted figures pass in front of the moon, he stiffened and shivered with fright. Both figures were hooded and carrying heavy tree branches on their backs. The first figure was a faceless female with eyes that suddenly glowed from under her hood. She stared directly at Noah as she continued up to the tamarind tree, only to disappear within. The second figure, a faceless male, followed her into the tamarind. But not before a deep, reverberating voice emanated from his lips—a mouth that momentarily glowed and faded to black again. His words: "Go back, my son. Go back." The stunned boy could only sink down onto the soft, thick grass of the grave and surrender to a deep sleep that lasted until the first feeble light of dawn.

Beyond dawn, burgeoning sunlight coaxed Noah into a slow awakening. He stretched both arms out to their limits and accidentally released a loud yawn. Only a minute later, footsteps on the pebbled path below gave him a start—had someone heard him? While he scurried to hide behind another large tombstone, the crunching pebble sounds stopped at a grave several tiers below on the hill.

Holding his head in his hands, Noah felt a disturbing emotional heaviness as he reflected on the haunting events of the previous night. *Why didn't I hear those stones last night when the two figures passed by? Was it a dream? Or,* he asked himself, *were they aumakua, spirits of the afterworld? Our own personal family gods? Our deified ancestors who had come to communicate with me? But why?* Then he remembered. His mother had told him how his birth parents had died—when a tree fell on their car the night of Hurricane Iniki. *Yes! The tree branches the figures carried. This is my connection to my birth parents.* A powerful sense of both anguish and wonderment enveloped him.

Noah heard the pebbles crunching once more as the person at the grave below him hurried away. He stood up and brushed himself off. Then he saw the flat stone he had tossed during his dream. It lay on the opposite side of the path. *Was it there all the time?* he wondered.

Any other abstract thoughts evaporated as his stomach cramped up from hunger. It would be only a short walk to the Manoa Marketplace and breakfast. He knew of one cafe that opened at seven, and he trotted there, praying nobody he knew would see him. He still had nearly thirty dollars in his wallet and another twenty folded into the heel of his left sneaker innersole. Luckily, Uncle Kekoa had paid him before the weekend. The cafe owners, a pleasant middle-aged couple, were friendly and didn't recognize him. He slowly downed their easy-over eggs and bacon then savored three delicious fluffy pancakes. Lingering over a glass of milk a sip at a time, he contemplated his predicament. *There's no point in going back to the cemetery. Sooner or later someone will recognize me. I have to find somewhere else to hide, but where? I don't have any transportation. Wait! My bike. I need to sneak by the house and get it.*

Noah set out on the mile-long hike back to the Wong home. He arrived a little before eight, in time to see his parents drive off in the family car. He wondered where they were going so early. Out looking for him? The garage door was shut and locked, as was the side door, but he knew the combination on the padlock that hung there. Just as he got the lock off its hasp and plunged inside the door, he felt someone nudge him into the darkness inside. Malia! She'd seen him sneak up the driveway from her bedroom window upstairs.

Barefoot and still in her cotton nightie, she threw her arms around him for a second or two, then took a step back. "Sssh!" she said. "I don't know if the *kupuna* are awake yet. Noah, where have you been?" She did a double-take. "Whose clothes are you wearing?"

"Uncle Kekoa's. I was a mess the other night."

Malia cupped her hands around his shoulders. "Everyone is so worried. They know why you're running. A police lieutenant came here looking for you. She wants to arrest you for murdering Duke Santos. What are you going to do?"

"Call Nina and tell her not to worry. All the evidence is scrubbed and thrown deep in the ocean." He reached up and took his ten-speed bicycle off its hook on the garage wall, then walked the bike back toward Malia. He needed to tell her goodbye. "Look, I've got to make tracks now before someone sees me. See ya."

"Wait a minute, Noah. Not so fast. Dad wants you to turn yourself in. He thinks it's for the best. He's even engaged a good criminal lawyer to handle your case. This lawyer thinks he can get you off for shooting Duke in self-defense."

"That's not going to work now that I got rid of the evidence. I've got to go back into hiding."

"Wait one sec." She spun about, bolted into the back hall, and returned with arms outstretched, carrying his UH warm-up jacket and bike helmet.

Sliding his arms into the jacket, snapping on the helmet, he couldn't help but smile. "You're the best, sis. Bye."

"Noah, please don't go!"

He walked the bike out the garage's side door and started pedaling down the driveway. He glanced up at the second-floor window just in time to see *Tutu* Masako, his grandmother, peering out at him with an expression of great sadness. He waved with a free hand. She threw him a kiss. Rolling into the street, he pedaled toward Manoa Road. At Beretania, he turned west toward Chinatown. He hadn't the slightest idea what he would do when he got there.

Chapter 20

Irritations

AN ANGRY Raimonde Portfia paced the floor of his grand office—up to the sweeping picture window and back toward the fully stocked wet bar, dropping live cigarette ashes on the imported oriental rug. He couldn't imagine anything more going wrong after the disasters of the last few days. *I've lost a good man to that asshole Wen Tse Fong. And Manuel being put in the crosshairs of Wen's snipers! I can't afford a gang war or anything that would get the nosy media all over my tail. That would be bad—bad for everyone, bad for business. And on top of it, even Lottie's bucking me now over keeping the family confined inside the compound until things cool down. Doesn't she see it's for their own good? Oh, and I miss my hot little bimbo. Quite a lay. I sure hated cutting her loose. Imagine the balls on that bitch wanting me, Rai Portfia, to finance her dancing career.*

Rai stopped pacing suddenly. He thought he'd heard something. He did, a sharp knock. "What?" he shouted at the door as if it alone were the enemy. "Who is it and what th' hell do you want?"

After a measured silence, Manny's voice penetrated his miserable thoughts. "Sorry to disturb you, Rai, but we need to talk."

Rai turned the key and jerked open the hand-carved wooden door with a vengeance. "Well, what is it now?"

Manny took a deep breath. "Can't we sit down like two brothers and talk story without you jumping down my throat?"

"Come!" said Rai. He pointed to the leather armchair beside his inlaid walnut desk. "Sit!" He swiveled his desk chair close to Manny's. "Talk!"

"This is exactly what I mean, Rai. Having a conversation with you is like listening to a bunch of barking commands. Like I'm your dog."

"Do you want this conversation or not, *brah*? I'm a busy man."

"Gee, you sure know how to put a guy at ease."

"Okay, I get it. Tell me what the hell you want."

Manny tried hard to tread lightly. "I got to thinking about what you said, Rai, when you brought me here to hole up. You have me worrying about the safety of my family. How can I protect them from in here?"

"I already offered you the first floor of Domo's house," Rai replied. "You can move them in any time. What more do you want from me?"

"You know damn well that Esme won't have anything to do with you or your enterprises. She'll never move in here."

"And just how is that *my* fault—that you, a wuss, married a priss."

"Stop it, Rai. I'm serious. You're the one that made targets of me and my family. I didn't start this war."

"Don't put this all on me, Manny. In a way you *did* start it. You needed a job, so you *asked* to come work for me. Your special requirements led to the Chinatown office and Wen's protection racket. No, you can't blame me when you can't be the master of your own household."

"Okay, okay, Rai, forget the blame. We still have a problem to solve."

"We?" repeated Rai. "What do you expect me to do? Force your family to move in here?"

"Couldn't you provide some sort of security at my place?"

"I'm already short one man as it is." Rai chewed on his lower lip as he thought about committing any more of his troops. "Tell you what: I'll send someone over after dark to baby-sit outside your house. I don't think Wen would dare try anything in broad daylight. I don't know what else I can do for you, *brah*."

"I appreciate it, Rai." Manny stood up, embraced his brother briefly, and left.

Rai slid his chair behind the desk once more. When he looked up, he noted that Manny had left the door open. He stared at the empty hallway, mulling over his commitment to his brother's family, when yet another figure materialized in the doorway, a full-bodied, brunette teenager clad in a peasant blouse and skimpy shorts. His beautiful daughter, Nina, stood there, with drooped shoulders and a sullen look on her face. She said nothing and started to turn away.

"Come in, sweetheart," her father said, rising. "Let's sit on the sofa. It's more comfortable."

Nina dragged herself across the carpet to the plush sofa, upholstered in blue velvet. She leaned over dutifully to kiss her father's bearded cheek before sitting down two feet away from him. She needed space between them to talk freely, knowing this was the hardest conversation she'd ever have in her life.

"What's wrong, sweetie? You look like you're bearing the weight of the whole world on your shoulders. At your age what could be so terrible?"

Nina slid a bent left leg up onto the cushion and turned her body to face Rai squarely. "Daddy, have you ever killed anybody?"

Where the hell did that question come from? I've never lied to her. How can I answer it? Who put her up to this?

"Daddy, have you ever killed anybody?" she repeated.

Nina's question stopped him cold. Her intense blue eyes were encircled by redness and shadows that he hadn't noticed before. *Has she been crying? Was she up all night?* "Why would you ask me such a question?"

"I know it's a weird thing to ask, Daddy, but I realize your business brings you into contact with some pretty yucky people. I've seen them here. They're always nice to me, but they creep me out. They look like gangsters, and it makes me wonder what your business is, but I'm not asking you that. Besides, you have a hot temper. I've seen you use it on Mama."

Rai bristled. "Mama? Did she put you up to this?"

"Of course not," Nina said. "I need to know for myself, that's all."

"Why?"

"If you answer the question, I'll tell you why."

"If you insist, yes. I've been known to defend myself and my business position from time to time. But if it's any comfort to you, I don't make a practice of killing people, and I assure you those who died at my hand or by my will were deserving of being snuffed. Frankly, I inherited this business from a long line of your ancestors. While I do take pride in what I do, I'm not especially fond of everyone and everywhere my business takes me. But remember—it does pay for the food we eat, the roof over our heads, and all the comforts we enjoy. It's what I do, baby."

"I'm not judging you, Daddy. I have my own sins to confess."

"You? Sins? I don't believe it," he responded with a chuckle.

"Daddy, I killed someone."

Rai heard the words, but their full meaning refused to sink in. "Now, dear, I'm sure those poor starving children in Africa would have died anyway. Besides, you can't help everyone. There's far too many unfortunates out there. A few Hail Marys should take care of that."

"Oh, Daddy, you're not listening. I killed a boy. He wasn't a starving African. I shot him dead with a gun. I pulled the trigger. My bullet killed a real human being."

"Is this some kind of game you're playing with me? If it is, it's sure not to my liking. Where would you get a hold of a gun in the first place? Wait! Was it one of my people? Who was it? Who gave you the gun? Give me his name. I'll kill the bastard."

"Stop, Daddy, stop it now!" She stomped her bare right foot on the carpet. "The gun belonged to the guy I killed."

"Sweetheart! Tell me did he…uh…Did he attack you? Did he hurt you? The son of a bitch deserved to die."

"Daddy, you're not listening. No, he did not rape me. In fact, he never even touched me. It was—"

"Then why would you do such a terrible thing?"

"Daddy, let me finish. The boy I shot was about to kill a good friend of mine."

"Just a minute," said Rai, with creeping impatience. "Who is this good friend—someone from school? What's his name?"

"His name is Noah Wong. Daddy, he's Malia's brother. Of course he's from school. He's in my World History class."

"Who's the boy you shot?"

"His name is Duke somebody. He and Noah used to be friends, but not any more. He was a junior and a real bully. Really mean."

"Okay, go on, sweetheart. Start from the beginning."

"After the movie my stomach was a little upset. I guess I had too many banana fritters at dinner, so I wanted to take a little walk in the fresh air. Noah offered to come with me. Halfway around the block he started looking over his shoulder. He thought someone was following us. We walked a little more and suddenly this guy jumped out of the shadows. Noah yelled, 'Duke, get away from us,' but Duke just started punching him, and actually knocked him down. They were fighting fiercely on the ground, and Noah was taking an awful beating. Somehow he managed to roll on top, but Duke pulled out a gun. Noah knocked it out of the way and it landed on the sidewalk in front of me. Then things got worse. Duke flipped on top—he was a lot taller and heavier and started slamming Noah's head on the sidewalk. He would've killed him. I screamed and yelled, but he wouldn't stop. I wasn't thinking clearly. I picked up the gun. And you know what? I've never even held a gun in my life. I tried to fire a warning shot over Duke's head. At the last second, he poked his head up and without meaning to, I shot him in the neck." Nina stopped.

"When did this happen?"

"The movie night."

"Are you sure he was dead?"

"Yeah."

"How do you know for sure?"

"Noah checked his pulse. None. He wasn't breathing, and there was a whole lot of blood."

"Who else knows about this?"

"Nobody. Wait! He told Malia."

"Why didn't you call me immediately? I have some experience in these matters—maybe I could have gotten rid of the body and any evidence that *you* were involved. By now, the police probably have the body and are already looking for a shooter. Where did all of this happen?"

"On Queen Street, a couple blocks from the movies. Noah took charge immediately. He took the gun and my sweater too. He said it might have some gun residue on it."

Rai's chest suddenly flared with a surge of heartburn. "Just a minute. I've warned you over and over about dating and boys, and you completely disobeyed me. But I guess all that's water under the bridge now. What's your relationship with this Noah Wong? Has he ever tried to kiss you?"

"Oh, Daddy. He was a complete gentleman around me. Always. In fact, he tried to convince me that *he* did the shooting and that *I* had nothing to do with it. That's why he took the gun and sweater—to get rid of them." With shoulders slumped, Nina hugged herself, as if chilled from her confession. "Uncle Alex drove me home this morning. He asked me what was wrong, but I didn't tell him anything."

Rai sat in silence for a moment, trying in his mind to sort the nightmarish details out. "Noah sounds like a smart kid. Maybe too smart for his own good. I'd like to know how he disposed of the evidence and make sure it can't be resurrected. I need to have a talk with him."

Nina shook her head and ran her fingers absently through her long, dark hair. "You can't, Daddy. I tried calling him at the bakery where he helps his uncle out. Maria answered. She sounded really upset, like she'd been crying. I explained that I was a friend of

Noah's. She told me he had run away. You know what? I think he's taking the blame for me. He's risking everything to protect me."

"You think so?" asked Rai, rhetorically.

"Why else, Daddy? Why would he suddenly run away?"

"How well do you know this boy? Is he being genuinely heroic? Or is there a possibility he could turn on you or even accidentally give up the evidence he has in his possession?"

"Gosh, Daddy, you're being so suspicious. He'd never do a thing like that. He's really very sweet and honest."

"Let me remind you, young lady, that you lied to me last night. I have a right to be suspicious. From your continued insistence, I assume you care a bunch for him—more than you've previously been willing to admit."

"Yes! I care very much. I'm sorry I misled you."

"I asked you before whether he had tried to kiss you and you refused to answer."

"The answer is yes and what's more, I kissed him back, and we held hands too. Oh, Daddy, isn't there some way we could help him out of this?"

"I don't know. It would have to be in some way that wouldn't put you in jeopardy. Sweetheart, I have to think of your well-being before I do anything. Also, I have to find him first. I don't even know what he looks like."

"I have a picture in my cell phone of the three of us—Noah, Malia, and me. I can email it to you and you can print it out."

"Okay. Then I'll have Domo and some of his men keep an eye out for your boyfriend."

"Thank you!"

Boyfriend! She didn't deny it, Rai thought with a stab of disgust. "By the way, young lady, you have to tell your mother all of this."

"I know," Nina mumbled with downcast eyes. "This morning when I got home, she asked why I'd been crying and where was my new cashmere sweater she'd spent a hundred dollars on."

"And you lied."

"Yeah. I said I forgot it at the movies." To soften the oppressive atmosphere, she sprang up from the sofa and threw her arms around her father's neck. "You're the best Daddy anybody ever had."

* * * *

Rai held up Nina's photograph of the three youngsters. *A good-looking kid, I'll give her that. I could ignore this whole nightmare, and maybe, just maybe it'll go away. But then I'd never know how the boy disposed of the evidence and whether he can be trusted at all. I sure don't want this thing coming back at us.* Rai impulsively reached across his desk to a beer tankard full of pens and pencils and retrieved a pair of scissors. He trimmed the photo, separating the two girls from Noah. Next he slipped the shot of just the boy into the flat bed of the office copier behind his desk and made a half-dozen copies of it.

Leaning back in his soft leather chair, he closed his eyes. *Being a father is sometimes harder than running a business. I simply can't deny my Nina anything. I hope I've made the right decision.*

"You wanted to see me, Rai?" The powerful form of the tall, dark-skinned Domo stood in the open doorway. The prominence of a mis-aligned jaw spoiled an otherwise handsome face. This souvenir of an earlier boxing career produced a sinister look that served him well in his present vocation.

"Yes, yes," said his boss. "Come on in and have a seat."

"If this is about finding Wen—the slippery bastard hasn't been seen on the streets since before the shootout on the rooftop. We've located his major gun, a lowlife named Zeke Young—a pretty dangerous dude. With Hugo out of the way, he's moved up in Wen's organization. We know where he lives and we're keeping an eye on his place. We could take him out anytime we please, but we're hoping he'll lead us to Wen."

"Sounds like a decent plan," said Rai. "Everything else running well?"

"Yeah, business as usual. Smooth as a baby's *okole*."

"There's something else I need."

"What's that, boss?"

Rai handed him the photocopies. "The kid's name is Noah Wong. He's on the run, hiding from the cops somewhere in Honolulu, or at least on Oahu. I want your men to be on the lookout for him. I need to have him found and brought in. I don't want him harmed in any way. I do need to have a talk with him though. He's probably the same age as Nina. I have to remind you that the Honolulu police are looking for him as well. Do not get in their way or make a fuss we can't clean up."

"Sure, Rai, I understand completely." Domo took the photocopies and left the room.

* * * *

The evening's last patron in the Sweet Choice and Coffee shop had just left. Bunny Kobyashi scooped the two singles tip into her apron pocket and began the last chore of her shift. Clearing off the dirty dishes, she whisked the tray off to the kitchen to be stacked in the dishwasher. When she returned to the dining room to wipe down the Formica tabletop, she noticed Leilani Wong still touching up her Hawaiian gods mural on the far wall. She stood for a moment to admire the artist's work.

"Get you anything, Miss Leilani?" Bunny asked. "Coffee maybe, and a piece a pie to go with it?"

"No thanks, Bunny, I'm fine," Leilani replied. "Don't want anything to keep me up late at night."

Bunny sat down at a nearby table to watch Leilani dab a few finishing strokes on Pele's mountain. Several minutes later Leilani joined Bunny at the table to spread out a protective towel and re-cap the open paint tubes. When everything had been put away in the black carrying case, Bunny broke the silence. "Can I ask you somethin'?"

"Sure, what did you have in mind?"

"Do you ever dream, Miss Leilani?"

"Of course I do, almost every night."

"I mean about those gods you paint and dead people, and their legends?"

"Since you ask," said Leilani, "I once had this dream about my Uncle Big John. He was murdered. He came to me like a little bright light that darted around my bedroom frantically, like he was trying to tell me—no, warn me—about something. Grandma *Tutu* Eme would have called it an *akua*, a truly good spirit. Is that what you mean?"

"Yes, that's it. Except, I'm sorta awake when I'm dreaming."

"So *you* are having these dreams." Leilani tilted her head in a show of interest.

"Yes. I was coming to work on the bus this morning. There were only a couple other people on it and they were sitting in the front. I didn't see anyone in the back when I sat down in one of the middle seats. After a few minutes, somethin' made me turn around and look that way. There she was: the White Lady. She wasn't there when I first got on. The bus never stopped—how did she get there?"

"White lady? You mean a *haole* lady?" Leilani asked.

"No, no! A young island lady dressed in white—a wedding dress maybe."

"Did you try to talk to her?" Leilani prodded.

"No way! She was spooky. I whipped around in my seat and stared straight at the driver the whole trip, and when I looked again, she was gone."

"Then it's just an illusion," explained Leilani. "In all likelihood you'll probably never see her again."

"Not true, Miss Leilani. I've seen her dozens of times—all in white, the Lady in White. Mama's seen her too—always in the same stretch of the road too. Mama thinks she was on her way to her wedding when a bus ran her down. Mama says there's proof some lady did die that way. The police, they know all about it, yes. Mama thinks the Lady in White is lookin' for the bus that did it."

"That's a fascinating story," said Leilani, as she looked at her watch. "It's ten-thirty. Time we locked up." She sighed deeply. Outside, relentless clouds blocked the moon. In thick darkness on the way to her car, she felt overcome by the day's horrific events, from beginning to end— exhaustion and emotional overload.

* * * *

Kekoa had locked up the bakery at seven, his usual closing hour. Upstairs, in their spacious, freshly renovated apartment, he stretched out in his La-Z-Boy recliner. Maria was nursing baby Rosa. The smell of *paniolo* chili in the Crock-Pot wafted into the living room. Kekoa brooded. He should have felt comfortable, satisfied with the day's volume of business. But, instead, his lower back ached, a symptom of his intense distress. Noah had run away, insisting he had no choice. Kekoa couldn't stop him. Which meant he would not have his nephew—strong, smart, and a quick learner—to help him tomorrow morning.

But there was another reason to worry, much more serious. Just four days ago, Noah had confessed to the shoplifting caper and had asked Kekoa for advice. In an overly generous, empathetic mood, Kekoa had spilled the story of his past, at the same age, on the run from a killer. Now he deeply regretted it. His nephew idolized him. Had he tacitly given the boy permission to act out and run away and hide, just as he himself had at the same age? Despite Alex and Leilani treating both children with equal love and affection, Noah had always exhibited rogue tendencies. To Kekoa, it didn't matter—*he* was the adult and had been irresponsible. He had fed his nephew information that the boy was too young and too unstable to handle. Now Kekoa blamed himself.

Chapter 21

Hiding

THE **FOUR-MILE** bicycle trip from Manoa to Chinatown should have taken Noah about twenty minutes, but this was Honolulu, the capital city on the island of Oahu. Nestled between the mountains and the great sea, the city of over 400,000 is plagued with almost a million cars and three rush hours. Noah had pedaled into the midday rush, construction, pedestrians, and potholes. Sweaty and fatigued from only a couple hours' sleep in the cemetery, he arrived on Maunakea Street in Chinatown shortly before noon. He hadn't eaten since breakfast in the cafe. But first he needed a hat and sunglasses to make him a little less recognizable and to help hide his black and blue bruises.

Noah unstrapped his helmet and stowed it in the wire basket hooked onto his handlebars. In his haste he padlocked the bike to a convenient, naked pole that had once held a parking meter, even passing the chain through the spokes. He entered the courtyard of the Chinatown Cultural Plaza, where vendors in booths displayed ethnic attire, scenic paintings, jewelry, and souvenirs. He chose a three-dollar, black peaked cap embroidered with *humuhumunukunukuapuaa,* the state triggerfish, and the word "Hawaii" in such tiny letters that it didn't look too touristy. Trying on a few pairs of six-dollar sunglasses, he selected the darkest pair. A five-dollar, light gray T-shirt with a *honu,* a sea turtle, on the back replaced Uncle Kekoa's white work shirt.

At Win Sum's Food Emporium he waited his turn and bought three *manapuas,* steamed buns filled with sweet *char siu* pork, and a bottle of water. Munching and sipping, he casually

196

strolled through the courtyard, then back out to the street, but halted with a sickening sense. He gaped at the empty pole where he'd parked his ten-speed bike. It was gone. Some thief must have lifted the bike up and over the pole, making off with Noah's only transportation—and his new helmet too.

Even in his dire situation Noah could hardly go to the police. He had no one with whom he could vent his frustration, so he started walking aimlessly, counting the hours until he could find a place to sleep, or at least rest. In the hazy, ninety-degree sun, he felt almost dizzy from fatigue. He walked past the Hawaii Theatre, where his parents had once taken him and Malia to the exhilarating Hawaiian version of *The Nutcracker*. At The Arts at Mark's Garage, petite bronze dancers pirouetted in the window. He passed his two favorite Chinatown restaurants: the Little Village Noodle House, on the first floor of a graceful Art Deco building. And Mei Sum, where the waitresses pushed carts loaded with round bamboo baskets that held steamed *dim sum*. He always ate two orders of a deep-fried variety he called "hairy taro."

Noah was overcome by a feeling of hopelessness. He wanted his family—even his father's scolding when he screwed up. He missed his summer job with Kekoa that had given him such a sense of pride—helping his uncle to make a real business run. Also, skipping the opening days of school. How was he ever going to catch up, entering tenth grade? And, through it all, he yearned for Nina. Would the two of them ever get out of this awful jam?

The endless day dragged toward dusk and beyond. Needing a place to hide, Noah found a deeply recessed doorway of a lei shop closed for the night. The boy sat down on the single concrete step and leaned against the glass door, setting off an in-store alarm. The Asian owner, who lived upstairs, came rushing down, screaming at him in his native tongue. Noah sprang up and moved on.

Noah found a doorway several buildings farther along the semi-lit street. Oddly, this door was not only unlocked, but slightly ajar. A flight of wooden stairs led to the second floor. He slipped inside and sat down on the bottom step, leaning against the wall.

He quickly fell asleep in the shelter of the warm stairwell and was aware of nothing until the next morning when he was awakened by someone roughly shaking his shoulder.

"Hey, kid!" the man's voice insisted. "What the hell are you doing in here?"

Noah shook the sleep from his head and replied, "Sorry, mister. The door was already open, and I needed a place to stay for the night. I've got no other place to go. Honest, I didn't break in and I didn't hurt anything."

The boy clamored to his feet and started to leave.

"Wait, kid. You wanna make some money?"

"What kind of money, and what do I have to do for it?"

"C'mon upstairs, and we'll talk about it."

Noah guessed the thin, wiry stranger to be Chinese. However, there was no inkling of any accent. The boy hesitantly followed the man upstairs to an apartment on the second floor. They entered a parlor with floor-to-ceiling windows overlooking the street.

Turning toward Noah, the stranger said, "My name is Wen Tse Fong. You can call me Wen. I'm a businessman. How about a hundred fifty a week to do errands?"

"You mean like a messenger?" Noah asked. He wondered why Wen didn't ask him what he was doing on the streets instead of being in school.

"Yes, like a messenger, only maybe also get groceries and deliver packages." The chiseled cheekbones and narrow goateed chin gave off the severe look of a man not to be denied.

"No drugs," insisted Noah. "I'm not gonna be a mule for anybody."

"Of course not," said Wen. "Have we got a deal?"

"One more thing," said Noah. "I need a place to stay, a place to sleep, at least until I can afford a place of my own."

"Sure, kid. You can stay here with me. You can sleep on the sofa and you'll find some extra bedding in one of the bedroom drawers."

"Well, Mr. Wen, was there something you wanted me to do right away?"

"Yes, indeed," he answered, while jotting something down on a pad. He tore the top page loose and handed it to Noah. "Go to this address. It's about six blocks from here, and tell my colleague—his name is Zeke Young—I want to see him. Quickly! Then I want you to go to a phone store. There's one on Beretania, and buy me one of those throw-away cell phones. And afterward stop at McDonald's and bring back a half-dozen Egg McMuffins for our breakfast. I don't know about you, kid, but I'm starved."

"What brand of cell phone, Mr. Wen?"

"Any kind as long as it works and it's cheap." Wen pulled out a wad from his neatly creased pants and peeled off two crisp one-hundred-dollar bills. He held them out.

Noah didn't move to take them. "Mr. Wen, do you have anything smaller? A storekeeper's gonna think I stole the money."

"Sorry, kid. Good thinking." Wen flipped through the bills and handed him two fifties and five twenties.

"You sure are a trusting guy, Mr. Wen," said Noah. "How do you know I won't run off with your money?"

At first, a moment of intentional silence, and then Wen's pupils appeared to grow smaller—weasel-like eyes. "I'd find you, kid. There's no way you could hide from me, and you don't want me to tell you what happens after that." A crooked smile crept across his gray lips, causing the boy to shiver.

Wen called after Noah halfway down the stair. "Hey, kid, shut the downstairs door."

Noah wondered what he was getting himself into. At least he had a job of sorts and a place to put his head down at night. He'd be earning money, not a beggar on the street.

* * * *

In her real estate office, Cindy Chou laid down the red pen she had been using to mark changes in a rental agreement. She stacked the papers atop an open file folder next to her laptop. She wanted to incorporate those changes into the formal computer

199

version, but found the excessive glare from the sunlit window too bothersome on her monitor screen. She stood and went to the window, intending to pull the vertical blinds. With her hands on the cord, she scanned the row of buildings across the street as a matter of habit. As her keen eyes perused the apartment house windows, they locked on one window in particular. A small man stood there. She recognized the face of Wen Tse Fong for several solid seconds before he turned away.

Cindy froze, recalling the horrible day he had terrorized her in this very office. He'd run scared from her office after their encounter. Her arm still ached from the bullet he'd fired at her. She shook her head, half-hoping his evil image would disappear and half-pleased that she could finally nail his whereabouts for the police. When she looked again, the figure in the window had stepped away from the glass. She saw the silhouette of a man, but could no longer make out the face. *Was it him, really Wen, or was it my wild imagination, my wanting so much for him to be caught? Should I call Gert or not?* Then she thought of Coland. *He'll know what to do.*

Half an hour later, Coland returned to the office after showing a prospective client a commercial suite in a brand-new office building. Tall and dignified, he still looked elegant no matter what time of day or how hard he'd worked. He'd hardly taken a seat at his desk when Cindy walked in and dropped her full dilemma into his lap.

"How can I know what you should do?" he blurted out in self-defense. "You're the only one who saw him, or at least thought so. What do you expect me to do—run across the street and confront the bastard?"

"Good idea, hon!" she said facetiously. "Well, maybe not exactly confront him, but at least get a better look at him anyway."

"Just how would I do that?" Coland asked, tilting his salt-and-pepper head to one side.

"You could try selling him some real estate."

"You're not serious. What if he recognizes me?"

"He's never met you, Coland, so how the hell is he going to

recognize you?"

"I might say the same thing. I've never met him, so how am I supposed to recognize the man and tell whether he's actually Wen?"

"That's easy: about five-six, thin, well-mannered in a creepy way, and speaks perfect English. He has an elongated face—bony cheekbones, narrow goateed chin. Brown hair, slicked back, a mole high on one cheekbone. A snappy dresser. Oh, and he should have a sore shoulder from where I hit him with the cough-drop jar and paper punch."

"Shall I ask him if it still hurts?" Coland grinned sourly.

"Don't be a wise guy. Shake his hand and see if he cringes."

"You really expect me to do all this?"

"It's the only way I'll ever find out if that was him in the window."

"Okay, okay, I'm going, but you'd better be watching from here so you can call in the cavalry if I get swallowed up."

An unhappy but obliging Coland collected his briefcase once more and exited the office. Cindy heard the street door slam and went to the window to see him cross. He stopped and turned on the sidewalk to look back up at her. She waved and blew him a kiss as he pulled open the street door and disappeared inside.

Coland almost tiptoed up the steps and found the door ajar. He knocked. The plastic nameplate read Henry Fu. He took one step into the apartment and called out, "Anybody home?"

From the bedroom Wen called back in a high-pitched falsetto, "If you're selling something, I'm not interested. Go away." Meanwhile, he scanned the room for some sort of disguise in case it was the police calling. In the closet he found a mandarin-style robe with deep, long sleeves and a matching noblehat.

"Sir, if you are the man of the house," called Coland, "it might be very profitable for you."

Wen donned the noblehat and robe and added a pair of horn-rimmed glasses he found on top of the dresser—glasses left by the unfortunate former occupant. One look in the mirror above the dresser, and Wen developed a pose: he crossed both hands into opposite sleeves, then shuffled out into the living room. "Good day to you, my fine visitor. How may I assist you? And what is this fortune you have for me?" His tone had a cloying respect.

"Mr. Fu, my name is Collin Smythe and I have some excellent commercial properties available. The owner is in a dire position and will sell them at a great loss. May I show you some pictures?"

"Oh, but no, Mr. Smythe. I can only wonder how you got my name, but I am certainly in no position to purchase real estate at any price, bargain or not. I must bid you good day and wish you the best of health." Wen actually enjoyed playing the part of a Confucian scholar once he learned he was not dealing with the police.

Coland checked off the attributes he'd been given against the man who stood before him. Fu's glasses hid what might have been a mole, and his deep brimless noblehat covered most of his hair. The garb he wore said nothing of his being a snappy dresser. His manners and speech were hardly those of a thug.

"Thank you for your time, sir. I'm sorry to have disturbed you. You have a good day also." He held out his hand for Fu to shake, but the man merely bowed slightly. Coland turned and left the room.

When he had reached the opposite side of the street, he turned to see if Fu was watching from the window. No one was there, so he started up the stairs to his own office. Convinced the man was not Wen, he had no fear of a chance sighting anytime in the future.

Cindy waited for him in the outer office. "Well?"

"It's not Wen. Not very likely anyway."

"Are you sure?"

"I just said not likely. I couldn't verify any of the attributes you listed; however, he doesn't act or sound like a gangster. Mr. Fu wore glasses, a mandarin robe, and a deep bowl hat. I think it's called a noblehat. What the hell was I supposed to do? I'm sorry, sweetheart."

"You did fine," she said. "It doesn't sound like Wen. I was probably imagining things. I'm sorry I put you through all this. You're a really good sport."

Then Coland remembered that Fu had refused to shake hands. *Could a sore shoulder have been the reason? No, it was more likely a cultural thing. Should I tell Cindy? Of course not—she'd only worry more.*

* * * *

In his apartment, Wen removed his costume and began to think about what had just happened. The idea of the man selling real estate remained a sticking point until he connected it with Chou & Rice Realty, where Mathew Saint met his end. He unconsciously reached for his sore shoulder. *I should have watched where Smythe went after he left here.* He thought about it for a few minutes more. *Naw, they don't have the balls for a stunt like that.*

* * * *

Often, either Maria or Kekoa ducked next door into the Sweet Choice and Coffee Shop to chat over a cup of coffee. Hank and Lori Pualoa also stopped by one or two afternoons a week, mainly to spend time with their granddaughter, Rosa Nani. Today Hank and Lori stopped in for lunch as well. Maria rolled the stroller beside their booth and returned to the display counter in the bakery.

Bunny Kobyashi came to wait on them. "Hi, folks. Howzit? What can I get you?"

Lori smiled up at her and launched bluntly into a friendly interrogation. "Maria tells me you've been dating the boss for a couple months now. Is it getting serious?"

"It already is. Were in love, but—"

"What's the matter?" asked Hank. "Andy dragging his feet?"

"Well, as a matter of fact," Bunny said, "he is. He wants to make sure the coffee shop is a success first. When I tell him it already is a success, he begs for a few more months."

"Maybe Andy is saving up for a ring," offered Lori.

"He doesn't need a ring. He gave me *this* as an engagement present." Bunny opened her gold heart locket and, lifting up the fine gold chain, pressed closer to the table to show them the pictures inside. "See?" she added proudly.

Hank stretched across Lori to finger the locket. He slowly turned it over and read the inscription on the back: "Love you always 18."

"Very nice, Bunny. Wear it in good health," Hank said as he released the locket to let it fall back on her chest.

Lori caught him rolling his eyes.

"Thank you. Now what can I get you? Papa Ballesteros is manning the grill. I bet he'll whip up a couple of dandy three-egg omelets with the kitchen sink in 'em. How about it?"

"Sounds great," said Hank, "and I'll have a mess of home fries and an order of Portugue' sausage with it."

"Haaank!" cautioned Lori in her sternest voice.

"Okay. Drop the home fries if we must," he said in an unconvincing voice.

"We'll have *just* the two omelets and two coffees." Lori patted Hank's slightly enlarged paunch above his belt as soon as Bunny had headed into the kitchen to place their order.

"Okay, dear, what's going on?" Lori said softly. "I saw the strange look on your face when you examined Bunny's locket."

"Lori, you're not going to believe this, but that was your heart locket. The one I got you for our eighteenth anniversary."

"You mean the one that was stolen from your truck at the construction site?"

"The very one."

Lori looked incredulous. "How can you tell? There must be a lot of similar lockets out there."

"The heart, the ladder-like gold chain, the inscription's wording, the number eighteen. I didn't want to say anything in front of Bunny."

Just then Rosa Nani woke up and began whimpering. Lori picked her up and held her to her breast. "You're right. You shouldn't upset the girl. After all, Andy is the one who has some explaining to do."

"Maria said he should be getting back before we're through eating," said Hank.

Bunny brought out their coffee and place settings. "Your omelets will be out in another five minutes." She stuck her fingers under Rosa's chin and "coochie-cooed" her. Lori cringed inwardly. Bunny was still holding a dishrag and went about wiping a few other tabletops.

A smiling Papa brought the omelets out himself and set them down in front of them. Lori immediately showed signs of fuming. Hank chuckled; Papa had added the potatoes and sausage back into the order, along with a stack of thickly buttered toast and two frosted Danish.

"Oh, my!" Lori wailed. Papa picked up her hand and, with a flourish, kissed the back of it. "Only da besta fo' m' family," he said with a wide smile under his brushy mustache. He returned to the kitchen before she had a chance to unleash a complaint.

Andy walked in the door just as Hank was savoring the last morsel of his sausage. Andy kissed the baby on the forehead and slid into the booth opposite them. "How was everything? Did Papa take good care of you while I was gone?"

"Too good," answered Lori.

Desperate to change the subject, Hank asked, "Where's Bunny now?"

Andy looked around and noted only one patron at the opposite end of the room. "Probably on break. If I were to guess, I'd say she was on the phone with one of her girlfriends. Why do you ask?"

"We wanted to speak to you privately on a sensitive subject," murmured Lori.

"Now wait just a minute," Andy objected. "Bunny is almost family. I've asked her to marry me, so I don't want to keep secrets from her." He reared up and got to his feet.

"You misunderstand, Andy," said Hank. "It has nothing to

do with Bunny herself. It concerns the pendant heart she's wearing."

"What about it?" asked Andy. "I gave it to her as an engagement present two weeks ago."

"We know," said Lori. "Bunny told us all about it. Congratulations, dear."

"Uh, thanks."

"Please sit down," said Hank. "I believe the locket is stolen property. It's exactly like the one that was stolen from me out of my truck last December—right down to the inscription on the back, 'Love You Always 18.' You see, I bought it for Lori for our eighteenth anniversary. We're not asking for it back, but we are kinda curious how you acquired it."

Andy bristled. "I didn't steal it, if that's what you're implying. Actually, I bought it from someone—that is, in a barter situation." He slid back into the booth and brushed back the cowlick from his forehead.

"I know you didn't steal it, Andy. Sorry to be so blunt. Talk to us," said Hank.

Andy's defensive stance relaxed a bit. "I have this sort of a regular customer who couldn't pay for his supper one night. He told me he'd lost his job, but would be on his feet again soon. I felt sorry for him and ran a tab on him for a few meals, but I couldn't continue that for very long. So I confronted him, and at that point he offered to settle up with the gold heart and chain. He told me he was going to give it to his wife, but she'd left him, and he hadn't any use for presents anymore. I didn't bullshit Bunny. I told her how I happened to get it."

"Does the guy still come in?" asked Hank.

"Not often...lately. I guess it's only when he has a dollar or two to spare."

"Do you remember his name?"

"Not offhand," said Andy, "but it should still be in the bottom of the register where I kept his IOUs."

"Was it Peshelli, Ernie Peshelli, by any chance?"

"That sounds familiar," said Andy. "Are you going to pursue the matter?"

Hank looked over at Lori, who was shaking her head. She placed her hand in his. "Darling," she whispered, "let's just forget it. Bunny is so happy."

Hank frowned, deepening the lines in his sun-weathered face. "Forget it? Maybe. Maybe not."

Chapter 22

Mischief

NOAH'S new job gave him purpose, but he sure could have used the royal-blue ten-speed bike on these messenger rounds. It'd been a gift from his parents on his fourteenth birthday. The theft left him blaming himself for not securing it properly. He moved cautiously through the busy streets of midmorning Chinatown—keeping his cap pulled down low over his forehead and turning away when passing anyone and altering his path slightly wherever crowding occurred. Although the boy wasn't familiar with all the street names here, he had a fair idea where he might find the address Wen had written out for him. He glanced down at the unfolded scrap of paper in his left hand to be sure.

Noah crossed the street to avoid a family produce market with its outdoor stands and boxes, heaped high with fresh fruit and vegetables: bok choy, radishes, dragon fruit, jack fruit, papaya, and more. He spotted a small shop on the corner with an array of cell phones in the window. *Just the thing Wen wanted*, he thought as he entered and wandered over to the display of phones and accessories. The elderly shopkeeper approached as soon as she saw him eyeing the locked case.

"You wanna buy?" she asked, her voice creaking with age and impatience.

"Yah," said Noah, eyeballing the price tags. He pointed to a flip-top model. "Is that the cheapest prepay phone you got?"

"Oh, yes, young man," she replied. "Plenty cheap."

"How cheap?"

"Twenty-nine dollah plus tax. You got thirty-tree dollah?"

208

He reached into his pocket and retrieved a fifty to show her. She snatched the bill from his hand and started to unlock the case. His money not only caught *her* attention, but the eye of the only other customer in the shop. The young Asian man appeared overly curious, making the boy nervous.

The shopkeeper asked, "You gonna want cheap calling minutes to go with that?"

"Sure, I need some, yah. How much for the minutes?"

"Anuddah thirty dollah, please. You git a hundred-fifty minutes fo' thirty-dollah, yes."

Noah pulled out his second fifty-dollar bill. The shopkeeper removed the phone and took it behind the counter to program in the necessary minutes. "You want I wrap?"

Noah looked over at the man whose eyes seemed locked onto him. "No, I'll just shove it in my pocket."

The shopkeeper handed him the phone, along with his change and receipt. Noah walked out of the shop and even a block in the wrong direction before looking over his shoulder to seen if the stranger was following him. At the end of the block he checked again; this time the man had dropped out of sight.

Ten minutes later, Noah found a narrow, almost-hidden block with a faded-out street sign, half a dozen old brick buildings, and, across the street, the number he sought, 817. A plain sign above the door read Royal Hotel. To Noah, it didn't look too royal. Just then, he noticed a car on his side of the street with two Hispanic-looking men. The guy in the passenger seat held a camera with a long zoom lens and took a picture of a man leaving the hotel, then another of someone entering. Noah waited and watched. A third man approached from the opposite direction and climbed into the back seat of the same car. Just as he bent to get in, the sunlight caught his profile. It was the man from the phone shop, the man who had stared at him.

Oh no. I can't have my picture taken, Noah thought. *What if they're the police?* He ducked down behind the parked cars and snuck by them one-by-one until he got opposite the four-story hotel. There was plenty of street traffic out front, including a lineup of delivery trucks. The boy timed his dash up the steps into the building with the passing of a UPS truck.

Noah found himself in a small deserted lobby with two stuffed chairs and a faded red settee, but luckily, no one behind the reception desk. A woman dressed in a shabby muumuu entered, passed him, and headed directly for the stairs at the rear. Wen had written the room number on the paper; Noah assumed that 304 would be on the third floor, so he hurried to the staircase and started up. Two flights up he opened the door and found himself in a maroon-carpeted hallway with at least a half-dozen numbered doors. He hesitated in front of 304 and knocked. With no response, he tried again. On the third try he heard movement on the other side of the door.

"What d' hell ya want?" said a sharp, angry voice.

"Wen sent me. I got a message for Zeke Young."

Noah saw an eyeball through the peephole. "Who the hell are you?"

"I'm Noah, Wen's messenger."

The lock clicked, the chain latch rattled, and the door swung open wide. A short, stocky, dark-complexioned man stood before him in nothing but polka-dot boxer shorts and black socks. Tattoos covered his beefy arms and hairless chest. The man beckoned for Noah to enter. The boy's eyes widened when he saw through to the adjacent bedroom, where a tiny woman with exceptionally full breasts hustled her body into an oversized white terry robe. Noah's jaw dropped. He'd interrupted something really personal.

"What's the matter? Ain't you ever seen a naked broad before? What's with this message already?"

"Are you Zeke Young?"

"Yeah. I wouldn't have even let your lousy butt in here except that you knew both my name and Wen's."

"Wen said he wants to see you—quick."

"So how come he didn't just call me?"

Noah shrugged.

"And what else?"

"I guess he's got a job for you."

"That's it, kid? That's all you got to say? You bust in here and you got nothing more?"

"No, sir," said Noah. "Except maybe—I saw three men downstairs in a car taking pictures of everyone coming in and out of this hotel." Noah crossed the room to the window and pulled the flimsy curtain aside for a view of the street below. "See there in the black SUV? That's a camera sticking out of their window."

Zeke followed him for his own look. "What the hell—you're right. Did you get a good look at them—were they Hispanic?

"Two of them could be," the boy responded. "The other man was a tall guy, maybe Chinese."

"Gotta go, sweet stuff," he said to the little lady. "Gotta take care of business." He squeezed past her into the bedroom. "Make yourself at home until I git back."

"Sure, Zeke." She stood in the doorway, allowing one skinny leg to part the folds of her robe for the boy's benefit. Holding the pose, she provocatively waved her knee back and forth as the folds of the robe parted. She deepened her breathing, stroking her breasts, taunting the boy until Zeke emerged. Fully dressed, he grabbed her fanny and planted a sloppy kiss on her lips.

"Come on, kid," he said. "Close your sorry jaw before it falls off. I know a back way outta this joint." He led the way down the stairs a half-flight below the lobby to a rear fire door that opened into an alley.

Noah remembered that he hadn't stopped for the Egg McMuffins. He looked at his watch: lunchtime. "We've got to stop and get Wen a bunch of burgers and fries. He'll be pissed if we don't, yah."

"He gave you money for it, kid?"

"Sure did."

"Good idea, then we'll let Wen treat us."

* * * *

Several days passed without interference from the law. Hugo and Mong plied their thievery slowly but steadily, building their going-home boodle from the southern Thailand tourists. They ate and slept quite comfortably on a modest budget. They also laid low whenever they saw a white police cruiser with its black fenders and crown light nose into the beach parking spaces. Two Thai officers would generally sit for a time, get out to question a few tourists and locals, then leave the sandy beach, all within thirty minutes. Hugo thought there might have been a complaint or two that initiated this law-and-order gesture, but the lawmen were overt and quick about it. Hugo saw no real threat to the thieves' own enterprise.

Their routine changed on the fourth day. Hugo and Mong were spotting and scooping up carelessly abandoned belongings on the beach. That day, the police arrived ahead of schedule and dropped off two plainclothes officers, who sat widely apart on the white cement wall in front of the hedgerow, overseeing the beach like a pair of Chinese guardian lions. Their identical Panama hats not only covered their heads, but branded them as local law enforcement.

"The complaints must have increased," Hugo told Mong. "It's time we move."

"But where we go, boss?" He had gotten accustomed to their current routine and its increased amenities.

"I hear the Phuket beaches are loaded with rich tourists," Hugo said. "Besides, we now have plenty of local money for *tuk-tuk* gas."

The thieves moved up the beach toward where they'd parked, circling right to avoid the police plants. Their path took them across a small hotel's beachfront, where they encountered a bear of a man in long surfing trunks and dark glasses. A bushy black beard covered much of his face. Outcroppings of unruly black hair sprouted on his head and barrel chest.

"Und ver do you tink yor goin'?" he challenged in a thick German accent. His giant stature almost matched Mong's.

"We're just crossing in front of the hotel on our way to the street," said Hugo, continuing along.

The bear shook his head and pointed in the direction from which they came. Mong shifted his lumbering body and approached the bear until they were face-to-face. "Why you stop us?" he asked.

"Private beach. Security! Dat's vhy!"

"We're just passing through. We're not making any trouble," Hugo piped up, as he noted that the closest policeman had jumped to his feet and was now looking their way.

"*Nein!* Go back!" the bear boomed. "Private property!"

Mong closed the gap and placed himself between the bear and the policeman. In a flash, he slid a switchblade out of his pocket and pressed the button to release the weapon, which now was about to puncture the bear's ribs. "You say nothin', *bruddah*," he grunted. "No noise or signs or fuss and you will live anuddah day."

The policeman, seeing nothing, or wishing to see nothing, lost interest. He spun about and began walking toward the other officer seated on the wall farthest from them. Hugo smiled broadly to indicate a friendly exchange among the three men.

"Now, *bruddah*," Mong whispered in the bear's ear, "you will follow my boss into da hotel, through the main lobby, and out onto the street—if you please." He had picked up a few polished speech mannerisms from Hugo and used them when necessary. For emphasis, he pressed the tip of the knife, without penetrating the skin, against the bear's lower back, causing the security guard to flinch in fear.

Hugo led the way, still smiling his toothy grin at the few tourists who bothered to notice them. Once the trio reached the road out front, they continued until they were out of sight and earshot of the police. At a perfectly timed moment, Mong surprised his hostage from behind. He cut the elastic cord to the bear's surf trunks and slit them clear down to the crotch. The bear howled with rage in German. Now he needed two hands to keep from exposing himself—in a word, rendering him harmless.

Hugo and Mong trotted away, occasionally glancing over

a shoulder to make sure the security guard wasn't following them. The escaping thieves kept up the pace until they came to the bushes where they had hidden their stolen *tuk-tuk*.

* * * *

Hank and Lori Pualoa lived in the community of Ewa Beach, twenty miles west of Honolulu on the south shore. Hank, the surviving partner of the original Finast Construction Company, had separated the family property from the business properties so he could live in the Ewa house where he and his brother, Big John, grew up. Finast Construction now flourished, work averaging near capacity for the last four years. Today, Hank sat at his home desk going over the monthly figures from the business when the den phone rang.

"Hello, Andy…He is?…He does? I'll be there in an hour."

Lori stuck her head in the den door. "You look bewildered. Who was that?"

"Andy. The guy he got the locket and necklace from, Ernie Peshelli, is in the coffee shop."

"What about it?"

"He says the guy wants to talk to me."

"I thought you said you were going to let the whole thing drop."

"No, Lori, *you* said we should let it drop. I didn't commit myself. Anyway, they're waiting for me so I'd better see what it's all about." Hank closed the accounting book and shoved it into the top desk drawer. He got up, kissed her quickly on the cheek, and headed out to his pickup.

* * * *

The last of the lunch crowd had gone, and Bunny was re-filling salt shakers when Hank came through the door. She was so busy humming away that she didn't notice him come in. He tapped her on the shoulder to get her attention. She jumped with surprise.

"Oh, hi, Mr. Pualoa. They're in the kitchen. Want me to get them for you?"

"Yes, please." Hank sat down at a window table for four and waited.

The man following Andy to the table hardly resembled the brazen bruiser of eight months ago—the day worker who had stolen his jewelry box out of his truck, tagged him with a black eye, and run off. This version of Ernie Peshelli looked thinner by thirty or forty pounds. His hollow cheeks had a pallid, shriveled look. His eyes were recessed and reflected a deep sadness. His step was deliberate, yet slow, as though he doubted whether each step would hold his weight. He and Andy took chairs on the opposite side of the table.

"Hank, I'd like you to meet a very repentant Ernie Peshelli. He's asked me to act as a go-between. I'll let him do the explaining himself."

Ernie laced his fingers together in his lap, as if to steady his nerves. "Thank you, Mr. Pualoa, for agreeing to see me. What I did was a criminal act, an impulsive and stupid act that changed my life altogether—for the worst. Although I'm glad you got your locket back, I'm terribly sorry to have caused you so much pain and frustration."

"Wait," said Hank. "I still don't have it. You bartered your meals for it with Andy here, and he gave it to his bride-to-be as a token of his love, so I'm certainly not about to ask for it back. I remain the loser, Ernie, but fortunately, it won't break me."

"I wish to make amends, Mr. Pualoa," said Ernie. "I don't have a job yet, but if and when I get one, I'll pay you for your trouble. I haven't been able to work for even a day since I stole the jewelry box from you. This isle is small and word in the construction firms gets around fast. I've been bunking with my sister, but it's tough on her. She's got four little kids, and me without a job I can't help with her expenses. I've started to go to church again. But I feel I can't resume my life unless I obtain your forgiveness."

"Ernie, I've already written off your so-called debt months ago, so you needn't worry about that. What does trouble me, though, is finding work for you in your present state of health.

You were a pretty good day worker, but now you're hardly fit for a construction job."

Ernie looked him straight in the eye. "I know. But Mr. Ballesteros said he would hire me as an assistant cook if I could obtain your forgiveness."

"I don't understand, Andy," said Hank. "What about your dad? Isn't he your cook?"

"Yeah, but Papa's seventy-five. It's getting harder and harder for him to stand over a hot grill for so many hours. Business is good enough, I think, that we can give him an assistant, a short-order cook. If Ernie works out and learns all that Papa can teach him, he might be able to take over his job eventually."

Hank squinted as he mulled the idea over. "Somehow I feel okay about that arrangement," he said.

Just then Bunny emerged through the swinging kitchen doors with four mugs of steaming coffee on a tray. She approached the table and set the mugs in front of them, before sitting down and joining the group. "I think we have something to celebrate here."

Stalling for time, Hank reached for his mug, poured in two sugars and three tiny containers of half-and-half, and said, "So you know the whole story?"

Bunny's plump cheeks flushed and her brown eyes sparkled with happiness. "Andy and I don't keep secrets from each other. He told me how he got the locket." She chuckled. "He had to tell me. I knew something was up when I saw the number eighteen on the back. And yes, now I know the whole story. Even these newly constructed walls have ears."

Chapter 23

Tactics

WEN, **ZEKE,** and Noah sat around a naked bridge table in the Chinatown apartment. Wen reached into the large white paper bag in the center and pulled out an obscenely large mushroom cheeseburger dripping with juice.

"Kid, I thought I told you to bring back Egg McMuffins."

"Gosh, I'm sorry, Mr. Wen. It got kinda late—past noon, so I thought you'd rather have something more lunchy. Besides, you said you were in a hurry to see Mr. Young here."

"Good answer, boy. I like someone who knows how to think for himself." Wen's beady eyes grew with anticipation.

Six burgers, a container of coleslaw, and three large bags of French fries disappeared in a hurry. When they were done, Noah collected the wrappers and deposited them in the trash bag under the sink.

"How about you take a walk, kid," Wen said. "I got some serious business to work out with Zeke here. Okay?"

"Sure, Mr Wen. How long should I go for?"

"Half-hour maybe," said Wen. "A couple times around the block should do it."

"The kid's shrewd and alert," said Zeke, once the boy had bounced down the stairs and out of earshot.

"How do you mean?" asked Wen. "I simply send him on errands while I'm cooped up in this shithole. It doesn't take much brainwork for that. He does have some common sense, though."

Zeke grunted. "The kid has more than that. He pointed out three of Rai Portfia's men watching my hotel from a black SUV.

He said they had a camera and were taking pictures of everyone going in or out. I saw it for myself. I think they intended to follow me to your place. They're looking for your ass, boss."

"And you let them follow you here? How stu—" Wen fumed.

"Of course not," interrupted Zeke, trying to soothe the dangerous temper of his meal ticket. "I never use the front door. I always use the rear fire door and the alley to the next block. They never saw us leave. All I'm trying to say is the kid's smart."

"Yeah, he's useful alright, I'll give you that."

Wen knew perfectly well that Noah was an underage kid who should have been in school, but didn't give a crap as long as the boy served his purposes.

"Especially now that we're shorthanded with Hugo and Mong gone," Wen added.

"What's happened to those two?" asked Zeke. "I ain't see them since a dog's age."

"They're in Thailand."

Zeke guffawed, "Thailand! What the hell!"

Wen's face soured. "I got this strange phone call from Hugo, telling me they got shanghaied there aboard a ship, and they need money, clothes, and passports to get home. He told me it was Portfia's men that crated them up and shipped them off to Asia."

"Did ya send them anything?"

"Naw. How could I? As much as I need those guys right now, I don't have that kind of money on hand since the cops froze my bank account and my protection business got shut down. Maybe later when things get back to normal."

Like never, thought Zeke, shifting his burly body from foot to foot. *The bastard's got ice in his chest where his heart should be. Hmm, does this mean I'm moving up?* "Gee, boss, that's rough. What are you gonna do about it? Is that why you sent for me?"

"I blame that Chou broad across the street for me having to hide out here, but most of all, I blame the Portfia brothers. Yeah, that's why I sent for you. The broad you can take out anytime." He self-consciously rubbed his tender shoulder. "It's the Portfia brothers I want to hit—where they really hurt. The bastards are trying to muscle into Chinatown. This is my territory. It was my Uncle Tsui's before me."

"So you told me, boss. Oh, by the way, I brought the new rifle just like you asked. I stashed it in the closet."

"Good," said Wen.

"I already took out a goon up on the roof," said Zeke. "I'm sure it was one of Rai's soldiers. How much closer do you want me to get?"

"Family!" said Wen with a mirthless grin. "You can't get any closer than real family."

"Shit, boss, you'll start a gang war. The police and the politicians ain't gonna like that. Neither will the locals. The papers'll have a ball wid it too."

"Like the man says, these are desperate times, and I've got to protect what's mine."

"Who do you wan me t' try and hit, boss?"

"If brother Manny's still holed up across the street, take him out. If not, see if you can catch any of Rai's kids outside the Portfia fortress in Salt Lake. Do what you can to make everything look like an accident."

"Okay, boss, I'll see what I can do." Zeke wasn't any too happy with the assignment until Wen handed him a fat envelope. He thumbed through the crisp bills.

"Hey, boss, I thought you were broke."

"I have a small stash nearby to keep going, but none to waste, and I put it to good use. Keep that in mind."

*   *   *   *

Later that same day. Gert Mahaila parked her unmarked cruiser in the alley behind the bakery and walked around to the coffee shop next door. She discovered the Wong family there. Leilani stood on a stepstool, working on her wall mural. She had just finished a *haku lei* of orchids that encircled the graceful head of Laka, the Goddess of Hula. Alex and their daughter, Malia, sat

219

with Kekoa at a table for six in a quiet corner. Seated next to Alex was another man. Gert approached. "Good afternoon, ladies and gentlemen. May I join you?" A rhetorical question. Her tone was friendly, but her gaunt face was stern.

Bunny had just set mugs of coffee down. "Can I get you something?" she asked Gert.

"No, thanks, I'm fine for now." She dropped into a vacant chair. Addressing the man with Alex, she said, "Lieutenant Gert Mahaila, Homicide. Aren't you Kurt Kenoi, the criminal defense attorney?"

"Yes. Alex has engaged me merely as an observer, not legal counsel as yet. I've promised not to interfere with your questioning, Lieutenant, but I admit this open arrangement would normally be contrary to my better judgment. However, as I understand it, getting the youngster off the streets is the primary objective of this meeting." The fiftyish lawyer had a receding hairline, square wire-rimmed glasses, and smoky gray, all-seeing eyes.

"I understand," said Gert. She knew him by reputation: seemingly mild-mannered, but a trial terror who sinks his claws in and doesn't let go.

Kekoa motioned for his sister to join them.

Leilani came down from the stool and wiped her hands with a cloth covered in solvent. She looked comfortable in paint-splattered overalls. A single thick braid flopped down her back, with stray wisps of dark hair escaping around her cheeks. She settled into a chair, her expression grave, her tall, substantial body tense. "Sorry about the smell on my hands. And I owe you an apology, Gert, for my temper when you last called on me."

"Me too, I was only doing my job," returned Gert. "It's tough mixing business with friendship. I hope I didn't cross the line."

"No, I guess I got a little too touchy. Is this nightmare with our son ever going to end?"

Gert had no answer. Turning to Kekoa, she asked, "What made you change your mind and decide to cooperate?"

"I'm worried about my nephew," he replied. "I believe he's extremely vulnerable out there alone, and he presents a hazard to himself and to anyone who might confront him."

"Is he armed?"

"No, no, nothing like that," said Kekoa. "Noah told me he had already tossed the gun and the girl's sweater into the ocean."

"But that's tampering with evidence, a crime in itself," protested Gert. "So why is he a hazard?"

"Noah may resist arrest," admitted Kekoa. "He's a born scrapper and knows how to defend himself. It's just that I believe he's innocent of the killing, and that he's taking the blame for the shooting to shield his girlfriend. That morning he came in looking like hell. His face was black and blue, his chest and arms were covered with bruises. Both cheeks and his upper lip were swollen and cut. Maria wanted to take him to a walk-in clinic, but he refused to go. After we finished the baking, he spilled his story, but not the truth. Noah said *he* shot Duke Santos, but I could tell the boy was lying—he was being heroic, I tell you, just to protect her." Kekoa paused, his big shoulders sagged, and he drummed his fingers on the tabletop as if to frame his thoughts.

"Finally," he continued, "Noah admitted to me that Nina fired the actual shot, but she did it to stop Duke from beating him to death. She and Noah are crazy about each other. She may have saved his life."

"Then where did the gun come from?" asked Gert while making notes in a spiral pad.

"Not from my Noah, I can tell you that much," Leilani blurted out.

"The gun was Duke's," said Kekoa, "At some point during the skirmish, the Santos boy lost his advantage and brought it out of his pocket, but Noah was able to bat it away. He told me Nina picked it up and pulled the trigger. She only meant to shoot in the air to stop the fight, but, instead, the bullet hit Santos in the neck."

Gert turned to Malia. "You were at the movies with them,

weren't you?"

Malia nodded. "And I wish the whole thing had never happened. My brother told me the same story only minutes afterward. He said Nina was upset because she thought she'd killed Duke. Noah told her *he* shot Duke, but he took Nina's sweater away from her anyway. She was coming to our house to sleep over, and Noah ordered me to have her take a long shower. Why would he say that if *he* fired the gun?"

Gert asked, "For the record, does Nina have a last name and an address?"

"Nina Portfia," said Malia. "She lives somewhere in Salt Lake."

"That's right," said Alex. "The next morning I dropped her off at her home in Salt Lake. It's a large compound surrounded by a high stone wall. But, unfortunately, I don't know the address—she directed me there with right and left turns."

"I think I already know the address," declared Gert. "And this complicates matters greatly."

"Why is that?" asked Alex.

"Nina Portfia is most likely the daughter of mob kingpin Raimonde Portfia. This puts a different spin on things."

"But why?" persisted Kekoa. "We're talking two fourteen-year-olds, not mobsters."

"But there is a mob connection between Duke Santos and Nina's father," claimed Gert. "The victim's uncle and guardian does routine odd jobs for the Portfia family. I talked with the man only this morning. We need to pursue that angle. It's imperative that we question Nina. The problem is, she's a minor, entitled to parental and legal protections."

"But what about our son?" said Leilani, a sob catching in her throat. "We're forgetting he's all alone on the streets, and we don't know where to find him."

"I have a feeling I know where the boy's gone," said Kekoa. "He's shown so much interest in my former exploits while I was on the run as a youngster, he's probably copying my journey. I think he's hiding out in Chinatown somewhere. There's plenty of places for him to get lost there."

"Just what are you suggesting here?" asked Gert.

"I'm proposing that you call off your BOLO or APB or whatever you call it these days and you and me walk the streets of Chinatown to find him."

"I can't do that," said Gert. "Technically, I'm looking for a murderer. All I can do is provide some special instructions to the beat officers to let them know they're dealing with an unarmed runaway." She got to her feet. "I appreciate your cooperation. However, I will need a more formal statement from each of you down at the station sometime in the next few days." She walked around the table to Leilani, bent over, and gave her a hug. "I'll do all I can to help."

Everyone watched as Gert the friend and Gert the police-woman strode away from their table and out the back door to the alley. Inside the cruiser she dug deep into a pocket of her black chinos, pulled out her hard red ball, and started squeezing it, all the while thinking, *What a God-awful predicament.*

"What do you think, Kurt?" asked Alex. "How bad is it?"

Kurt took a sip of coffee, grimaced because it was luke-warm, and pushed the mug away. "As I see it, the boy can defi-nitely be found culpable for intentionally removing and destroying evidence. If it can be established that he did *not* bring the gun to the scene, any form of murder—premeditated or not—is off the table. If it can be established that he didn't fire the gun, he won't be tried for manslaughter. However, Malia says he told her he fired the fatal shot. In point of fact, that constitutes only a third-party hearsay confession. Unless he reiterates that so-called confession in public, we should be able to discredit it. If we can't, he'll be tried for manslaughter. If he feared for his life, it will be a simple case of self-defense."

Kurt folded his arms across his chest. "Any assault charges would depend on who started the skirmish and who stalked whom. The defense would have to convince a jury that your son would not have brought his girlfriend on a stalking mission. It would depend on establishing where the two were beforehand."

"Five of us were at the movies together immediately before they went for their walk," said Malia.

"What kind of relationship do Noah and this Nina have?" asked Kurt.

"Nina called their get-togethers non-dates because her parents didn't allow her to date yet," said Malia. "They always met at the movies or ball games and went home separately afterward. That night they sat together at the other end of our row. When the lights went out, they held hands and kissed a lot. Her dad would've blown a fuse if he'd seen them together like that. What will happen to Nina when they prove Noah didn't fire the gun?"

"Her lawyer would have to prove a lack of malicious intent and that her only motive in firing the fatal shot was to save Noah's life," said Kurt. "Other factors would include her firearms experience, whether she knew her victim, how she felt about him, and what was going on in her head at the time. Even then, it would depend on jury and judge to determine her ultimate fate."

"Thank you, Kurt," said Alex. "If you're willing to take the case, I'll come to your office in the morning with a retainer check and sign your representation contract."

"I am, and tomorrow morning will be fine," said Kurt, offering a handshake.

* * * *

Rai relaxed in a beach chair beside the pool reading a James Patterson novel and sipping a vodka collins. Avoiding the scorching sun, he always waited for the late afternoon shade cast by the house. His usual routine included twenty-five quick laps in the pool beforehand. Today he'd stretched it to thirty. He glanced at Raul and Salvadore playing Ping-Pong at the far end of the courtyard opposite his office. He noted his two men on the roof providing the usual security for the family compound.

"Hey, Dad," yelled Raul. "I hear your private office phone ringing off the hook. Should I get it?"

"Yeah, pick up and tell them I'll be there in a minute."

Rai set the glass and book aside on the mosaic tabletop. He stood, hiked up his trunks, and tied a large beach towel around his waist as he walked on the flagstone path to the office. Entering, he asked Raul, "Who is it?"

"Some broad. She asked for you, but wouldn't give me her name." He handed the cordless receiver to his father.

As Rai accepted the phone and listened, a flood of anger washed over his unshaven face. "Who the hell is this and how did you get this unlisted number?…Oh! Police! Lieutenant Mahaila." His voice adjusted to a civil tone. "Do I know that name? Ah, we've met before." *So much for paying for a private line*, he thought. "You want to interrogate my daughter? No way, José, she doesn't have to talk to you. A warrant? You wouldn't….You did? Tomorrow afternoon at two? I'll let you know…. It's a firm appointment?…Yes, ma'am."

Rai put the phone down, dialed a two-digit in-house number, and waited for his chief underling to pick up. "Domo! Get down here! We've got a major crisis brewing."

"Sure thing, boss."

Rai turned to Raul, who had stayed to listen. At age twenty-four, he felt entitled. Some day soon he hoped to get into the family business.

"Raul, where is your sister?"

"Upstairs in her room, moping. Mom's with her. The poor thing's been up there all day, Dad. I don't think she's even come down to eat. Want me to get them?"

"Wait a bit. I want to talk to Domo first."

In a matter of minutes Domo appeared in the office and shut the door to the courtyard. "What's this new crisis, Rai?"

"Have you had any luck in locating the Wong boy, the one in the picture I gave you?"

"Not yet," replied Domo. "I thought you wanted me to concentrate on finding Wen and taking him out first."

"I did, but now the priority has changed. That nosy police

lieutenant wants to interrogate Nina about the Santos shooting."

"You mean that Mahaila broad that's always squeezing the rubber ball in her fist?" Domo asked.

"Yeah, that's the one," said Rai. "But you'd better stop calling her a broad. She's in HPD Homicide and she's got clout. We have to be at police headquarters tomorrow afternoon at two. She wants to question Nina about the shooting, to find out whether she meant to harm the vic or even knew him. I've got to protect her, and there's no time to lose. Our first priority right now is to find the boy and bring him in here by tomorrow morning. I need to hear his story."

Rai didn't often feel vulnerable, but at this moment his entire lean body turned cold. And not from his still-damp swim trunks. He believed that Nina, his only daughter, had told him the truth—that she had killed that young hoodlum. Now his little girl was in deep trouble. It was time to call a criminal defense attorney.

Chapter 24

Three Strikes

THE SUN had retreated between the buildings, making it harder for Noah to read the magazines he'd found in the basket by the worn vinyl couch. The boy was restless, confined to the mind-dulling apartment most of the day with nothing to do. He had a spasm of self-pity, wishing he and Nina hadn't taken their walk that fateful night—at least not gone where they were so vulnerable. *Damn, I'm missing out on my life!* Noah sighed. *I wish I could taste some of Auntie Maria's ensemadas right now, and I sure could go for two whole slabs of her Filipino chocolate bread pudding cake.*

Noah noticed that Wen seemed to have lost interest in him except at mealtimes. Going outside more than necessary wasn't really an option—too risky, increasing the chances of his being recognized. The boy suspected that the boss was planning something big with Zeke Young. There was an air of secrecy about them—a lot of whispering when he was around. Whatever it was, he had a feeling it might take place within the next few nights. Maybe it was something illegal, but since he wasn't a part of it, he didn't care as long as he had a place to hide until his own problems blew over. And he believed they would blow over when everyone stopped looking for him.

"Hey, kid, you're gonna lose your eyesight reading them girly magazines in the dark like that." Wen reached over his head and turned on the floor lamp. "That better?"

"Yah, lots," said Noah, wondering about the sudden attention. "Thanks, man. You gonna want some food tonight? It's five-thirty."

"Yeah, I'm getting hungry even thinking about it," said Wen. "I've got an old menu here from the Little Village Noodle House. Do you know where it is?"

"Sure do. I've been there."

"I'll phone an order in, and you can pick it up. Anything special you like?"

"Nope, it's all good with me," replied the boy. "Wait! How about spring rolls and some orange chicken?"

Noah dropped the girly magazine back in the basket. He'd had an unpleasant morning trapped with the boss. Wen paid him well and treated him decently enough. But Noah always sensed a sinister edge under his smooth-talking surface. Wen had asked him why he didn't have a bicycle. He confessed that it had been stolen. Wen had insisted on the details, then lashed out at him: "You want to work for me? Stop being careless and stupid." The Adam's apple in his skinny neck had bobbed up and down as he delivered those biting words.

After Wen called in the food order, Noah started down the stairs to the street. He stopped short just outside the street door. He suddenly became aware of two strapping men, decked out in muted aloha shirts and black trousers, coming toward him on opposite sides of the street, checking into every storefront and alley. *They're definitely looking for something or someone. Is it for me? Are they cops? They don't look like cops—more like bozos.*

Alerted, he quickly stepped back inside, turned the latch on the outside door to the locked position, and backed against the wall mailboxes, out of sight, until the two hoods had passed. Then he undid the latch and periodically peeked out until he saw them reach the next block. Finally venturing out, he was clever enough to slip from door to door, hugging the buildings' shadows. Reaching the corner, Noah hesitated once more to look around. The two thugs had disappeared.

At dusk, the Chinatown streets were coming alive: theatergoers on their way to early dinners; workers finishing their shifts and drifting into bars with loud music; restaurant owners out front beckoning to tired shoppers. An old, bent Chinese man scurried from corner to corner. Two attractive teenage Japanese girls, with straight black hair falling down their backs, chatted nonstop as they crossed the street in front of him. A clutch of eager tourists crowded around a lei shop with its escaping fragrances. It could have been any or all of these distractions that led to letting his guard down.

Crossing in front of a narrow alley, Noah didn't see the two arms reaching out. Large rough hands locked about his waist in an iron-tight grip. He stiffened. The hands were trying hard to lift him off his feet and pull him into the alley. When Noah found that he couldn't wriggle free, he used the back of his head to smash into where he thought his assailant's face might be. He knew he'd found his target when the arms suddenly dropped away and a string of oaths followed. In a flash, Noah understood. This guy was one of Raimonde Portfia's men, another bozo sent to bring him to the compound, by force if necessary.

Noah leaped up, pivoted, and threw a round-house right fist to the man's left cheek, a staggering blow. His clenched fist, with the force of a brick, followed with an uppercut that smashed into the attacker's nose. Blood gushed everywhere. One straight-up punch to the gut sent the guy down on one knee, mixing roars of pain with gasps for air. He held up a hand in a motion of surrender.

Noah backed off and sized up his attacker—likely *hapa*, Filipino and Hawaiian, and dressed darkly like the two other stalkers. When the boy looked up and saw he had the attention of a crowd across the street, he turned away, bolted through the alley, and ran several more blocks. He was running so hard his chest hurt, and his mouth and throat were parched. He slowed to a walk. Reasoning supplanted his athletic prowess as he surveyed his surroundings. He'd gone blocks out of his way from the restaurant.

Noah's knuckles and the front of his polo shirt dripped with blood. He pulled it over his head and used it to wipe the sticky blood from his hands as best he could. Then he dropped the balled-up shirt into the nearest trash curbside receptacle. *But I can't enter a restaurant like this,* he thought. After a short search, he found a souvenir vendor just closing and pulled a T-shirt down from its display hanger. When the shopkeeper complained, Noah handed him a five-dollar bill. The boy literally had to stretch the too-small shirt over his head and broad shoulders. With this fit, every muscle and ripple in his upper body stood out like a roadmap. Worse, two tiny rips began to unravel under his armpits. The shopkeeper grinned and disappeared behind the panels as he finished shuttering his storefront. Noah shrugged and refigured the shortest route to the Little Village Noodle House.

He started out in that direction, but he seemed to be attracting a lot of attention from passersby—not exactly what he needed. He just assumed it was the tight fit that prompted their admiring smiles. But when the reactions continued, he looked down at his new T-shirt. He knew it bore a slogan, but had not bothered to look. Reading it upside down, he discovered why he'd gotten such a reaction: "We Hawaiian Girls Have More Fun." He drew a bunch of giggles and smirks at the restaurant as well, but he soon had two large paper bags to carry that blocked the embarrassing message from sight.

As soon as Noah set the bags down on the bridge table, Wen and Zeke guffawed at the hilarious shirt. At a loss to explain what happened, he marched into the bedroom and filched an undecorated T-shirt from what must have been the former occupant's array. For the rest of the evening Wen and Zeke kept up their relentless teasing.

Around ten Zeke left the apartment, saying he was tired and going back to his place. But something about the way he and Wen were interacting told Noah that this was the night, the night of the secret caper they'd been planning together.

* * * *

Cindy Chou slid the breakfast plates and mugs into the dishwasher and tidied up the rest of the kitchen. Coland remained at the table poring over the *Wall Street Journal* insert in the *Hono-*

lulu Advertiser, grumbling about the state of the stock market.

"Down for the third day in a row," he declared.

"Put the paper away, dear," Cindy said. "It's 8:15. Time to leave."

"I know, I know," he said. "We have a property settlement at nine sharp."

"I'll get the car keys, you get the briefcases—"

"and we'll meet in the hall," he said. They found they were finishing each other's sentences more and more often, a comfortable sign of a solid marriage.

They rode down the high-rise elevator to the parking garage, where their new navy-blue Lexus awaited them. At the exit, Coland pressed the remote, and the high-security gate rattled upward to its radioed command.

Only minutes later they were in a Chinatown parking lot; Cindy chose an all-day stall. At the edge of the lot, Coland poked a ten-dollar bill through a slot in a pay-box that corresponded to their stall number. They walked to the corner. Nearby, a car engine started up and gunned, but that in itself was nothing unusual. As they stepped off the curb, tires screeched behind them. Nothing strange about that either. The next thing Cindy knew, she was thrust toward the opposite sidewalk, where she wound up on her hands and knees.

Coland did not fare as well. The front right fender of the errant car caught him on the left side of his buttocks. The impact spun him around and threw him onto the street. The car's right rear wheel ran squarely over his leg just above the left ankle. The driver did not stop. The car sped to the next corner and turned out of sight. An angry stranger's voice shouted after it, a woman screamed, and other enraged witnesses yelled "Stop!"

"He's hurt. Call 9-1-1!"

"It's an old rusted Chevy."

"Did ya get the license number?"

"No. It happened too fast."

"The car was blue."

"No, I saw it was green."

"The creep didn't even stop."

"Wasn't the driver a man?"

"I don' know."

"Did you call for an ambulance?"

A young man helped Cindy to her feet. She started to thank him, but then reeled toward the street and saw Coland sprawled out. She realized that the husband she loved was the person who most probably had saved her life by pushing her to safety. Coland was unconscious. His left leg was splayed out in an unnatural way. Cindy began to shake and feel dizzy until someone sat her down on the curb to wait for help.

Eight minutes later the ambulance arrived. The EMTs quickly immobilized Coland and loaded him onto a gurney. Cindy struggled to her feet. "Please! Can I ride in back with him to the hospital? He's my husband."

"Lady, you don't look so good either," said one EMT. "Maybe you had better get in back." He helped her up the step and onto the bench beside where Coland lay, closing the door behind him.

As the ambulance began to move, the second EMT addressed her scrapes and checked her vital signs while the first EMT attended to Coland, hooking up an IV. Cindy felt the swaying and bumping motion as the vehicle swung right and left around corners and over potholes. She tried to look out the tiny rear windows, but the unreferenced motion nauseated her. Another six minutes brought them to the Emergency Room entrance at Queen's Medical Center.

Coland was transferred to a hospital gurney, and quickly disappeared through the double doors. The second technician, concerned about the wife's condition, helped her down from the high vehicle and led her to the ER waiting room and an admissions desk. Cindy insisted she was fine, thanked him, and settled into a chair to wait. Then she remembered their important appointment, the closing of a commercial building sale; she called the client to postpone.

Half an hour later, a doctor came out and informed her that Coland was headed for the OR. "In addition to shattering both leg bones just above the ankle, your husband has also fractured his ilium, one of the three large bones in the pelvic region. The ilium is immediately reparable. However, some kind of custom prosthetic device will be needed to permanently fix the leg bones. X-rays and surgery should determine just what that will be. Meanwhile, we'll fit him with a cast. It'll be several hours. There's a small waiting room just outside the recovery room. A nurse's aide will take you there."

"Thank you, Doctor," Cindy said weakly. The moment he left, she began sobbing helplessly, so filled with anxiety for Coland that she completely forgot about her own sore knees and scrapes.

* * * *

Gert Mahaila sat at her desk poring over the crime scene photos and the medical examiner's report. She selected a photograph that showed a long trail of sneaker-heel marks along the ground: evidence that the victim had been shot on the sidewalk in front of the body shop and subsequently dragged behind the stack of tires. Another photo of the sidewalk flagged six blood samples. A corresponding lab report indicated that two different blood types were present.

A second report stated that there was next to no gunshot residue on the victim. Gert mulled over this observation. *This means the gun had to have been fired from at least a few yards away. If the two fighters continued grappling at close range, a third party must have been present to fire the shot.* She tried to imagine several shooting angles with each combatant on top at different moments as each one struggled to gain dominance. *Yes, there must also have been a third party present, the shooter, who was facing a moving target.*

Gert sat back in her chair, removed her red rubber ball from a pocket, and began rolling it on the desktop from one hand to the other and back again while she thought. *Kekoa and Malia may be right, the girl may well be implicated.* She captured the ball in her right hand, squeezing it slowly at first and then a little harder and faster. *I'm interested in hearing what this young lady has to tell me.*

"Hey, Lieutenant, your visitors are here," said the uniformed officer at her office door. "They're in Interview Room One."

"Thanks, Corporal Harris." Gert slid all the photos into a large file folder and used the three-hole paper punch and the metal tabs at the top to attach the reports to the folder. She locked her purse in the bottom drawer of her desk and stood ready to go. With the file under her arm, the lieutenant marched down the hall to Interview Room One. She stopped cold outside the glass doors. Father and daughter were not inside. Instead, a seated man in a suit, white shirt, and tie waited there. Gert checked the number painted on the glass. "One." She angrily swept into the room.

"I'm Lieutenant Gert Mahaila of HPD Homicide. Sir, my warrant specifically named Raimonde Portfia and his daughter, Nina Portfia. What are you doing here?" She took a seat opposite him at the government-issue gray steel table. "This is an unwelcome surprise. And who might you be?" she asked, eyeing him, knowing full well what was coming.

"Alonzo Paxton, attorney for Nina Portfia and her father, Raimonde." He held out his hand. Gert ignored it.

"I'm the legal representative of your specifically named subject," announced Alonzo, setting a business card down in front of her. "Due to an incapacitating illness, Miss Portfia could not attend and sends her apology instead. I believe this statement will answer any questions you might have for my client." He pushed a single sheet of white bond paper across the table.

Gert accepted the formally typed statement and read: "On Friday evening, the fifth of August 2005, I, Nina Elena Portfia, attended a movie at the Ward Theater Complex with three of my friends, namely, Malia Wong, Noah Wong (her brother), and Sally Tailor, plus Sally's friend I only know as Peggy. We remained together inside the movie from 9:30 p.m. until 11:10 p.m. Afterward, Malia, Sally, and Peggy went into Dave and Buster's Restaurant while Noah and I went for a walk a couple blocks away to Queen

Street. We returned to the group after the walk and waited for Malia's father to drive Malia and me to the Wong home, where I was spending the night. I have no recollection of any violence taking place at any time that evening."

The statement was signed by Nina, Raimonde, Alonzo Paxton, and a notary.

Gert's blood boiled. "Counselor, this is not the face-to-face interview that I expected to have with your clients. I have my own questions to ask. I would like specific and personal answers to those questions. Not prepared hogwash. In my professional opinion, you are non-responsive to my warrant."

"Lieutenant," said Alonzo smoothly, "I completely understand your position here, but Nina Portfia is a minor, not to mention that right now she is undergoing a serious bout with the flu. Her folks and her family physician caution against her leaving the house."

"Mr. Paxton, I intend to pursue this as soon as your client is fit. Consider this an open warrant until she responds in person with proper parental representation."

Alonzo's voice hardened. "My client has cooperated and sent you her statement, saying she has no recollection of violence. As long as she is neither a witness nor a suspect, any further action on your part might be construed as harassment."

Gert's metal chair scraped on the bare floor as she sprang to her feet. "Bullshit! Counselor, we're done here for now. I'll be in touch."

Chapter 25

Two Outs

IN THE SURGERY waiting room at Queen's Medical Center, Cindy abandoned the idea of trying to read a newspaper or magazine. She compulsively watched the computer-controlled status board for a progress report on Coland. "Benfield-Rice" had been truncated to "B. Rice" in white letters on the dark screen. Five patient names were listed in various stages of progress. After thirty minutes Coland's status had gone from PRE-OP to OP-RM. Six hours later, to Cindy's relief, the screen shifted to RECOVERY. She leaped up and hurried to the Nurses' Station.

"Your husband isn't awake yet," she was told, "but he came through the operation with no further complications. If you wish, you can be there when he wakes up. Through those doors and behind the curtains of Recovery Station Four."

Cindy found herself in a corridor of drapes, mostly closed. She pulled aside the curtain at Station Four to find Coland asleep flat on his back, with his left leg elevated in a plastic trough about a foot off the bed. Cindy sat down and waited, trying not to doze off, but failing under the stress. A quarter-hour later, she heard a simple moan. Coland's eyes were open and staring at the ceiling. She stood, looked down at him, and smiled. "Hi," she said.

"Hi yourself. Why can't I move my left leg?" he asked in a small, worried voice. "Is it still there?"

"It's there all right, but let's say it's all tied up for the present. Don't you feel it?"

"Uh, yeah, I do now. That's quite a contraption down there."

"They tell me it's only temporary."

"What happened to me?" he asked. "All I remember is parking the car and the two of us walking to the office. I feel like I was hit by a bulldozer."

"A car hit you from behind and didn't stop."

"Why don't you tell me about it."

"Well, for one thing, you saved my life by pushing me toward the curb. The-hit-and run car got you instead. Knocked you down and ran over your left leg. The driver was targeting me, not you. You hero you."

"Then why is my hero bum so sore? Is that where he hit me?"

"Yes, my dear, in fact, you have a cracked ilium in your pelvis."

"Were you hurt at all, honeybunch?"

"Just a few scrapes and bruises," she replied. "Nothing to worry about."

"How long am I going to be off my feet?" He groaned and tried to shift his body slightly but couldn't.

"The doctors are supposed to order some contraption to connect the ankle bones across where they were crushed. As soon as it arrives, they'll install it. Eventually, you'll be able to walk without a limp."

"Not another operation?" he complained.

"Yes, I think so, dear. The surgeon's coming in to see you this afternoon. He'll tell us everything we need to know. I'm guessing you'll be on crutches for a time and then a course of physical therapy, like any other broken-bones patient."

He remained silent and closed his eyes for a few seconds to allow all this information to sink in. Then something else occurred to him. "What about the police? Shouldn't they be notified?"

"I saw a police car pulling up to the scene as the ambulance was taking us away. I just assumed they'd interview the crowd. Wouldn't that be sufficient notification?"

"Except this was no damned accident," he said weakly.

"Attempted murder is what it was. We need Lieutenant Mahaila. Shouldn't we call her?"

"And what would we tell Gert?" posed Cindy. "We don't know anything more now than before the attempt."

"Don't we?" Coland asked, surprising his wife with his clear, analytical thinking so soon after major surgery. "What if it was ordered? What if someone at the scene could tie the hit-and-run to the gang leader who tried to take you down in your office—Wen Tse Fong?"

"Oh my God, Coland. Why didn't I think of him? Then we could nail the slime, take him off the streets. Even if it doesn't pay off, Gert might be able to use the information. I'll call her now."

* * * *

Hugo and Mong had driven the *tuk-tuk* about seventy miles mostly south and southeast on the Thai Peninsula's coastal road. The *tuk-tuk's* lack of shock absorbers made for a bumpy. uncomfortable ride that soon took its toll on their bodies. Their original destination had been the Phuket Island resort beaches, but on the way they came upon a nameless beach full of European tourists. A row of vacation homes lined the road opposite the unspoiled bleached sand. Fresh faces and scant policing made it seem the perfect place for their petty thievery practices. Indeed, the next few days yielded more than they had collected in all their earlier efforts. Their loot even included three passports: two Australian and one Singaporean.

On the third day, while returning on foot to the parked *tuk-tuk*, Hugo and Mong happily talked about their newest booty and bragged to each other of the cleverness they'd used to obtain it. They didn't notice the unmarked police cruiser following them because it hung back at a cautious distance. The faithful *tuk-tuk* fell into full view as the pair strolled into the public parking lot. The cruiser closed the distance and pulled into the lot alongside the two thieves. Two plainclothes officers jumped out of the cruiser, guns drawn, yelling a string of Thai insults and accusations. Hugo and Mong, taken completely by surprise, raised their hands high in the air in response. They were quickly handcuffed with their arms behind them.

At this point the rear door of the cruiser burst open. A tiny man with a neck brace and a bandage wrapped around his head like a turban emerged, spitting Thai words out faster than they could be interpreted. He ran toward the *tuk-tuk*, turned to face Hugo and Mong, and shook his fist at them with all the accusing words and phrases he could muster. He was the *tuk-tuk* taxi driver Mong had left for dead up north almost a week before.

"You gimme key, *tuk-tuk*," he demanded in broken English.

Mong couldn't reach it with his hands in cuffs, so he lowered his large head, indicating his right-hand cargo shorts pocket.

The driver reached deep into the pocket and yanked out the key. Then he looked straight up into Mong's face and scolded. "Mistah, you veddy bad man. Why you heet me, steal me *tuk*? I drive you anyplace you wan."

Mong shrugged in resignation as he and Hugo were shoved toward the cruiser. One officer placed his hand on Hugo's head, pushing him down into the back seat. When it became Mong's turn, the officer reached upward with his whole arm, but far short of Mong's towering height and bulk. Mong merely grunted and obliged him by bending over double like a jackknife and squeezing into the back seat. Through the open rear window they heard the *tuk-tuk* being coaxed from an ugly start to a sputter and then to a rhythmic putt-putt that gave the vehicle its name.

The little taxi man chugged off in a cloud of thick blue smoke, pleased to have recovered his place in the local manner of things.

The police cruiser did a U-turn and exited the lot in a northerly direction on the same coastal road. The two thieves eyed each other in disgust. Their successful, satisfying game was over. With their hands cuffed behind them, Hugo couldn't even reach into his pocket to bring out a wad of bills for a bribe. It was bad enough that the officers had already confiscated their take for the day, tying it up in a paper evidence sack and tossing it in the cruiser's trunk. Hugo and Mong knew their entire prior stash would be appropriated in their rented room down the road. Not knowing the local language, of course, they couldn't communicate with the arresting officers. They knew nothing of Thai justice. They would soon learn.

Chapter 26

Taken

NOAH KNEW he was in a trap of his own making, a fly caught hopelessly in a spider's web. Obviously, the police wanted to talk to him. After all, he was a murder suspect. But he now knew that someone else, some stranger out there, seemed to have more than a passing interest in him, someone willing to play rough. He had his suspicions. *Maybe Mr. Portfia? Who else? But why would Nina's father be so interested in me? After all, I'm actually protecting his daughter, trying to keep her out of the picture altogether. So why? Is it because he just doesn't want me dating his daughter?*

Being Wen's delivery boy wasn't all that bad. Noah had gotten used to the routine. The work was easy and the cash and sleep-in benefits suited him to a tee. Tonight's expedition involved Wen's desire for pizza, which brought Noah to the edge of Chinatown near Nuuanu Street. In the guest parking lot of a high-rise condo, he spotted a yellow Porsche Boxster Spyder with the top down. It wasn't the first time he'd seen it—and Noah was pretty sure Nina's brother, Salvadore, owned it. Nina had described the convertible, her father's gift to Sal on his seventeenth birthday. Nina had also told him that Sal's girlfriend lived in one of those high-rises.

Noah's keen senses were honed to pick up on the unexpected. He knew it was possible there were a few other yellow Boxter Spyders in Honolulu, but he didn't think so. Not in the same guest parking lot. *Some wheels, all right*, he thought. *Oh-oh, there's someone opening the hood, but it doesn't look like Sal.*

Noah retreated into a dark doorway across the street to watch. In less than five minutes the hood went down again. The figure, in a gray sweat jacket, wiped the hood with his right forearm sleeve, using it like a cloth rag, then looked from side to side to see if he was being watched. He left the Porsche and crossed the street to Noah's side, continuing from about a half a block away toward Noah. From the distance it was difficult to see who it was, but something seemed familiar about the approaching figure and the agile way he moved. Noah sank deeper into the shadow of the doorway. As the man passed by, he recognized Zeke Young. *So this is what Zeke and Wen were planning so secretly. Zeke's tampering with Sal's car. I wonder why. What's the connection? Should I warn Sal? And just how would I do that? How would I even find him?*

Right now Noah needed to pick up the pizzas Wen had ordered. When he returned with the pies, the boy could hear talking inside the apartment on his way up the stairs. One of the voices belonged to Zeke.

"Dat pretty car is there almos' every night," said Zeke. "It was a sittin' duck."

"Did you get the job done all right?"

"Sure, boss. Ain't dat what ya pay me for? Yah!"

"Shhh!" ordered Wen. "I think I hear the kid coming up now."

They went silent as Noah entered the room. He set the two large pizza boxes on the bridge table, took three paper plates down from the cabinet, and set them out as well. From the fridge he pulled out three bottles of Wen's favorite Sinkiang Black Beer. Noah placed two of them on the table and took a sip from the third bottle before putting it down.

"Wow!" he declared. "Strong stuff." It was the first beer of his life.

Wen seemed oblivious to the fact that he was serving alcohol to a minor. Even if he had thought of it, he wouldn't have cared.

"Hey, plenty good beer, yah," agreed Zeke. As he pulled out a handkerchief to wipe his nose, a red waxed paper wrapper fell on the floor.

Noah bent over, picked it up, and tried to return it to its owner.

"Nah! It's just trash, kid," said Zeke. "Toss it."

On his way to the wastebasket under the sink in the kitchen, Noah read the writing on the wrapper. "DANGER. Contains explosive squibs. CAUTION. Keep leads connected until ready for use." The wrapper had a paragraph of additional fine print he would like to have read, but there was too little time, so he checked to see if either one of the men was watching him before he stuffed it into his jeans pocket. Noah knew that squibs were small pyrotechnic devices used to ignite a charge. He suddenly realized: *They're gonna blow Sal up in his car!*

With a controlled, casual stroll, he returned to the bridge table, sat down, and took a large slice of pepperoni and sausage from the box. The sickening lump in his throat made it hard to swallow. Somehow, he did manage to get it down with the bite-and-sip help of the Chinese beer.

Wen pushed the box toward him. "Have another slice, kid. There's plenty left."

"I'm full."

"You usually put away three or four slices," said Wen. "What's wrong, kid? You don't like sausage?"

"Sure I do, but I ate a sandwich late this afternoon."

"Ain't like ya, kid," added Zeke.

"I think I need some air now," said Noah, getting up from the table. He headed for the stairs, rumbled down, and pushed the door out to the street.

Noah knew what he had to do. The first step was to call the Portfia family to warn Sal. But he didn't even know Nina's number, and certainly not her dad's or Sal's. *Maybe I should go to the police and tell them about the car bomb, but the cops would only arrest me for killing Duke. I'd wind up in jail for being the good guy. Damn it, I need to think this out before I make the wrong move. Wen's been good to me, but he and Zeke are gangsters and I'm gonna get caught up in what they're doing. Dammit, I don't know whose side I'm on.*

Noah's anguished thoughts were so drawn inward that he failed to notice the two men in black attire scouring the streets. They came up from behind him, surprised at their own good fortune, and pulled him into the dark empty hall of a vacant one-story building. The first thug shoved Noah up against a stucco wall. The second thug pulled both of the boy's arms behind and cuffed him with plastic tie straps. Noah executed a backward kick, but the thugs were prepared, one of them having been his victim in the alley the last time around. Each time he kicked, they kicked the standing leg out from under him, buckling it until he almost fell. When the kicking stopped, they slipped a black cloth bag over his head to disorient him. One thug held him against the wall while the other went to fetch the car, which was parked several blocks away. Whenever Noah tried anything too ambitious, he got shoved against the stucco wall again and, eventually, he turned passive.

Noah was forced into the rear seat of the car, and one of the thugs sat in back with him. Sitting in a moving car with his hands bound behind him proved painful. He wasn't about to complain. He'd learned the hard way that these guys played really rough, so he had no desire to challenge them again physically. He tried to figure out where this car ride would end. After all, he still wasn't sure who they were or what they wanted from him. While his imagination wandered over the possibilities, none of them made any sense.

* * * *

"I wonder where the kid is?" said Wen. "It's after midnight and he left here at ten."

"What? You're motherin' da kid now? He's probably got some girl, yah?"

"That's a good one, me mothering anybody," Wen replied. "I've gotten used to him, that's all. I need someone to do all my errands as long as I'm holed up in here. The cops are still looking for me since Mathew Saint got himself killed. I have to stay cooped up here for another couple weeks anyway. The boy's hiding from someone too."

"Do ya s'pose it's da cops?"

"It's possible," said Wen. "Do you think he'd turn me in?"

"Don' know, boss, he's your guy. You picked 'im. Maybe he squeal on me too."

* * * *

Noah could hardly breathe inside the hood covering his head. He could see only blackness and inhale only the stale smell of fabric sucked against his face. The old scar over his left eye ached. He figured they'd been driving at least half an hour, when the car made a sharp left and continued on slowly as though it had entered a long driveway. It stopped. The engine went silent. He heard the rear door open and felt someone yanking him out of the car and onto his feet.

"Okay, kid," a new voice said. "No one's going to harm you. The boss only wants to have a serious little talk with you. If you cooperate, we'll return you to where we found you. Will you cooperate?"

"Sure. What have I got to lose?" The hood came off. Noah gratefully inhaled genuine fresh air, shook his head to free his thick, matted hair, and blinked in disbelief. They were inside a high-walled compound. "What is this place, a fort or something?"

"No, it's a family residence." The voice came from a dark-complexioned man with a full head of silvery gray hair that seemed at odds with his hulking, muscular physique.

"What do I call you?" asked the boy.

"You don't." He placed one hand on the boy's shoulder and steered him toward a large house with white columns and a front door carved in koa wood. Up the steps they went, through the sweeping lanai, down a hall into a paneled room furnished like an office.

A man in a white short-sleeved shirt sat behind a massive desk. *Tawny-skinned, Filipino-Hispanic*, Noah thought. He had sharp eyes set too close together, slicked-back black hair, and a clipped short beard.

"Come in, young man. Have a seat." He spoke softly yet with authority, the kind of commanding voice one dared not ig-

245

nore. He motioned to the chair next to his desk.

Noah turned around to show that he still had his hands tied together. "It's a little uncomfortable to sit this way."

"For chrissake, Domo, I didn't tell you to handcuff the boy. What the hell is wrong with you? Cut him free." The reprimand from the man behind the desk sliced like a knife. He waited while Domo clipped the bonds before Rai asked, "By any chance do you know who I am?"

Noah rubbed his sore, reddened wrists. "No, sir." He settled into the plump side chair.

"My name is Raimonde Portfia. I'm Nina's father. You know Nina, of course."

Noah felt the blood freeze in his veins. His words came out weak. "Yes, sir. Will I be able to see her, sir?"

"That all depends on what you have to tell me. I expect to hear nothing but the truth from you, no matter how difficult that may seem or who is actually to blame. Do you understand what I am saying?"

"Yes, sir."

"First, tell me in your own words what happened that night you went to the movies with my daughter."

Noah began his narrative and continued to the point where Duke produced the gun.

"Are you positive this gun belonged to this Dante Santos person?" asked Rai. "He brought it to the scene?"

"Yes, sir," replied Noah. "I don't think he actually wanted to shoot me. He wanted to pistol-whip me with it. Otherwise, he would have shot me right away."

"I see. Go on."

"I picked up this chunk of iron pipe I found on the ground and smashed it into his knee. He dropped the gun and then I snatched it up and shot him in the neck. That's the way it happened. Honest!"

"Where was my daughter while all this was occurring?"

"I don't know," replied the boy. "I think she ran back to the theater when our fight broke out. She wasn't even there when I got up."

Rai's black eyes shot thunderbolts. "Young man, you're lying to me. I want the truth out of you—not some heroic bullshit." His manicured hand, adorned with jeweled rings on three fingers, slapped down hard on the desk. "You understand me now?"

Noah shivered. "Yes, sir." The chips were down and he knew it. His fists clenched the arms of the chair until his knuckles turned white. "Okay, I didn't pick up the gun and shoot Duke Santos. The pipe I hit him with knocked the gun out of reach and out of sight. That was the last I saw of it 'til afterward. Duke got on top of me then and began punching me right and left in the face. I couldn't stop him. Then I heard the shot that probably saved my life. Duke collapsed on top of me. I think he was dead right then and there. He wasn't moving. It was like dead weight pushing him off of me"

"Young man, I mean business. I'm going to ask you one more time. Where was my daughter while all this was happening?"

Noah's diaphragm tensed. Air felt trapped in his lungs. "I...I heard her crying somewhere. I didn't see her right then, but she must've been there the whole time, watching. After I pushed Duke off of me and stood up, I saw her standing half in the shadows with the gun in her hand and her arms hanging by her sides. She had a stunned look, and I took pity on her. Duke was my problem, and she didn't have to get involved. But she chose to save my life, and I'll always owe her for that. I decided to take the blame for the shooting."

"Are you absolutely certain Nina fired the shot that killed Santos?" Rai was testing the boy. Nina had already confessed the truth to him.

"The gun was in her hand, and there was no one else around. Almost positive, sir."

"What did you do then?"

"I took the gun and her sweater—I thought her sweater might have gunpowder on it."

"Yeah, gunshot residue, GSR," agreed Rai. "Then what did

you do?"

Noah answered with painful honesty, but Rai's questions went on for another half hour.

"Is that everything?" he asked. "Have you left anything out that I should know?"

"Not about that night, but there is something else. Do you know where your son Sal is, sir?" asked Noah.

"I assume he's watching TV in his room. Why? How is he tied into this?"

"Not tied to the shooting, but I think I saw his Porsche in Chinatown earlier this evening."

"He better not be in Chinatown," Rai snapped. "I have this family on lock-down. No one leaves the compound without my permission. How do you know the car was his?"

"How many new yellow Boxster Spyders are there in Honolulu, sir?"

"I imagine just his," said Rai. He looked toward the door where his *numero due* stood at attention. "Domo, what do you know about this?"

"Sal was warned not to leave just like the rest of the family," Domo replied. "Although he's been quite serious about some broad living in the high-rise behind Kukui Plaza. Rai, I suppose he snuck out to be with her. I didn't see him leave or I would have stopped him."

Rai turned back to the boy. "How is my son's presence in Chinatown of interest to you at all?"

"I'm pretty sure I saw a man put a bomb under the hood of your son's car."

"A bomb? How did you know it was a bomb?"

"When I got back to the apartment where I'm staying, this guy dropped a red wrapper on the floor. It fell out as he took out his handkerchief. I don't know why, but I picked it up and stuck it in my pocket and read it afterward. It said DANGER, explosive squib and something about keeping the leads in contact until ready for use. What do you think it was?"

Rai's unflappable demeanor was melting fast. He turned back to Domo. "Quick! Get word to Salvadore to stay away from his car. Bring him back to the compound even if he's kicking and screaming. Take all the help you need."

"Got it, boss." Domo left.

"Noah, did you follow this man or did he follow you back to your place? And why would he be so interested in you?"

"Actually, I didn't have to follow him. I recognized him as Zeke Young when he passed me on the street. We met back at the apartment."

"Zeke Young?" repeated Rai. "He's an SOB hit man for Wen Tse Fong. So that's what this is all about."

"You know Mr. Wen Tse Fong?" asked Noah.

"Oh yes, if this Wen character thinks he's a competitor of mine, he's mistaken. The man's a real pain in the ass, a dangerous, disruptive type who won't mind his own business. What matters here is—how do you know these people?"

"I suppose Nina told you I've been on the run from the police ever since the shooting. Mr. Wen caught me sleeping downstairs in the front hall of his apartment. He said he needed someone to run errands for him, and I needed a place to hide. It seemed like the perfect arrangement. Mostly, I fetched takeout meals for him and sometimes for Zeke. I didn't know what kind of business they were in until I saw the explosives wrapper. Then, I just wanted out of there. That's when your men grabbed me."

"You actually know where the little weasel is living?" asked Rai.

"Sure, but I didn't know he was hiding too."

"Oh, yes," said Rai. "From both the police and me. You'll tell me where this apartment is, won't you?"

"Uh, yeah," said Noah. "Only now I'm gonna have to find another place to hide out myself."

"You can stay here at the compound until we get this shooting business straightened out."

"Will I be able to see Nina?"

"Oh, yes, I almost forgot about your request," Rai picked up the compound's intercom phone and punched in a series of numbers. "Lottie, dear," he said in a honeyed voice as if nothing at all were wrong, "would you locate Nina and bring her to the office?…Thank you." He hung up and turned to the boy once more.

"Who else knows that you did *not* shoot Santos?"

"You're not going to do anything to him, are you, Mr. Portfia?"

"Of course not, son. I just want to contain that information—keep it from going any further. Maybe have a little talk, that's all."

"Only my uncle, Kekoa Pualoa. I work for him in his bakery. At least I did."

The double doors to the office pushed open. Mother and daughter entered, Nina in a plain tank top and cutoff jeans. At the sight of Noah, her face flushed and her deep blue eyes filled with tears. Joyously, she screamed his name. She wanted to rush to him, but stern looks from both her parents and her mother's hand on her shoulder held her back.

Rai rose out of his chair and assumed command. "Tomorrow afternoon, I'm calling in Hawaii's best criminal lawyer here, and the four of us are going to sit down and map out a strategy that's best for both of you kids. Tonight, I have to concentrate on getting Sal home safely. Lottie, it's nothing for you to worry your head about," he said as if his wife were ten years old. Now run along and find a bedroom for Noah. He'll be staying with us for a few days. I'll explain everything in the morning."

"Thank you, sir. But…" Noah hesitated. *My parents. I need to tell them where I am. Mom's prob'ly crying nonstop now, Malia too. And Dad's going nuts trying to figure it out.*

"But what, son," Rai inquired.

"I was just thinking about my parents," replied the boy.

"You run along with Nina and her mother. You can call them tomorrow after we sort this all out with the lawyers."

"Yes, sir." Noah followed them out into the hall.

Rai's antique clock ticked off another forty minutes to 2:15 a.m. before the phone rang again. It was Domo, informing Rai that Sal and his girlfriend were safe, already in a taxi headed home to the compound. Domo had also engaged a former HPD demolitions expert to defuse the car and return it to the compound.

Rai sank back into his swivel chair and undid another two buttons of his custom-tailored silk shirt. He could breathe easier now. But the pleasure lasted only a split second as a fearful thought flooded his brain. *After Wen learns that his plot to blow up Sal's car has failed, he'll look for another Portfia family target—maybe Esme and her children!*

Chapter 27

Unexpected Alliance

AT SEVEN the next morning, with less than five hours sleep, Rai rolled out of bed and pulled on his clothes. The mob king-pin normally summoned people he needed to see to *his* office, so he could conduct business on *his* turf. But this morning's business was far too important to wait. He hurried to the second floor apartment of Domo's house, where he had installed Manny—a bedroom, a tiny sitting room, and a second bedroom converted to a small office of his own. Without ceremony, he swung open the door. Manny was already on the computer, working on Rai's business books. Rai informed Manny that his wife and children were in imminent danger, explaining the threat and the need to act on it without delay. "Esmeralda, Frank, and Delores must move into the compound immediately. We have plenty of room in the guest house. They'll all be safe here."

* * * *

Esme was sipping tea in their cozy kitchen when Manny's call came. Despite his urgent tone and dramatic explanation, it took twenty minutes for his wife to absorb the fact that their lives might be threatened. With the phone to her ear, she tried to scribble a list of her options. Squirming, slouching, and adjusting her bottom in the captain's chair, she rejected the options one by one. Finally, this mother of two had to agree. *The safest place for my kids and me is in that monster fortress that Rai and Lottie call home. But should I make Manny pay? Continue punishing him by leveling another layer of guilt on him?* After ten more minutes, her ice-cold anger thawed and she decided not to agitate him further. Besides, what if this really were a matter of life and death? *We're going to be living under the same roof again, and it might as well be in peace.*

"Manny, if the kids and I are moving to the compound, we all have to pack some clothes and personal things to take along. Did Rai tell Carlotta that he issued this invitation to us? We can't just barge in uninvited. I don't know what I ever did to that woman, but she sure has it in for me. I've been getting dirty looks from her since day one."

Manny tactfully refrained from reminding his wife that she herself started the inter-family feud. She exuded nothing but disdain for Rai's business world—and for the luxury benefits that Lottie reaped from it. Manny suspected that Esme was also jealous of their lifestyle and wished that her husband earned a better living. He couldn't blame her for that.

"Don't worry, dearest, it's Rai's invitation that counts, and he rules the roost in that house. I'll tell him right now that you accepted. Then I'll drive home to help you pack. Don't worry, the transition will be smooth. I love you, baby."

Esme's cup clattered into the saucer as she finished her last sip of tea. "Okay, Manny, you can stop with the icky endearments now. I know you want to get back into my good graces, but I'm still pissed off at you. Nothing's changed. This gangster vendetta against the Portfia family did not have to include the four of us. You put us all in danger, and now we have to ask your brother for favors."

"Esme, if that Chinatown mobster Wen Tse Fong hadn't started in with his protection racket, none of this would have happened. There are some things I just can't control."

Thirty minutes later Manny parked at the curb of their modest home in Makiki and came inside. At the bottom of the stairs he boomed up: "I'm in the living room when you need me, guys."

Upstairs in Delores's room, Esme dropped a suitcase on her daughter's bed and spread it open. "Pack only what you need for the next few weeks. Remember, this is a temporary measure, not a permanent move. Make sure you include all your day-to-day toiletries. And of course all your schoolwork and books."

"Mom, is Daddy going to be living with us there?" asked Delores. "I miss him terribly."

"I miss him, too," Esme answered. "I'm not sure what the arrangements will be at the compound, but I'm sure he'll be somewhere close. Don't worry, you'll be able to spend time with him."

"Why aren't you and Daddy sleeping in the same bed anymore?"

"Your father and I had a disagreement. He betrayed my trust and went to work for your Uncle Rai."

"I think you don't like Uncle Rai. But why is working for him so bad?"

"Your Uncle Rai runs a mob of gangsters that do bad things and break the law and sometimes hurt people." Esme laid a stack of neatly folded bras and panties on the bed next to the suitcase.

"He seems like such a nice man. He's always been good to me and Frank. It's hard to believe he does bad things." Delores refolded two pairs of jeans and a skirt and added them to the pile on the bed.

"Your father knows full well your uncle is a bad person, and he went to work for him, anyway."

"Does Daddy break the law and hurt people too?" She added three blouses and three pairs of surf shorts to the clothes on the bed.

"Uh, no. Your father does some accounting paperwork and bookkeeping for him. I assume the work he does is legal. I'm not entirely sure, though."

"If Uncle Rai is so bad, why are we going to live with him?"

Esme dropped a pile of socks next to the undies. "An angry rival of Uncle Rai's threatened your cousin Salvadore. Apparently, somebody was trying to hurt Daddy too. Your father seems to think we'd all be safer inside Uncle Rai's compound—for now, anyway."

"Oh, Mommy," Delores cried, rushing into her mother's arms. "Now you're scaring me."

Esme stroked her daughter's hair. "Now, now, I don't want to scare you, honey. We'll be safe there with the high wall around us and all of your uncle's men out there to protect us."

"Why can't we just go to the police for protection? Can't they just arrest this rival bad guy?" Delores held up a floral-patterned, one-piece bathing suit in front of her and then laid it across the pillows.

"If only it were that simple," said Esme. "Honey, we can't prove that this evil crook tried to do these things to us. In the case of anonymous threats, the best the police can do is send a patrol car by the house a few times each day. That's why we have to rely on Uncle Rai's hospitality and the protection that goes along with it."

Delores let it go for now and placed her beloved guitar in its case. An eighth grader in middle school, she had an appealing confidence drawn from her musical gifts as a player of the steel guitar and singer of Hawaiian songs.

When Esme finished helping Delores pack, she shut the suitcase and set it on the floor. On her way into the hall with it, she encountered Frank leaning against the frame of the bedroom doorway.

"How long have you been standing there?"

"It didn't take long for me to throw my stuff in my camp duffel, so I heard most of what you told Del."

Frank had an athletic body and reddish-brown hair. As a high school freshman, he was making his mark as a talented basketball player, even this early in the school year. His goal in life at this moment was to be All-State.

Esme found her son's bulging duffel already at the top of the stairs. "I suppose you have your own questions?" she asked him.

"Not really," he replied. "Except maybe, what would it take to get you and Dad back together again?"

Esme suppressed a sigh. She had raised the kids to be intelligent, independent thinkers—a mixed blessing, she was discovering. "For one thing we'd have to get past this crisis first. Then your father would have to stand on his own two feet and hold down a decent job, free and clear of Uncle Rai's influence. Now come here you two." Esme took both children in her arms, and all of them embraced in a hug of warmth and hope. "We might need your help to make it work," she added. "Frank, take my two suitcases downstairs, okay?"

In the living room the kids hugged their father, then Manny helped load the car, and they all piled in. No one spoke during the twenty-minute drive. The atmosphere was heavy with apprehension. As they pulled up in front of the guest house to unload their belongings, Lottie and Rai came from the main residence to welcome them. Rai explained that they would have exclusive use of the two-bedroom guest house, with two queen-size beds in each bedroom. "You'll have complete privacy, and at the same time, protection. My trusted soldiers are dormitoried in the gray two-story house close by. If you need anything, Domo's next door. And I'm usually here. Just ask."

Lottie brought fresh linens inside the clean and orderly guest house. Esme and Delores began making the beds. Before Manny had a chance to put in his two cents' worth, Esme threw him a curve. She decided that he and Frank should share a room. She also decided that Delores would bunk with her. A startled Manny shook his head in disappointment.

"But..." Delores started to object.

"It's only temporary," said Esme, quickly squelching her daughter's complaint before it evolved.

Lottie watched and listened. *I see the seeds of dissent in the child's face. Maybe I can throw a little fuel on the youngster's fire.* "Delores, there's a vacant bedroom in the main residence next to Nina's if you wish a room to yourself."

"I...uh, better not," said Delores, seeing her mother's stormy scowl.

"Okay, then," Lottie said with a half-smile, half-smirk. "Make yourselves comfortable." She headed back to the residence kitchen, where she needed to give last-minute menu instructions to the chef.

Chapter 28

Unfinished Business

THE PORTFIA breakfasts were not exactly typical. The daily buffets set up on the lanai of the main residence were prepared by a full-time chef and two undercooks. Those in the guest house and the employee residences would normally take their food back to their own quarters. The immediate family ate in the formal dining room. Despite Rai's late-night vigil for Salvadore's safety, he had risen early that morning and now he simply wanted to enjoy some quiet time alone with his newspapers in the dining room.

Noah slept deeply in a first-floor bedroom behind the kitchen, and awoke to the clattering and clanging of breakfast preparations. He swung out of bed and looked for his clothes. The filthy, ripe clothes he'd worn for the past several days were gone. How was he going to explain to Kekoa that the clothes his uncle had lent him had been thrown out? Well, he'd worry about that another time. He found fresh clothes from one of Rai's sons neatly laid out on a leather bench at the foot of the bed: a polo shirt, nearly new cargo shorts, briefs, and even designer socks. He showered and dressed, then headed into the kitchen.

"Oh, nooo," said one of the cooks, smiling. "You go dining room, eat wi fam'ly."

Noah would have preferred the friendly kitchen, but he made his way down the long hallway, amazed by the sheer number of paintings: landscapes, seascapes, and portraits in carved gold frames lining the walls. There were polished koa doors, too, mostly shut, along the way. The hallway ended in the grand dining room with its floor-to-ceiling windows and Rai at the table with his back to him.

"Come on in, young man," Rai said, sensing his presence. "There's food out there on the lanai."

"Good morning, sir, thank you."

Returning with a full plate, Noah found the dining room intimidating, especially the white tablecloth edged in ivory embroidery. *What if I spill something?* He chose an upholstered chair near the opposite end of the long table and was about to put his plate down, when Rai shook his head.

"No, down here where I can see you."

Noah moved closer, deciding to put at least one chair between them as a buffer.

"Ah, much better" said Rai. "Noah, isn't it? Now we can talk."

"Yes, sir. What about?"

"Later this afternoon we will get some legal advice that hopefully will get you and my daughter out of the royal can of worms you two made for yourselves."

"I'm grateful for all that you're doing for us, Mr. Rai."

"And I'm grateful to you—that is, for your looking out for Nina, taking the so-called fall for her."

"It wasn't her fight. Nina shouldn't have to take the blame for defending me."

"You're absolutely right," said Rai. "You're a brave young man with heroic ideals. I appreciate that you chose to hide from the cops rather than betray my daughter. It's been a hardship for you, no doubt. However, I don't like the fact that it's drawing undue attention from the law. I have business interests to protect."

"I don't like being on the run from the police either. Being here is much nicer, but—" Noah hesitated. He didn't want to rock the boat with this man; the conversation was almost too pleasant, and besides, he had a problem. "Mr. Rai, my dad is getting a lawyer for me. And I really need to call my folks. They have no idea where I am."

"We'll work on it," Rai said evasively. "While we're at it, I have a favor to ask of you."

"Yes, sir, anything!"

"Last night you mentioned that you knew the whereabouts of Wen Tse Fong and some of his associates."

"Uh, yeah."

"Would you be willing to tell me where I can find them?"

Noah felt chicken skin growing on his forearms. "That would depend on what you'd do with that information. You'd have them eliminated, wouldn't you?"

Rai was taken aback by the sophistication of the reply—a street-smart wisdom unusual in a kid so young. A frown merged his thick eyebrows, turning them into one bushy, black caterpillar. "You're saying you're feeling some kind of loyalty to these people for sheltering you and paying you wages. I can understand that, but let me tell you, these men are bad. Worse than bad. They've already killed one of my best men. And they've also tried to kill my brother, Nina's uncle. The police are looking for them regarding other crimes. You needn't be so loyal to that kind of trash."

Noah gobbled up a few forkfuls of egg and a bite of sausage while he waited for Rai to finish. But he had to press his point. "I can understand your wanting revenge, sir, but it wouldn't feel right for me to be contributing to their deaths. That would make me a murderer too. I now know what they do and what they're capable of, so it's not a sense of loyalty I feel. It's what I think is right. I'd sooner turn them over to the authorities, but the police are out there looking for me too."

Just then Nina sailed into the room, barefoot, wearing a tank top and miniskirt. Balancing a plate of waffles and syrup, she leaned over and grazed her father's forehead in an almost-air kiss. Pointedly, she took the empty chair between them. "Good morning, you two grumpies." Her soprano voice vibrated with false cheeriness.

"Good morning, daughter," Rai said. "Noah, we'll talk later. I'm sure you'll come around to my way of thinking." He picked up his newspaper again and seemed to be reading in earnest.

Noah snapped back, "I don't think so, sir." He was surprised by his own outright defiance, and even more when Nina's hand draped over his at the table.

A gutteral, near-animal sound emanated from behind the raised newspaper, perhaps Rai clearing his throat. Noah wasn't sure, but Nina suddenly pulled her hand back. She knew perfectly well what it meant.

* * * *

Cindy Benfield-Rice combed through her purse for the key to their real estate building, and unlocked the glass downstairs door with its wrought-iron anti-burglary bars. As she stepped inside and turned to close the heavy door again, her eyes locked onto a slight male figure leaving the doorway across the street. A Panama hat, pulled down, obscured much of the man's profile, but she felt compelled to watch him proceed to the corner. Just before he reached that intersection, he turned his head and tilted his hat up to see if anyone had followed him. "It's him!" she said aloud. "Wen Tse Fong!"

Cindy stumbled twice while hurrying up the stairs to her office. At the top she glanced at her watch—eight-thirty. Her clients were scheduled to be there at nine to sign leases in a new high-rise office building. There was still time to call Gert. She dropped her purse and keys in the middle of her desk, flipped her cell phone open, and speed-dialed her friend.

"Hey, Cindy, what's up?"

"Are you interested in knowing where Wen Tse Fong has been staying?"

"You bet, girl," replied Gert.

"There's an upstairs apartment directly across the street from our office. I saw him coming out of the building not five minutes ago. He walked to the corner toward Maunakea. There's no question that it's Wen. A few days ago I thought I saw him in the window there, but I couldn't be certain. I sent Coland over to check—on the pretext of selling him some insurance, but he'd never seen Wen before so he couldn't be sure. Anyway, I think he's

261

living there."

"I can't believe Wen would hole up so close to where he hustled you and Coland and then tried to shoot you, girl."

"I guess he figured to hide right under our noses where you wouldn't think to look for him," replied Cindy.

"I'll get an unmarked car over there to keep an eye on that front door."

"Maybe you'll get the bastard this time."

"By the way, Cindy, I hope Coland's recovering well. It's a good thing you told me the hit-and-run was intentional. Attempted murder puts that case in my hands too. I talked with the first-responding officers and got a list of the witnesses and their statements. Between them I got a fair description of the driver. Zeke Young has done time for being a robbery wheelman and he's a suspected hit man, although we've never gotten a conviction. He's also a known associate of Wen Tse Fong."

"So why haven't you picked him up already?" asked Cindy.

"I'm afraid that he's also gone into hiding, but there's a fleabag hotel we're keeping an eye on."

"Good. I've got to go now, Gert," said Cindy. "I hear my nine o'clock coming up the stairs."

* * * *

At precisely three o'clock that afternoon, a late-model Mercedes coupe pulled up to the Portfia mansion. Two men got out of the car. Rai was on the lanai to welcome them. Attorney Alonzo Paxton was a short man with thinning hair swept to one side in an obvious attempt to cover up baldness. He wore a business suit, white shirt and tie, wing-tip shoes, and a gold tie clasp with a diamond in it. Alonzo served as Rai's full-time attorney, specializing in both criminal and business law. They shook hands in a brotherly manner.

The other man introduced himself. "I'm Kurt Kenoi. I was hired by Alex Wong to represent his son, Noah Wong." They followed Rai down the hall and into his paneled office. At the far end, he ushered them to be seated at an oval cherry wood table that served for conference meetings.

Alonzo skipped the small talk. "Kurt is an excellent criminal defense attorney," he told Rai. "Alex Wong made a wise decision hiring him. Kurt and I agree that the children need separate representation. They could wind up with opposing legal interests, but I don't think it will fall out that way. I certainly hope not."

Rai listened closely, "I sent for the kids as soon as I saw you pull up. They should be here any minute."

They heard a light rapping at the door. Nina softly stepped in. At her mother's insistence, she wore a demure long-sleeved beige blouse and matching pants.

"Sweetheart, we're over here. Gentlemen, this is my daughter, Nina Elena Portfia. Sweetheart, where's Noah?"

"I don't know for sure, Daddy. I think he left the compound."

"Why would he do that?" Anger lines spread out from the corners of Rai's mouth. "He told me this morning that he was happy to be here."

Nina's composure crumpled. "It may have been something you said, Daddy. I mean, something you asked of him. He was quite upset at the breakfast table. He worried that you were going to force him to do whatever it was you wanted."

"I just wanted a little information. I can't imagine why he's so upset." Rai lied easily.

"Shall we go on without the boy's presence?" asked Alonzo.

"Yes," declared Kurt. "I think I know enough of what happened from what Noah's family imparted to me. We met on Wednesday in Kaimuki."

"Good. Nina, dear, Come sit next to me. This is Mr. Alonzo Paxton. I've hired him as your attorney. And Mr. Kurt Kenoi here is Noah's. Suppose you tell us what you can about the shooting."

With her right hand, Nina brushed her long hair away from her face, a delaying tactic she often used when confronted with something unpleasant. She quietly told all the preliminaries about the non-date at the movies. "My friends went into Dave and Buster's for something to eat. I didn't feel very well. Noah said he'd take a walk with me around the block, but…uh…we walked a couple blocks farther, on Queen Street. We both kept hearing, like, shuffling noises behind us. When we got in front of a car repair place, we decided to go back, but this big guy jumped out of the shadows. Noah yelled, 'Duke, get away from us!' but when this Duke guy came at Noah, he yelled at me to run away or he'd hurt me too. Noah shouted at me to go and find the others." Nina paused. Her belly spasmed; she wished she hadn't eaten so many waffles at breakfast. It was scary, these three men staring at her, silently sucking in every word she said.

"I was frozen in my shoes. All I could do was stand clear and watch them fight. When they were on the ground, Duke fought his way on top and started punching Noah over and over again. His face jerked from side to side and was bloody. I was so scared he was going to kill him. I looked down at the ground and I saw this gun, so I picked it up. I tried to aim it over Duke's head to frighten him off. I had no intention of hurting anyone. How could I know he was going to rise up at that very moment? I pulled the trigger and Duke collapsed on top of Noah. I…I don't remember anything after that."

"Nina, didn't you have to take the safety off the gun?" asked Alonzo.

Kurt held up one hand, his palm facing the others. "Excuse me, but I must interject something important here. When I met with the Wong family on Wednesday, Lieutenant Gert Mahaila of HPD Homicide joined us. She shared information she'd just received: the Dante Santos autopsy report. The bullet lodged in the victim's neck was a .38-caliber. What was left of the rifling indicated that it may have been from a revolver. And to be clear, there's no safety on revolvers. Oh, and one more thing: the boy's uncle informed me that it was Santos's gun—a good indication that he came with intent to kill Noah."

"Most likely, Kurt," said Alonzo. "Nina, have you ever fired a gun before, maybe at a carnival or a shooting range?"

"No way! I'm afraid of guns."

"One more question. Why did you fire in Duke's direction?"

"I wanted him to stop. I told you—I was afraid he would kill Noah."

Alonzo turned to Kurt. "How does this stack up with what you learned from the boy's family?"

"The two stories line up pretty well," said Kurt. "If the two of us were to go to the State's Attorney's office and plead together, I'm pretty confident this case will never go to trial."

"What about Lt. Mahaila?" asked Rai. "She wants to depose Nina, and I've been putting her off, saying she's sick."

"I believe the lieutenant will be sympathetic," said Kurt. "She seemed to be when we met on Wednesday with the Wongs. In fact, I understand she has some connection or other to the family."

"Then I think we're done here for now," said Alonzo. "But I do want to be present whenever the lieutenant deposes Nina. In fact, I'll set it up myself. You'll need to be there too, Rai."

"Of course," he said.

They all rose from the table, and Rai led the two men to the front door. Reluctantly, Nina tagged along. On the lanai, Rai put his arm solidly around her shoulders and together they watched the two lawyers climb into the Mercedes and drive off.

Nina took a deep breath, wriggled out of her father's grasp, and faced him. "Daddy, what did you ask Noah to do?"

"I didn't ask him to *do* anything. I merely asked him for the address where he was staying before he came here."

"And why would that upset him?"

"Perhaps it was because he was staying with some business rivals of mine."

"Perhaps? Daddy, I know when you're fudging. You mean some business rivals you'd like to be rid of?"

"Well, yes, but it's not quite that simple, sweetheart."

"Daddy, you swore to me that you don't kill people."

"But I don't."

"So you have one of Domo's soldiers do it for you. It's the same thing."

"I only want to halt more killing. Those thugs have already killed one of my men—and, I'll have you know, they tried to kill your Uncle Manny too. They have got to be stopped."

"Daddy, all of it has to stop, but only *you* can do that."

"Honey, I've got a major business to run. A lot of people depend on me and my leadership." Rai despised arguments with any family member, and his daughter had just stepped over the line. His narrow face turned dark. "Nina, you're beginning to sound like that boyfriend of yours—the boyfriend you have no business having in the first place. If you had obeyed me and not lied to me about your so-called casual friends just going to the movies, none of this would have happened."

"Oh, Daddy, you're impossible," Nina shrieked. She stomped off to her room in tears.

* * * *

With the advent of the cell phone and all its smart relatives, the public telephone booth was rapidly becoming a dinosaur. Only a few were left in Chinatown and Noah had trouble finding even one of them after several hours of looking. He'd ridden a bus from the Portfia compound back to Chinatown, but he feared he'd become a little too well-known there. He finally found a bright orange phone booth emblazoned with red, green, and white dragons. The booth had been strategically placed for the tourist trade. He punched in a familiar number, but not the one he really wanted. Calling his parents would be far too emotional, and he might not accomplish what needed to be done.

"Osaka Family Bakery," answered Maria. "How may I help you?"

"It's Noah, Auntie. Can I talk to Uncle Kekoa?"

"Noah!" she cried. "Honey, where are you? Are you okay? Your parents are worried sick."

"Please, Auntie, can I speak with him?"

"Sure, honey." The phone went silent for several minutes.

"Hello, Noah, you okay, son?" asked Kekoa.

"Yeah, I'm fine, but I need to talk with you."

"I'm listening."

"I'm running out of ideas of what to do and I don't know where else I can hide."

"It's time to turn yourself in," said Kekoa. "Where are you now?"

"In Chinatown. The problem is too many of the wrong people know I'm here and are looking for me."

"I thought you might wind up there. If you tell me exactly where you are, I'll come get you and bring you home."

"What about the police?"

"The police won't be a problem if you don't resist them. Your father has engaged a highly respected criminal lawyer. Your parents and I had a meeting with him. Everyone agrees that the worst crime you've committed is evidence tampering."

"What about the murder charge?" asked Noah.

"You didn't fire the gun, did you?"

"No! I told you I didn't. But I won't testify that Nina shot Duke. No way, Uncle."

"Noah, listen to me. Nina has already admitted to the shooting. They're calling it accidental homicide, or at the very least, justifiable homicide. No jail time involved."

"How do you know that?"

"Your father is keeping me in the loop."

"I still won't testify that she shot Duke."

"Again, I ask you to listen to me. Perhaps you'll reconsider when you hear what both of your attorneys agreed on at a meeting this morning."

"What's that, Uncle Kekoa?"

"They're going to plead both cases to the State's Attorney. They believe that the case will never go to trial—although there may be some judgments involved."

"Judgments?" Noah's voice trembled. "What does that

mean?"

"It means something other than jail time," said Kekoa. "Now give me an address where I can pick you up. I'll leave in five minutes."

"I'll be on the *makai* side of King Street at Maunakea in fifteen minutes. Don't take too long. Two men may be out there looking for me."

"You mean the police?" asked Kekoa.

"No, two gangsters, Wen Tse Fong and his sidekick, Zeke."

"Why would they be looking for you?"

"I left them kind of suddenly, so they may think I'm double-crossing them. I'll tell you more when I see you."

Chapter 29

Contested Loyalty

NOAH HAD plenty of time to walk the three short blocks to the designated pickup corner. At the first intersection, while waiting with a dozen other walkers for the traffic light, he glanced across to the other side. Zeke Young stood on the opposite curb, facing him. They were likely to meet head-on in the middle of the street. Noah panicked. *I wonder if he sees me. I can't risk a run-in with him now that I'm heading home and nearly out of this whole mess. What can I do?*

The light changed to green. The crowd pressed forward to cross. Noah resisted the momentum. He wheeled about and hurried back, dodging pedestrians coming at him and edging in front of those heading the same way. With each purposeful shift and dodge, the boy felt he was extending the distance away from Zeke. *Is it possible he's really not following me? Maybe he didn't even notice me.* Noah glanced over his shoulder to check out this notion. No, he's not there. In that moment of carelessness, he ran smack into the arms of an oncoming pedestrian. Not just any pedestrian— Wen Tse Fong, with a humorless smile fixed in stone.

"Ah, kid, I've been looking all over for you," said Wen, nimbly half-turning so he faced the same direction as Noah. He locked his bony fingers around the boy's bare left forearm and pushed him forward until they reached the sidewalk. "Where have you been?"

"Uh…nowhere, Wen." Noah lurched desperately to his right, wriggling sharply to release his arm from Wen's grip. Instead, the boy felt Wen's hand tightening, with his fingernails cutting into the boy's flesh.

"You weren't planning to desert me after I gave you a home and all those meals, were you?"

"Of course not, Wen. The cops are already looking for me. I just didn't want to get into deeper trouble."

Noah was uncertain whether his lame answer would do, so he marshaled his strength and wrested free, but only to feel the tip of a knife blade in the small of his back. A disturbing warm breath blew across his neck from behind. Zeke had caught up with them.

"Relax, kid, an' ya won't git hurt, yah," said Zeke.

"You weren't think of turning us in to the cops, were you?" said Wen, grinning like a toothpaste ad.

"I wouldn't do that. The cops are looking for me too. They'd have me locked up already, and I wouldn't be out here on the street with you. Why would I do a thing like that?"

"Maybe t' save your own butt wi' da cops," answered Zeke, with a devilish smirk on his fat face.

"No! No, no. You treated me decently. I wouldn't turn you guys in."

"We're drawing too much attention out here," Wen said. "Let's take him back to the apartment. We'll deal with him there."

Zeke withdrew the knife, pocketed it, and placed his hand on the boy's shoulder as if they were pals. The trio walked the several blocks back toward the apartment. As they reached the last corner, Zeke stopped short.

"Hey, boss, that's a different car out front. And they ain't Rai's boys. More da kine cops, yah."

"Can we go around and get in through the back door?" said Wen.

"Across da fire escapes," said Zeke. "Come on, this way, yah."

Instead of turning onto their usual street, Zeke led them around the corner. He halted at an alley he intended to enter, but a high wood fence, splashed with graffiti, denied them access. He hustled past an abandoned storefront streaked with soot from a long-ago fire. At the front of the second building in from the corner, they came to a steel door. The deadbolt had a broken-off key in it, but Zeke seemed to know in advance that the door would swing open freely anyway.

With a sinking feeling, Noah realized that Zeke made it his craft to know every escape route in Chinatown, and that's why the thug always wore solid-black T-shirts and cargo pants: the dirtbag usually came prepared for sneaking around.

They trudged up the worn, splintered stairs to the second floor. Zeke opened a fire door to a long hall that led to the rear of the ell-shaped apartment house. At the end of the ell, he raised a window and stepped out onto a rusty fire escape. Through the early shadows of nightfall, Noah stared at the flimsy rails. Would they hold his weight? Zeke slung his bare, tattooed legs over the hand rail and stretched across a three-foot separation to a second fire escape, on the adjacent building. Noah peered down. The two retracting fire escape ladders merely led to the ground floor—and entrapment in a no-way-out space littered with garbage. Two rats darted among orange peels and Styrofoam fast-food boxes. A panicky thought struck Noah. Were they planning to kill him down there?

Apparently not. With an unfriendly shove from Wen, he stumbled along behind Zeke. They followed his lead through the unlocked rear door of Wen's commandeered apartment.

"Wait!" cried Wen. "Don't turn on the light. The cops'll be able to see it from the street."

"Sure, boss, we can go in da bedroom an' shut the door and turn on the light."

"Good idea, Zeke."

"What do you want from me, guys?" asked Noah. "I didn't do anything to you."

"You turned us in to da cops, that's what you did. We saw 'em down there. Now you pay for it," Zeke grunted.

"That's right, kid," said Wen. "If you didn't tell them where I'm holed up, who did?"

"I swear I didn't tell anybody where you are," claimed

Noah.

"Then where did you stay last night?"

"I slept in a doorway down the street," Noah replied quickly.

"Yer lyin," said Zeke.

"Zeke's right. Why are you lying to us?" asked Wen.

"Because if I told you the truth, you wouldn't believe that either."

"Try me," said Wen.

"I spent the night at my girlfriend's house in a real bed with clean sheets. In case you haven't noticed, I've got clean shorts and a different shirt on."

"Must be big girl to wear *da kine* shorts, yah?" Zeke laughed. "Right, boss?"

"These clothes belong to her brother, stupid," said Noah. Before he could catch himself, he felt sausage fingers reach up and crawl around his neck.

Zeke bared his yellow teeth and said, "You shut yer mouth or yer dead meat." His eyes looked as though they'd leap from their sockets. Ten powerful fingers squeezed and released, pulsing like a wild beast poised for the meal after the kill.

Noah tried to pry the slimy fingers off his throat. When that failed, he threw a round-house punch to the gut with his left fist. Zeke doubled over with a loud "Ooof." Leading with a flexed heel, Noah followed through with a kick to the groin. It sent Zeke through the flimsy bedroom door, blasting it off its hinges.

The bedroom's ceiling fixture cast its forty-watt beam into the living room, just enough to expose the whereabouts of someone inside. Wen switched it off. "The nightlight in the bathroom will have to do," he muttered.

Zeke lay writhing on the threadbare carpet. Noah's broad chest swelled imperceptibly with pride at his own strength and skill, but the victory didn't last long. He found Wen's weasel eyes boring into him—and a weapon in his hand, trained on his belly. Noah guessed it was a semiautomatic pistol—too dangerous to defy him.

Zeke crawled to his feet. "I'll keel da little bastard."

"Enough, the two of you," commanded Wen. "Zeke, you can get even another time. Right now I need you to go up on the roof and keep an eye on that car across the street. I'm hoping they didn't see the light from the bedroom. Take the new sniper rifle with you just in case. It's in the closet. Kid, sit down on the bed until I tell you to get up."

Still sore from the kick to his groin, Zeke, with the sniper rifle slung over his shoulder, dragged himself out the back door and up the fire escape to a vantage point on the roof.

* * * *

"Homicide, Lt. Mahaila."

"Lieutenant, it's Kekoa. I got a call from Noah a little over two hours ago. He wanted me to pick him up, but when I got to the designated meeting place in Chinatown, he wasn't there."

"You think he changed his mind?" asked Gert.

"No, I'm pretty sure I convinced him to turn himself in. He's worked for me for months and he trusts me. Something's happened, preventing him from being there. I just know he's in trouble. He did say someone by the name of Wen and someone else were out looking for him, and he had to be careful."

"Wen? Not Wen Tse Fong?" asked Gert.

"Yeah, I think that's the name he mentioned," said Kekoa.

"Where are you now?" she asked.

"I'm in Chinatown," replied Kekoa. "I just pulled over to the curb. I've been circling the streets here up to now. Where are you?"

"Not far from you, but I can't respond right now. Stay where you are. I need to deal with some urgent police business first. We have some action at one of our police stakeouts, and I'm waiting for backup before we go in. I'll give you a call when this is all over."

"Good luck," said Kekoa, but Gert had already clicked off.

* * * *

Lt. Mahaila folded her cell phone and stuck it in the breast pocket of her short-sleeved blue shirt. She waited in her parked vehicle, and several minutes later, a tall armored panel truck with Honolulu Police Department markings passed her. Gert reached out the driver's window and placed a flashing bubble light on the crown of her unmarked cruiser. She pulled out of her parking space and stopped diagonally in the middle of the one-way street, intentionally blocking the flow of all traffic. She exited the cruiser and removed a shotgun and bullhorn from her trunk, then trotted quickly down the street to the unmarked car opposite the apartment. She slipped into the rear seat.

"What's the status?" she asked the plainclothes officer in the front passenger seat.

"We haven't seen anyone go in or come out, but we know somebody's up there. We just don't know whether it's Wen or not," he said. "We saw a light go on briefly in the apartment."

"Is there a back door?" she asked. "Anybody check it out?"

"The back door leads to a fire escape, but that only leads to a boarded-up alley," he replied. "He'd only be trapped inside."

"Can it be breached?" she tried again.

"It's pretty damned high, and there's barbed wire on top of the fence. I'd say not very likely."

Gert left the unmarked car and moved toward the armored panel truck. Police in helmets and body armor were being rapidly deployed to their tactical positions. They also erected a pair of spotlights. Big mistake. As soon as they were turned on, two crisp shots smashed into both of them, causing most everyone to leap for cover. The rest dropped to the ground and crawled to safety to keep from being the next target.

"He's got a weapon," yelled one voice.

"No shit," yelled a second voice.

"Those shots came from the roof over the apartment," yelled yet another voice.

"Where the hell is that damn negotiator?" Gert said to the officer next to her. She laid her shotgun against the fender of the panel truck and leaned across the hood.

"How the hell should I know, Lieutenant," he replied.

Gert gave him a nasty look, then put the bullhorn to her lips. "Wen Tse Fong, we don't want to hurt you. Put down your weapon and come out with your hands high where we can plainly see them. We have you surrounded and outnumbered twenty to one."

A light came on in an herbal medicines shop behind the officers. The innocent light was the oblivious proprietor opening for business. More shots came from the rooftop across the street. Though one was a near-miss, the second shot found its mark in an upper arm. The injured officer grabbed his arm and sank down to the sidewalk until aid arrived. A third shot smashed through the herb shop window. The light inside was quickly doused.

"Officer down," someone cried.

"Responding," another replied.

The sergeant in charge of the roof snipers knelt down and spoke into his tactical radiophone. "Do you have a clear view of the shooter?"

They heard a burst of static and then a response. "We have at least three clean shots at a small view of the target on the roof across from us. We've seen it move through our night lenses and have seen gun flashes from the approximate area. Do we have a green light?"

The leader of the tactical team looked over at Gert for approval. She nodded. Once more he spoke into his radiophone. "That's a go."

It didn't sound like three individual shots. It sounded more like one deafening shot. The lump of shadow across the way jerked up for an instant, then slid from view altogether.

"Report!" commanded the tactical officer.

Another blast of static and they heard: "Three confirmed head shots, more than likely a kill, sir. No visible after-movement."

"Well, that's over with," said the tactical commander. "I suppose it could have been a lot worse."

Just as he started to stand tall, his radio phone told him otherwise. "I have movement inside the apartment. One, no, maybe two persons inside." A burst of static. "Confirm second person. Unable to identify either party. We have a shot at one of them, but because of the window glass, there's room for error. Do we take the shot?" Once again the tactical commander, a sergeant, turned to the lieutenant for clearance.

"No," said Gert. "The man on the roof was most likely Fong's henchman, Zeke Young, a for-hire assassin, an expert with a sniping rifle. If Young survived the hit on the roof, he could be the second person they spotted. On the other hand, it could be a hostage."

"Why a hostage?" challenged the sergeant. "The man on the roof is most likely dead. My men are excellent shots. Couldn't it be another Fong henchman?"

"The problem is, we can't be sure. I have intelligence that leads me to believe the third person is a hostage, a youngster named Noah Wong. Somehow, the boy's mixed it up really bad with Wen Tse Fong's bunch. Fong was out looking for him with a vengeance. Now we know for sure the boy's missing. That information was reported to me less than an hour ago."

"If the window shot isn't a go, do we try a frontal assault up the front steps?" The sergeant was getting antsy. "Tear gas and all?"

"Probably, but hold off for now," said Gert. "Put a couple of armed men around the corner to be sure there's no way out on the back street. Right now I'd like to try contacting him again."

Another officer handed her a scrap of paper with a telephone number on it. "Good, just what I need. Thanks."

Gert put the bullhorn to her lips once again. "Wen Tse Fong, we don't want to see you or anyone else get hurt. Let the Wong boy go free, and we'll take that into account. Put down your weapons and come out of there with your hands high where we can plainly see them. I repeat, we don't want anyone else to be harmed." She waited a few minutes and spoke again. "I'm going to dial a telephone number for your apartment now. When it rings, please pick up. I'd like to talk with you, Wen. Obviously, there's something you want from us. Maybe food or a drink or even some talk. Let's hear about it. Maybe we can end all of this amicably, so pick up." She put down the bullhorn. Then she removed the cell phone from her breast pocket and punched in the numbers she read from the paper scrap. Endless ringing, but no one picked up. She terminated the call, waited a few more minutes, and then punched the redial, with the same result.

She hung up the second time and turned back to the sergeant. "Give me ten minutes more. I want to be sure. If Fong still leaves us no options, try the frontal assault, but remember, no shooting unless he threatens the boy or any of your men. In fact, if he threatens at all, back the hell out of there. We don't need any more casualties."

Chapter 30

Uncovered

SUDDENLY, bullhorn messages resounded, loud and clear. Wen listened to the first one with disdain, but his gun hand twitched and lowered slightly. Noah sensed his vulnerability and thought of making a move on his captor while he was still distracted. But he knew Wen had quick reflexes, and the bullhorn message proved too short for him to try. By the time Gert's second, longer message reverberated, Wen had already made up his mind to try an escape. He trained the gun directly on Noah with renewed purpose.

"Okay, kid, get ready. We're gonna back out of this joint the same way we came in, through the rear door." He issued the order in such a loud, gravelly voice that they both missed hearing the part of the message that a phone call was coming.

Noah was rattled. "You can't leave. The place is surrounded. They told you it was."

"You can't believe everything the cops say," snapped Wen. "They can't know our escape route. Besides, that other building offers me a lot more options than this one." He pressed the muzzle of the gun in the boy's back. The phone rang in the front room. It rang again and continued to ring.

"You gonna answer it?" the boy asked.

"Hell, no," Wen said. "I put one foot in that room and I'm a dead man. Shit! Look at all them red dots moving around the walls. They're searching for nobody but me. We're getting the hell out of here, now!" Wen placed his hand on the rear door knob.

"You go out first, kid, and make sure nobody's out there.

Be sure to check the roofs and the fence over at the street." The phone continued to ring.

Noah cautiously stepped out onto the fire escape and honestly answered, "I don't see or hear anything." His body turned cold with fear. *Damn! Wen's setting me up, a bull's-eye target. What if they shoot me by mistake or even for real? Maybe the cops still think I'm a murderer.*

"Any little red dots running around out there?" asked Wen, edging slowly out the door, tailgating closely behind the boy, using him as a shield.

Noah scanned once more, then thought to check his own chest—nothing there. "Nothing." He lifted one muscled leg over the rail onto the narrow ledge, then the other. Holding onto the near side rail with one hand, the boy reached for and clung on to the opposite rail. He stretched his first leg across the three-foot span and wedged his sneaker toe securely between the vertical bars on the opposite side. He transferred the second hand to the opposite side. As he brought his second leg across, Noah's mind suddenly filled with a flash of hope. The transfer from rail-to-rail could be the same for Wen, but with one exception. The boy sized up the situation and waited for his opportunity.

Wen was shorter than Noah, skinny, and not at all that athletic. He would have to stretch much farther, with his shorter arms, to reach across the three-foot gap while wedging his sandals between the vertical bars on the opposite side. Noah's heart quickened as he observed that Wen didn't have the foresight to tuck the gun in his belt or pocket. Having to maintain his finger on the gun's trigger would only complicate matters. While Wen reached across with his right hand, he needed to grab the second rail and still hold onto the weapon; he had to divide his fingers between the two grips.

Not very likely, Noah thought. The boy extended his arm as if he wanted to help. He knew his captor had to lean forward and release his left hand from behind himself just as he reached out. When his captor did so, Noah swung his open arm and slammed it into Wen's outstretched arm, knocking it away from the second rail, preventing him from ever reaching the opposite side.

Caught in mid-air, there was no place for him to go but down. The gun fell out of Wen's hand as he wildly grasped for open space. His elongated scream echoed in the silence between the two buildings. He fell the one-story distance as a dead weight, smacking the back of his head squarely on a chain-link fence that surrounded a sump-pump installation attached to the building next door. Unconscious, Wen slipped out of sight another six feet below-ground into the sump-pump reservoir and nearly a foot of standing residue water.

Noah didn't wait to see, nor did he care, what happened to Wen. He raised the window to the hall and stepped on through. Once inside, he decided to close and lock the window and draw the curtain across it. He wasn't sure why he did this. Perhaps it was to symbolically shut out the life-threatening drama from which he had just escaped. Once more, he had another person's death on his conscience, even if it was done to save his own life. The boy turned and ran through the long ell-shaped hallway, then scrambled down the stairs to the street.

The front door to the apartment house represented real freedom. He bounded through the steel door like a missile. The second his two feet landed, his arms were grabbed from both sides, and he was forced to lie flat on his stomach on the concrete side-walk. He felt his wrists being strapped together behind him and his body being searched from neck to ankles. *Oh no,* he thought. *Nina's father's guys again, out of the frying pan and back into the fire. Maybe I shouldn't have run away from the compound. He must be pissed at me for leaving.*

But when the two men in black lifted Noah to his feet and he saw the word "POLICE" written in white across their body armor, he relaxed. *I'm tired of running. Besides, Uncle Kekoa said I should turn myself in.*

"Is there anyone else inside?" asked one officer, looking him straight in the eye.

"I can't tell you about the rest of this building, but Zeke Young is on the roof, and Wen Tse Fong fell off the fire escape into some kind of hole below. I don't know if he's alive or dead."

"Does he have a gun with him?" asked the officer.

"He did have," said the boy. "He may have lost it during the fall."

"How do I find him?"

Noah described the way back to the fire escape and how to get down to the ground level. One officer remained behind to guard the building entrance. The second officer pulled back the steel door and disappeared behind it.

"What's your name, kid?" asked the remaining officer.

"Noah, Noah Wong."

The officer spoke into his shoulder mike. "Lieutenant: The boy is safe. Young is on the roof and we have reason to believe Wen is dead from a fall."

"I just gave the order for a frontal assault," returned Gert after a burst of static. "Hang on to the boy until I get an all-clear from the assault team."

* * * *

Four men in full armor, two with clear face protectors, and two more with gas masks, a battering ram, and a four-foot standing shield started up the staircase. At the top of the stairs, they broke the door in. They saw no one in the front room. Under cover of the shield, two canisters of tear gas were tossed deep into the small bedroom. The tiny kitchen and bathroom looked empty. The two men in gas masks checked out all the rooms and both closets as well—no sign of anyone. They checked out the back door and saw no activity there or in the long dead-ended alley to the street either.

Two of the men with armor climbed the fire escape to the roof level and continued their search there. Behind the front edge of the roof, hidden from the street by a twelve-inch-high brick ledge, they found the bloodied body of Zeke Young with three entry wounds closely spaced in the middle of his forehead. His right arm was still wrapped around a sniper rifle equipped with telescopic sights. Both men, overheated, removed their helmets. One kicked the rifle out of the dead man's reach and then stepped closer to pick it up. On their way down, one of them straddled the space across to the adjacent fire escape and tried the window to the hall. It was not only closed, but locked from the inside. Shining a flashlight down into the pit below he saw a figure lying there with his face in the water. He continued down the moving ladder to the ground level and entered the chain-link fence via a gate. He assumed the body was Wen Tse Fong's.

When each of the assault team leaders relayed the all-clear back to Gert, she asked that the boy be brought to her. An officer escorted him around the corner, across the street, and over to the unmarked car. As they got nearer, he saw a familiar figure step out from behind the car and walk toward him.

"Noah? Noah Wong, I hardly recognize you. You've gotten so tall," said Gert. "Say, weren't you Wen Tse Fong's hostage inside the apartment?"

"Yes, ma'am."

"So how did you get away?" she asked.

"I blocked him from getting across the two fire escapes," said Noah. "And...and he fell into some kind of hole in the ground. He screamed once, but I didn't hear him after that."

The escorting officer intervened. "The boy has already told us how to find him. We're uncertain of his current condition and whether he's still a threat, but he's trapped below the fire escapes out back."

"I already have confirmation of his death. I'm just waiting for the details."

Noah continued to explain to Gert how he managed to escape from Wen and what the connection with him had been in the first place.

"Can't you take these off?" he asked, twisting his body half-around so she could see the plastic cuffs cutting into his wrists.

"Are you through running away?"

"You bet, Lieutenant."

"There's still a BOLO out on you, young man," said Gert. "I would be breaking the rules if I took the restraints off altogether, but I can re-cuff you up front, and you'll be far more comfortable." As she re-cuffed him, she also read him his Miranda rights. "Now that you're officially arrested, I can give your Uncle Kekoa a heads-up and your parents as well."

Gert allowed Noah to sit down on the rear running board of the armored panel truck to wait for one more team report. The officer had just left the building and was crossing the street as she finished speaking to the boy.

"Lieutenant? We found the bastard at the bottom of a sump reservoir with his head in the drink. His head was twisted like his neck had been broken. We couldn't determine whether he died from the broken neck or drowning."

"Thank you, good job. The important thing is that the gangster is dead," said Gert. "His death saves the state the expense of a trial, and we'll let the medical examiner worry about how he got that way."

"What about Zeke Young?" asked Noah, fearing the answer. "He was up on the roof with a rifle."

"Oh, our snipers took him out over an hour ago," said Gert. "He's well on his way to the morgue by now."

"What's going to happen to *me* now?" asked Noah, as soon as he saw the assault team pulling off their armor and packing up.

"First, I'm going to make those phone calls to your parents and uncle. I'm sorry, Noah, but procedure requires us to take you down to police headquarters and officially book you. We'll have your family meet us there and arrange for bail. They've hired an excellent lawyer for you. I'm assuming he'll be there too. Hopefully, you won't be locked up for the night."

* * * *

Noah sat rigidly on a bench in a holding area as he waited for his family and attorney. His body, his whole being, ached from feelings of misery, shame, and dejection. How had it all come to

283

this? His wrists, reddened and chafed, were still restrained in front of him. He had been officially searched, fingerprinted, and booked by the desk sergeant. When the double doors swung open and his family came through, he broke into his first smile—in how long? He couldn't even remember. Moments later, he was caught up in a bear hug between his parents. Leilani took one look at the wrist restraints and choked back tears as the shock of reality closed in on her.

At 11:30 p.m. Kurt Kenoi walked through the door carrying his briefcase. "Sorry to keep you waiting. You're Noah, I presume? Your parents hired me to represent you." He checked his watch and realized Night Court was about to end. "Oh-oh, Judge Terumi Fujita will be winding up for the night. Excuse me! Let me see if I can persuade him to hear one more preliminary arraignment and bail case." Kurt hurried down the hall, rushed inside, and approached the bench.

"Please, Your Honor, will you take just one more hearing? The boy is only fourteen, and if you don't hear his case tonight, he'll be in lockup all weekend."

"Counselor, who is the arresting officer and what are the charges?" asked the judge.

"Lt. Gert Mahaila is the arresting officer. She says the boy was being held hostage at gunpoint and was instrumental in assisting a police assault on a Chinatown mob leader earlier today. The mobster, a Wen Tse Fong, fell to his death in what the lieutenant called a justifiable homicide—perhaps even more likely, the boy's self-defense."

"I know the lieutenant," said the judge. "I've also heard of this Fong mobster in connection with an alleged protection racket."

"That's him," said Kurt. "The police also took out one of his henchmen, Zeke Young, a known hit man for Fong's mob. Young fired on the police, wounded one of them, and died during return fire. Your Honor, I'm here to represent Noah Kaleo Wong. With your permission, I'd like to have him released on bond. He's been a hostage long enough."

"Wong, eh?" repeated the judge. "A common name in Hawaii. Are the parents here, along with all the principals?"

"Yes, Your Honor," replied Kurt. "They're down the hall."

"Well, what are you waiting for? Bring them in." His gray head was lowered as he leafed through one of his courtroom logs, when all the hearing participants arrived and took their seats in the Night Court room.

Judge Fujita accepted the paperwork from Kurt and read through it. He was startled when he finally looked up and saw them. "Leilani, Alex, Kekoa! This is quite a surprise! Leilani, is this hearing for your son?"

"Yes, Judge," Leilani said passionately.

"Your Honor is familiar with the family?" asked Kurt.

"Oh, yes," he said. "My father and I drew up and managed the Pualoa children's trust for Leilani and Kekoa. Our firm also took part in unseating one of the other trustees, a murderer, who was also misusing that trust for his own purposes. In fact, I may have to recuse myself from sitting on the case."

"But Your Honor, this is only a bail hearing, and hopefully not an arraignment," pleaded Kurt.

"We'll start and see how things go," said the judge. "What is this second charge, evidence tampering? Does it have to do with another shooting, a different one? If so, this complicates matters."

"Your Honor," said Kurt, "the evidence tampering relates to an entirely separate case. You may have read about the shooting near the Ward theater complex a week ago."

"Yes," acknowledged the judge. "Was the boy also the shooter in that case?"

"No, Your Honor," replied Kurt. "Noah was the victim of a mugging and attempted murder."

"So who was the shooter?" asked Judge Fujita. "The suspense is killing me."

"Noah's fourteen-year-old girlfriend, Nina Portfia," replied Kurt. He then described the entire horrific night with meticulous care.

"Are you implying the attacker brought the gun to the scene with intent to kill?"

"Yes, Your Honor. Nina's attorney, a colleague of mine, has her confession verifying these facts. We are preparing a joint presentation to the Assistant State's Attorney a week from next Monday. It is our joint opinion that this case will never go to trial."

"You're saying Noah Wong was a victim and not a perpetrator in that case?" asked the judge.

"Yes, Your Honor."

"So noted," said the judge. "Then what is this evidence-tampering charge all about?"

Kurt replied, "In some deep expression of loyalty, protection, and affection for his girlfriend, Noah foolishly tossed the gun and her sweater into the ocean—from the seawall at Magic Island. Then he went into hiding, thinking everyone would believe he was the shooter. While the crime of evidence tampering is generally serious, youthful folly and foolhardy ideas of gallantry do present extenuating circumstances."

"Noah Kaleo Wong, please stand. Do you disagree with any of these facts presented in my court?"

"No, Your Honor, everything Mr. Kenoi told you is true."

"Now then, is there any reason why you can't tell me exactly how Wen Tse Fong died?"

"No, Your Honor. But I need to tell you what happened first, if that's okay."

"Of course, son," said the judge.

Noah had never stood before a judge before. The black robe, the high bench-podium were so intimidating. He ran his fingers through his wild hair and pushed the unruly strands back from his forehead. He wished he'd had a comb to make himself more presentable. The old scar on his forehead itched. Softly he began, determined to tell the truth. How he'd gone into hiding, being an errand boy for Wen, and how he tried to get away. "I was on Maunakea Street, on my way to meet Uncle Kekoa. He was going to take me home, so I could turn myself in to the police. Wen kidnapped me off the street at knifepoint and forced me to go with him to his place, then he held me there at gunpoint. The police were out front with a loudspeaker, begging him to surrender. Wen decided to escape, but he made me come along. He wanted me as a shield and then when he didn't need me anymore, I think he was going to kill me." An anguished Noah recounted every moment and move of his ordeal.

When he had finished, Judge Fujita asked Gert, "Lieutenant, do you have any reason to doubt the boy's story?"

"No, Your Honor, I don't," replied Gert. "In both cases the boy was the victim and he demonstrated remarkable courage. In fact, Noah helped to neutralize a very dangerous felon."

"Remember, this pre-arraignment hearing is not a trial," said Judge Fujita. "Guilt or innocence cannot be judged here. However, it is within my power to render decisions on probable cause. In the death of one Wen Tse Fong, I find a clear case of justifiable homicide. A hostage, fearing for his life, kills in self-defense in order to escape his captor. Therefore, there is no probable cause to bind him. On the other hand, I find a clear case of evidence tampering—destroying and disposing of evidence, I do find probable cause there. However, I must admit there are extenuating circumstances."

Judge Fujita leaned forward, lacing his fingers together, to speak to all assembled. "I've made my decision. There are general guidelines for setting bond. One is based upon the risk of flight. To that end, the boy's family members are here, not only to support him, but as well-known and respected members of the community. In addition, the arresting officer also vouches for him. Another guideline is based upon the severity of the crime, which, in this case, is a felony. Taking into consideration the extenuating circumstances, I set bail at $5,000, along with a recommendation for a more formal arraignment hearing with a state's prosecutor present." He addressed Alex. "You may pay cash to the court cashier or obtain the services of a bail bondsman."

"Thank you, Your Honor," said Kurt.

"Does this mean I can go home and sleep in my own bed tonight?" asked Noah.

"Yes," replied Kurt. "Just as soon as your parents arrange for bail."

Noah wouldn't allow himself to cry, but his relief was so overwhelming that he felt like it.

Chapter 31

Resolved

(Monday, August 22, 2005)

JUDGE FUJITA recommended a "more formal arraignment hearing." The word "more" was key here. It allowed for special considerations: the fact that both Noah and Nina were juveniles with no police records and both had pleaded unusual and extenuating circumstances to each charge levied against them. To that end, Assistant State's Attorney Loren Fiske held a meeting in his office exclusively for the criminal defense lawyers, Kurt Kenoi and Alonzo Paxton. It was their responsibility to successfully defend the teenagers. The children's futures hung in the balance.

The two families waited in the hall, blanketed in an atmosphere of suffocating anxiety. Noah sat between Alex and Leilani on a koa bench. Nina sat on the bench across from them, between Carlotta and Raimonde. A full two hours passed, and still not a word. The walls revealed nary a sound. All they could hear was the distant din of other court comings and goings. The early minimal conversation had long since ended. Simply where to fix one's gaze became a problem. The window at the end of the corridor was too far away. One could study the generic framed landscapes on the walls only so long. With so much riding on this hearing, no one dared to doze off.

From inside the office, they suddenly heard the scraping of chairs being pushed back, and the sound of three male voices floating near. Six heads jerked up. The office door opened. Parents and children, alert and terrified, leaped to their feet.

Fiske held the door for the two defense lawyers, then followed them out into the hall, and nodded his permission to Kurt to announce the State's findings.

A solemn Kurt delivered the news. "There will be no trial and no jail time," he declared. "Wen Tse Fong's death was confirmed justifiable homicide, and Dante Santos's death was considered accidental without malice. Regarding the charge of evidence tampering, an appropriate decision has been reached. Noah, you must perform 300 hours of community service within the next twelve months."

Fiske peered out at them from round glasses in black frames, like a wise, kindly owl, and summarized the State's conclusion. "Neither child will be burdened with a criminal record."

All four parents surrounded him with heartfelt thanks and grateful handshakes. Afterward, Leilani and Carlotta hugged, forgetting they'd been strangers. Both mothers sobbed with relief.

Kurt stepped forward, determined to have the last word. "Noah? Nina? Please listen carefully. From now on, you will respect your parents, obey them, and behave yourselves!"

The two kids clasped hands and, almost in unison, replied, "I promise!"

Epilogue

NOAH AND NINA plunged into their sophomore year in high school, tackling piles of makeup homework for the weeks they had missed—grateful for a normal life once more. They dated frequently, but not exclusively, all through high school and beyond. Noah received his Associate's degree in business at Kapiolani Community College and went to work for Hank Pualoa's Finast Construction Company, where Hank started grooming him to someday take over. Nina got her KCC degree in liberal arts. After two off-and-on engagements, Noah and Nina finally married, and, a year later, she gave birth to the first of their two children.

Leilani Pualoa Wong launched her career as an artist with gallery shows of her Hawaii-themed paintings and began earning commissions. Alex's much-in-demand CPA firm grew until he gladly took on a partner.

Malia Wong graduated from the University of California at Berkeley, Leilani's alma mater, excelled at Stanford University Law School, and now practices law in San Francisco.

Nina's father, Ramonde Portfia, suffered through a battle with pancreatic cancer and died a few months after her wedding. It was a mutual wish that neither of his sons continue his business, which eventually disintegrated in the incapable hands of Domo Martinez.

Raul Portfia went on to medical school at the University of Hawaii and became a doctor specializing in oncology. He never married. Salvadore bought a karaoke bar and married one of his pole dancers.

Sam Osaka, the bakery's founder, passed away quietly in a nursing home with Kekoa and Maria at his side. With pride and peace of mind, he had left the bakery to Kekoa, knowing it was in skilled hands that he himself had trained and nurtured.

Manny Portfia cleaned up his act and made a success of his office cleaning service. Within two years, he bought the Chinatown office from brother Rai. Esmeralda was overjoyed to have him back now that he was legit.

In five years Frank Portfia apprenticed with Kekoa in the bakery.

Andy Ballesteros married his waitress, Bunny Kobyashi, and together they made a success of Sweet Choice and Coffee. Papa passed away a week before the wedding. After waiting so long, they decided to go ahead with the wedding anyway. It was another five years before they had their first child, a girl. Ernie Peshelli regained his health and continued to work the kitchen for them.

Hank Pualoa happily and confidently turned over his shares in Finast Construction to Noah six months before he died. His wife, Lori, died a year later. They had led a happy life together.

Masako Wong beat her cancer rap. She and Paul exhilarated in their retirement from teaching, often babysitting their grandchildren—with loving reminders on good behavior.

Cindy Benfield-Rice and her husband, Coland, ran their commercial real estate firm profitably for only six years. Coland's lower leg problems took eighteen months to heal once the bone fixture was installed. Afterward, he walked with only a slight limp. Wealthy and worry-free, they traveled for at least three months every year.

Oh, yes. Hugo Set Tran and Edward Li Mong both died before finishing their long prison terms in Thailand.

All *Pau*

Rosemary and Larry Mild, cheerful partners in crime, coauthor mysteries and thrillers. Their short stories appear in three anthologies: *Dark Paradise:* Mysteries in the Land of Aloha; *Mystery in Paradise:* 13 Tales of Suspense; and Chesapeake Crimes: *Homicidal Holidays.* In 2013 the Milds waved goodbye to Severna Park, Maryland, and moved to Honolulu, Hawaii, where they cherish time with their children and grandchildren. The Milds are members of Mystery Writers of America, Sisters in Crime, and Hawaii Fiction Writers.

Rosemary is also a member of the Society of Professional Journalists and the National League of American Pen Women/Honolulu Branch, where Larry is an official Friend.

Visit them at **www.magicile.com**.

Contact them at **roselarry@magicile.com**.

Also by Rosemary and Larry

The Paco and Molly
Mystery Series

Locks and Cream Cheese—In scandal-ridden Black Rain Corners, a Chesapeake Bay mansion harbors locked rooms and deadly secrets. A wily detective and a gourmet cook tackle the case.

Hot Grudge Sunday—Bank robbers and conspirators derail the sleuths' blissful honeymoon at the Grand Canyon. Can they nail the suspects after they themselves become targets?

Boston Scream Pie—A teenage girl's nightmare triggers a sinister tale of twins, two feuding families, and a blonde bombshell who hates being called "Mom."

**Available on Amazon.com
and as E-Books**

Also by Rosemary and Larry

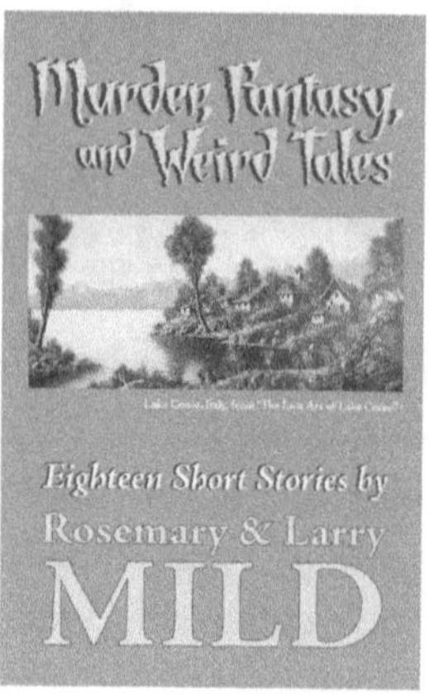

Murder, Fantasy, and Weird Tales—
Delve into tales of the brave, the foolhardy, and the wicked on their journeys to
the unknown in Hawaii, Japan, Cambodia,
Italy, and elsewhere. Art lovers, hit women,
a vampire, a lively hologram, and others
reveal their secret compulsions.

***Cry Ohana, Adventure and Suspense
in Hawaii—***A car accident and murder
tear apart a Hawaiian *ohana* (family). Danger erupts at a Filipino wedding, a Maui
resort, and amid the Big Island's volcanic
steam vents. Can the family re-unite and
bring down the killer?

***The Misadventures of Slim O. Wittz,
Soft-Boiled Detective—***"If you're looking
for a truly bumbling gumshoe, you want
me, Slim. I'm rarely in charge, frequently
behind the eight ball and seldom paid;
but in spite of all that, my case record is
remarkably shaky."

**Available on Amazon.com
and as E-Books**

Also by Rosemary and Larry

The Dan and Rivka Sherman Mystery Series

Death Steals A Holy Book—Dan and Rivka inherit a rare Yiddish translation of a 14th-century holy book, but it is stolen and their book restorer is murdered. Can they recover the book and nail the culprit?

Death Goes Postal—Priceless 15th-century typesetting artifacts journey through time, leaving a sinister imprint in their wake. Dan and Rivka risk life and limb to recover the treasures. Not quite what they expected when they bought The Olde Victorian Bookstore.

Death Takes A Mistress—After 23 years, Ivy Cohen seeks revenge on the lover who killed her mother. She follows the clues from London to Maryland, where she makes a shocking discovery.

**Available on Amazon.com
and as E-Books**

Also by Rosemary and Larry

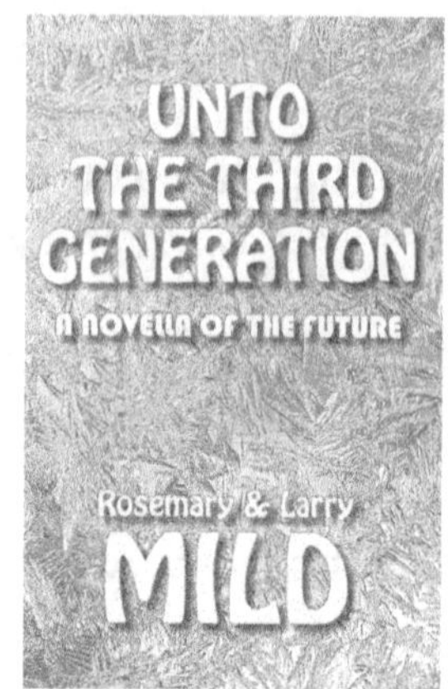

Unto the Third Generation—Two young people, each unaware of the other, volunteer to become cryonauts—physically frozen in a life-suspension experiment. Leonard, a high-steel worker, and Francine, a waitress, postpone their destinies for untold generations. But their continued existence is in jeopardy—depending upon two world-shaking events.

Also by Rosemary

Miriam's World—and Mine—Miriam Luby Wolfe, a junior at Syracuse U., spent her fall semester in London exploring her talents: singing, dancing, acting, and writing. But she never made it home. A terrorist bomb destroyed her plane over Lockerbie, Scotland. Learn about Miriam, the Pan Am families, the bombers, and the political fallout.

Love! Laugh! Panic! Life with My Mother—Rosemary's hilarious and heartwarming story of her super-achieving mother. Luby Pollack was a journalist, popular book author, and psychiatrist's wife. Always the Heroine, and sometimes the Villain, from the viewpoint of her loving but ornery daughter.

**Available on Amazon.com
and as E-Books**